WANTON DESIRE

"Why would I want to leave your cousin alone?" Paul asked, watching the play of emotions across Emma's face.

"Because you're not right for her!" Emma shouted.

Amusement colored his tone. "Who am I right for? Perhaps a sabre-tongued temptress who smells of lilacs and has hair the color of honey?"

His finger grazed her throat and moved to her earlobe, and she tingled beneath his touch. "How can you play games with my cousin's heart? Don't you have any sense of decency?" Emma asked, struggling for control.

"None whatsoever." His arms circled her waist and he pulled her to him. Then slowly he tilted his head and whispered her name as his lips touched hers.

He explored the texture, the taste, the shape of her mouth, and a shudder of emotion ran through her. An emotion that was wonderfully wanton, but to enjoy his embrace was wrong. He was the type of man to trifle with a woman's affection; she couldn't let him know how much he affected her. She wrenched free of his arms, drew her hand back and cracked her palm across Paul Rousseau's jaw. . . .

MAGNOLIA NIGHTS
MARTHA HIX

ZEBRA BOOKS
KENSINGTON PUBLISHING CORP.

ZEBRA BOOKS

are published by

Kensington Publishing Corp.
475 Park Avenue South
New York, NY 10016

First printing: September, 1988

Printed in the United States of America

To five great authors . . .

*Barbara Catlin, Kathryn Davenport, Karla Hocker,
Emma Merritt and Evelyn Rogers*

. . . and with love to Leslie and Sharon

Chapter One

New Orleans, February 1842

"Pardon me, sir."

First Lieutenant Paul Rousseau of the Texas Navy halted in his tracks and turned to the St. Charles Hotel's concierge. "Yes?"

Rounding a gilt desk, Castillo templed his meaty fingers in front of his chest. "A lady is waiting in your room."

Paul's curiosity was roused. "Oh?"

The clerk smirked while digging into his pocket to produce a twenty-dollar gold piece. "I'm sure you won't mind that I allowed her entry."

"Why would I mind?" A lady caller was an intriguing proposition, but this pasty-faced hare was a man who could be bought. Disgusted, Paul began to walk away as the festive tune of strolling musicians filtered from the street into the lobby, and a nearby clock chimed midnight. But Castillo's nasal whisper transcended the sounds, stopping Paul from leaving. "She claims to be your sister."

Sister? Paul had no siblings. A lazy smile played

7

across his sun-weathered features. Since sailing into the crescent city to deposit a manifest of American survivors from a Campeche Bay shipwreck, Paul had favored no woman except Marian Oliver, and his purpose for seeking her out had been two-fold. Her brother was his naval commander, and Paul had unfinished business with him. But more important, Marian was his archenemy's widowed daughter-in-law. A whip of resentment lashed through Rousseau as he thought of Rankin Oliver.

"Will there be anything else for you this evening, sir?" Castillo asked, palm up.

"No."

Paul dug into his pocket, as his thoughts turned to Rankin Oliver. The man had murdered his father, but he hadn't been able to prove the duel had been unfair. Oliver had too craftily hidden the evidence of his guilt. For thirteen years Paul had futilely harbored his hatred; then, recently, in the Yucatán village of Sisal, he had learned Oliver was selling munitions to the Centralists in Mexico City. Once more, however, Paul had been thwarted. He had been unable to bring the miscreant to justice—and an innocent woman had died at Oliver's hands during the attempt.

For the ten thousandth time Paul vowed to blacken the Oliver name for eternity.

Then Castillo cut into his thoughts by asking, "Shall I have champagne sent to your quarters, sir?"

"No."

Paul dropped a picayune into the center of that soft palm, cleared his mind of Castillo's interruption, and glanced up to the second floor.

8

Marian, he was certain, waited in his room. Though she didn't excite him inordinately, Paul planned to get close to her, as close as possible, and gain her confidence. In order to extract the vengeance he sought against her father-in-law, he needed to track Rankin's activities. What better way than through a member of his household?

Paul strode away from the lobby. Though Marian didn't send his blood racing with lust, she was fairer than most women. So why look a gift horse in the mouth? Yet his unhurried steps belied that line of reasoning as Paul ascended the curving staircase leading to his quarters.

Emma Frances Oliver had been waiting in the hotel room for over thirty minutes. She felt she must speak with Paul Rousseau in private, and she prayed the man she knew only by hearsay would be more reasonable than her cousin by marriage. Marian had fallen in love at first sight with Étienne Rousseau's son. But Olivers did not love Rousseaus. It just wasn't done. Good people did not cavort with bad.

Why, Emma asked herself, couldn't sweet William's widow understand that? But Emma knew why. Marian had been behind a door when brains were passed around.

Emma didn't care much for William's widow, but she had promised him she'd look out for his wife. And Marian was family, so this was a matter of family honor. Above all else, Emma would look out for an Oliver.

Right now she wanted nothing more than to

appeal to Rousseau's sense of decency, providing he had any, and be on her way. She nodded, as if to verify the validity of her reasoning. And if Rousseau wasn't honorable, she had an alternate plan that was certain to appeal to his type of man.

Despite her warm wrap, gooseflesh rose on her arms. The room was damp and chill, the flames from the fireplace long spent. Only the dim light of an ornate mantel lamp lit the room. With her usual impatience Emma eyed Rousseau's possessions, perusing each in turn, while walking the floor and rehearsing her speech. Next to the huge tester bed, where Rousseau no doubt planned to debauch poor dumb Marian, rested a sea chest. Emma wondered about its contents but chose not to risk being caught snooping, for that act would surely loose a swarm of trouble on herself. Rousseau might return at any moment. But, oh, Pandora's curiosity was aroused!

"Admit it," she muttered. "You're curious about Rousseau, too."

Since arriving in New Orleans two days previously, she had heard nothing but Paul this and Paul that from Marian, who had rattled on and on as if the man were a god. Emma had been ready to tear her hair from its roots. She couldn't help but bemoan the fact that Uncle Rankin was in St. Martinsville, and it would take days to get word to him. If he were in town, he'd put a halt to the goings-on.

By all that was right, it was Emma's duty to save her kinsman's widow from weakness of the heart.

Bored with her wait, Emma centered her attention on the silver dish on the bedside table. Her curiosity aroused, she plucked a gold-and-diamond brooch from it and walked over to the lamp.

Like unexpected claps of thunder, the echo of footfalls reverberated from the hallway and a key rattled in the lock. The door swung open with a creak.

Drat! There was no time to return the pin to its rightful place, for a man's shadow cut across the rug and up the back of Emma's emerald-green skirts. Pulse racing, she dropped the brooch into her cloak pocket, painfully pricking her skin as she did so. Then she whirled to face Paul Rousseau.

"What the devil?" Startled as he was, his voice held a faint trace of a French accent. "Who are you, *chérie?* What are you doing here? Not that I'm complaining . . ."

Emma lifted her determined chin. This elegantly attired man had a confidence about him that threatened to overpower her if she let it. Short of stature but long on mettle, she refused to allow him to stop her.

"Are you going to answer?" He appraised her with speculative interest, and crossed the room. "Sister dear."

She stepped back and spoke quietly. "Mr. Rousseau, my name is Emma Frances Oliver."

"Emma . . . *Oliver?* I recall Marian's speaking of you. You're her deceased husband's cousin, right?"

As she responded in the affirmative, Paul relinquished his plans for Marian. Emma fascinated him, particularly due to the impropriety of this visit. Furthermore, he had seen her slip something into her pocket. What in this room was small and easy to steal? Following a hunch, his eyes traveled to the silver dish. Ah, ha! She had stolen his mother's brooch. He was certain it would be returned to him. Paul Rousseau held on to his possessions, and this little thief, not Marian, was his quarry now.

He shortened the distance between them, his gaze raking her. "She neglected to tell me you're blond and beautiful."

Looking at him, Emma forced back a grin. Marian had also neglected mentioning Rousseau's pleasing appearance; it had probably been an oversight. But a handsome face did not a gentleman make.

"Hasn't your *maman* warned you of the perils of visiting a man in his hotel room?"

"I'm twenty years old. My mother doesn't run my life."

Emma realized her reputation, what little was left of it, was compromised, but the gravity of the situation warranted drastic measures.

Not only was this man an odious Rousseau, he had plundered and pillaged the high seas before associating himself with the Republic of Texas. Texas—ha! Uncle Rankin had told her about that place. It was peopled by nothing but cutthroats, liars, and misfits.

Though the local newspapers were generous with praise for him, and though Marian was fascinated by his supposedly heroic endeavors in the Texas Navy, Emma doubted Rousseau was a hero.

"I wanted to speak with you in private," she said.

"Ah! Then you have my attention. We're quite alone. And I always have time for my . . . sister."

She opened her mouth to speak but closed it as he

12

captured her hand, lifting it to his lips. Instead of kissing her fingers in the gallant manner, he turned her wrist and pressed his lips gently to her palm. Fighting the strange warmth his touch evoked, Emma looked downward and jerked her blood-dotted hand away. Oh no, the brooch! Be calm, she warned herself. But what was she going to do about that pin?

His eyes riveted to hers, and she hid the incriminating crimson evidence behind her back. "Now, about Mrs. Oliver—"

"Did she ask you to call on me? I'll wager she didn't."

"Well, no, but I—"

His eyes boldly cruising up and down her body, he interrupted again. "I think it's interesting you're here at midnight to discuss your relative."

Rather than incur Marian's fury Emma had decided to visit the man in secret, and after the Oliver household had turned in for the night she had ventured from Magnolia Hall to accomplish her mission. "I, um, I thought it more prudent if we had privacy for this discussion."

"Did you now? Privacy. You mentioned that a minute ago." He rubbed his chin. "I'd say Marian doesn't know you're here."

Emma refused to grant him the pleasure of an honest reply.

"I think you wanted to find out for yourself about the man who has Marian, shall we say, intrigued."

"Marian's intrigued with needlework." Emma sniffed. "But that doesn't mean I have an interest in her pastimes."

In truth Emma had a hankering for needlework, but she planned to use her sewing skills on mending wounds. Her goal was to be a physician, but . . . She reminded herself not to be sidetracked by her own desires.

"No," he said dryly, "I don't imagine you find needle and thread interesting."

She squared her shoulders. "My interest lies with Mrs. Oliver. For her sake, please take leave of her."

"No."

"Be reasonable, Mr. Rousseau. You and I both know there's bad blood between our families. Your courtship of her is destined for trouble."

"Bad blood? I've come back to New Orleans prepared to put the past away. After all this time, surely your uncle bears no grudge against my family. But if he does, I pray to mend yesteryears' fences." His look was genuine, though he skirted the truth. "It's time this matter was put to rest."

Emma's reservations eased—a bit. "Are you squiring Mrs. Oliver solely to redeem yourself with our family?"

"Not in the least." Paul could say that with sincerity. He heard Emma sigh in relief. He wouldn't tell her, or any other Oliver, that redemption was not his purpose. Not yet. Making Rankin Oliver pay, according to the letter of the law, and bringing down the house of Oliver was his goal.

"My uncle may take much convincing," she said.

Paul cocked his head and furrowed his brows. "A busy man such as he must have matters other than a duel of days gone by to fill his mind."

"Your father slandered his name and undermined

his business ventures. Those misdeeds are difficult to forget."

Paul forced himself not to grimace at those falsehoods. "Surely Rankin Oliver doesn't blame me for the trouble between himself and my father. I am certain his time is occupied with more noble pursuits. A family is most time-consuming, and don't his sugar-planting and cotton-factoring interests carry him far and wide?"

"Of course."

"I thought so. I heard he was in the Yucatán just last month, and now I'm told he's on extended business in St. Martinsville." He paused. "But then, I don't suppose he bothers you with such details."

Proud of the trust Uncle Rankin placed in her, Emma replied, "As a matter of fact he does."

Paul drew a cheroot from a tabletop humidor, struck a lucifer, and took a contemplative draw of smoke. He now saw Emma in a whole new light. "I recall Marian speaking of the great love between you and your uncle." He dropped his hand to his side. "Please go on. I'm interested in what you have to say."

"I think not. We've gotten away from the subject, Mr. Rousseau. We were discussing Mrs. Oliver."

He parted his lips. "I'd rather discuss you."

Those lips might have been sculpted to perfection by Michelangelo, Emma decided before checking her errant thought. He wasn't going to snare her in the same net as Marian! "I demand that you leave Mrs. Oliver alone."

Waiting for his reply, Emma watched him with all the inquisitiveness he had accused her of. From his appearance she could understand why Marian was attracted to him. His hair, black as pitch, was trimmed in short curls that barely brushed the top of his collar. His amber eyes were turning ebony as he stared at her. His face was rather long, rather angular. A jagged scar along his right jaw marred his features. Or did it? His nose was a bit crooked, but, oh my, that only enhanced his appeal.

He strode toward the fireplace. Muscles strained the material of his silk shirt as he drew off his frock coat and tossed it across the back of a chair. His shoulders were broad, his waist slim, his hips narrow. One finger loosened his neck cloth, then unfastened the top button of his shirt. Black chest hair sprang from the V. Emma tried valiantly, unsuccessfully, not to smile as she wondered about the range of that fine down.

A smile grooved his cheeks. "Have you finished undressing me?"

"You flatter yourself."

As if he delighted in her overt regard, he grinned and bent to light the fire in the hearth.

Emma touched a finger to her lips and closed her eyes. Except for the plates of male cadavers in her father's medical books, she had never seen an unclothed man, and she mused over what Paul Rousseau looked like in the flesh. No doubt finer than those likenesses of shriveled dead men.

With that thought she tried to gather her wits. Rousseau was walking toward her now, the dancing flames behind him casting his physique in golden relief. Her heart missed a beat. But refusing to allow herself to be charmed, she took a step backward.

It was on the tip of Paul's tongue to tell Emma there was nothing to worry about, insofar as Marian was concerned. But he didn't. Why not let Emma dangle on a string for a while? He was enjoying the game, and responded to her earlier demand with a question. "Why would I want to leave Marian alone?"

"Mr. Rousseau, I don't want to see her hurt. As you probably know, my cousin William passed away three years ago. Marian is lost without him—she stayed in mourning too long. She's quite . . ." Emma had started to say featherbrained, but had thought better of it. Poor Marian craved attention with a pitiable vengeance, and she hadn't turned her yearnings in the proper direction. "She's vulnerable and thinks she's in lo—" Emma swallowed the last of the word. "I'm sure the feeling will pass if you'll take your leave. Then she'll accept attention from New Orleans gentlemen, and all will be well."

"What a snob you are. You're saying I'm not good enough for her. That's for Marian to decide." A muscle twitched in his jaw as if he held himself in control by the thinnest of threads. "Yes, she's fond of me. Perhaps she loves me. She's possessed of a warm rather than insulting nature."

"I didn't mean to malign you." Emma certainly didn't need to alienate him.

"If that's an apology," he said after a half-minute of silence, "I accept it." The angry set of his features turned into a smile of superiority. "I'm sure Marian could have her pick of admirers, but don't forget whose name is on her lips." His tone became smooth and suggestive. "Once a woman's tasted the wine of a

17

real man, it's difficult to be content with the sip of water a gentleman offers."

"I'll wager no one's ever accused you of being arrogant!" she charged facetiously.

"Never? On occasion." He was standing near . . . oh so near. Crooking a finger under her chin, he forced her to look up at him. His nail grazed her jaw, eliciting a shiver from her. "And what of you, *chérie?* Have you . . . savored wine?"

"I despise wine!" Unsettled by her lie and by him, Emma swatted his hand away. "You dare make an advance to me while you refuse to quit my cousin's company!"

"An advance?" he teased, then mocked her earlier words. "You flatter yourself."

"Oooh!" Losing the battle with her temper, she jabbed the tip of her forefinger into his chest. "Stay away from her. You've nothing to offer. It's a well-known fact your father was a no-good gambler, and you sailed under the skull and crossbones of piracy—"

"Letters of marque," he corrected.

"Pirate, privateer—I see no difference between the two." Emma thrust her arm down. "You may have Marian fooled with tales of your so-called noble endeavors with the Texas Navy, but I'm not so gullible. You're nothing but a lowly vagabond!"

"Who keeps the Mexican Centralists from blockading the Gulf sea lanes." He perused her form. "Thus allowing the import of fine silks to cover full breasts . . . and tiny waists that can be spanned with two hands."

She wouldn't be sidetracked. "You're not right

18

for her!"

Amusement colored his tone as he retorted, "Who am I right for? Perhaps a sabre-tongued temptress who smells of lilac and has hair the color of honey? Maybe a vixen with irises like the first blush of green in April, yet full of the storminess of March?"

His callused finger, not the finger of an aristocrat by any means, grazed the curve of her throat and moved upward to her earlobe. Beneath his touch she tingled.

"Such a comely woman spellbinds this lowly vagabond, making me itch to pull those ivory combs from her hair."

"How can you play games with Marian's heart? Don't you have any sense of decency?"

"None whatsoever." His fingers loosened the tie of her cloak, and it slid to the floor at their feet. "There are many varieties of wine, Emma. Perhaps you've never tasted a fine French vintage. Would you like a sip of one?"

As her eyes collided with his, his arms circled her waist, pulling her to him. He was strong, she realized; his strength, no doubt, hewn from physical labor. Heady aromas clung to his clothing—the manly scent of tobacco interlaced with his flesh's warmth. Then slowly . . . ever so slowly . . . he tilted his head, his nearness assailing her senses in a strangely intoxicating way. He murmured something in French that she didn't understand. Yet it sounded wickedly seductive.

Once, and then again, he whispered her name as he lowered his head to touch his lips to hers. He explored their texture, taste, and shape as if her mouth were a precious delicacy. Then, groaning, he slid his tongue past the barrier of her teeth to claim the intimate recesses. A shudder of emotion ran through her, grand and wonderfully wanton.

But to enjoy his embrace was wrong. He was the sort of man who trifled with a woman's affection, and Emma refused to allow him to dishonor her or William's widow, or to let him know how much he affected her.

She wrenched free of his arms, drew her hand back, and cracked her palm against Paul Rousseau's jaw.

Chapter Two

The sting of Emma's hand reddened Paul's cheek, but his composure did not waver. Never would he give her the satisfaction of knowing she could inflict pain, though she packed a mighty lick for one so small!

She rubbed his kiss from her lips. "Step back, Rousseau."

"I'll not." He renewed his grip, his eyes delving into the light-green ones that mesmerized him. She felt good in his arms, and he was pleased that she had responded to his kiss ... before having second thoughts.

He smiled as she protested the embrace and twisted in his arms. He smiled at his luck. Ah, yes. She was much fairer game than Marian. He would enjoy himself while wooing Emma, which was not possible with her empty-headed kinswoman.

He would entice Emma to him ... and keep her innocent of his motives.

"Let me go ... please," she murmured.

That simple request was appealing, and he allowed space between them. With a sweeping gesture, he then bowed from the waist. "Your wish is my command, Mademoiselle Oliver," he declared, yet his voice held the scrape of sarcasm. "For the moment."

"Mr. Rousseau, if I cannot appeal to your sense of decency, may I appeal to your monetary sense? I'm prepared to offer you the sum of one thousand dollars in return for your agreement to leave New Orleans straightaway."

Paul was stunned. The conniving little wench! Of course he should have expected nothing less from an Oliver.

His pride injured, he squared his shoulders and ran splayed fingers through his hair before wheeling away. In two steps he was beside a marble-topped bureau. Did she think him a man who could be bribed for a few coins? This viper must think all men as easy prey as the concierge.

And what of Emma Oliver? How far would she go in her quest? He knew her to be a woman without scruples. She had visited his chambers sans chaperon, which showed this tiny spitfire was less than virtuous. Though he had been bored with Marian's prattle, Paul now confirmed one choice tidbit he'd gleaned from her: Emma lacked respectability. He watched her as she paced back and forth, glancing at him from time to time.

Back in Virginia, Emma had been jilted by her fiancé, Marian had said. Paul surmised the man had discovered her lack of virtue and propriety. That mattered not.

What did matter was that she was unscrupulous. A thief. Surely there was a maxim that described a person of means who stole for the thrill of it, but the word escaped him.

The piece of jewelry in her pocket was worth much more than money could buy, certainly more than her bribe. Save for a miniature portrait, the pin was the only tangible reminder Paul had of his mother.

Yet he had said nary a word at the time it was stolen, and he wouldn't now. The theft might prove advantageous.

Emma abandoned her pacing and stood her ground five feet from Paul. He leaned back against the bureau, crossing one ankle over the other.

"One thousand dollars, Mr. Rousseau."

"I heard you the first time. I suppose that kind of money is mere pocket change to you."

"I'm not wealthy in my own right, if that's what you mean. The money is a large part of the inheritance I received from my cousin William. I believe he'd approve of my spending it for his widow's benefit."

"Aren't you noble?" Paul asked coolly. "So you think I can be purchased like fruit at the market." He straightened, and his laugh was low and cynical as he strode toward her. The air crackled with tension. "Well, I can be," he lied, intending to find out just how much she was willing to sacrifice. "Everyone has his price. But one thousand dollars isn't nearly enough. If I deny myself Marian's pleasure, how much is it worth to you?"

"I'll not give you a cent more."

"Then let me name my figure. My price is one evening with you in that bed over there."

"You snake! Your black heart will burn in hell before—"

"My, my, such language from a lady. But you're

23

not a lady, are you?"

"And you're certainly no gentleman!" Emma gritted her teeth. "I'll have the money delivered on the morrow."

"Money isn't a part of the contract." He watched her glare at him. "When will you deliver yourself to me, Emma Oliver? Now perhaps?"

Retrieving her cloak, Emma clutched the garment to her and charged across the room.

"Well, when?" he taunted.

"Never!" The word was punctuated by the slamming of the door as she exited.

Her answer echoing in his brain, Paul threw back his head in laughter and then dropped onto the bed. *Oh yes, you will.*

The vixen thought she had the better of him. That wasn't so. Relaxed and confident, Paul relit his cheroot. He ought to hate her, ought to loathe anyone with Oliver blood. For some odd reason, he didn't. But he warned himself not to let his feelings for Emma get out of hand. After all, she was an Oliver.

Since she had stolen the brooch, he'd have a reason to see her again. That appealed to Paul. Closing his eyes, he chuckled. She deserved to be prosecuted for her thievery, yet if he turned her over to the police, his plans for the Olivers would be torn asunder. Such a move would gain him nothing. And the thought of her comely little body behind bars held no appeal, but she didn't have to know that. Her thievery, Paul decided, even more confidently, could be used to his best advantage.

And though Emma tantalized him, arousing his passion, he would never trust her. But what a

24

delightful little *lagniappe,* a delectable little bonus, she'd be in his pursuit to vindicate his father.

Wanting to get as far from Paul Rousseau as possible, Emma hurried through the long corridor and down the hotel staircase. The very idea of him! It galled her, his suggestion that she compromise her virtue to his blackmail. What did he take her for, one of those painted strumpets who paraded along the levee?

"An evening in his bed," she muttered under her breath, as she sailed past the venal concierge who had demanded a twenty-dollar gold piece before producing a key to that scoundrel's room, "I'd rather cuddle an alligator."

Once in the pungent-smelling night air, she whipped her cloak around her shoulders, tied it beneath her chin, and checked her pocket for the brooch. Drat! She'd be forced to see Rousseau again when she returned it.

Looking down St. Charles Street, first east, then west, she searched for her carriage. It was nowhere in sight. Over the sound of street music, a group of drunken sailors called to her. Their message was obscene. Well, what did she expect, since she was unaccompanied?

She detected heavy steps behind her just as a body lurched against her. Reeling, Emma grabbed her attacker's skirt. A woman! The young female, whose hazel eyes were as bright in the gaslight glow as her face was beautiful, shoved Emma forcefully, and Emma stumbled into the clutches of the woman's corpulent male accomplice.

"Get your hands off me!" Emma struggled against his grip, eager to be away from his whiskey-fouled breath.

"Hear that? She wants me to unhand her, Katie." The wrinkled man sneered, showing his gapped, rotten teeth. A filthy black patch covered one eye, and he peered at his captive with the other. "I want not to unhand the pretty little piece."

A carriage turned the corner at nearby Common Street, and Emma spied Uncle Rankin's majestic grays in the leads. "Miss Emma!" she heard Jeremiah yell. The hoofbeats clomped faster. A savior, saints be praised!

"Packert!" The woman pulled frantically at the big man's arm. "Let her go! We must leave."

"Get away from her," the coachman roared. Jumping down from his seat, he flew to Emma's aid, yanking her away from the cutthroat.

Emma tried to strike Packert, but he and the woman disappeared into the shadows, the ruffian jeering.

"You okay, Miss Emma?" Jeremiah asked as he opened the carriage door and handed her into the interior.

"I . . . I think so, thank you."

Emma dropped onto the seat, exhaled a loud breath, and disregarded the sniff of disapproval of her companion in the carriage. As the horses set a pace for the three-mile journey to the Oliver plantation, Emma's equanimity returned and she gave thought to the disturbing situation of how to deal with Paul Rousseau's demands. How could she protect Marian from him? How could she protect herself from him! Obviously he was a man who wouldn't quit without a fight.

Moreover, he was not above pitting two women of the same family against each other. She shivered. Oh, how she despised him. Paul Rousseau was rotten to the core, as rotten as that awful ruffian's teeth!

Since Rousseau had proven he had no sense of decency and he had spurned her offer of money, Emma realized she must confess all to Marian. Surely then William's widow would see the light. Nonetheless, it pained Emma to think about bruising Marian's fragile emotions. And it would be humiliating to recount an adventure in which Emma had, once more, shown a lack of social decorum.

But it had to be done.

"Went and got in trouble, didn't you?"

Emma glanced at her mammy, who sat straight as a pencil on the seat beside her. "Where have you been, Cleo?" Not giving the woman a chance to answer, she chastised her. "And a lot of help you were when you did show up. I could've been killed, and you wouldn't have stuck your nose out the window."

"I know exactly where not to stick my nose." Cleopatra, her face set in a scowl, crossed her arms over her spare chest. "Besides, I knew you'd be all right. Satan hisself'd know better than to tangle with you."

"Thank you for your kindness," Emma replied caustically. "As usual you've no qualms about 'tangling' with me."

"Somebody's gotta try to keep you in line. And

listen here, missy, you be entrusted to me when you were a babe—oh, such a pretty little thing you were then!" The servant smiled, then shook her head in disgust. "But you ain't been nothing but trouble since the day you was born. I've had twenty years of your sassing and talking back, not to mention your habit of taking in every stray you can find."

"Spoken by a person elevated at an early age to the high station of mammy," Emma shot back. "A free woman of color with faint regard for the unfortunates of society."

She might as well have saved her breath; Cleopatra ignored the comment.

"Now you've taken it upon yourself to mind Miss Marian's business, and—" Cleopatra curled her lip—"been visiting a man in his hotel room to do it."

"Hush." Emma sighed. Cleopatra had been especially testy of late due to the haste in which the two women had left Richmond. Emma didn't want to think about the events that had led up to their departure.

"Ain't gonna hush! Why, in the first place, the very idea of you huffing up, then leaving your poor mama and daddy was disgraceful. And your coming to this wicked city and taking up the ways of white trash makes me sick, plumb sick."

"I had my reasons, and you know them," Emma reminded her.

"Huh! Reasons, my foot. You just got a streak of rebellion running through you. You been raised to be a lady, but what do you do now? I'll tell you what you done; you ain't in this town two days and you be sneaking around to meet Miss Marian's man."

Emma squeezed Cleopatra's hand. "You're making it sound worse than it is. My only motive was Marian's welfare."

"That be Master Rankin's responsibility."

"Well, he'll be in St. Martinsville until who knows when." Emma clenched her fist. "No telling what Marian or Rousseau—especially Rousseau!—might've done between now and then." Or what he might still do, she added silently.

"If you were so set on talking to him, why didn't you wait till he come out to Magnolia Hall?"

"As I told you before, I have to help Marian, and it was best not to bother her with my . . . with my—"

"Meddling," Cleopatra finished for her. "Still think you done right? You gonna tell her now?"

"I don't know. And yes."

Minutes later Cleopatra tilted her head. "Well, is you or ain't you gonna tell me what happened?"

Emma had never kept a secret from her beloved mammy, but she sometimes kept her in suspense. "Did anyone ever tell you that you're a busybody?"

Cleopatra's eyes drilled into Emma. "Just a certain youngun I know who needs a good switchin'!"

"If anyone needs a switchin', it's Marian." Emma rubbed her brow. "If she had the sense God gave a goose, my calling on Rousseau would not've been necessary."

Although innocent of the intimacies shared between men and women, Emma was woman enough to know the importance of physical love to happiness. She wanted William's widow to find contentment again, but not in the arms of a

29

Rousseau. A Rousseau who was a lecher at that! Why was Marian so blind to Howard O'Reilly's attention? He was a man of sensitivity and grace; and being noble and solicitous, he'd provide a strong shoulder for the dependent Marian to lean on.

"You heard her, Cleo. She refuses to listen to reason—"

"Sounds familiar."

Emma continued undaunted. "She sees absolutely nothing improper in the advances of that . . . that . . ." She couldn't think of a name nasty enough.

"Miss Marian's old enough to know what she wants and how to handle it!" Cleopatra smirked like a Cheshire cat. "Just like you're not old enough to figure out what's good for you."

That particular look spelled Franklin Underwood, and Emma's former fiancé was a subject best avoided. "Rousseau tried to molest me," she said quickly.

"You be as dumb as Miss Marian. He's a man, ain't he? It wouldn't be natural if he didn't get the wrong idea. Hmmph. I remember him from when I visited here in '29 with your mama and daddy. Why, that beanpole come to Magnolia Hall and wanted to call Master Rankin out! 'Course the master laughed in his face, said he didn't duel with children." Cleopatra chuckled. "That black-eyed Frenchie ain't nothing for either one of you to be troubled over. He be ugly as those mud-sucking crawfish they's always eating around here."

"Well, he's not ugly or skinny now." Try as she might, Emma couldn't suppress a grin. "He's tall and quite handsome. Furthermore, he was born on American soil, not in France, and he's a citizen of Texas."

"I've heard about those Texians—they's rough as cobs."

"I'll allow he lacks gentility." Why she was going to the scoundrel's defense, Emma didn't know. "But for your information, Marian told me he's her brother James's second-in-command on the schooner *San Antonio*."

"You've sure changed your tune, missy. Sounds like you're smitten just like Miss Marian."

With all her heart Emma hoped not. Yet she couldn't forget the feel of his lips . . . his tongue. She pushed that remembrance aside. "You know why I'm worried about her. When William was in Virginia, dying of yellow fever, he made me promise to look out for Marian's interests. She's my duty."

"He *musta* been sick."

Ignoring the pointed barb, Emma spoke. "Not so sick that he didn't want to protect his widow from the likes of Rousseau."

"Umm-hmm."

"Oh, Cleo, don't be so smug." Emma looked out the window. "Right now I wish we'd never left Virginia."

"You be mad 'cause things ain't turning out the way you want 'em. Just like when you got mad at your poor daddy when he told you to get that doctoring notion outta your head."

Cleopatra had struck a nerve. Emma shuddered. She hadn't been angry with her physician father—he'd been furious with her. He had caught her in his laboratory distilling sulfurous ether, and the bowels of hell had burst forth. When they'd argued over her dream to work by his side as an equal partner, Emma had known she was defeated; he had sons to carry on his profession, and he'd never change his mind about her ambitions.

Uncle Rankin was the only person supportive of her goal. Emma's heart filled with love. Anytime she needed a sympathetic ear, Uncle Rankin was there for her. When she had told him of the distress she'd suffered from sitting helplessly by her Cousin William's deathbed, he had understood. To him, she had first confessed her desire to follow the profession of Hippocrates. From Uncle Rankin she had received blessings . . . and a small black bag of medical necessities.

"Won't do you no good to ignore me, missy." Cleopatra adjusted her *tignon*. "Women carry babies not medical bags!"

Emma cupped her ear, tilting her head toward her mammy. "Do I hear an echo in this carriage? Babies, not medical bags? Is my father present?"

Cleopatra still had a point to make. "When you ever gonna learn you can't please Master Quentin by defying him?"

"Please don't start on my father again!"

"Hmmph. The very idea of a woman pining to be a doctor. It's foolhardy, foolhardy, I tell you. You should've stayed home and married that nice Mr. Franklin."

Emma cringed at the name. Her mother wished her married to that yawning bore, and both her parents had pushed her into the engagement. It was a good match, familywise. The Underwoods had been in Virginia since Jamestown, and their land holdings were extensive, which had impressed Noreen and Quentin Oliver. Emma couldn't have cared less. "You're not getting any younger," she had been told over and over. So, despondent over the fruitlessness of her doctoring dreams, and to please her father, Emma had consented to wed. She loved making Dr. Quentin Oliver happy, but walked just short of the altar. To preserve Franklin's pride, she had allowed him to break the engagement, which hadn't helped her reputation.

Thus, Emma had planned this visit to Louisiana. It wasn't that she wished to run from her shame. She simply wanted to be in Uncle Rankin's company.

Her voice was low and anguished. "You just don't understand."

"I understand something you don't know. Leave Paul Rousseau be. If Miss Marian wants him, you'd best let her have him. A lady doesn't steal another lady's honey."

"Oh, hush. I'm not stealing anyone or anything." Suddenly remembering the brooch, she dug into her cloak pocket, first one, then the other, searching frantically. "Cleo, the brooch is gone!"

"What are you talking about?"

"Those two on the street—Katie and Packert, they called each other—must've stolen it." For a second she considered ordering Jeremiah to turn the coach around and chase the pickpockets, but realized such an action would be useless. The dark streets of New Orleans teemed with people.

"What are you talking about?" Cleopatra repeated.

In an agitated voice, Emma explained the

33

situation. ". . . and I didn't mean to take it! Why, oh why, didn't I simply hand the pin to Rousseau? Rogue that he is, he's liable to press charges when he discovers it's lost."

"Oh, baby." Cleopatra put her arms around Emma, hugged her as if she were a child. "We be in a heap of trouble."

"I'm a—" Emma swallowed hard—"I'm a common thief, just the same as those two."

"What are we gonna do?"

Emma had no idea. It was a fine predicament she had gotten herself into. The brooch was lost forever, she realized. Of course it would have to be replaced, but she doubted Rousseau would be chivalrous about that. He could—probably would—throw her into jail and tell the whole world she had visited him on the sly.

"Baby, what are we gonna do?" Cleopatra asked again.

"Let the devil take him." Defiance gleamed in Emma's eyes. "I'll deny everything."

"Why are you trying to deny it?" Paul asked heatedly.

"You're being insubordinate, Mr. Rousseau."

Captain James Throckmorton, Marian Oliver's brother, sat opposite Paul in the open-air French Market café. Paul was determined to sway Throckmorton's thinking on the *San Antonio* situation. Before dawn he'd taken a longboat to the anchorage, and had found the marines aboard in a vicious mood. Now as morn waned, Paul's mood wasn't the

34

best, either.

"Granted I'm insubordinate. But I'm doing what has to be done!" Paul curled his hand into a fist and knocked it on the tabletop, sloshing his superior officer's cup of café au lait. Late morning diners turned their heads, and Paul lowered his voice. "Our sailors need shore leave. We've taken a pounding from Santa Anna's men, but we've taken a harder pounding from our own president."

Paul sneered as he thought of the Republic of Texas's president, Sam Houston—past president, Mirabeau Lamar, had called him the Big Drunk. Paul didn't know whether the accusation was true, but the appellation pleased him.

"Houston's got it in for our commodore," Paul said. "And he's taking his jealousy of Ed Moore out on all of us."

"Hold your tongue, mister!"

"I refuse." Paul's voice was resolute. "Our men haven't been paid. We're marooned in the Mississippi River. Morale, sir, is at an all-time low. At least allow our crewmen some time to themselves."

"Quit crusading, Rousseau." Captain Throckmorton polished off his milk-laced coffee. "Besides, if I allow them to go ashore, those dockside harpies are just waiting for them. Then trouble'll start."

"The *trouble* is anchored offshore, Captain."

"Sorry, Mr. Rousseau. I can't chance it."

"Mark my words. There'll be a mutiny."

Throckmorton scoffed at Paul's warning.

Galled, Paul watched him bite into an éclair. "The least you can do, sir, is order decent food for the men."

35

"There's no money for extra provisions. We had to feed those Americans from the *Sylph* that the *Austin* picked up in Campeche and gave into our care, you know."

"They've gone ashore, along with the ranking officers," Paul reminded him. "Our marines deserve better than wormy hardtack and salt meats, sir."

"Good God, man, you don't expect me to dig into my own pocket to feed them, do you? They deserve worse than their lot! Have you forgotten, Mr. Rousseau, that less than a month ago, when we were replenishing water supplies at the Isla de Mujeres, they threatened to seize the ship and sail it to those Centralist bastards in Mexico?"

"I haven't forgotten, sir."

Paul clenched his teeth. Commodore Moore had signed an agreement with the Yucatecan rebels in Mérida the previous September, providing that the Texas fleet would patrol the waters of Campeche, freeing the rebels from Santa Anna's Centralist vermin. The $8,000 per month the Navy received for its services was the only source of revenue available to keep seven warships—such as they were—afloat.

"I haven't forgotten what drove our men to desperation, either," Paul said, not mentioning Throckmorton's brutality to the marines. "Have you forgotten the anger we all felt upon learning Quintana Roo negotiated a treaty between his fellow Yucatecans and the Centralists in Mexico City?"

"No. But that peace agreement isn't ratified yet."

"If it is, Texas loses not only its financial sponsor but its only ally south of the border."

"Yes, yes. I know."

36

"That's all you can say, sir? Need I remind you that Santa Anna is spoiling for a victory?"

The Mexican tyrant had been humiliated at San Jacinto, then the Pastry War with the French had taken its toll—his pride and his leg. But he had risen from the ashes of defeat to plague Paul's adopted Republic once more.

"Baudin's troops kept the menace from our borders for a while, but no more. As you know, the Santa Fe expedition was captured to a man—and they're being brutalized in the dungeons of Mexico City."

"I need no reminders of our dire straits. Would that we could rid ourselves of that one-legged jackal." Throckmorton chuckled. "If I'd have been ol' General Baudin, I'd have lopped off more than his damned leg!" Then, more seriously, he added, "Sam Houston should've killed Santa Anna when he had the opportunity. After we beat them in '36, you know."

"Leave that for the scholars to decide." Paul frowned. "Whatever the case, Santa Anna is back in power. And the point I'm trying to make is that the whole of Texas is in danger."

"Undoubtedly. If we're not there to stop him, he'll blockade the Gulf first thing, and he's sure to move his army overland. Sure as I'm sitting here." Throckmorton clicked his tongue. "But Houston says we can't afford the Navy."

"The way I see it, sir, we can't afford *not* to have a naval armada."

"If it were left up to you, we'd be beating for our rendezvous with the commodore in the Arcas Islands,

37

but we of the *San Antonio* won't go against our President's recall order."

Houston's recall order was the reason they were becalmed in New Orleans. Upon arrival in Galveston they'd been told to proceed there with the *Sylph* survivors and await further instructions.

After his December inauguration Houston had ordered Moore to continue fulfilling his duties to the rebels on the Mexican peninsula. Yet he had issued a new order: Moore and the fleet were to return to Galveston. Apparently the communiqué hadn't been received, or it was being ignored. Knowing Ed Moore, Paul figured the latter to be closer to the truth. In all probability the fleet was staying put to protect the Yucatecan ally. And who would protect Texas?

"With our army disbanded last year, if the fleet is laid up for lack of money, Santa Anna will attack our citizens," Paul said. "The Republic of Texas may be no more."

Unresponsive, Throckmorton replaced his spoon.

"Our seamen know this, sir." Paul crossed his arms. "They couldn't take the blow to their morale. That's why they threatened mutiny. And they haven't had a chance to alleviate their animosities. Give them something, sir—some crumb of consideration to renew their spirits!"

"Well, I'll be damned before I'll feed the lot of them with the fruits of my own table." Throckmorton shrugged. "Anyway, the problem will be taken care of. Houston won't allow the Navy to be laid up. He'll sign an appropriation bill to keep us afloat."

"I'll believe it when I see it." Paul leaned his chair back on two of its legs. "In the meantime I'll pay for the men's provisions."

"Damn good of you, Rousseau. But don't waste your funds. They've sailed under the Lone Star flag this long without charity food. As long as I'm in charge, they will continue to do so."

Rankled, Paul shook his head. Commodore Moore budgeted food money for all the ships. From beef to vinegar to spirits, the men were to be fed well. As Paul saw it, Throckmorton was paying exorbitant prices for what few provisions he stocked.

Naval life was never easy, especially at present, due to frontier politics and the Mexican menace, but Paul was damned sick of fighting for the men's rights. A leader owed his subordinates decent treatment, though that concept was foreign to Throckmorton. Paul didn't wish for ease. It was the regimentation of Navy life that caused him to long for the freedom he had enjoyed as a privateer. But that wasn't the present issue.

"I will have provisions sent aboard," he stated, brooking no further conversation on the point and courting a possible court-martial for insubordination.

Throckmorton gave up the argument. "Do as you wish. Waste your money with my blessings." He wiped a smear of chocolate from the corner of his mouth and motioned for another cup of café au lait. "By the way, I understand you're escorting my sister to the Mardi gras ball tomorrow night."

Paul lifted a shoulder nonchalantly. The idea of revelry held no appeal. He felt like a traitor for considering frivolous undertakings when the men were stranded offshore. Hopefully the food would appease them.

Still, the masked ball had one thing in its favor. Emma was certain to be there. The little spitfire had been on his mind constantly, and just the thought of her was enough to entice him into cheering inwardly for the festivities. He needed another opportunity to win her over, needed a clue about Oliver—any clue. Then he would take it from there.

"You seem rather ambivalent, Rousseau old boy. What's the matter?" Throckmorton laughed heartily. "You haven't let that gossip in the *Picayune* about the masquerades being outlawed dampen your spirit, have you?"

Picturing Emma, Paul smiled. "Not at all."

Suddenly Throckmorton said something that Paul didn't comprehend. "Excuse me, sir. What did you say?"

"You have the look of a man enthralled with a lady. Is my sister the lucky woman?"

"If you don't mind, sir, why do you ask?"

"Never mind."

Paul pulled himself up. Since Throckmorton offered no help, Commodore Moore had to be apprised of the morale situation. Already mentally composing the letter, Paul said, "If you'll excuse me, sir, I'll see to ordering food for our men."

"Of course, of course." Throckmorton waved a hand in dismissal. Interested only in filling his big stomach, he took another bite of his éclair.

Chapter Three

"You sure do have a marvelous appetite," Marian gushed.

A few slivers of braised liver; two hot rice cakes, *calas tout chaud;* and all the wine Paul Rousseau could drink—if that was what Marian called breakfast, then he was guilty as charged. Oh, his appetite for food was appeased; what he had a hankering for was Emma Oliver. So far she hadn't made an appearance in Rankin Oliver's opulent breakfast hall. But if Paul could stomach Marian's coquettish behavior, he could damn sure wait for the vixen to appear from wherever she was hiding.

"I'm so glad you received my invitation to breakfast, Paul." Marian touched a napkin to her Cupid's-bow lips. "I was afraid you'd forgotten me. I haven't seen you in days!"

Seated across from her in one of the twelve rococo chairs, Paul was trying unsuccessfully to give her his full attention. Emma was all he could think of, and he ached to ask about her.

He directed a forced smile at the pretty brunette. "Wonderful breakfast," he complimented. "You set

41

a fine Creole table, Marian."

Right then, he would have much preferred Virginia ham to Creole fare.

"Oh, Paul, how you do go on. But thank you, kind sir!" Marian dropped her lashes. "My late husband, God rest his soul, always complimented my table. How I've missed planning meals for a man." Her mind seemed to wander to another place in time. "It's so frightening being alone."

"Now, Marian," he scolded in a soothing tone, "you're not alone. You've many around you to lessen the grief, and you can't tell me you don't find abundant pleasures in society life."

"I am blessed, and you are right." She forced a smile. "Isn't it a beautiful morning? Rather cold though. Oh! James tells me you sent food out to your ship. Isn't that irregular?"

Paul didn't reply. He had no wish to discuss naval matters with Marian.

Her fingers fluttered to her mouth. "I forgot to tell you, I had the most marvelous note from my mother yesterday. She lives in Richmond, you know."

"That's wonderful." He stood, then walked around the polished dining table to assist Widow Oliver from her chair. "By the way, have you had any news from your father-in-law? I would think he'd be returning from the bayou any day now."

She shrugged. "I've no idea."

He wasn't surprised, and for the first time, Paul wondered why he had ever thought her useful. "You will let me know when word of him arrives?" he asked, figuring he might as well have saved his breath.

42

"My goodness, yes." Marian caught her lower lip between her teeth. "Now, Paul, you're not frightened he'll call you out for courting me, are you?"

Frightened to be called out? Hardly. Paul would welcome the chance to cross swords with Rankin Oliver. But it would never come to that. Paul thirsted for more than blood. He wanted the Oliver name sullied, wanted to see his adversary swing from the gallows. "He won't challenge me. Peace of mind is what I'm after."

Her doldrums gone, Marian said, "Splendid! I'm so pleased we'll be able to put all that nasty business about your father in the past and get on with *joie de vivre!*"

"Right." Paul swallowed back a defense of Étienne. "You haven't spoken a word this morning about your cousin from Virginia."

Marian took the bait. "You mean Emma?"

He coughed behind his hand. How in the hell many cousins from the East does she have visiting? he thought with disgust. Marian's lack of conversational skills got on his nerves. The vinegary little Emma knew how to converse. "Yes."

"Oh, I never see her until afternoon. She doesn't take breakfast. She much prefers a morning ride to food."

"Does she now?"

"Oh, yes." She tucked her arm through his as they headed to the foyer. "That Emma! As much as I care for her, I'm relieved she didn't bring her menagerie of dogs and cats with her on this visit. Those horrid creatures make me sneeze."

"I'm so sorry to hear of your malady," he replied,

masking his indifference and edging toward the door. But he filed away the tad of information about Emma. If she behaved in his arms, he would reward her with a flop-eared puppy. "Tell me again about Emma's broken engagement."

"Oh goodness! I shouldn't've mentioned that." Marian appeared ashamed. "It was wicked of me to spread gossip."

"Don't think ill of yourself, Marian." Paul was not going to give up. "It's just that . . . well, the story is so interesting, I haven't been able to put it out of my mind. Gentlemen don't break engagements. Surely he was either a man without honor or she's a woman in need of it."

Marian's back stiffened. "I don't care what people back home say, Emma couldn't be at fault. She's a dear person. Surely she's done nothing morally wrong." She colored. "I'm not acquainted with her former fiancé, but his reasons must've been groundless."

I'll bet, Paul thought. "Forgive me for prying, Marian."

A sly grin stole across Paul's features. Any guilt that he had felt about following up on his intentions toward Emma—there hadn't been much—flew out the window. Marian had said more with her weak defense than she could have by telling him the whole story.

That chatterbox now said, "Though Emma defies convention she's a lovely person."

"How so?"

"She goes out of her way to please others."

He hoped Emma would go out of her way to

44

please *him*. Of course he wouldn't mind reciprocating.

"I think it's because she's caught in the middle of a large family," Marian was saying. "Two older brothers, an older sister. And a younger one, too."

"Her parents don't give her the attention she needs?"

"Do not misinterpret my words. Quentin and the poor crippled Noreen are fine people, and they love all their children, but I think Emma behaves wildly because she needs someone who is all hers. Like a man."

"Wallflower, is she?"

"Heavens, no! Emma's the belle of Richmond. Or she could be. Well, could've been . . . before this awful scandal with Franklin arose."

"And she made this trip to New Orleans to get away from it?"

"Probably. But I hear tell that she had an argument with her father over something to do with her ambitions."

"She's ambitious? For what . . . a husband?"

"All women want a husband, sweetness! My goodness, that's what we were put on this earth for." In puzzlement, Marian bit her bottom lip once more. "But I don't think that's why Emma was fighting with Quentin. She agreed to attend finishing school and do all the other things proper for a lady, but she has a notion for higher education. Why, to hear her talk you'd think she was a man!"

During his interlude with Emma, Paul had never once likened her speech to a man's. He smiled. She was all female, and he was all male and he wanted her.

"Paul, sweet, enough about her. What about me? You're not throwing a bit of attention my way."

Since it seemed unlikely that he'd see Emma that morning, Paul saw no reason to stay at Magnolia Hall. "Thank you for breakfast, Marian, but I really must get back to the city."

"Must you leave so soon? I do want you to meet my dear cousin. She's so special to me—and to my dear departed William . . . or was." She withdrew her arm from his and steepled her fingers under her chin. "Perhaps we could join Emma for her morning ride."

Paul's senses became alert. "I suppose I could stay awhile longer."

"I'm so-o-o-o pleased. Excuse me. I must change. I have a new coffee-brown riding habit. Do you like brown?"

"Adore it," he replied, half hearing.

"Wonderful! Well, wait for me right there, darling." She pointed to a settee in the foyer. "I'll see you have more wine."

He raised a palm. "I've had enough, thank you." His demur was for naught.

"Becky, oh Becky!" Marian craned her neck around a doorway. "Get Master Rousseau a refreshment. Where is that good-for-nothing? Probably lazing about in her quarters with those children of hers."

Paul shook his head. Marian didn't have children, so he supposed she had no maternal instincts and couldn't understand her servant's need to be with her offspring.

46

"I'm so excited about tonight." Marian started up the stairs, blowing him a kiss from the landing. "I just love Mardi gras!"

It was amazing. Marian had the ability to talk about several things at once, making little sense of any of them. Except when it came to gossip. But he supposed she was a necessary evil for now. He needed her to get to Emma.

He figured Emma Oliver wouldn't show up in his room again without a fight. But she would be there! Soon. And as for her morning ride, she could ride him or he would ride her, or preferably they'd take turns. Whatever the lady preferred.

Emma had spent two sleepless nights and one long day worrying about that brooch—and about Marian. Not to mention herself. Each time she thought it propitious to mention her meeting with Paul Rousseau, she had been interrupted. The longer she hesitated over making an explanation, the harder it got.

As for her offer of money to Rousseau, the previous afternoon Emma had written a note to the banker who held her Letter of Credit in New Orleans, instructing him to release one thousand dollars in currency to Cleopatra. The mammy had then gone straight to the St. Charles and had left the cash with Paul Rousseau, demanding a receipt.

Since he had said nothing about the pin to Cleo, Emma decided Rousseau didn't know it was missing. Forcing herself to be cheerful, she looked on the bright side. The morning was sunny, albeit

47

brisk. What good would it do to fret? This was a perfect day for an invigorating ride atop a magnificent stallion.

At the bottom of the outdoor staircase that descended from the gallery Emma stood motionless, her heart beating wildly as her stiff fingers clutched her riding crop. Paul Rousseau, and Marian, stood in the carriageway!

How dare he show his face at Uncle Rankin's home? Emma fumed. She had paid him in currency to quit his claim! But why was her heart fluttering at the sight of him?

Marian slipped her arm through the crook of Paul's elbow, Emma noted, then touched his midnight-blue coat at the breadth of his wide chest. Emma wished to tear him limb from limb!

"Good morning, dear," Marian said to Emma. Her brown eyes dancing, she smiled up at Rousseau's arrogant face, made hasty introductions, and rattled on.

Rather than snap at her cousin, Emma clamped her teeth and marshaled patience. Marian was such a silly, helpless twit! But she was family, and family was paramount to Emma.

Her attention was suddenly caught.

". . . and isn't it lovely that Paul and I will be able to join you for your morning ride?"

As far as Rousseau was concerned, Emma silently determined it wasn't.

"Did you sleep well, cousin dear?" Marian asked.

Emma hadn't.

"Oh, I'm so looking forward to tonight's ball. I mentioned that Paul will be my escort, didn't I?"

48

"It slipped my mind." Emma couldn't even enjoy the prospect of the upcoming event since he'd be present, his pockets stuffed with her money.

"Paul sweet, don't be rude. Please say something to my darling cousin."

"Believe me, I didn't mean to slight you, Mademoiselle Oliver," Paul said in his rich baritone as he stepped away from Marian. "I have the strangest feeling about you." Mockingly he bowed toward Emma. "You know, as though I'd met you somewhere before. Have you ever had that feeling?"

"Certainly not," Emma replied haughtily. She'd have given her eyeteeth to let fly with the scathing truth about Paul Rousseau, but this was neither the time nor the place.

"Isn't he absolutely charming! And, Paul, doesn't my cousin look stunning this morning?"

"Absolutely charming," he replied, a low tone to his voice that could have been a tease, or a caress.

Marian touched Paul's arm possessively, but spoke to Emma. "I never thought the clouds would part and I'd have sunshine in my life again. Oh, cousin dear, isn't life grand? Isn't *Paul* grand? Now, now, don't be embarrassed, sweetness. And you, Emma—I do hope you'll find someone you can love, someone even half as stupendous as Paul makes me feel!"

"Marian, for heaven's sake, don't place me on a pedestal," he admonished. "Some call me less than virtuous."

She threw back her head and chuckled. "Woe be to the one who speaks false of you!"

Emma realized Marian's last words had been

49

spoken in jest. Yet a chill penetrated her bones, for obviously Marian loved this scoundrel, and the truth about him would crush her. How could she tell her cousin what he was really like?

Until Emma found a way to thwart Paul, she could only hope that Rousseau's advance to her had been made in a weak moment. Two days had passed since his proposition and despite his covert words spoken only moments before, Emma held on to the hope that she had made a mountain out of a molehill.

Marian plucked a blossom from a bush. "My goodness, aren't the azaleas beautiful? They're blooming early this year," she chattered, dancing out of earshot to garner another bloom from a different bush. "I do hope my costume will be ready for tonight!" she called over her shoulder.

Paul stepped closer to Emma and inquired in a whisper, "What fashion will you be wearing this evening? Courtesan? Ah, yes, something gold adorned with diamonds would do wonders for your, um, complexion."

"Get away from me."

"Now, now. Why not wear the split breeches of a thief?" They'd be tailor-made for you. Wouldn't you agree?"

Gold adorned with diamonds. Thief. Emma's heart sank. He knew about the brooch. "I don't know what you're talking about, Mr. Rousseau."

"Don't you now?" He winked and said teasingly, "I don't blame you for wanting a remembrance of our first meeting. I'm counting the hours until our next one . . . then I'll have something of yours."

She had been wrong a moment ago about Rousseau. "You have something of mine already. One thousand dollars. Either return it, or live up to the stipulations."

"I believe this is yours." He reached inside his coat, withdrawing an envelope. "And my word stands."

"You're out of your mind." Emma tried to disregard the bold cast of his eyes, the dark shadowing of his cheeks. How did he get that scar on his jaw?

"Undoubtedly."

His big hand tucked the money in her jacket, at the rise of her breast. The familiarity of his touch was outrageous, provocative.

"Out of my mind lusting for you," he whispered.

Standing so near to him, Emma's senses were aroused. His scent was alluringly warm and slightly herbal. Why couldn't he have bad breath or body odor or some repugnance befitting his low caliber?

To Emma's relief Marian returned. "When are we going to start for the stable? And what were you asking my cousin?"

His eyes never left Emma. "About her costume for tonight."

Emma met his gaze defiantly.

"Oh, Paul." Marian giggled. "Don't be silly! You know it spoils the surprise to tell."

Still centering his attention on Emma, he grinned sardonically. "Something tells me I'll never cease to be surprised by you."

"Why, Paul Rousseau," Marian cooed, daintily lifting the hem of her skirts a mere inch, then

51

pirouetting. "What a wicked one you are."

"Truer words were never spoken," Emma mumbled to herself.

Thankfully the conversation was broken when a young servant boy ran up and tugged on Marian's hand. "Mistress Tillie's lookin' for you and Massah Rousseau. She feelin' poorly agin. She be needin' you to cheer her up!"

Although Emma adored her aunt, she knew this latest disorder was nothing to be concerned about. Aunt Tillie was always "feelin' poorly." From clandestine reading of her father's medical books Emma had long since diagnosed hypochondria in its purest form.

But what a marvelous excuse to get away! With a quick "Pardon me" she passed the two and made for the stable. If she was lucky, she'd be gone before Rousseau and Marian returned from cosseting Auntie!

Walking the path to the stable, Emma railed against Paul Rousseau. Apparently he had no intention of making an exit from Marian's life. Or from hers. Drat him! He held the trump card—the theft. She had to buy time, hire a detective, do whatever it took to find Katie and Packert. After all, Rousseau hadn't seen her take the jewelry; any number of people had access to his room. He suspected her but couldn't pin the theft on her.

Emma was infuriated with Rousseau and with Marian. But mostly she was angry with herself. She was, as Cleo had charged, smitten with the man. With his black hair, dark eyes, and rakish appearance, Paul was certainly attractive, but only on

52

the outside. For he was less than genteel, and he was a lecherous rake. Emma Frances, surely you have better taste in men than that! she chided herself.

Pressing her lips together with determination, Emma decided that though she was curious about, and fascinated with, Paul Rousseau, she was going to ignore him when they met again.

A few feet short of the stable, she felt a tug at her headdress; then it was pulled from her head. Swinging about, she placed her hands on her hips. Rousseau had her hat in his hand, twirling it around his forefinger.

"Running away, *chérie?*"

Chapter Four

"I don't run from anything or anyone."

"Don't imagine you do." Paul grinned at the spunky woman.

Emma looked beautiful, from her blond sweep of hair to her narrow calfskin boots. The holly green habit fit her shapely body like a glove.

Running the tip of his finger along the silly leghorn hat's plume when he'd have rather been stroking her velvet-smooth, oval face, he said, "I don't run from anything or anyone, either. In my thirty years of living I've never backed down from a challenge, and I don't intend to start with you."

"Is that so?" Emma raised her riding crop slightly.

"I ask no quarter," he replied. "And give none, either."

"We'll see about that."

Paul eyed the riding whip, which she was now waving, then directed his attention to her light green eyes. "If you think lashing me with that thing will do it, you're mistaken." Moving closer to her, he placed the hat on her fetching blond curls. "You know the terms, *chérie.*"

She reached up to secure the hat pin. "I cannot meet your price, Mr. Rousseau."

"Let me help you . . . with your hat, that is." He started to assist her, but she swung away from him and made for the stable. He was right behind her. Once inside the building, he said teasingly, "How nice we're alone."

"Not in my opinion." Glaring, she whirled around. "Two thousand dollars cash, and that's my final offer."

"Your money doesn't interest me. You interest me." He lessened the space between them, taking her tiny hand between his callused ones. "And I don't want to take anything away . . . I'd rather give than receive. In this case I'll give you pleasure that won't cost a picayune."

She wrenched her fingers free of his grasp. Holding her head high, she whipped the crop against her skirt. "The only pleasure I could possibly derive from you is lashing this quirt across your ugly face!"

He knew the little spitfire was angry enough to do it. The thought didn't frighten him, but he decided to ease up on her. "I've never had a taste for suffering, *chérie*."

"Only inflicting it," she retorted hotly.

"You're wrong." Paul crossed over the straw floor to a stall where a white Arabian stallion was penned. Patting the horse's sleek head, he addressed his next words to the animal. "Say, boy, how are you today? Ready for a ride?" The stallion whickered and bobbed his head twice, as if he'd understood. "Yes, the pretty lady with the blond hair will accompany us, *mon ami*. I'll saddle your lady friend for

Mademoiselle Emma Oliver."

Emma's brows drew together. It was perplexing to hear him speak kindly to an animal. Considering the trouble he had given her and Marian, Emma never thought a horse would bring out his gentle side. And despite her anger, she was interested in Paul's behavior, both laudable and despicable.

Her tone lacking its previous edge, she commented, "I didn't think men of the sea were horsemen."

Paul warmed to the soft sound of her voice. Leveling his gaze with hers, he saw that she was peering at him quizzically, and realized there was much to be learned about this woman who mesmerized him with the fire of her personality. She could be cunning and devious. Yet he did not fault her for either; life had forced him into the same path, for survival and to achieve his goals.

He wanted to know more about her inquisitive side, and her tender one. Answering questions about himself didn't hold much appeal, but it might help him get close to her . . . and gain her confidence. "I haven't been a sea dog all my life."

"I'd argue the 'dog' part." The twinkle in her eyes matched the mirth in her voice. "I've heard many things about you," she said seriously. "You seem to be an enigma."

Paul folded his arms in front of his chest. "How so?"

"I've been told you've been a pirate—uh, privateer —yet you're now on the right side of the law, insofar as your naval adventures are concerned anyway."

Paul was reluctant to defend his past, yet he didn't

want to lose ground with Emma, even though he enjoyed the positive turn this conversation had taken. "I don't deny I've been a privateer, and I feel no shame about my years in that pursuit. I'm on the right side of the law, as you put it, because of the patriotism I have for the Republic of Texas. I won't bore you with the details."

"Who says I'd be bored?"

He chuckled and leaned back against the stall gate. "When I was seventeen I set sail from this place and ended up at Jean Lafitte's old port of call in Galveston. Learned to love Texas almost as much as I love a salt breeze at my face and the roar of the ocean in my ear."

Texas had given shelter to his troubled heart. Paul had been lonely and alone after his parents died. On the heels of losing his mother and then his father, his grandfather had turned him off the family sugar plantation—with good reason. Texas had been a good place to come to grips with himself and get on with being a grown man.

"Is that all?" Emma asked. "Tell me why you became a part of the Navy."

"The war with Santa Anna came along, and I signed up with the first fleet. We Texans were victorious at San Jacinto, so I went back to privateering."

"But you're now in the Navy. What happened?"

"I met Ed Moore down in the West Indies. Over a bottle of my best cognac we discussed our mutual interests—Texas's problems with the Mexicans being at the forefront. President Lamar was looking to reinstate the Texas Navy, and he'd offered Ed the post captaincy. By the time we got to the bottom of the bottle, Ed decided to accept the offer. And I gave him my word I'd serve under him."

"Marian's brother is your commander on the *San Antonio*." She lifted a brow. "I would've thought you'd be in charge of your own vessel."

"When the next ship is commissioned . . ." Paul hesitated. There was no use saying another ship probably wouldn't be commissioned, thanks to the Big Drunk. "When the next one's put in service I'll be at the helm."

"You're very sure of yourself and your endeavors."

"Granted," Paul said calmly. Yes, he was sure of himself. Of the Texas Navy's future, he wasn't as confident.

"James tells me your president doesn't approve of the Navy."

"Sam Houston is a legend in his own time, and he's given his all for the betterment of our Republic; but he's a mountain man and an Indian fighter. He's not perfect."

"You don't like him?"

"I respect him. For the most part I admire his leadership abilities. I don't agree with his policy toward the fleet."

"There's not much you can do about it, right? He gives the orders for you to follow."

"That's the scheme of naval life, *chérie*." With the toe of his boot Paul pushed aside several blades of straw. "Enough about that. Tell me about you."

"I'm not through with *you*." She placed the quirt on a shelf. "I've only heard one side of the story about your father. Pardon my saying so, but he was disgraced here in Louisiana, yet you're welcome in society. I find that strange."

Disgraced? Paul begged to differ, but he had no urge to discuss Étienne Rousseau, especially with Rankin Oliver's blood kin. He admitted inwardly that his father had had faults, but then who didn't? Étienne had been weak in many ways, spoiled by his mother, fine looks, and too much money, which had been spent unwisely at the gaming tables. Nonetheless, strength had been a part of his character, too. He was loyal to his friends and country, kind to all and fiercely loving of his son and his wife Angélique.

As for society circles, Rankin—an interloper, a tinker turned planter and merchant—had done his best to malign Étienne's character, but most people had taken the slurs for what they were: petty backstabbing. However, if Paul were to call Emma's attention to the truth, she'd know he harbored ill feelings toward her uncle. "This isn't your home in Virginia. New Orleans makes its own rules."

"How do you know I'm from Virginia!"

"When your name is mentioned, *chérie,* I'm all ears." He grinned mischievously. "Perhaps you'd like to hear all I know." He hoped he could get her to discuss Rankin Oliver with candor. And—who was he trying to fool?—Paul Rousseau wanted to get Emma Oliver alone so that he could enjoy more of her. "The St. Charles would be a good place for further discussion."

"There won't be a time and place!" In exasperation she dropped her arms. "This game of yours has gone far enough." Her determination was voiced in each syllable. "I'm going to tell Marian that you're playing her false."

"I forbid it!" Paul needed to end the charade with Widow Oliver, and quick. It was causing more pain than gain. Almost sorry for Emma's change from curiosity to anger, he stepped closer and took her elbows; she didn't pull away. Rather than taunt her, he ached to make love to her, but time would take care of that. "If you do, I've my own story to tell."

"What are you implying?"

He felt the small quiver of fear that ran through her. "Emma, you seem to have forgotten something."

She drew her shoulders back. "I've forgotten nothing."

"What about the property you took from my room?"

"I . . . I don't know what you're talking about!"

"The devil will take you for lying, Emma Oliver."

She swallowed hard. "I didn't take your brooch."

"Au contraire. You did." A wide grin spread across his face. "I never mentioned it was a brooch."

"Drat," she muttered. Defeat seared through her. "I didn't mean to take it." Her voice was quiet. "You startled me when you walked in, and I dropped it into my pocket. Unfortunately it was stolen by two pickpockets when I left the St. Charles." Looking him squarely in the eye, she added, "I'm prepared to make restitution in the event it can't be recovered."

Paul had been confident that its return would be simple. Now it had become complicated. He might never see the brooch again. He should have said something about it the moment it was stolen. "How do you put a price on a family heirloom? It belonged to my mother and to my father's mother before that."

"Oh no," she whispered, dropping her lashes, then looking up at him once more. "It *will* be found . . . somehow."

"I'd say the prospects of that are doubtful." Lifting her chin with his forefinger, he stared into her troubled eyes. He would give no quarter. "I'd say you now have two reasons to visit me at the St. Charles. To make me forget Marian, and well . . ."

"Why are you doing this to me?" she asked pleadingly.

"Because I want to make love to you."

"I should slap you for saying that."

He winked devilishly. "You won't."

"What makes you so certain?"

He stepped even closer. "Your words lack conviction."

"Well, then let me put some conviction into my words. I'll *never* allow you to make love to me!"

"Never is a long, long time." The desire to kiss her overwhelmed him. He took her hat from her head once more and dropped the leghorn onto the straw. "Emma, beautiful Emma . . . let's not argue."

His palms framed her face. He parted his lips slightly and tilted his head down to hers. She was braced between him and the wall, and he loved the feel of her warm, soft, womanly body. Her lips were sweet and tinged lightly with coffee; her lilac-scented skin drove him wild with desire. He heard her moan as he kissed her tenderly, felt her arms steal around

61

his back. A flash of heat swept through him and settled in his groin, and he wanted her more than he had ever wanted another woman.

"I dreamed of you last night," he whispered between kisses, confessing the truth. "You were lying naked in my bed. Your skin was hot from our lovemaking, and you called out my name as I made you mine. Say it, Emma, say my name."

"No," she murmured brokenly, moving her face to the side.

"Say it." He pressed his body solidly against her, forcing her to look at him, and kissing her once more. "Now."

"Paul," she whispered in surrender, her fingers curling into his shoulders. "Paul."

Her words poured through him like rich cream, and he ached to take her right then, right there. But he wouldn't. He wanted her in his bed, with all the time in the world for each of them to savor the delights of their lovemaking.

"I'll call for a carriage," he said huskily.

Defiance flared in her eyes, as she stiffened her shoulders. "Don't be absurd!" She ducked under his arms and grabbed her plumed hat. Several feet separating them, she crumpled the brim in her palm. "Do you always have two women at the same time, Rousseau? Two women of the same name, this time. Have you considered the pain you'll cause Marian by trifling with her affection?"

"Marian who?" Paul walked slowly toward Emma.

"Oooh! You are a rotten blackguard, Rousseau."

She thrust her hand out. "Get out of my way and let me pass."

"Have you forgotten you're indebted to me?"

"Mr. Rousseau, I'm indebted to no one."

"Ah, but you are. To me. Of course we can settle the matter at my hotel."

"I won't go!"

"Yes, Emma, you will."

"Over my dead body!"

"Your dead body is not what I want."

She started for the door, but he caught her arm. "If you're not willing to share your *warm* body, then I'll call the police when I return to the city . . . about the matter of the brooch, you know."

"I'm not frightened of you or of your extortion. You can't prove I took the pin. It's your word against mine."

"Then you're not as astute as I had pegged you. I have a material witness." He paused for emphasis. "The night you visited my room, you bribed the concierge with a gold piece. He remembers you. And he'll gladly testify you were in my quarters," Paul fibbed. "It's two against one."

"You vulture. I'm not surprised you've drawn that venal hotel clerk into your wicked scheme. He's as reprehensible as you." She curled her lip. "My mother always says birds of a feather flock together!"

"Then you and I are a matched set of lovebirds." He extracted a piece of parchment from his coat pocket. "This note, written by Castillo at the hotel," he lied, "implicates you as a thief."

Wordlessly she grabbed the document, ripping it to shreds and stuffing the remnants into her skirt pocket.

"Remind me to check your pockets often." Arms akimbo, he chuckled. "He'll be more than agreeable to sign another one."

"I don't doubt that for a moment." Emma clenched her fists. "I can't return the brooch unless I find it. Give me time to search for the thieves, and you'll get it back."

"Why should I give you time?"

She glanced at the ground, then up again. "Because I asked for it."

Paul could feel himself being wrapped around her finger, and he pulled away from that velvet bond. Shaking his head, he said, "Your time is up."

"Do you have any redeeming qualities?" she yelled.

Remembering Marian's words about Emma's love for dogs and cats, Paul answered, "I've never been cruel to animals."

"Too bad that quality doesn't extend to humans!"

"All right," he acquiesced. "I'll give you three days to return the pin. Three days, and that's all. I'll expect you at the St. Charles by Tuesday evening, no later than sunset." Bending down, Paul gave her a quick kiss on the cheek . . . and it tasted like more! "Do keep your dance card open tonight. I'll expect a waltz with you—if I'm not completely occupied with your dear cousin, that is."

He whipped around and left the stable. Perhaps he had been unnecessarily harsh, but Emma could take it. Of that, he was certain. He had the distinct impression that she was the type who wanted a challenge, just as he did. He was beginning to rethink his assessment of her former fiancé. In all probability, the man had been so enraptured after he'd lifted Emma's skirts that he had started following her around like a little puppy dog until she'd given him the boot. If Paul were to start yapping and begging, letting her think she had won about Marian—which she had—and about the brooch, she'd lose interest in him.

Paul didn't intend to let Emma lose interest. Not yet. Not until her words ceased to deny him and she succumbed to the wanton language of her body.

A voice in the back of his brain screamed, "You're letting desire get in the way of logic! This isn't courtship, it's war. If you want information on Rankin Oliver, you need to play the game Emma's way." Yet he couldn't, for realization hit him. He yearned for her body as much as he yearned to right the wrongs Rankin was imposing upon the Republic of Texas—not to mention his obsession with avenging the deaths of Karla Stahl and Étienne Rousseau.

Marian Oliver had hurriedly hidden around the corner of the stable. She had heard everything, and her mind was in a dither. So much to comprehend! Pursing her lips, she attempted to sort through those overheard revelations.

Since Paul was obviously so taken with Emma, she supposed she should be insulted, but she wasn't. Well, she couldn't allow anything to upset her, not

65

with tonight still ahead! Who could be angry when there was a Mardi gras ball to attend?

And Howard O'Reilly would be there. Oh, what a lovely thought that was! But Howard was such a stick at times, he didn't see that she had played up to Paul Rousseau simply to make him jealous.

Heavens, she hoped he'd recognize her disguise tonight. Venus, the goddess of love, was going to get Mr. O'Reilly's attention—and his betrothal!

Emma certainly had Paul's attention. Such a strumpet, that one was! But Marian upbraided herself. Emma had been kind to her, always, and sweet William had loved Emma. Poor Emma just didn't seem to realize when she was bringing disgrace on herself. Falling back into her former way of thinking, Marian decided that surely Emma realized it was sinful to steal, and certainly she had gone to Paul's room to protect her. But didn't she realize how shameful that was!

Oh, if Marian didn't love Emma so much, she'd go straight to Tillie with the information. *Poor thing.* Tillie was in such frail health Marian expected her to pass away any sundown!

Heavens, when that happened she'd have to go back to wearing dismal mourning weeds! Marian frowned. Black did nothing for her coloring, and she had, at Rankin's insistence, mourned William's passing for three long years. Not that she didn't pine for him—she did. But black!

Emma, since she was fair-complected, looked lovely in black. Let her do the mourning; let her hold Rankin's hand! On second thought, Marian wouldn't wish that on her worst enemy. She decided, with a nod, to visit her mother as soon as propriety allowed.

But that was no good. If Marian left for Virginia, how would she get to see that red-haired attorney? She chewed at a fingernail. She'd stay. And since Emma—Howard's niece, it shouldn't be forgotten—was in residence at Magnolia Hall, why should Marian not avail herself of each and every opportunity to see her future husband? Marian was extremely proud of her decision.

Oh, my gracious, yes! She and Howard O'Reilly were made for each other, just as Emma and Paul were. Marian had seen the sparks flying between those two! Fluttering her hands, she conjured up images of a double wedding. It was about time Emma settled down and married, Marian reflected sanctimoniously. The poor thing was twenty years old! Paul would save Emma from spinsterhood.

"Oh, won't that be delightful," she whispered gleefully.

A beautiful gown—no, two of them!—would have to be commissioned. Champagne and delicacies and a stringed quartet would be arranged for the nuptials. She was going straight back to the drawing room to start work on a wedding gift for Emma—a nice embroidered handkerchief would be lovely.

The widow Oliver literally danced back to the house.

Chapter Five

In the privacy of her room, Emma sat down at the writing desk to ponder her predicament. Drat Rousseau! Drat him and everything he stood for, which was the miserable Texas Navy.

He had admitted more than once to being less than honorable, and she cringed at the thought of languishing in a prison cell! What was the answer to her dilemma? Emma didn't want to lose her virtue to him of all people. That should be preserved for her future husband.

She wanted a home and husband someday. She doubted that a tall, dark, handsome stranger would sail into her life and sweep her out of her slippers. Even if some man did, he probably couldn't and wouldn't accept her radical ambitions.

The devil transposed her thoughts: Paul. Sail. Tall, dark, handsome. Rousseau had sailed into New Orleans; he was everything a maiden dreamed of—in a rugged way. Emma grimaced. Yes, he was all those things. But the nays outweighed the yeas. He was a Rousseau—and a double-crossing woman-izer at that.

So much for girlish musings about the ideal man. No, he wasn't for her or for Marian.

And if it became common knowledge that Emma was a felon, no sensitive man—was there such for her?—would take her to wife. Should she give in to Paul Rousseau?

After taking three deep, calming breaths, she felt much more rational. Suddenly the clouds in her mind cleared and sunny skies broke through. An attorney! That's what she needed, legal counsel. But the only lawyer she knew in New Orleans was her mother's brother, Howard O'Reilly. The mere idea of confessing all to him sent chills through Emma.

But Paul had given her three days' grace. A decision about speaking with Howard could wait. What about the planned talk with William's widow? It was out of the question now. If she did that, Paul Rousseau would take his pound of flesh.

She needed to occupy her mind. Betsy had been absent that morning, and this worried Emma. Dependability was Betsy's watchword. The servant had been a gift from Emma's father to the Louisiana Olivers, and since she had a special place in Emma's heart, a visit to the slave quarters was in order to call on the house servant and her children. Emma waited until Paul was safely away from Magnolia Hall before walking to the row of small houses situated two hundred yards from the big house.

The quarters were clean but Spartan. Two cornshuck mattresses; a walnut crib and rocking horse, both of which had been gifts from Emma's mother; a rough handmade table; and two chairs were all the furnishings. A few garments hung on nails sticking from the whitewashed walls. Emma's heart went out to the family as she took little George onto her lap and handed the toddler a piece of toffee.

"I wish my mother could see your children, Betsy," she said earnestly. "Your babies are beautiful!"

"Thank you." The mulatto woman, who was about Emma's age, got a faraway look in her light-brown eyes as she rocked her sleeping baby. "Sometimes I miss being in Virginia, and I sure would love to see Mistress Noreen! Your mama be the finest lady I ever met."

That was true. Emma's mother, despite her handicap, did much with her life. Maybe too much. Noreen Oliver gave her all to husband, duty, and children. But there were too many young Olivers. Emma was merely one more daughter to marry off. She tried not to think harshly of that. Her mother loved her, she was certain.

Brushing aside these thoughts, Emma said, "Are you happy here at Magnolia Hall?"

"Oh, yes'm, I'm happy. Jeremiah and the chil'en make me real happy and proud." The baby began to fret, and Betsy held her youngest even closer to her chest. "My Jeremiah . . ." She smiled bashfully. "Having a man who make you get all shivery inside is just about the best thing in the world."

Emma cleared her throat. The only man who had ever made her feel that way was . . . *Forget that scoundrel!* she warned herself.

Stroking George's soft cheek, Emma observed his mother. "I missed you at the house this morning, Betsy."

"Mistress Tillie," she replied, her voice barely above a whisper, "she gave me a free morning."

"Something's troubling you. Please tell me."

"It's little Rose here." Tears sprang to the woman's eyes. "My babe's sick!"

Emma set George on his feet, crossed the room, and bent to touch the infant's feverish forehead. She could hear the child's rattled breath now, could see that its minuscule nostrils were clogged. "Has a doctor been called?"

"No'm."

"Why not!"

Betsy ducked her head. "Mistress Tillie say she can't afford to be calling doctors ever'time one of the slave babies takes sick."

Her teeth clenching, Emma looked away. How dare Aunt Tillie neglect her charges!

"The 'remedie' lady was here last night. She helping my baby."

Shocked, Emma said nothing. Though Betsy had been reared in Virginia, apparently she had taken up the ways of voodooism. It was best not to tangle with these superstitious beliefs, not when the infant needed immediate medical care. "Let me see her."

Emma took Rose from Betsy's arms and placed her inside the crib, taking the bindings from the child to check her tawny body for telltale swelling. Rose wailed in protest. It was a pitiful sound, congested and weak. Emma crooned, "Poor baby, it'll be all better."

She drew the sick child into the comfort of her arms. "Put a kettle of water on the hearth. Then go to my room and find the small black bag in my armoire. I'll need a fine-woven blanket, too."

"What you gonna do, Miss Emma?"

"I'm going to doctor this sick child."

The mulatto's hand flew to her mouth, and her eyes widened. "No'm. Doctoring's for menfolk."

"It has been in the past, but that will change." Emma forced herself to be patient. "You trust the gris-gris lady, don't you?"

Betsy nodded.

"She's a woman; I'm a woman. Women can be healers." Emma's tone brooked no challenge. "Now do as I instructed."

Cowed, Betsy ladled water into the kettle. That finished, she started for the door. Then the baby began to bawl, making her tense with concern.

Remorseful for the harsh tone she'd used to her, Emma thought better of her plans. As well as giving attention to the child, she needed to reassure the worried mother. Wasn't that what her father called a "good bedside manner"?

"Wait," Emma said gently. "Have Jeremiah fetch Dr. Boulogne posthaste. I'll pay for his services." Emma swallowed. "And if you'll allow me, I'll do my best in the meantime to make your baby daughter comfortable."

The mother brightened. "Thank you, Miss Emma. I'd be mighty pleased if you'd take care of my Rose till the doctor get here."

Emma sprang into action. Putting the baby back into the crib, she propped up little Rose's upper body, swabbed her nose, and bathed her torso with an alcohol-soaked rag. Meanwhile, George made noisy use of the rocking horse and of an assortment of cooking utensils. Betsy returned with Emma's bag and blanket, and Emma rubbed a mixture of camphor and lard on the tiny chest. Then she concocted a sugar teat to disguise the foul-tasting elixir she had secretly taken from her father's apothecary one night. Despite her attempt to make the medicine go down easier, Rose cried from its bitter taste.

"Just a little, sweetheart," Emma coaxed, tickling the child's throat. "That's a brave girl."

Now that Rose had acquiesced, Emma began, with Betsy's assistance, to fashion a tent over the crib and the nearby table. "We need to keep steam in here," Emma said, pouring water from the kettle into a wide, flat pan. "Hold the blanket up a tad, and I'll set this inside."

Thus began a vigil of drawing and boiling water, and replacing the pan inside the confine. Despite alternating chores, there was more than enough to do to keep both women busy. Emma was again in the process of coaxing the sugar teat past Rose's toothless gums when Dr. René Boulogne arrived.

The doctor, a man who appeared to be thirty-five but was probably older, had a winning smile and a shock of strawberry-blond hair. Step by step, Emma explained the procedures she had taken, and he nodded his approval of each one. Then he opened a well-worn medical bag, taking a stethoscope from it. Emma's fingers itched to touch the gadget, to put it to her ears and listen to Rose's heart and lungs. *Someday, Emma Frances. Someday . . .*

The doctor rose from his ministrations. "The child will be feeling better." His words carried the accent of his homeland, France. "The right procedures, mademoiselle, you did." He turned to Rose's mother as Emma sighed in relief. "The fever will break soon," he stated, and then he gave instructions for the child's care.

"I be mighty thankful to you both," Betsy said.

Dr. Boulogne motioned for Emma to follow him.

"Mademoiselle Oliver," the doctor said as they walked toward his buggy, "please allow me to know where you acquired the tools of doctoring."

She gave him a short description of some of her readings, and Dr. Boulogne chuckled. "Make a fine nurse, you will."

"Thank you, sir. I've always had a calling to help the infirm—but not as a nurse. I wish to be a physician. No! I don't merely wish it, I intend to be a doctor."

Shaking his head, he chuckled anew. *"Impossible.* No medical school in America accepts *les femmes* for admission!"

"I know that." Emma slowed her steps. "But I hope someday that will change . . . and in the meantime, I pray a physician will take me on as apprentice."

"Maybe so, maybe not." They were at his gig now, and he stopped before stepping in. "You dream the impossible dreams. But you are devoted, so you'll make a fine plantation mistress; and look out for her slaves, a good mistress does."

"I've no intention of marrying." Emma did not add *unless I can find the right man.* "I'm devoted to my calling."

He shot her an astonished look, an expression

74

very male in his blue eyes as amazement turned to amusement. "Better you marry, mademoiselle. If you do not, you will have no time for your devotion; your days will be too full with turning away your suitors."

"Please don't make light of me. I write and read Latin quite well, and I've studied the principles of medicine at length. I take my studies very seriously."

"Offending you was not my purpose. It is apparent you are serious. So I will be as well. Nurse the sick, Mademoiselle Oliver. The world needs you."

"The world needs more doctors, sir." She remembered the way he had nodded approval of the care she had taken with the baby, and she was encouraged by the thought. "How do you feel about the possibility of a female doctor?"

He raised a shoulder and turned up a palm. *"Les femmes* I have nothing against. They sometimes have more understanding of suffering than men."

At that moment Emma made up her mind. She was going to convince Dr. René Boulogne that he needed her as an apprentice. And if it took a bit of temporary compromise on her part, so be it. She smiled and spoke mildly. "You're right. Maybe I should think in a more practical way, but, Doctor, how will I learn to nurse the sick if I don't have someone to teach me?"

He raised a brow before settling into the buggy. "Tomorrow at ten I will check on the infant." He doffed his hat and picked up the reins. "I would not complain if a certain young lady were to assist me once again. . . ."

The buggy pulled away, leaving Emma ecstatic.

Clapping her hands, she whirled around in a circle. Dr. Boulogne would help her fulfill the first step to her goal! She was on the road to practical experience, and it was wonderful to think that someday she'd be a physician.

On the path back to the house, she indulged in the dream, forgetting her problems for a while, and when she entered the drawing room, she found Marian caught up in her embroidery.

"Oh. There you are, Emma dear. Have you seen that lazy Betsy?" Not waiting for an answer, Marian went on. "What do you think of these lovebirds?" She held a handkerchief aloft. "Aren't they exquisite?"

Emma nodded affirmation, but the design called to her mind Paul Rousseau and her problem with him. In the stable he had called them "lovebirds." Her happiness suddenly vanished, and three days seemed like three hours as Emma worried over how she was going to get her hands on the brooch . . . and keep Rousseau's hands off *her*.

Cheered by his good fortune, Paul tightened his hand around a mug of rum, bringing it to his lips. Less than an hour after leaving Emma at her uncle's plantation, he had found Henry Packert, who now sat opposite him in the corsair's three-room shotgun house on Carondolet Street.

"So, ya been looking for me, have ya?" the pirate asked. "Well, old pal, whatcha need?"

Paul studied the reprobate. Henry Packert probably wasn't as old as he looked, with his wrinkled face, dirty eye patch, and rotten teeth. But he was definitely past middle age as evidenced by his thick, filthy body that appeared as if it would deflate if punctured.

Paul had never liked him, but the two men had been brethren on the high seas, and several times he had come to the pirate's aid. Though the single-eyed Packert sailed his leaky corvette with admirable finesse, he was possessed by a sickness the likes of which infected Emma Oliver: thievery for the sport of it. But Packert had two things on his side: he knew the goings and comings of the port of New Orleans, and he hated Rankin Oliver.

Nevertheless, Paul rued the situation that was forcing him to turn to this man.

"Tell me," Paul implored, "what you know about Rankin Oliver's dealings with the Centralists."

Packert patted tobacco onto a cigarette paper, licking an edge, before rolling a smoke with two thumbs. "Rankin Oliver ya say. Hmmm." His brown-stained fingers stuck the cigarette between his blackened teeth. "Seems to me I recall he and yer pa dueled it out some time back. Does your interest have anything to do with that?"

"To be honest, yes. But it has to do with patriotism, too. I'm back with the Texas fleet now," Paul explained, and Packert indicated he was aware of it. "I have reason to believe Oliver's running guns to the government in Mexico City."

Packert brought a candle flame to his cigarette. "'Reason to believe'? Got any evidence proving it?"

"If I had hard evidence, I wouldn't be here talking to you." Crossing his arms, Paul leaned his creaking chair back on two legs. "A couple of months ago, down in Merida, I met Oliver's mistress. After a while Karla told me that he was on Santa Anna's payroll. She wanted to be free of her so-called protector, but he kept her dependent. We made a deal. In exchange for passage back to the Rhineland she'd help the Texan cause by gathering evidence on her protector's activities. Last month she sent word to me—success was at hand; she had papers to prove it. I went by"—Paul paused, renewed anger flashing through him—"I went by her hacienda later that night. I found her dying, her skull crushed. Her last word was 'Oliver.'" Grimacing, Paul ran his hand through his hair. "Needless to say, the papers couldn't be found."

"Don't surprise me none." Packert scratched the gray stubble of his beard. "Word has it several crates of guns and powder be on their way down the Miss'sip'. Stamped for Oliver's sugar plantation in the West Indies. I'd place me bet 'twill end up at his factor house . . . temporarily."

Paul's line of sight swept across the small room that was surprisingly clean, considering the occupant. "When will the shipment be here?"

"Next few days." The older man shook his head. "Can't say for certain."

"Figure Oliver'll be back from the Bayou in time to meet the shipment?" Paul asked.

"Doubt it." Packert took a swig of rum and wiped his mouth with his palm. "Oliver ain't one to make a move that'd put hisself in jeopardy. He'll have an alibi, good and proper. He lets others do his dirty work."

78

Something didn't add up. If Oliver's minions carried out his odious deeds, Paul wondered why he had taken Karla Stahl's life with his own hands. But looking on the other side of the coin, Rankin Oliver had left her for dead, her one word being the only clue to her assailant. "Who in particular is helping him."

"Don't know."

"Packert, don't hemhaw with me."

"I ain't." Packert poured himself another glass of spirits and squinted his eye at Paul. "Gotta be a body he trusts, I reckon. And he ain't a trusting man. Don't imagine it's anybody at his factor house, though. Too close for comfort, if ya know what I mean. *You* tell *me* who he trusts"—he raised his glass in a mock toast—"and then we'll both know."

"I will find out." Paul raised his own glass and downed the burning liquid.

"And I'll keep me ears peeled. Let ya know what turns up, that I will."

"Good." As far as Paul knew, Rankin Oliver was close to Emma Frances Oliver. Was her arrival in New Orleans timed to meet the shipment from up North? It seemed too preposterous for thought, involving a young niece, but Paul refused to dismiss any possibility.

Emma. Paul rose to his feet and walked over to the window. Two whores passed by and waved to him, but he ignored them. His thoughts were on thieving, lying little Emma. And the brooch she had stolen from him. Packert was a thief, too. A talkative thief. "Packert, there's something else. I—"

"Henry, I'm home," a woman called, interrupting

the conversation, from the back of the house. Her arrival was punctuated by the slam of a door. "Where are you?"

"Up front, Katie me love." Packert smacked his lips, as if in eager anticipation of his woman. "Come meet our company."

When Katie swept into the front room, Paul was completely unprepared for the sight of the tall, cloak-draped woman. He had expected a hag. Yet she was young and lovely, and had a proud bearing. Her hair was a rich, deep shade of brown, her eyes hazel. Her heart-shaped face and olive complexion were set off by a smile that revealed healthy, even teeth. She was almost, Paul thought, as lovely as Emma Oliver.

"This be me ol' mate, Paul Rousseau," Henry said, expanding on the truth. "And this be Katie."

"Monsieur Rousseau . . ."

Packert was quick to add: "Used to be abused by her old master, but them be days gone by. Been bought and paid for by me, so keep your hands to yourself."

Bought and paid for? There was but one explanation for that: she was a former slave, a woman of mixed blood. Paul damned the owner who had seen fit to offer such a fine *femme de couleur* to the likes of Henry Packert.

Respectfully he offered his hand. "Pleased to meet you, Katie."

"And you. But I prefer to be called Kathryn, if you please."

"Kathryn . . . may I assist you with your wrap?"

"Don't be starting that honey-talk with me

80

woman!" Henry roared, jumping to his feet and nearly knocking the table over in the process. "Be me own right to get her cloak."

Stepping back, Paul acceded, "Naturally, Pack—" His voice left him. His pulse surged. At the bodice of Kathryn's modest gown was *Angélique Rousseau's brooch!*

"Where . . . where did you get that pin?" Paul asked, his voice strangled.

"We'll never tell," Henry responded, chuckling. "Me woman likes nice baubles. Pretty, ain't it?"

"It's exquisite." Paul took his eyes from the heart-shaped pin, with its pavé of diamonds, to drill a look at Henry Packert. "But you stole it."

"Is that a fact?" Henry asked as Kathryn stepped back.

"It is. That piece of jewelry is mine; I'd recognize it anywhere. It was stolen last week."

Henry sneered. "Ya wouldn't be saying that it was me who done took it from ya?"

"No, I'm saying you stole it from a woman—I believe it was in front of the St. Charles Hotel. She had just filched that brooch from under my thumb."

Henry's high-pitched laughter filled the small room. "That be rich! Ya let a trollop steal from ya. She musta been a sweet tart in bed, I'd allow."

Paul saw red. For some odd reason he would not condone disrespect of Emma. He lunged forward to grab Packert's lapel. "Be careful of your words."

His eye bulging as he held up a palm in surrender, Packert begged clemency, which Paul allowed and stepped back.

Kathryn pushed away from the wall she had been

81

hugging. "If it's . . . if it really belonged to Monsieur Rousseau, then we must return it in the name of friendship. Isn't that right?" Her last words were more of an order than a question.

"Now, gal, don't be minding me business." Packert ran a finger under his dirty eye patch. "The way it looks to me, the brooch be me woman's now. 'Tain't fair to take it away from her."

"Packert—" She clamped her mouth shut when he raised a palm in a gesture of demanding quiet.

"If me gal was to turn it over, how much would ya give me for the inconvenience?" Packert picked up a knife from the table and ran his thumb down its face. "The brooch belongs to us now. But I might be willing to part with it for a couple hundred . . . seeing's how it's me old buddy Paul Rousseau."

The vicious implication of the blade wasn't lost on Paul. In three steps he was across the room again. He grabbed Packert's wrist, yanking it until the knife clattered to the tabletop. "Seeing's how I'm your old buddy Paul Rousseau, I'm willing to give you the two hundred dollars. But get something straight right now. You and your threats of violence don't scare me." He slammed the pirate's arm to the table.

Packert screamed in pain when his skin made hard contact with the knife handle. "Damn you, Rousseau!"

Paul stepped back and reached into his coat pocket. After counting out the required number of bills, he ordered, "Get the brooch."

Packert lumbered over to Kathryn and wrenched the brooch from her bodice to fling it toward Paul, a

82

diamond popping from its setting when it landed on the floor.

Two minutes later Paul rode away from Carondolet Street, the piece of jewelry in his possession. He supposed he should tell Emma of its recovery; it was the decent thing to do. On second thought he decided against it.

Now that he had some firm information, it was unnecessary to press her regarding her uncle's doings.

Instead he would turn his attention to Emma Oliver, the woman, and tonight at the masquerade ball he would have the perfect opportunity to do so.

Chapter Six

The last Saturday evening before Lent was a night of gaiety in New Orleans. While music flowed as freely as the champagne fountain, a thousand candles cast dazzling lights throughout the crowded ballroom and over the fun-seeking revelers. The tunes were lively, befitting the occasion that was almost the zenith of New Orleans social life.

Emma had a difficult time enjoying herself. Though Betsy's infant was improving, she had other matters on her mind. Most of the ball attendees spoke the crescent city's Gallic tongue, but her French was poor, Latin being her interest. Oh, the entourage of eligible bachelors who swarmed around her, like flies to watermelon, had graciously spoken English, but they meant nothing to her.

For the third time in the space of ten minutes, Emma lost track of the conversation. Her escort to the masked ball, Howard O'Reilly, was saying something to her. She didn't reply. Not that she wished to be rude to her mother's brother—Emma just wasn't paying attention. Her thoughts, her line of sight, were squarely on Satan.

Dressed in a red hood, a matching cape, and scandalously close-fitting tights, the devil was swinging Venus through a reel. No one but Paul Rousseau would have the gall to wear such a disguise. Emma seethed with disgust and vowed for the hundredth time that evening to erase him from her mind.

Pasting on a smile, she turned to her escort. "Pardon me. I didn't hear your question."

"Might I fetch you a cup of punch?" Howard inquired. He was dressed as a hyena.

"Yes, please," she replied politely, her eyes returning to Satan. "On second thought, I could use a glass of champagne."

The reel ended. Marian, frocked as Venus, headed toward the table at which drinks were dispensed. Cozying up to the hyena, she smiled into his furred face. Satan struck up a conversation with a medieval queen and her court jester. Then— Oh no! The devil left the queen and strode toward Emma.

Paul's gaze never wavered as he crossed the room. He wasn't deceived by the gold demi-mask she wore. Emma, sabre-tongued Emma, was dressed in flowing white silk, and emeralds twinkled amid the honeyed locks of her hair. Her gown, which was fastened at one shoulder and left the other tantalizingly bare, was adorned with embroidered metallic-green leaves across the bodice. In the guise of Daphne, Emma was the most comely female in the ballroom. No, Paul corrected that thought, she was the most comely female in the world. He longed to breathe in the fragrance of her fair skin, to touch and to taste it as well.

He knew she was doing everything in her power to disregard him. She laced her fingers, her arms pointed downward. Her demeanor spoke of innocence and vulnerability. But looks could be deceiving, Paul's brain reminded his heart.

He had promised himself that he wouldn't dance, not even once, with Emma. Until that moment he had done an admirable job of pretending not to see her. Outwardly, at least. He was well aware of the scores of panting admirers who had danced attendance on her all evening, and he couldn't blame them.

A sorry excuse for the god Neptune stepped in front of Paul, and sidled up to Emma, a grin splitting his face. "I believe you've promised this dance to me, mademoiselle."

Paul cut in front of him and snarled, "Weigh anchor, Jolly Roger." He captured Emma's hand. "She promised this dance to me." Without giving either party a chance to protest, Paul whirled Emma onto the dance floor, leaving Neptune gaping like a flounder.

"It's a shame—" he said.

"Yes, you are shameful," she interrupted, "holding me so close."

"Granted. But, my beautiful goddess, it's more of a shame I didn't wear the disguise of Apollo. What a joy it would've been to pursue Daphne, thus causing the fair nymph to turn into a laurel tree."

"Oh, you would love to rest on a laurel, wouldn't you? But that won't happen. Besides, I think your devilish disguise fits you quite well." She held herself slightly away from him; her gaze moving down his physique. "Yes, you are shameful," she said again.

Paul's body responded to her closeness and to her bold perusal. He was drunk on her, and he wished never to sober up. Yet he disliked, distrusted, and damned his recalcitrant heart. He wanted to hate her, wanted to hate himself for falling easy prey to an Oliver.

"And what of you?" Still stepping in time with the waltz, Paul pulled her even closer, his loins growing hot with passion. "Don't you know better than to leer at a man's private parts?"

"I did no such thing!" She glared up at him, but he read her embarrassment, sensed the wildfire of excitement sweeping through her. "I hate you," she spat out.

"Yes you did. And no you don't."

Fighting fire with fire, she said, "Well, sir, as you stated the other night, perhaps I'm not a lady."

"Have you known many men in your life, Emma Oliver?" he asked quietly, wondering about her former fiancé.

"Maybe I have, maybe I haven't." She lifted her chin haughtily. "It's really none of your concern. And I'm warning you, stay out of my business!"

"I'm thinking you have," he stated, uncowed by her first words. "Tell me about your broken engagement."

Her green eyes widened, and she missed a step. "How do you know about Franklin Underwood!" When Paul didn't reply, Emma darted an angry look at Marian. "Never mind answering!"

"Franklin Underwood." He pulled out each syllable as if it were a nasty taste in his mouth. Teasing her was a habit that was growing on Paul. "Oh, sweet vixen, it tears at my heart to think of you giving your beautiful body to someone called *Franklin Underwood!* I promise to banish all memories of that beast from your mind."

She stomped on his toe, but Paul wasn't about to let on that it hurt.

"I despise you, Paul Rousseau!"

"You're beginning to sound redundant, *chérie.*" His next words were down-soft. "Must you always fight me, sweetheart?"

"I'm not your sweetheart!"

"Ah, now, I'd rather love you than fight you."

"Love?" Her voice was tight. "You don't know the word's meaning. And for your information, I'd rather swallow belladonna than dance with you, much less let you love me."

"You didn't protest, *amoureuse,*" he reminded her, pleased that he'd called her sweetheart in a language she didn't understand.

"You didn't give me the opportunity."

"And that, my temptress, is the way you need to be handled."

Emma didn't reply. When was this waltz going to end? Parrying with Paul was futile. She decided to finish the dance with as much dignity as possible, and then promptly request that Howard take her back to Magnolia Hall.

Yet the moments turned into heavenly minutes as Paul led her around the streamer-festooned ballroom. She gave up her anger, her resentment, as she allowed herself simply to enjoy the dance. For a tall man Paul was amazingly light on his feet, and he moved with easy grace, as though he had waltzed a thousand times or more. His body was strong and stirring—more intoxicating than champagne. And when his palm slid to her bare shoulder, she knew she should demand he remove it, but she didn't. He danced her toward an exit, and she considered protesting as they entered the shadows. But she didn't. The final notes of the waltz crested, then faded. Yet he didn't release her, and that was going too far!

"Let me go," she exclaimed. He didn't obey, and she declared, "You're being quite disgraceful."

"It's quite disgraceful what you're doing to me."

"I'm doing nothing to . . ." Her voice trailed off. Through the thin folds of her gown, she felt what she had done to him, and crimson dotted her cheeks. "Oh . . . no."

"Don't be ashamed. It's a natural reaction when a man holds a woman. Didn't Frank—"

"Do hold your tongue about Mr. Underwood. And as for your 'natural reaction,' have you said that same thing to my cousin?"

"Emma! You're jealous."

Saints preserve her, she feared he was right. Nevertheless, she answered, "You're mistaken."

"Rest assured, I've never been in a position to utter those words to your kinswoman." His hands moved to caress her shoulders, to pull her closer. "I hope you are jealous, little vixen. Then I'll know you have feelings for me." His voice lost its sarcasm, and assumed the mellow tones of a lover. "You're the only woman I desire. What I'm feeling right now is just between you and me."

That's not all that's between us. "Please leave me be," she whispered raggedly, warring against the mesmerizing effect he had on her.

"I can't. I won't." Their eyes met and held. "Don't

fight this attraction we both feel. I want to make love with you. And when I hold you in my arms, as closely as two people can hold each other, I won't relish the idea of having blackmailed you into them. When you're in my bed, it would pleasure me no end to know you want to be there."

"If that's what you want, you're going about it the wrong way." She cringed at her own words. What had made her say that? She had Marian to consider.

"Tell me then, Emma, what approach do I need to take?"

"Just leave me . . . and Mrs. Oliver . . . in peace," she whispered. "That's what I want you to do."

"Impossible. I can't leave you alone."

His words were the fruition of her girlhood dreams. To be desired beyond reason was a heady thing. Oh, if the situation were different . . . If Paul were different, and free of a former attachment . . . But he wasn't.

"It's very possible," she said. "I'm not going to meet you Tuesday night."

With a tug, he pulled the ribbon of her mask. "Can you look at me and deny you want what I desire?" His gaze flowed over each of her features in turn, then amber brown eyes welded to leaf green ones. "Can you?"

"No, I cannot deny it," she murmured finally, truthfully, as the tip of her finger touched the scar on his jaw.

Marian forgotten, Emma was caught up in the magical web he had woven around her. She wanted nothing more than to experience his lovemaking. She was wicked and wanton, and she didn't care. He wasn't the man of her dreams; he had a shadowy past. He was a blackmailer—and worse! Suddenly those things didn't matter. Though she both wanted him and hated him, she was filled with a pagan desire for Paul Rousseau.

He stepped back, a tender smile touching his features as he brought her fingertips to his lips and his warm breath fanned across her skin. A delicious shiver ran the length of her spine when he said, "Until we meet again."

Drawing his cape around him, he turned on his heel, moving toward the shadows. Then he stopped. "You've won, my love. Tonight I cease my attentions to Marian Oliver." And he was gone.

Emma wilted in thankfulness. No longer would she worry over Marian's welfare. Instead she'd revel in these heady moments, enjoying the primitive urges he'd evoked within her. And she *would* see him again.

Feeling empty without Paul nearby, Emma returned to the ballroom. Her previous determination to leave the festivities early was squelched, and she yearned for the feel of his arms around her once again.

"Emma, Emma," Howard said as he walked up to her and cut into her thoughts. "Where have you been? Your champagne's growing tepid. Are you ill, dear girl? You look as if the devil has possessed you!"

Oh, yes, Satan has possessed me. She thought of Tuesday evening when she'd be in the arms of the devil himself.

By dawn Paul hadn't slept a wink. As he had

tossed and turned on his big bed, visions of Emma had crowded his thoughts. Ah, comely Emma! The beautiful witch had cast a spell over him, and it had taken every ounce of his willpower to ignore her after they had parted at the masked ball. But he had. He was proud of himself.

He also gloried in his strategy for next Tuesday evening. Taking all the time in the world with Emma, he would feed her from his fork and they would drink champagne from one fluted glass. Or better yet, a fine French wine, he decided as he remembered teasing her on the night they'd met.

He'd make love to her slowly, tenderly, gently, and they would savor each moment of their love-making. Ah, yes, the night would become a memory both would cherish a lifetime, he thought confidently as a thin ribbon of smoke curled from his cheroot toward the hotel ceiling. He would bury her memories of past lovers forever.

But he must never forget she was his enemy's beloved niece. Between now and Tuesday Paul intended to keep an eye on the Oliver cotton-factoring house and an ear tuned for a clue to the operative's identity. Tuesday night, however, was going to be devoted to matters of the heart.

Drawing his brows together, Paul remembered Howard O'Reilly's words on the previous night. The attorney had called Paul aside at the masked ball, saying he had business to discuss.

"Another time," Paul had replied, keeping Emma in sight. She was surrounded by a cadre of admirers, and he was experiencing an unhealthy amount of jealousy.

Howard lifted the hyena mask from his face. "I

92

say, old chap, you can't put me off forever."

Since Paul had no intention of joining Emma's faithful corps, he turned his attention to the lawyer. "What is it?"

"It's about your grandfather's estate. As you know, I'm the executor of Remi Rousseau's will, and it must be settled. You're one of the beneficiaries."

Paul frowned as he thought of his grandfather who had passed away the previous September. "Old *Grandpère* didn't say a kind word to me in more years than I care to remember. Strange he should leave me a legacy."

"I daresay it carries stipulations."

"No doubt." The Rousseau patriarch had disinherited his only son, Étienne, over bad judgment at the gaming tables. Upon catching Paul in a compromising situation with the old man's young mistress, Remi Rousseau had banished him from the family sugar plantation. His parting words to his sole heir had been a threat to disinherit him. But that was years ago—in 1829—not long after Étienne had lost his life. Paul had attempted to atone for his indiscretion, had written his grandfather; but old Remi had ignored the letters. Eventually, Paul had given up, and he had never returned to St. Martinsville.

"Would you care to hear the stipulations?" Howard asked.

Paul lifted a shoulder in an offhanded manner. "Not particularly. His crumbs don't interest me."

"It's more than crumbs, actually. Quite a bit more. It's a sizable estate." As Marian started toward the two men, Howard said, "Please come by my office Monday morning, and we'll discuss this further."

Remembering he'd promised Emma to break off his relationship with Widow Oliver, Paul gave in. "All right. Monday morning."

Marian grabbed each man by an elbow. "Shame on the two of you! This is a party, not a men's social! Paul, I do believe you owe me this dance."

"Uh, sure."

"And, you—you naughty hyena," she continued, releasing Howard's arm and turning into Paul's. "Go see about your niece. Emma told me she's anxious to leave."

Taken back, Paul made no move to dance with Marian. Emma was Howard's niece? Then his attorney and Rankin Oliver were of the same family. Damn. If that bit of information had been available to him before he'd started the whole mess with Marian, the situation would be different. He could have asked Howard about Rankin Oliver's activities, and he could have met and pursued Emma in the normal fashion.

"You never told me you're related to the Olivers," he said.

"You never asked." Howard, who was starting across the ballroom, waved a hand at Paul. "See you Monday!"

Suddenly a knock sounded against Paul's hotel-room door, yanking his thoughts away from the previous night and back to the St. Charles. He heard again the incessant beating of fist against wood.

Was it Emma? Considering her honeyed reaction at the costume ball, he wondered if she had decided to advance the timing of their meeting. Paul certainly hoped so. Not wishing to appear too eager, he took his time grinding out the cigar, then wrapped a towel around his middle and cut across the rug.

He was disappointed when he caught sight of Captain Throckmorton, hand poised in the air as if to knock again, in the hallway.

"Oh, there you are!" James Throckmorton dropped his arm. "Thought I might've missed you."

"Where did you think I might be?"

"With my sister, I suppose. It is a glorious morning—weather's warmed up a bit, I might add."

"As you can see, I'm not with Marian."

"Yes, yes." The man brushed past Paul, tossing his gloves onto a table. "We've got troubles on the *San Antonio*, Mr. Rousseau. Bad troubles."

Paul slammed the door, then strode over to the sea chest to grab his breeches. "What happened?" he asked while pulling them up over his hips.

"A fracas developed between some of the men."

"Can't say I'm surprised."

"Watch your insubordinate tongue, Lieutenant Rousseau. Might I remind you that I'm your commanding officer?"

"I need no reminder of my position . . . sir."

"Good!" Throckmorton grabbed an apple from a bowl of fruit that had been left by a chambermaid the previous day. Biting into it, he said around a mouthful of pulp, "Go out there and take care of it for me."

"What's the problem now?" Paul asked, as if he couldn't guess. Clearly the men wanted more than decent food to keep them satisfied. They needed to assuage their lusts for women. Paul could identify

95

with that, at least as far as one particular woman was concerned.

"Those no-goods threatened to hang Ensign Stewart from the yardarm!"

Those so-called no-goods are mighty handy during skirmishes with the Mexicans, Paul was tempted to say as he hurried to collect the rest of his uniform. He felt that sorry excuse for an ensign probably deserved the punishment, but now was not the time for petty bickering.

"I'll take the longboat shipside." Paul finished buttoning his shirt. "What concessions are you willing to make, sir, to the men?"

"An extra ration of rum all around ought do it."

Paul hiked a black brow. "I'd say a ration of woman-flesh all around would be more apropos."

"Spoken like a true Gaul." Throckmorton wiped his mouth with the back of his hand.

"Be that as it may, I speak the truth."

"Well, I won't allow any harlots aboard!"

Paul drew on his coat and stood his ground. "Then grant me authority to give our men shore leave."

"No!" Throckmorton shook his head vehemently. "Why, Houston might send sailing orders any tide. An extra ration of rum for each man and that's all."

"Are you looking to see *me* swinging from the yardarm?"

"Of course not, Mr. Rousseau!" Sneering, Throckmorton asked, "You're not afraid of those rascals, are you?"

"Not in the least, sir. But I fear what will happen if we aren't lenient."

"It's my place to concern myself with that. I issue the orders, and I'm ordering you to take care of the matter."

"Aye, aye, Captain."

Within an hour Paul was in a longboat, headed for the *San Antonio*'s anchorage. A chilled, salt-scented breeze whipped against his face as, feet spread wide and rooted to the deck, he crossed his arms and looked southward. A wicked grin stole across his features when he glanced at the cargo. Throckmorton would more than likely court-martial him if he discovered the contraband being taken aboard the schooner, but Paul shrugged away his concern.

Singing bawdy lyrics, six members of the world's oldest profession sat atop six casks of rum.

As the boat cut across the river, between their songs, they tried to entice Paul into sampling their wares. He didn't partake. The only woman he wanted to assuage his heat was Emma Oliver, and he wondered what she was doing at that moment.

His thoughts of her were cast aside, however, when Coxswain Merritt yelled, "Mr. Rousseau, sir, look port side." He lowered his scope. "It appears to be Captain Throckmorton!"

Paul uttered an expletive as the captain's longboat approached them at fast clip. Fearing it was too late already, he nonetheless bellowed: "You women, hide!"

And that's what Throckmorton's going to have of mine—my hide! he thought wearily.

97

Chapter Seven

Rustling through the moss-draped oak trees, the wind gave a mournful cry as cold mist fell on St. Martinsville cemetery and twilight deepened into Sunday night. The French settlement along the Bayou Teche was quiet, peaceful; her inhabitants resting before another week of work in the sugar country of south Louisiana. St. Martin de Tours Church shadowed the graveyard where a lone figure cut around the stone crypts.

Rankin Oliver shook off the eerie feeling of being alone with the dead. His demeanor in public didn't lend itself to the morose, but now in private . . . Still, this hour of evening was the only time he could go undetected, could be alone with the grief that hadn't diminished with the passing of time.

His Angélique rested in the Rousseau family vault. No, Rankin thought, Angélique wasn't *his*. He had claimed her maidenhead, but she had not taken him as husband. At the time he'd been but an Englishman, a tinker without a pot to call his own, which had mattered not to Angélique. It was her parents who had been against him. Royalists who had escaped from the guillotine in France, the

98

de Poutrincourts wanted their daughter wed to one of their own background, their own way of life, their own religion—and to a man with money.

French losers they had been, Rankin thought sourly, like ol' Louis XVI and his queen, Marie Antoinette.

Yet Rankin had been determined to become socially acceptable. He'd even considered taking up papist ways, as his brother Quentin had done to marry that cripple Noreen O'Reilly. But he hadn't.

Money, he'd figured was the key. Money had the power to cross the line. But before Rankin had earned his fortune, Étienne Rousseau had asked for Angélique's hand, and she had bowed to family pressure.

They were all gone now, the de Poutrincourts and the Rousseaus. With the exception of Angélique's son. Thankfully Paul Rousseau had let Rankin be, for the most part, after Étienne had been put out of his misery. But the stripling had been nobody's fool; he had guessed correctly that there was foul play involved in the duel between Rankin and Étienne. Still, he hadn't been able to prove it. Ha! Once more Rankin had triumphed.

Rankin laid a bouquet of flowers before Angélique's resting place. This wasn't his first visit to his beloved since her death in 1828. On many occasions he had journeyed up the Bayou Teche to pay homage to her. Indeed, his holdings in the area had been expanded so it would be easier to do that.

"Awgh," he cried all of a sudden, and swiftly brushed ants from his leg. "Blast ye, ye bloody bastards!" Rubbing his ankle, he moaned, "Ye never allow a man one moment to his grief without feeding on his flesh."

"Ants love cemeteries, didn't you know?" a croaking male voice called from ten feet away. "'Tis a feast that lies ready for them."

"I'll not have ye talking such, Simon Dyer! Ye've no respect for the dead."

Moving forward, the diminutive man ignored the comment. "Well, at least you're hearing what I have to say now, old man. I called your name twice."

"I heard ye not." Rankin straightened. "And I'll not have ye calling me an old man. My years are three less than yer fifty-eight." Glancing at the expensive clothing that covered his trim frame, he reaffirmed that he could still turn a woman's head. "Not bad for my age, either."

"You're nothing but an old peacock. Listen to the truth for once: your blond hair's gone gray, and you're old and wrinkled."

Rankin hunched his shoulders as he shook a fist at the shriveled shadow of a man. "Be gone with ye."

"Why, old fool? So you can fall to your crypt-talking?" Simon scratched his thin beard. "Ha! I've heard you yammering to Angélique as if she were still breathing."

"Enough!" Rankin raised a hand to strike Simon, but it was caught between the man's bony fingers.

"I wouldn't do that if I were you." Simon dropped his hand to his side. "I got the goods that could put you behind bars, remember? 'Twas me who fixed the firing pin so's Étienne's pistol wouldn't discharge, remember?"

Rankin drew back. "I remember it well. The guilt falls on yer shoulders as well. Ye were his second . . . his trusted friend."

"My memory hasn't departed me. But you'd do well to recall another point: I've nothing to lose. You do." Simon picked a tooth with his thumbnail but stopped when a deep cough racked his body.

"Look at ye—sick! Ye'll be worthless next Tuesday night."

"You're . . . worrying for . . . nothing." Simon took a restorative lungful of air. Recovered from his spell, he waved a hand. "My health'll hold up. And there's something I need to tell you," he wheezed. "In case word leaks out about the shipment, I'm sending phony crates to your factor house. The *Ransomed Princess*'ll pick up the cargo in Baton Rouge and carry it on to Vera Cruz."

"The factor house? I don't like the idea of it. I don't like the idea of any of this."

"Well, it's too late to stop it now." Simon snickered. "For all my extra work I believe I'm entitled to another thousand in gold."

Rankin's plans for Simon and for the Mexican government vanished at those last words. "Ye blackmailing leech! I ought to kill ye and be done with it."

"But you won't. I still have my uses."

"Ye do, Dyer. Ye do. Damn ye to hell."

Dyer had first become useful when Rankin wouldn't leave the duel between himself and Étienne Rousseau to fate. Though he was the better shot, he'd wanted to make certain he, not Angélique's widower, walked away from the confrontation. For years he had waited for that duel, and had done everything humanly possible to provoke it.

At Elkin's Club one summer evening he'd got his chance. Rankin had insisted on joining Étienne's

101

table for a game of faro. For once the no-good gambler had been winning, and Rankin had accused him of cheating. The accused, being a spineless jellyfish, had laughed away the insult. Angered to the point of desperation, Rankin had then done the unthinkable: he'd sullied Angélique's name.

"Conscience hurting you?" Simon asked, mean as a striped spider.

"No!"

Rankin fell once more to recollection. By chance he had learned that Étienne's best friend was guilty of bigamy. If that fact had become known, Simon Dyer would have been cast out of society, if not Louisiana, and he would have lost his beloved wife, who spent money as if it grew on trees. So Rankin went to Étienne's trusted friend and threatened to expose him unless he agreed to tamper with the firing mechanism of Étienne's pistol.

Rankin had sweetened the pot with cash. Through his silence and his financial support, Simon had then been able to continue his seemingly monogamous life as a respectable sugar planter. The spendthrift Mrs. Dyer had gone to a greater reward some time ago, but Rankin still had Simon in his pocket. Money *was* power.

Waving his hand in a gesture of dismissal, Rankin said, "Be gone. I'll bring the money on the morrow."

"Figured you would." Simon laughed before repeating his words. "Figured you would."

He disappeared around a crypt, leaving Rankin Oliver to delve once again into the grief that consumed him.

*   *   *

102

"Paul Rousseau has caused me all the grief I'm going to allow," Emma muttered to herself as she prepared on Tuesday morning for her trip into the city. Away from his mesmerizing presence, it was easy to be strong. Though she was attracted to him—and there was no denying that!—Emma was ready to put a stop to it. She wouldn't allow fascination to rule over sound judgment.

The only way to ensure that was to consult with Howard O'Reilly. This was not a decision made in haste. After mulling the problem through first on Sunday, then on Monday, and again this morning, and gaining a headache in the process, she had decided that although her reputation was going to take a further battering when her transgressions became common knowledge, she needed legal assistance—if not a buffer between herself and temptation.

Marian, of course, would hear of the whole dirty business, but if that entailed another price for Emma's impetuous acts, so be it.

Funny though, she couldn't help wondering why neither she nor Marian had heard one word from Paul since the masked ball the previous Saturday.

Emma plucked a gray bonnet from the armoire in her bedchamber and placed it on her aching head. For a moment she wondered if she was making the correct decision about consulting Howard. Perhaps Paul had seen the light, in view of his absence.

"Emma Frances," she muttered aloud, "don't be absurd."

Paul Rousseau wasn't the type to give up easily. And why should he? At the masquerade ball she had admitted that she desired him. After her encouragement hadn't he every reason to believe that she would meet him at the St. Charles by sunset that evening? He was simply biding his time.

Miraculously she dodged Cleopatra's chaperon-age and traveled by carriage to the attorney's Canal Street firm. Sweeping into the office, she slammed the carved door behind her with a resounding thud. The rooms were empty, save for Howard O'Reilly, and Emma was thankful for the confidentiality of her visit. The grandfather clock struck three as she faced the russet-haired senior partner of O'Reilly, Blake & Dupré.

As Howard made welcoming chatter, Emma gave him the once-over. Her mother's younger brother was tall and gaunt. His coat and trousers could accommodate additional pounds on his thirty-five-year-old frame. Despite her resolution, Emma couldn't help comparing him to Paul Rousseau. That blackguard's clothing always fit as if each stitch were tailor-sewn to his muscular physique, and he easily topped Howard by several inches. Her uncle's eyes were brown, as were Paul's, yet they lacked the spirit and expression of the naval lieutenant's. No, Howard wasn't one iota as attractive as Paul Rousseau. Funny how positive thoughts of Paul kept creeping into her mind at the most inopportune moments.

"What a pleasant surprise," Howard said warmly, his voice holding little of the Irish brogue of his childhood and quite a bit of an Englishman's clipped speech pattern. He glanced at the clock. "I say, though, if you had arrived but five minutes later, dear niece, you'd have missed me."

This was Fat Tuesday, the final day of Mardi gras.

104

Naturally he intended to celebrate the day before Lent's onset. "I know you're busy, Howard," she said, "but . . . this matter is of the gravest importance. Please indulge me for a moment or two."

He lifted a brow. "Certainly I can spare a few minutes for my niece. Let me take your wrap; then have a seat—do have a seat."

Emma smoothed her gray woolen skirt and allowed him to assist her into a leather arm chair. She prayed that he'd be patient.

After hanging her cloak on a rack, O'Reilly perched his thin frame on the edge of his highly polished desk. "Capital you came by, Emma, though I am in a rush. This morn brought a post from your mother. You'll be happy to hear the news!"

If Emma were to be *happy* about any news from Virginia, the letter must not include any reference to herself. When she departed the James River for these parts, her mother had been in a fit of motherly concern—and temper. "Oh?"

Howard had the guileless look of a child. "Noreen informs me that your fiancé has booked passage for New Orleans!"

Oh no! Emma felt her blood rush downward. "Franklin is my former intended, and I couldn't care in the least what he does or where he goes."

"I am sorry, Emma." His hand reached out to squeeze her fingers. "I didn't mean to ruffle your womanly pride. I'm sure Mr. Underwood wishes to atone for any wrong done to you."

"I couldn't care in the least. Franklin and I are finished." Drat him! It was just like Franklin to turn up and spoil her visit to New Orleans. Spoil her visit? Ha! By no stroke of the imagination had it been moonlight and magnolias. "Perhaps we should get to the point of my business."

"Of course!" Evidently Howard was pleased to change the subject. "Pray tell, Emma, what brings you to my humble office?" As was his custom, he minimized the sumptuous surroundings.

"It concerns Paul Rousseau." Her words were clear as a bell, belying the nervousness that quivered within her.

"Decent chap, that fellow," Howard said, clamping his mouth shut. Yet there was a cryptic cast to his eyes. "Always liked him, yes I have."

"Oh, Howard, how can you be so blind?" Her temper got the best of her. "That man has you hoodwinked as surely as he has Marian—" Emma flushed at this slip of the tongue. But on second thought, maybe it was time Howard had his eyes opened. It was far beyond time for him to make his feelings known! "Rousseau has turned her head."

Howard stood, moved slowly around to his chair. Emma watched him brush shaking fingers across his thin lips. She knew he was shy in matters of the heart, and not given to discussing his feelings with others.

"I'm aware she holds him dear." He forced a benign smile. "Certainly she'll do what she believes right."

"Certainly. But, my dear uncle, you don't have me fooled. I know you love her."

He reached for a stack of papers, shuffling them as a mantle of red spread from his neck to his hollow cheeks. "Emma . . . Emma, you speak out of turn."

"Guilty." Lifting a brow, she frowned. "But if you let him continue in his attentions, there's no telling what will happen." She received no response. "I fear she'll be hurt by Rousseau. I believe his affection for her is but a figment of Marian's imagination."

"That was not my impression."

"It is mine." Emma prayed for courage to continue. "Howard, I'm in a terrible fix with Mr. Rousseau."

"What have you done *now,* Emma?"

"It's what Rousseau is doing."

Thoroughly disgusted with herself, she proceeded to explain the events leading up to her visit that afternoon. His eyes wide and his face white, Howard was clearly shocked, both by her impetuous visit to Paul's hotel room and her inadvertent theft of the brooch. She hadn't yet gotten to the details of the blackmail.

Planting the heels of his hands on the desktop, he leaned forward. "Whatever the case, Emma, Paul is a reasonable man. Although his legal position is quite solid, I don't think he will press charges."

"Don't count on it!" She pounded the heel of a fist against her knee. "You must agree to be my emissary. I need a private detective on the trail of those thieves. Furthermore . . . well, I'm not without guilt over the brooch's loss, so I'd like you to negotiate a settlement with Paul—I mean, with Mr. Rousseau. I cannot allow him to badger me any longer."

"Badger you?"

"Yes. He's blackmailing me."

"Heavenly days, Emma Frances Oliver, explain yourself!"

Nervously she picked a piece of imagined lint from her sleeve. "Paul Rousseau is guilty of

107

duplicity, and . . ."

"Em*ma!*"

"That libertine made advances toward me." She hesitated. "In payment for the brooch he demands that I rendezvous with him tonight at the St. Charles Hotel."

"Oh?" Howard leaned back in his chair and touched a finger to his upper lip while watching her. His familial demeanor had been replaced by a strictly professional one. "When he threatened you, was it before or after you danced with him at the masked ball?"

"Before."

"I see. What did Marian say when you confronted her with these tales?"

"I haven't told her. I wanted to, but I just never found the right opportunity. Then he threatened to expose details of the theft. . . ."

Rolling a pencil between thumb and forefinger, Howard appeared to study it closely. "I daresay affection is strange, my innocent Emma. Did it ever occur to you that he simply found you more to his liking than he did Marian? Perhaps his ploy is but to woo you."

"By underhanded trickery? Then he doesn't know beans about me."

Howard rose to his feet and walked the length of the office and back again. "If Lieutenant Rousseau were in this room with us, would he be able to say in all honesty that you've done everything in your power to thwart his advances?"

"If he were being honest."

"And if you were being honest, Emma dear, could

108

you deny that you were enraptured with him at the aforementioned ball?"

"Well . . . I . . . What makes you ask that?"

"Are you forgetting that I was your escort?" He was quick to add: "Did you know you were in love with Lieutenant Rousseau before he took your arm in that waltz?"

"Not true." Her answer wasn't nearly as forceful as she intended, and it was even less forceful when she added, "I'm not in love with him. My feelings go no deeper than wanting him to cease his attention to me and to Marian!"

"Then you aren't concerned as to his whereabouts at this moment?"

"Not . . . not in the least."

His brown eyes studied her for what seemed like eons before he said, "My advice, then, is simply to let the matter go. Stay home tonight. Lieutenant Rousseau won't miss you. He's indisposed."

"What do you mean?"

"I don't believe I stuttered." He pulled a gold watch from his pocket. "Pardon me for cutting our chat short, but the hour grows late and I've a legal matter to attend to. Please let me see you to your carriage."

"Wait! Explain yourself. And don't pull any of that fancy lawyer talk on me."

"You said you weren't concerned about his whereabouts."

"Well, I am!"

Silence fell. Howard leveled a sharp look Emma's way. "Captain Throckmorton arrested Paul last Sunday afternoon. He's in dire straits."

Chapter Eight

Her uncle's statement hit Emma with the force of cannon fire. Paul was in dire straits. He was her tormentor, yet she wished him no ill.

She grabbed the arms of the chair. "Surely you are joking."

"Not at all." Howard bolted up from the desk. With fingers laced behind him, he walked across the room and back again. "Paul's in Throckmorton's custody."

"How do you know? Have you seen him?"

"This morning. He missed an appointment yesterday, and I went looking for him. When he wasn't in his room and no one knew his whereabouts, I went down to the dock and spoke with the coxswain. Then I prevailed upon him to row me out to the schooner."

Her wits returning, she asked, "What did Paul do to bring such measures upon himself?"

"In one sentence, he tried to look out for the marines aboard ship. Lieutenant Paul Rousseau is a man who wishes the best for his subordinates. Apparently our Marian's brother isn't of the same mind." Howard went on to explain Paul's actions on

110

the men's behalf. "He's prepared to accept a court-martial for his actions."

For the first time Emma felt a deep respect for Paul. He was not as unprincipled as she had believed. "James is despicable."

"Then you've taken Paul's side in the affair?"

"Not in the least. What affects the Texas Navy doesn't affect me." She wanted to judge Paul harshly for trying to bring women aboard his ship, but she couldn't. "I'm speaking from a strictly humane point of view."

"Personally I believe Paul is blessed with admirable qualities."

"That's your prerogative," she said. "But, plain and simple, wouldn't it have been easier for him if he'd just followed orders? It would've saved him a lot of trouble."

"It would have saved him more than trouble." Howard paused a moment so his words would sink in. "Paul was whipped for insubordination, and he's presently locked in the hold of the *San Antonio*."

Emma inhaled sharply. "How badly is he injured?"

"It's difficult to determine. But he's a man of hearty health, so I see no reason why he won't recover . . . in time."

"That's for a doctor to decide. Has he had medical attention?"

"Come now, Emma. Throckmorton isn't conducting a tea party. Paul's incarcerated on a ship of war!"

"For how long?" she asked, blood pounding in her ears.

He turned a palm up. "Until a trial is convened,

111

I suppose."

"Is there anything you can do?"

"Naval law is out of my jurisdiction, but I'm going to try." He stopped near her chair, and looked down at her. "I was on my way to see James Throckmorton when you arrived. I intend to call in a marker."

She met his gaze. "Why would you do that for Paul?"

"I have my reasons." There was a vague, mysterious tone to Howard's voice. "And they don't concern you."

Whys weren't of paramount importance to her at the moment, so she didn't pursue the subject. "All right. In the meantime, I'm going to tend his wounds."

"Don't put him in legal jeopardy," Howard cautioned. "Let me speak with James, uh, Throckmorton, first."

"I'll give you two hours, Howard O'Reilly." Emma sprang to her feet. "If I haven't heard from you by then, I'm going out to that ship. Paul needs me."

Howard watched her pace the room. Then he said his goodbyes and departed. Perhaps he had played an underhanded trick, a ploy he had used in court more than once: turn the tables on an accuser. He had endeavored to make Emma realize how much Paul meant to her, and apparently he had been successful.

He wanted the best for Emma. Always had, always would. She deserved to love and be loved. And Paul deserved the same. Being the Rousseaus' family counselor, Howard was privy to certain information about them, and he knew that Remi

Rousseau had treated his only son and his only grandson in a raw manner.

Hailing his barouche, Howard continued to justify his actions. Emma was the product of a loving family, though one too large for individual attention. Paul was the sole descendant of a family gone wrong. Both Emma and Paul needed the succor of love—and those two were meant for each other. Together they could heal the past's deficiencies. And if it took a small push from an outsider, what was the harm?

Of course, Howard realized his motives might be selfish. He loved Marian, loved her with a passion. He wondered if she could ever care for him, even an iota? Could she see past his staid front, his less than heart-stopping exterior, to the passionate, adoring man who had trouble expressing his emotions?

"In the words of Shakespeare," he muttered to himself, "'all's well that ends well.'"

He hoped this would end well for Emma . . . and for Paul.

The hold of the *San Antonio* smelled of gunpowder and mildew. It was hot and dank and putrid. Sounds seemed to reel around Paul: the tide's lap as it battered the ship, men's steps on the deck above, a rat squealing as it scurried across the planks. Lying on his side, he stretched his aching muscles. Sweat rolled across his back, its salt eating into one of the wounds that laced his flesh. He gnashed his teeth against the throbbing discomfort.

Despite his physical pain, he remembered with marked clarity Throckmorton's wrath. The captain

113

had jumped from his longboat to Paul's, nearly falling into the river as he'd done so, and had banished the women and the spirits to the shore. Then Paul had been piped aboard the *San Antonio*.

"Let this be a lesson to the lot of you," Throckmorton had barked, his mean beady eyes sweeping across the top deck and the thirty marines he'd assembled to witness the fruits of disobedience. "I'll tolerate no disrespect for my authority!"

The weather was clement, the sailors inclement. As the Mississippi lapped at the hull, the sun beat down on the schooner, its rays accenting the weathered deck, the polished pivot gun near the bow.

"Six lashes," Throckmorton said, thrusting his big belly forward as he paced the deck. "One for each harlot."

Paul proceeded down the deck to the pivot where Sergeant Seymour Oswald waited, cat-o'-nine in his beefy hand. The sergeant didn't meet Paul's stare.

Marshaling his dignity, Paul unbuttoned his jacket and discarded his shirt. The chill air stung his bare torso. "Mete out the punishment, Sergeant."

Oswald swallowed. Hocker and Tampke each took a step forward in silent protest.

The captain, so enraged that spittle frothed at the corners of his mouth, stomped over to them. "Shall the two of you take a double turn after Mr. Rousseau?"

They retreated, one step.

Paul bent over the pivot. The youngest of the crew, a lad named David Montgomery, was commanded to restrain him. The boy's fingers shook as he laced the straps around Paul's wrist.

114

The planks creaking beneath his feet, Throckmorton took his stance. "Commence!"

Rawhide bit into his wrists, but Paul refused to close his eyes.

"One!"

The cat snapped through the air, sinking all nine of her fangs into Paul's shoulder blades. He clenched his teeth against the fiery pain that radiated from his wounds to his head, toes, and fingers.

"Two!"

The lash ate into his back.

"Three!"

As flesh ripped away, Paul willed himself not to faint. Not then, not later. And when the cat was through with her feast, Paul somehow managed to walk under his own power to the hold.

That had been Sunday. This was Tuesday.

The hatch flew open. Paul's dilated eyes protested the invasion, but his heart was glad for it. For three days he had languished in this prison. Three days without sustenance or human contact, save for the few minutes of Howard's clandestine visit.

"Oswald here," the sergeant at arms called down to him. "Got grub for you." The sounds of his feet hitting the planking echoed through the hold.

Paul's eyes began to adjust to the light. He forced words past his dry throat and cracked lips. "Did the captain give you permission to bring me food?"

"Nay," Seymour Oswald responded, "'tis my conscience giving the permission. By the by, the grub 'twas bought by your purse. 'Twas the least I could do."

Paul shifted awkwardly into a sitting position. Arms outstretched, Oswald offered him a plate of beans and bread and a tin cup of rum. Paul hated to consider the contraband's source, but with his knotted stomach growling with anticipation, he wouldn't argue the point. The finest delicacies from New Orleans kitchens had never smelled better!

"You'd best be gone, Sergeant. If Captain Throckmorton finds you here, you'll have a taste of the cat, too."

"It wouldn't be the first time, Lieutenant. But I've no fear o' him or o' the lash. And he went ashore. The Mardi gras ball." Oswald bent down, resting his weight on his heels. "Eat up, afore the rats come a-callin'."

Paul downed the rum, its fire eating a path to his stomach. Then he took the plate and spoon, and began shoveling the vittles into his mouth. Sopping up the last of the bean juice with a crust of stale bread, he popped that into his mouth. He could feel his strength begin to return. "Thank you, Sergeant Oswald," he whispered, handing the plate back to his benefactor. "Return to your station."

Oswald set the plate on the dirty boards that were Paul's bed. "Begging your pardon, sir, but I've something to discuss with you."

Paul nodded.

"Me and the lads signed on with the commodore in good faith, sir, but our treatment ain't been right under the Cap'n. No, sir. Not right at all. You know that, Lieutenant Rousseau, else you wouldn't've sent grub out for us and you wouldn't've gotten in trouble over them women you were thinking to bring aboard. Ain't none of the men, no sir, that don't want you on our side. We got a musket from the wardroom, and we'll give the cap'n a lot o' what

116

he gives."

"That's enough!" Paul held up a hand. "Seymour," he used Oswald's given name in the hope of gaining the man's trust, "Seymour, I guarantee you, if you and the men overtake this ship and sail down the Mississippi, you won't get past Balize before you're captured. And you know the punishment—the yardarm."

"'Twill be a cold day in hell. We'll make it," 'specially with you at the helm."

"I'll have no part of a mutiny, Sergeant Oswald." Paul leaned back against a crate and swallowed his pain. Looking the man straight in the eye, he said, "And I've no use for mutineers."

Oswald drew in a deep breath. He rested an elbow on his knee and covered his mouth with a palm. A minute passed before he responded. "Mr. Rousseau, sir, Texas is my home port—I got a warm feeling for the place. I want to be loyal to the Lone Star ensign, and 'twould do me fair if we was to face Santa Anna's fleet head-on. I believe I speak for all the lads on those counts, but put yourself in our place. We've been months without pay. Ol' Sam Houston don't support the fleet. The food . . . well, we're men o' the sea, and we can abide the fare sorely served, though we much appreciate the kindness you showed in that direction.

"But we're men," Oswald continued. "Not machines. We've no braids on our shoulders or say in our destinies, but we need the comforts a warm woman and a cold mug provide. Can you understand that, Lieutenant?"

"Very much so." Paul paused. "But keep something in mind. Even though I went against my superior's mandate, I do believe in upholding the oath I gave to the Republic of Texas—a pledge to abide by the law and to follow orders. I also believe in due process."

"Then you're in agreement with Throckmorton and Houston about the recall order?"

"Not at all. But I believe we should go through the channels of command to voice our complaints." Paul pointed southward. "A merchant ship sailed four days ago for Campeche, carrying a letter to the commodore. As soon as he hears about conditions aboard this schooner, he'll set sail for New Orleans. Matters will be set to rights."

"'Twill take weeks!" Oswald protested.

"Yes. But you and the others must tough it out, Sergeant, until Commodore Moore reaches these waters. The honorable thing will be done. I promise you."

Seymour Oswald seemed to consider Paul's words. He opened his mouth to comment, but the sounds of heightened activity above drew his attention.

"Laddies, 'tis a lady coming aboard," Paul heard a youthful voice shout, then a cheer arose from the others.

The thump of the rope ladder as it was cast down the starboard hull reverberated throughout the hold. Neither Paul nor the sergeant spoke. Oswald grinned. Paul merely listened.

"Give this note to the marine in charge, and then take me to Lieutenant Rousseau," Emma Oliver could be heard to demand. "Right now, young man, before I report you to Captain Throckmorton."

"Get topside, Oswald," Paul ordered.

118

"Aye, aye." The sergeant hurried up the quarter ladder.

Paul stared at the hatchway. Emma, a vision in gray wool and white lace, made her way toward him, a small black bag in her right hand. He didn't know whether to be mad or glad for her presence; he didn't want her to see him in this condition. He wanted her to see him naked and clean . . . and strong. But she looked damned good to him. So good.

"Paul," she said, and with an anguished cry, she knelt before him. "Oh, Paul, you were so foolish. Why did you go against James's orders!"

Angered, Paul cast away the hand that moved to touch his cheek. "Is that why you came out here, Emma? To rap my knuckles for being a bad boy?" At her shocked expression, he continued. "Go ashore, woman, and leave me be!"

She drew away. "Don't you dare talk to me like that, Paul Rousseau! I'm here to doctor you."

"Doctor me? I doubt it." He sneered, disliking his words as he said them yet unable to keep them back. "I think you're here because you didn't want to break our date. This is Tuesday. And it's"—he looked toward the hatchway, then back at her— "almost dusk."

"Oh, yes, it's always been my secret wish to cavort with a half-naked, filthy, injured man. I just love rotting hulks of ships and rotting specimens of men."

"Beneath the filth I'm the same man who waltzed with you last Saturday night." He leaned forward. "Would you like me to prove it?"

"I doubt you could."

"Try me."

"Unfortunately you are the same man. To the bone. There lies the problem." She cut him an icy glare. "And the next time you see him, you can thank your friend Howard O'Reilly for your freedom. He interceded with James and secured your release. It seems you have Howard duped as to your wicked ways."

"Don't change the subject," Paul said, nonetheless grateful for his attorney's actions. *"Ma chére,* it's more in order to thank you for this rendezvous."

"Oooh!" She jabbed her finger downward. "I'll hear no more sass from you. Turn over!"

"No."

"Yes!" She grabbed his forearm and yanked with all her might.

In his weakened condition Paul swayed forward before pulling away, but not before she saw his back.

He heard the sharp intake of breath she tried to hide, and he didn't want her sympathy. "You've seen the sideshow—now go home. Go."

She didn't comply. Instead, her equanimity regained, she unbuckled the satchel. "I want to help you, Paul. You need medical attention. If you'll allow me, I'll treat your wounds."

"This doesn't involve you, and I don't need you to champion my cause."

Her silence was heavy with affront. "Very well," she finally said. "I'll be going. Goodbye."

Feeling the loss even before her departure, he said without sarcasm, "Wait! I . . . I'm sorry. You've no business here, and I've no business accepting your help, but I do appreciate it."

She studied him for a moment, then said, "Good." She unpacked a jar of salve and a clean, white rag.

120

"And it's good to see you humble—for once."

He got a whiff, just a whiff, of her flowery perfume. It was wonderful. She was wonderful. He didn't want to wonder if she had ulterior motives. "I didn't know you were a nurse," he said, for lack of something better to say.

"Don't call me that." She punched the rag into the jar of salve with more force than necessary. "I'm not a nurse."

"Why do you protest? Most women would be honored to be called an angel of mercy."

"There are a lot of things you don't know about me, Paul Rousseau."

"I'd like to know them." He offered his back. "I'd really like to— Awgghhh! What the hell are you doing?"

"Applying salve." She stopped her ministrations long enough to place a piece of horehound candy between his lips. "Shhh, it'll be all right."

He yearned to hold her fingers to his mouth, but she drew them away.

"I'll try to be more gentle," she murmured as she touched his torn flesh once more.

The bitter mint, sugared by the sweetness of those fingers he longed to kiss, worked its way around his tongue, and he felt no more pain as Emma eased the medication into his wounds. Her touch was as soothing and mild as sweet Havana tobacco. She took the chill off places that not ten minutes earlier he had doubted would ever be warmed again. No woman this kind, this alluring, could be as rotten as he had supposed.

He reached behind him to cover the top of her hand with his palm. Turning his head, he locked his

121

gaze with hers. "You're very good at this."

"Do you really think so?"

"Absolutely."

A smile lit her face. It was the first genuinely happy smile she had given him. He wanted to see more of those smiles. A lot more.

"Thank you," she said, her tone strangely hoarse.

She took his fingers, and her hand was soft yet strong; he was transported away from the miserable surroundings. Instead of misery there was beauty all around him. There was Emma.

Unaccustomed to kindness, Paul relished the moment. And he made a decision. He would give up blackmailing her over the brooch. When he held her in his arms, it would be because she wanted to be there, not because he had forced her into it. "Emma, about the brooch . . ." Her shoulders stiffened, and he hurried to add, "Let's pretend it never happened."

"You're willing to forget I stole it from you?"

"Stole what?" he asked innocently. "I don't know anything about a theft."

"You're benevolent, too? Wonders never cease." She shook her head in amazement and got to her feet. "Do you . . . are you strong enough to walk out of here, Paul?" she asked, and he loved the way she spoke each syllable.

"Yes," he answered. "But where are you taking me?"

Smiling, she held her hand out to assist him. "To the St. Charles."

Chapter Nine

They reached the hotel well after dusk. While Emma was glad that Paul had released her from worry over the brooch, she was not pleased by his physical condition. Dr. Boulogne couldn't attend him, and she had dismissed the idea of taking Paul to the hospital. Hospitals were no place to be sick.

She led him to bed and pulled back the comforter. "Lie down."

As she tugged the boots from his feet, he didn't protest. His body hit the mattress heavily.

"I'll get the lamps," she said.

She moved about to light the room. In the street below revelers were making the most of Fat Tuesday, but as soft candlelight cast a golden glow over the room, Emma had no wish to celebrate this final evening before Lent. This was her place, here with Paul, seeing to his injury.

In a swish of gray woolen skirts, she turned to him. Aboard ship she had seen his sorry state; nevertheless she wasn't prepared for the shock of seeing him in the full light. His eyes told her not to pity him, as he rested on his side, but the gauntness of his cheeks accentuated the jagged scar on his right jaw, despite the bristles of his three-day-old beard. His black curls were plastered to his head, and ribbons of sweat separated the thick dark hair on his bare chest, woven through with crusts of grime. Paul's blue trousers now seemed a size too large. She was determined to make him well again.

"Don't look at me like that," he said gruffly.

"I must look if I'm to treat you."

"I'm all right. Feel better already." A muscle working in his throat, he levered himself up on an elbow, but the movement was too much and he fell down against the pillow. "Shouldn't have come here," he said. "There'll be trouble at the ship. Need to be there."

"It'll have to wait." Her tone brooked no defiance. "Right now you're going to have a bath, medication, and more to eat."

As if to reinforce Emma's edict, the chambermaid arrived with a pail of hot water and a kettle. The kitchen maid following on her heels bore a tray laden with a bowl of thick gumbo, a loaf of bread, a pitcher of purified water, and a teapot of hot water. The two women left the provisions and departed.

The liquids had to be taken first, Emma insisted, so he drank a glass of water in two long gulps. As he handed her the empty glass, she touched his skin. It was hot. Too hot. Fear sliced through her with the force of a cat-o'-nine. An infection could kill him! Were her pitifully few doctoring skills enough?

She withdrew a packet of herbs from her bag—the brewings for a fever-fighting tea—and dropped them in the teapot. Once the brew was down his throat, she perched on the edge of the bed, bowl in hand, to spoon the piquant okra stew between his lips.

He pushed her hand away. "I can feed myself!"

"All right." She had to leave him some pride, so she returned the spoon to the tray. The room was chilly, so she set about making a fire in the fireplace. Too soon she heard the spoon clatter to the bowl.

He groaned, pushed the food tray away, and turned onto his stomach. His white-knuckled fist eased open as sleep, deep and heavy, overtook him.

Emma carried the pan of water to the bedside table. This was her first opportunity to assess the full extent of his injuries. Pulling up a straight chair, she sank onto its velvet-covered seat. Six gashes cut through his once-smooth back, puffy and red. First, these wounds had to be cleaned. Emma took up a soapy rag and touched it to a gash on his shoulder. He flinched and groaned but didn't awaken, and she breathed a sigh of relief.

Paul was peaceful now, and her heart opened to him. Even in his deplorable condition she found him handsome. She smiled, took up the wet rag, and cleaned his back. Then she coated it with salve, and washed his neck and face. That done, she found a jar of talc and began to comb powder through his coarse, ink-black hair; those strands felt nice, so nice beneath her fingers. His ear—she could only see one—was finely shaped, and the ebon-hued lashes that lay on his cheeks were thick and curled, perhaps too much so for a man but not too much for Emma's pleasure.

In his fretful sleep he rolled onto his side and she

125

seized that opportunity to cleanse his chest. His neck was tanned a rich bronze, as were his torso and arms. It seemed strange to see a body darkened by the sun. Undoubtedly he stripped to the barest necessities when sailing the Gulf of Mexico.

"Papa," he mumbled, "Help you, Papa."

Emma's hand stopped. Why was he dreaming of his father? She told herself not to be silly. Even though Étienne Rousseau had been her uncle's nemesis, he was Paul's father. It was natural for a person to dream of a departed loved one.

She wondered about the type of man Paul was. Had tears ever moistened those lashes? Surely they had. After all, he was human. Had he ever been in love? Jealousy, pure and simple, reared its head.

Just that afternoon Howard had accused her of loving Paul. She felt . . . She felt what? It couldn't be love. She respected his principles, insofar as the men aboard the *San Antonio* were concerned, but she admired many people. And she didn't feel this way about them!

It was physical attraction, that was all. She couldn't deny it. Wanting him was a hurting thing. No man had ever touched her naked flesh, yet she ached for Paul to do so. A primitive urge heightened her awareness of the tense aching in her breasts and in the secret place of her womanhood. She was his for the taking.

Her palm slid over the corded muscles of his shoulder, and she murmured, "Oh, Paul . . ."

Waking from pain-heavy sleep, he heard her dulcet voice, felt her hands on him. They were cool, yet warm, and sure and gentle. They aroused him.

He didn't move for fear she would cease stroking him. She was making love to him by running her fingers down his right forearm, closing them around his wrist. His breath was shallow now, his blood hot for her as her seductive skills held him spellbound.

The big fingers of his right hand closed around her small hand, bringing it close to his hips. He felt her knuckles move to the bulge of his manhood. Then breath left him as she ran them across it. He removed the pressure of his hand, and her shaking palm cupped him. Paul, his heart stilled, believed that death had taken him and he was in heaven.

He opened his eyes, and Emma leaned forward on the chair beside the bed. It was dark in this place; only the dancing flames from the fire haloed the lovely honey-blond hair falling around Emma's shoulders. Those enchanting green eyes of hers watched him closely. He was just this side of heaven.

She moistened her lips, and he was dying to taste them. Later. If he didn't slow down, Paul realized their lovemaking would be over too quickly. Getting what he desired was a heady thing, even though he had imagined it differently. But there was more than his own pleasure to consider. For Emma he would take it slow and easy.

"Come closer, sweet angel of mercy. Know what I want?"

She blushed. "I . . . I—"

"I want a shave."

"A shave!"

"Yes." He locked his gaze with hers. "I'm going to kiss you . . . and more, you know that. And when I do, I don't want these chin bristles getting in the way.

127

Will you shave me, Emma?"

She grinned. "I have kept the water hot."

"My, uh, gear's in the top drawer of that bureau over there. No need to strop the razor," he added, glad for his habit of sharpening it after each use. He wanted her close to him, with no further interruptions.

He watched her cross the room, her delectable rear swaying as she moved, and his manhood responded even more—how was that possible?—to her movements. Paraphernalia in hand, she returned. As she lathered his brush, her bosom swayed. He swallowed hard. Damn the high-neck dress she wore! His hands were aching to touch her generous breasts. Yet he gave thanks for the buttons that went from her neck to below her waist. Buttons were made for provocative unfastening. Still on his side, Paul laid his head against the pillow and presented his throat.

"I've . . . I've never shaved a man before." She knew he was unaware of her studies and of her work with Dr. Boulogne. Would Paul make jest of her if he knew her usually sure fingers were now unsteady? "Aren't you afraid I'll cut you?"

Responding to what he figured to be innocent hesitancy, he replied, "Not in the least."

Totally enraptured, he reached up to lift a lock of hair from her shoulder, his hand lingering on the curve of her throat. "Just use the same touch you used when you bathed my back. Nice upward strokes. Take it slow and easy."

She grazed the brush across his throat, his cheeks. "How did you get that scar on your jaw, Paul?"

128

"Don't think I'll tell you. It wasn't honorable."

"I've never thought you honorable, anyway"—she tugged on his earlobe—"so go on."

"A mistress's dagger, my sweet." His hand moved to cup Emma's cheek. "Hell hath no fury like a woman scorned."

"You've scorned many," she surmised aloud.

"Not nearly as many as you imagine. I'm particular about those I take to my bed."

"Liar."

"Guess it would appear that way to you." With his thumbnail he outlined her delectable lips. "Now, how 'bout that shave?"

Wordlessly she set to his bidding, and he forced back a grin. The tip of her tongue was caught between her teeth, and her thinly arched brows were pulled together in a frown of concentration. The razor moved up Paul's neck, and her motions were smooth as glass. She was close, so close. He savored the scent of her perfume, enjoyed the sensuous "Oh my" that escaped her lips once, and then again. His eyes never left her face as she carried through his request. The ache in his loins was bursting for release.

"There's something very intimate about shaving a man," she said, avoiding his gaze.

"And there's something very intimate about being shaved. It's a trusting touch."

"I'm surprised you trust me," she said, setting the shaving gear aside. "After the brooch, you know."

"What brooch?" he asked, seeking no reply and hoping to remind her that the pin was past remembering. "Thanks for the shave," he said, to change the subject.

"You must shave often." She studied his face. "Your beard grows heavy on your cheeks."

"Does that bother you?"

"Oh no. I think it's very manly." She laughed. "I'm going to give you a terrible case of conceit."

"No, *amoureuse,*" he murmured, sliding his hand past her waist. She wasn't wearing a corset! She didn't protest when he cupped her derrière and urged her to the bed beside him. Levering himself above her, he leaned over to say in her ear, "You're going to let me kiss you."

And she shivered with delight.

His pain and fever forgotten, Paul possessed the lips that fascinated him beyond reason. Moving to deepen the embrace, he gripped Emma's hair. There was fire between them, a fire that raged into an explosion of desire. His leg was between her thighs and her muscles gripped him. How long they savored the tastes of each other's mouths, Paul didn't know. It could have been seconds, but it was probably minutes. It was wonderful. He leaned away just enough to unfasten her dress. Her fingers cut into the flesh of his arms. With his chin he pushed away the fabric, exposing the thin chemise that covered her womanly treasures. Then his lips trailed kisses along her collarbone, and down to the rise of her breasts. Through fabric, he captured a swollen peak. Laving, tasting, cherishing.

She held his head to her breast. "So good," she moaned.

"So good," he echoed, gathering the folds of her skirt between his fingers. At last he found the sleek

130

skin of her thigh, and skimmed his palm along its rich satin. "I want you, my sweet," he whispered in French. His mouth slanting over her lips anew, he continued in English. "Want you so much."

He was touching her most secret place, and she experienced a moment of panic. Her palm flew to the top of his hand, stilling the caress. She wanted this lovemaking, but wasn't there pain—a lot of it—the first time?

"What's wrong?" he asked tenderly, looking into her eyes.

"I . . . I've never been with a man before."

"You're not serious."

"I am." She closed her eyes to shut out his shocked expression. "I didn't mean to spoil it. Maybe if you kissed me again . . ."

From the moment he'd met her, Paul had figured Emma to be a woman accustomed to lovemaking. And blushing maidens didn't fondle a man's private parts, as she had done. Yet she couldn't be lying. The proof of that would be apparent only too soon. Should he claim her maidenhead?

He wanted it—oh how he coveted it!—yet he refrained. Women and society were strange about virginity claimed. But binding ties were not Paul's primary concern. Honor stood in the way. Maidenhood hadn't stifled him in the past, nonetheless he would not dishonor Emma.

He sought revenge against her uncle, not Emma. He intended to avenge his father's death and be gone. Out of New Orleans, and most certainly out of Emma's life. And though she had offered him a woman's most treasured gift, he wouldn't take it.

She deserved better than the terms he could offer.

"What's . . . what's wrong?" she asked.

"I don't make love to virgins."

Her face registered disbelief; then a flush crept onto her face. "I see," she said, her voice brittle. She got off the bed and buttoned her dress. "How wise of you."

Was it? Paul was regretting his chivalrous behavior already; the fever must have gone to his head. And he was sorry for bruising her ego. More than anything, he yearned to tell her that he wanted her—craved her more than he had wanted any other woman. But he wouldn't.

"I'm, uh, feeling a little weak," he lied, rolling onto his back. "Awwgh! *Sacre bleu!*"

Serves you right! she fumed inwardly. She had never imagined that he would turn away from her. What had she done wrong? Surely men enjoyed the conquest of maidenly females! What was wrong with her? Why didn't he want her? She wasn't ashamed to touch him intimately, and hadn't he seemed to enjoy it?

Anyway, that was a bother she didn't need. Her aim was to be a healer. Period. It was best not to forget that. Why, if they made love, it might overtax Paul, and she'd have that on her conscience.

Rising up, Paul set his feet on the floor. "Emma, it's getting late." He lowered his head as if he were dizzy. "You'll be missed at Magnolia Hall."

She realized he was hoping to get rid of her or offering her a chance to restore her torn pride. But run she wouldn't.

"Until your fever breaks you're stuck with me. I

sent word I had a patient to attend to."

"Patient?" he asked, bemusement in his tone. "You told me you aren't a nurse."

She held her proud head high. "I'm studying to be a doctor."

"And a good one you'll be."

Don't flatter me with your tongue, hold me in your arms! she wanted to rail at him. Instead, she turned from him, walked to the fireplace and lifted the kettle from its hook. "I only know one physician here in New Orleans. I sent word to him that he was needed, but he had an emergency at Charity Hospital. Too many Carnival injuries, you see. If you'd like, though, I'll find another doctor."

"That won't be necessary," Paul replied, the timbre of his voice heavy and low. "You're all I need, Emma."

How dare he entice her with belated charm? Did he think to mark her for a fool anew? She forced casualness into her tone. "It doesn't worry you that a female is tending your wounds?"

"It's unusual, but it doesn't bother me." He grinned. "Matter of fact, Madame Docteur, I like the idea. I've been told you have ambitions, but I never dreamed you had such a calling in mind."

"Well, I do." At least Paul was on her side on one score. At any other time that might have pleased Emma. She poured another cup of herbal tea. "You'd better drink this. You mustn't allow your body to go without fluids."

The air was tense between them.

"Emma, I have to get back to the ship."

"Why?"

"Duty. There's unrest out there. There'll be a mutiny unless someone appeases those men."

"You may be right"—she shook a finger at him—"but you can't be the one to help them."

"Have to. I'd lay down my life for the Texas Navy."

"No doubt. Valor is a weakness men are heir to."

"And for that I have no apology," he said. "Haven't you ever loved something or someone enough to sacrifice yourself?"

Hadn't she just done that? Still angry at his rejection, she went for a nerve. "If you're referring to your love for anything connected with Texas, please don't expect me to commiserate. Why anyone would love a frontier nation peopled by the misfits of society is beyond me."

"Yes, it is beyond you." He lurched to his feet, but swayed as he put one foot in front of the other. "Got to go."

"You'll kill yourself if you do. Need I remind you of your fever? And your back looks like a side of beef hanging in a butcher's window."

"Praise me no more with your fishwife's compliments."

"Forgive me for sounding like a physician," she said, drawing out the last word for emphasis, "but I forbid you to leave. It's three o'clock in the morning! Give yourself until daybreak, at least. With any luck your fever will break, and you'll then have the strength to tend to your duties. You are *weak,* you know. You told me so yourself."

"I knew I'd eat those words," he muttered.

"So be it." Emma wished to change his mind

134

about going to the ship . . . and about making love to her. She pointed to the bed. "Get back there."

In spite of his convictions a trace of a grin curled the corners of his mouth. "And what about you? Fevers take a while to break."

"I'm staying. I told you that."

"Then take the bed," he offered. "I'll sleep on the floor."

Nonplused by his complete change from predator to lamb, she felt . . . Felt what? Disappointment. While she was innocent of certain aspects of intimacy, she perceived that he had desired her. So what if he took her virginity? She was offering it, and—by darn!—he was going to get it.

"Thank you for your generous offer, my good man, but I'll not hear of it. That bed is big enough for both of us." She combed her fingers through her hair, and moistened her lips. Her voice was low, teasing and enticing, as she said, "I intend to make you suffer for not making love to me. From here on out, you're going to be lured and tempted and tantalized to the nth degree."

"What did I hear you say?"

"You is disgusting, purely disgusting." Cleopatra hitched her nose toward the ceiling of Paul's hotel room. "I figured you was up to no good when you didn't show your face by the time Miss Marian came home. But I waited—yes, ma'am—just in case you hadn't been lying about Dr. Boulogne."

"I didn't say anything about Dr. Boulogne. I sent word I had a patient."

135

"Patient? Hmmph. That's what I'm trying to be—patient! But you, missy, would try the patience of a saint." Cleo pursed her mouth. "Laying up in bed with that man—the very idea!"

That had been true, but Cleopatra had not caught them together. Emma crossed to the window and pulled back the drapery. The first light of dawn had begun to ribbon the sky. Where was Paul? Probably on board the *San Antonio*. While she was dozing, he had slipped out of the room. A doze was all it had been. She had spent a tortured night lying next to him. He had barely moved a muscle, and he certainly hadn't touched her. But oh, how she had wanted him to.

If there was anything to be thankful for, it was that Paul's fever had broken. Which was not much consolation.

"Well, ain't you got anything to say for yourself?" Cleopatra pressed.

"I wasn't 'laying up in the bed with that man.'" Not in the real sense of the phrase.

"Hmmph." Cleopatra huffed over to the place in question and pounded her forefinger on the sheet. "I got eyes, missy, and you was laying up right here, bigger than Richmond." She drew back from the smears of blood that streaked the top portion of Paul's side of the bed. "That man done compromised my baby."

"Cleo!" Emma laughed. "It's not what you think. And if you'd paused to consider, you'd have realized it would've taken acrobatics for me to put that blood there. We'd have to have been standing on our heads. Hmm"—she patted a forefinger against her

136

lips—"that's an interesting concept."

"You hush, missy." The mammy drew herself up to her full height of four ten. "I don't know where you get talk like that, but I guess it be from those nasty medical books. The Lord knows I never taught you such filthy mindedness!" Cleopatra stomped back across the room and leveled a glare at Emma. "But don't you fall to thinking I'm addlepated. I know about man-and-woman ways, and I also know what can, and can't, be done on a mattress."

Emma feigned shock. "Are you saying you aren't as pure as the driven snow?"

"That be my business." A flush heightened Cleopatra's mahogany cheeks. "And don't you be switching the subject on me." She motioned behind her, indicating the bed. "That one gonna marry you. I'm gonna see to it!"

"Oh? If the 'one' you're referring to happens to be an inanimate object commonly known as a place for sleeping, you'll have a difficult time getting it to sign the marriage registry. Four legs, but no fingers. Sorry, Cleo." Smoothing the wrinkles from her skirt, Emma swept past the fuming mammy. "Now leave me be. I need to brush my hair."

Amazingly, Cleopatra said no more.

Emma searched for a hairbrush. None was atop the furnishings. She checked drawers, fruitlessly. Surely Paul had a means for combing hair. Her eyes stopped on the sea chest. "I doubt there's one in there," she said, more to herself than to Cleopatra. But she was curious as to the contents.

"I be staying outta that if I was you. Didn't that brooch teach you nothing?"

137

"Thank you, dear conscience." Irresistible curiosity got the best of her, and Emma tried the lock. It was fastened. "Loan me a hairpin, please."

Scowling, Cleopatra reached under her tignon and pulled a sturdy pin from her hair. "Guess you learned lock-picking somewhere, too."

"Actually I don't know the first thing about it, Cleo. But I can't go out in public with my hair mussed."

"'Cause people'd know what you been doing." Cleopatra shook her head, and her next words were laced with uncharacteristic dejection. "Where did I go wrong? I always wanted you to be a nice lady like your mama, but . . ."

Emma, feeling guilty for causing her mammy's depression, took Cleo's thin hand and squeezed gently. Cleopatra had been more than a nursemaid, much more. She was the sister Emma could depend on, the mother she had sometimes needed, the friend who could be relied upon . . . and an occasional partner in antics. In short, Emma loved her.

"Don't blame yourself for my behavior. I failed you; you didn't fail me." She pressed a kiss to Cleopatra's cheek. "I wish I could be the proper lady you want me to be. But lately . . . lately I no longer know what's proper and right."

"Time's a woman be thinking like that, she be in love with her man."

"I fear you're right."

"Me right? Must have wax in my ears!" Cleopatra exclaimed, her old self returning. "I ain't been right in weeks, according to you." She put her hands on what would have been the curve of her hips, provided she had some angles. "Well, baby, let's get that chest opened so you can get to brushing that hair. Won't have that man of yours coming back and thinking I raised a slovenly gal!"

Cleopatra sank to her knees in front of the chest, her deft fingers picking the lock in the blink of an eye. The heavy lid creaked open, and the scent of cedar burst forth.

Emma took the top tray onto her lap. It held a small velvet pouch, which she felt no compunction about opening. An emerald ring surrounded by diamonds winked up at her. She replaced it. There were also letters from a New Orleans bank, a sextant, a spyglass, brass buttons, several coins. And a gold watch; its inscription was in French, but Emma believed it had belonged to Étienne Rousseau.

"Take a look at this," Cleopatra implored, holding out a miniature portrait.

Emma absorbed the woman's exquisite features. She had black hair and eyes, a lean face, and a bearing that resembled Paul's. "She must be his mother. Angélique, I think she was called."

Suddenly contrite for invading Paul's privacy, Emma returned the items to their rightful places. "Funny, what a person's possessions say about him. A rank stranger would know Paul is a man of the sea . . . and that he loved his parents dearly."

"That's true, but you ain't found a hairbrush yet."

"Also true." Remorse forgotten, Emma dug into the chest. A pair of cropped breeches and neatly folded shirts were stacked in it. She moved those aside, and spreading her fingers to the left, hit a

139

metal object. What is it? she wondered. It feels like a . . . Surely it isn't the . . . Her fingers closed around the object. Shirts flying, she pulled the brooch from the trunk. It was the same piece of jewelry, minus one diamond, that she had taken from Paul Rousseau's room!

"How . . . What is going on?" she said aloud, the much-needed brush now forgotten. "Drat him! He tricked me!" She threw the hated pin on top of the now wrinkled shirts. "He won't get away with this, Cleo. Lieutenant Rousseau is going to answer to me!"

"Tee hee," Cleopatra chortled.

"I'll need a boat to row me out to his ship," Emma thought aloud as she gathered her medical supplies and dropped them into the black satchel. "Maybe Uncle Rankin has one at the factor-house wharf."

"You ain't ducking me this time, missy! I'm going with you."

"As you wish."

The mammy patted her tignon and got ready for action. "I'm gonna hear those firecrackers go poppity-pop!"

Chapter Ten

Calling himself forty kinds of a fool for leaving Emma alone and untouched in his hotel room, Paul reached the levee guarding the city of New Orleans from the silt-lined Mississippi River. He was on a course for the *San Antonio*'s longboat, tied up at the wharf now six streets away. He had to get back to duty, and away from desire. Though his flesh bore testimony to the injustices of ineffectual command, he was first and foremost a lieutenant in service to the Republic of Texas.

Yet he ached for Emma. There was no cure for it, save for man's oldest method of declaring superiority over women—sex. Which he had renounced the night before. Honor be damned! If he had the night to do over . . .

Paul told himself not to think of her, but it was impossible. He wanted to make love to her. The shirt and coat of his tight-fitting naval uniform rubbed the wounds on his back, but the pain he felt for Emma overshadowed his physical discomfort.

He turned the corner from Common Street. Yet each step he took, in a northwesterly direction, was haunted by the memory of the previous evening. Memories of her. Emma caring for him with her healer's hands and heart; Emma with her lovely hair falling around her shoulders, and with breasts eager for his lips; Emma yielding to him. Why, for once in his life, had he been gallant? Could it be that he was falling in love with her? Absolutely not.

He stopped at the longboat's usual mooring, which was the Oliver Factor House wharf. Where was the boat? Shading his eyes, he looked both ways across the river, but didn't sight the longboat. For a second he considered borrowing the Oliver skiff but dismissed the notion.

"Been waiting for ya to show your mug." Henry Packert stepped in front of Paul. There was a wicked gleam to his lone eye. "Got word on them crates."

"Later," Paul said, brushing past the pirate. "I'm headed for my ship."

"Planning on swimming? There ain't a dinghy in sight." Packert hooked a thumb toward Oliver's small boat. "'Cept that one."

Paul grimaced. "Never mind."

This part of town was very quiet. Though it usually teemed with beggars, bitches, and boatsmen, most of these were probably sleeping off the effects of Fat Tuesday. Until the longboat returned to its station, Paul was stranded ashore. "All right, Packert, let's hear it."

"Oughtn't to tell ya, seeing's how ya shamed me in front of me woman the other day, but I guess I will. You came to me rescue a couple o' times out in the Gulf, and I ain't one to forget good turns." Crooking a thumb toward Rankin Oliver's cotton warehouse, the hulking pirate sidled closer to Paul. "Got something to show ya. Follow me."

It didn't take much for Paul to guess what was in store. Earlier Packert had gained entrance to the frame building, so he led Paul to a high-silled window. The old pirate's face turned florid as he struggled to climb upward. In spite of his injuries, Paul easily swung himself through the opening. The light was dim, for the warehouse was large and its big freight doors were fastened. That one window near the front provided the only illumination. Packert lit a lantern. Amid the cotton bales piled high on the floor were twelve wooden boxes, each marked COPPER PIPING—OLIVER SUGAR MILL, HAVANA. Paul's suspicion was confirmed. The contraband ordnance for Mexico had arrived.

"They was off-loaded late last night," Packert said. "Guess Oliver figured nobody'd pay no nevermind, since the whole town was celebrating."

"You're probably right." Paul walked closer to inspect the outside of a crate. "Have you opened any of them?" he asked doubtfully. From the looks of the boxes, they hadn't been touched. "Let's make certain they contain gunpowder and weapons; then I'll go for the police."

"Police? No use bringing them into this," the older man protested. "We can take care of the matter ourselves."

"What do you mean?"

Packert chuckled, a mirthless little sound. "We'll torch 'em good and proper. This whole place'll blow to kingdom come."

"No! Think straight, Packert. If you set this

143

warehouse afire, you'll be guilty of arson."

"Not if I don't get caught. And consider this, me ol' friend: the explosion will be evidence in itself. It'll put Rankin Oliver behind bars, that it will."

"There's no need for fire." Going against the law to avenge Étienne Rousseau's death was not Paul's intention. He could have done that years ago! And an explosion might set off a chain of fires. "Let's get this crate open."

"All right," Packert finally grumbled. "There's sense to it."

A nearby shelf held an assortment of tools, crowbars among them. Wishing for his usual strength, Paul took one and handed another to Packert. He wedged the flat end of the bar under the lid. Suddenly he heard the other man move behind him. "Wha—"

With a swiftness belying his girth, Henry Packert swung the steel bar in a wide arc. The blow caught Paul on the shoulder, in the uppermost lash wound. Stunned by the pain, Paul fell and grabbed his back.

The aged corsair used the moment to his own advantage. He threw the lantern atop the bale closest to the crates. Running forward, he shoved his weight against the side door. It gave.

He turned to Paul. "Didn't mean to hurt ya, but I couldn't see going to the calaboose boys. Rankin'd find a way to get outta trouble."

He was gone.

Realizing it had been futile to try to reason with an unreasonable man, Paul struggled to his feet and got out of his jacket. He beat at the flames with the coat, acrid smoke filling his lungs. But the fire raged.

There was no stopping it!

Still holding his jacket, Paul raced for the door Henry had forced open. Outside and well away from the building, he turned, chest heaving, and raced onto the levee. The skiff was gone. Shielding his eyes with a soot-blackened hand, Paul peered to the right, then the left. He caught sight of Packert rowing downstream, fast and furious.

He rubbed away the perspiration threatening his vision. "Damn!"

With no time to think, he threw his coat over his forearm, then sprinted down the embankment and alongside the factor house. Just as he cleared its corner, he halted in his tracks. Emma Oliver and her mammy stood not ten feet from him. Both women were like wooden statues, but Paul saw the horror, and anger, in their eyes.

"Get back," Paul shouted. "I couldn't put out the fire. Get the hell away."

"What are you doing here?" Emma asked, ignoring his warning.

"Damn it! There's no time for talk." Grabbing each woman by an arm, he pulled them across the street.

The building did not explode. Not then, not later. Yet despite the efforts of the fire fighters from Dépôt des Pompes, Rankin Oliver's factor house burned to the ground. Paul realized neither gunpowder nor weapons had reached the warehouse. It must have been a dummy shipment, but what had happened to the first one?

When the flames died to embers, the fire wagon and its men departed. A group of police investiga-

145

tors walked around the rubble now. Whispering and pointing, a small crowd of thrill-seekers stood at the street's edge.

"I don't care what you say or what you told those firemen," Emma accused, "you set that fire!"

"Care to give me the benefit of the doubt?" Paul asked.

"No." She crossed her arms and glared at him. "As surely as I'm standing here in front of my uncle's burned-out business, you're to blame."

"We seen it with our own eyes," Cleopatra put in. "You was running 'round the corner of that building."

"Ladies, ladies. Please listen! I came down here to look for the Texas longboat. I saw the side door swinging on its hinges, so I went in to investigate—and found the fire. I tried to stop it." He held up his jacket. "Tried to stop it with this." It was a flimsy excuse, even to Paul's own ears, but he wouldn't incriminate Packert; the pirate would answer to Paul and Paul alone. "It was the least I could do for the Oliver family."

"Why didn't you simply run for help?" Emma asked.

"I wasn't thinking clearly. Please trust me."

"Don't you know trust has to be earned, Paul Rousseau?" Emma asked through gritted teeth. She took one step back. "Why would I put faith in your word? You've tricked me since we met." She receded another step. "You blackmailed me over that brooch—when it was in your possession all along!"

Paul groaned inwardly. "I just got it back."

"Save your explanations," she demanded. "I don't

have time to waste on lies. A terrible crime has been committed against my family, and I'm going to see that it doesn't go unpaid."

A realization, hard and cold, filled Paul's mind. He had blackmailed, lied to, and scorned an Oliver. That was an error in judgment which might lead to his undoing.

"Yessir, and you'll answer to the police." Cleopatra shot him a glowering look that could have started a fire. "And to Master Rankin."

"I look forward to it."

On the first score, Paul got his opportunity not two minutes later. A tall policeman, with curly blond hair and hazel eyes, alit from his horse and strode over to the investigators. Afterward, he walked over to Paul and the two women.

"Detective Daryl Watson here." Ignoring the mammy, he turned to Emma. "Miss Oliver?" She nodded and he continued. "My men tell me you're an eyewitness to the fire."

"Yes, I am."

"Did you see anyone or anything suspicious?"

Paul squared his shoulders. Would Emma accuse him publicly?

Emma didn't want to believe Paul guilty of arson. Even now, knowing he had duped her about the brooch, she wanted to believe in him, but she couldn't.

What was his motive? she asked herself. Paul slipped his jacket from his arm, turned, and shook it. Was that an unsubtle signal, a reminder he had tried to extinguish the flames? she wondered. The white linen of his shirt bore traces of blood, especially

147

near his right shoulder. Why would an injured man try to save an unpeopled building from destruction? Watching him push one arm and then the other into the coat sleeves, Emma yearned for the truth. The night she had met him he'd sworn he wanted to mend fences with Uncle Rankin, and there had been his pain-filled rambling of the night before: "Help you, Papa."

"Miss Oliver, did you hear me?"

There was only one reason why Paul could have committed this crime. He had lied from the onset about his intentions toward her uncle. He blamed Rankin for his father's death.

He deserved punishment if he had lied about the fire; and if so, the Oliver family needed to be protected from him. If he had told the truth, then the truth would come out. She had to testify to what she had seen.

Emma nodded. "Yes, I . . . we saw him." Her shaking finger pointed at Paul. "He says he's not guilty, but—"

"Who?" Watson hitched a thumb at Paul. "This one?"

Emma forced a yes past her frozen throat.

She had done it. Accused him. Paul wondered why as he held up a palm. "You're wrong. I'm innocent."

"He ain't," Cleo put in.

"What do you have to say for yourself?" Watson asked Paul, while motioning the other policemen forward.

"I've said it. I'm innocent." Paul glared at Emma as he made his explanation. "She mistook me for the culprit," he added.

The detective didn't appear any more convinced than the two women, much less the three policemen who had come forward to circle the group. Watson gave Paul the once-over. "And you didn't see anyone leave the building?"

Paul swallowed. Identifying Henry Packert wasn't to his benefit. "No one."

"You got a name?" Watson asked.

"Rousseau. First Lieutenant Paul Rousseau. I'm second-in-command of the Texas schooner *San Antonio*."

Watson's eyes widened. "That so? Well, I'm surprised you aren't with your ship."

Giving full attention to the detective, Paul said, "I was on my way there when I spotted the fire."

"Were you on the ship last night?"

"The, uh, early part of the evening. Why do you ask?"

"I think you're guilty. Guilty as sin." Watson rubbed his jaw. "Me being a detective, I see a lot of human nature gone sour. Times like those, men take their hostilities out in unusual ways."

"I beg your pardon?" Paul asked.

"In case you don't already know, which I think you do, I'll tell you. About midnight last night, your men mutinied."

Paul's shoulders slumped. Worse had come to worst on the schooner. Could there have been anything he might have done to prevent the mutiny?

"We've got eight of them behind bars," a youthful policeman disclosed.

Watson nodded. "That's right. But your mates

149

injured a couple of the officers before they were collared. Seems the crew of a U.S. revenue cutter heard the gunshot that killed your captain, and—"

"James?" Emma interrupted. "Are you saying Captain James Throckmorton is dead?"

"Yes, ma'am. The crew of the *Jackson* brought his body ashore."

Emma's hand flew to her lips; Cleopatra's mouth dropped open.

"Damn!" Paul squeezed his eyes closed and lowered his head. His hands were clenched at his sides. He had had no use for Throckmorton, but he believed his death unjust. The mutineers would be brought to justice!

Disgust filled Paul. He had compromised the oath he had given to the Republic of Texas when he'd left the *San Antonio* . . . on Emma's arm. If he'd spent less time seeking revenge against her uncle—and pursuing Emma, he might have discharged his duties with success.

Raising his head, he said, "I give you my word as an officer of the Republic of Texas I did not torch that warehouse."

Watson peered at the ground, then back again. "The Texas Navy's pretty popular in our local press. All the citizens of New Orleans—well, the upstanding ones, anyway—support what you fellows have been doing out in the Gulf."

"Can you appreciate the necessity of my taking command of that ship?" Paul asked.

Emma interjected her own question. "You're not going to let him leave, are you?"

Cleopatra put in, "If you do, his next stop'll be

Jamaica or somewhere."

"See here"—Emma glared in the detective's direction—"I demand that you arrest Rousseau immediately."

Anger raged within Paul. Damn her! She'd have him *jailed!* This was typical Oliver behavior.

Just this morning he had imagined he was falling in love with Emma, though the night before she had said he'd suffer for not making love to her. Now he'd be kept from his responsibilities. Was this her revenge?

"Have to consider public opinion," Watson said, almost to himself, as he rubbed his jaw again. "I'll order a police boat to row you over to your ship."

"No!" Emma and Cleopatra protested in unison.

"Hear me out, please." Watson patted the air in a gesture of conciliation. "I'm giving you this chance, Lieutenant, but don't make too much of it. I'm going aboard with you. Better find someone you can trust to take the helm. And don't take too long doing it, because you're under arrest for arson."

Forty minutes later Paul, wearing the singed jacket, descended the companionway to the *San Antonio*'s gun deck. Second Lieutenant William Seeger followed him. Watson did not accompany them, for he stayed topside.

The deck wasn't long by naval standards—less than one hundred feet from bow to stern—but what the schooner lacked in length, she made up in speed. Of course she wasn't a-sail now, but Paul fondly recalled the way she could skip over waves as if she were a pebble. How long would it be before he'd sail her again?

"Attention!" he ordered, vowing not to think about the morning, Emma, or his own future.

Ten of the eleven sailors remaining, each dressed to varying degrees in ducking and stripes, rolled from hammocks strung above the six twelve-pounder batteries. Faces bruised, the marines stood straight and tall. Salutes were exchanged. These men, Paul had learned from Seeger, had courageously defended the Texas ensign against the mutineers.

Paul eyed the remaining seaman, the man who hadn't risen at his order. The youngest of the group, he was the wet-eared lad named David Montgomery who had tied Paul's wrists to the pivot. Now he yawned and stretched his arms. Though Montgomery was a lie-abed, Paul knew him to be loyal and true, and a fine young man to boot. Paul cleared his throat, a commanding sound.

"Huh?" David lifted his head; it was battered black and blue. "Oh! Uh, Lieutenant . . ." He, too, rolled from his hammock, but caught his toe on a nearby eating-table's leg. "Ouch!" Hopping on one foot and holding the other within his palms, he said, "Sorry, sir."

Paul stifled a grin. His hands behind his back, he trod across the planks. "Men, as your commanding officer, I thank you for your valor last night. The Republic owes you a debt of gratitude." He paused. "I've been informed that all but six of the mutineers were apprehended by the New Orleans authorities. Those few escaped across the river to Algiers, but they will be caught!"

A cheer rose from the group.

"I deeply regret that I wasn't aboard last night when the incident happened. But you have my word that I'll do everything in my power to see that the mutineers receive their just deserts."

Paul would do that, provided he was given the opportunity. He stopped near the bow, turned, and locked eyes with one man, then another, each in turn. What he was about to say took a lot of faith on his part, but these men needed the trust and support of their commanding officer.

"For a number of months you have not been paid for your services. The lieutenant"—Paul nodded toward Seeger—"has been instructed to rectify that inadequacy. At three bells this afternoon he will issue back salaries." When Paul had boarded the schooner he had hastily penned a note giving Seeger the authority to draw funds from the Rousseau account in the bank. "After which, all but *one* of you shall be granted a liberty permit until sunrise on the morn."

Questioning expressions on their faces, the men stared at one another.

"I'm asking for a volunteer to man the ship," Paul said.

"I'll do it, sir," said a whiskered sailor.

"Ah, Davenport, you're touched in the head! You grouse more'n any o' us about needin' a woman," Jay Johnson pointed out. "'Cept for Jims Hocker."

The boatswain's mate limped forward. Karl Tampke was a big German, grizzled and ugly, especially with one eye swollen shut. "I stay here," he

153

slurred. Two of his front teeth were missing now. "De vimen just vant my geld. I save for old age."

"From the looks of you, you'd better spend it while you can, Tampke. You'll never make it to dotage." Paul grinned. "You'd better get to sick bay."

"I haven't yet grown accustomed to wine and sport." David Montgomery stepped forward. "I'll keep watch, Lieutenant."

Paul expressed his appreciation. But the most difficult part was yet to come. Wrestling with his conscience, he stopped at a twelve-pounder and ran his palm along its metal firing vent. Right now he was at the crossroads of duty or disobedience.

As an officer in service to Texas now in charge of a schooner of war becalmed by politics, should he obey his president or his commodore? In the past he was able to see the black and white of right and wrong. Presently he had trouble distinguishing the shades of gray between the two. Sam Houston believed his actions to be just. Stalwart in his convictions, Edwin Ward Moore felt the same. Paul's sympathies were aligned to Moore's, but disobeying Houston could bring further jeopardy upon himself. Still, he had to protect the Republic's citizens and to honor those who had fought for Texas independence.

"When you return from shore, I am ordering this vessel to set sail for our rendezvous with Commodore Moore in the Arcas Islands."

"But . . . but I thought we were to stay here until further orders from President Houston," Montgomery said, then added, "Meaning no disrespect, sir."

154

"None taken." Paul glanced at Lieutenant Seeger and back again. "I take full responsibility for the repercussions."

"The commodore must be apprised of our situation," Seeger offered.

Glad for that show of support, Paul said, "On the voyage to those waters, Lieutenant Seeger will be your officer-in-charge."

"What about you?" Montgomery asked, his dark brows furrowed.

"Pressing matters detain me in Louisiana." Skating around the truth rankled Paul, but he felt it judicious not to mention his legal problems. It wouldn't be good for morale if the men thought their superior officer might be guilty of a criminal deed. "That will be all."

"Yes, sir."

Paul clipped a salute and swung around, meaning to climb the companionway. But before he did, he turned his head to the sailors. "Good luck, men. My heart is with you."

He ascended the ladder and pushed the companionway hatch closed. The wind curled at his neck. Not a strong gust, but he relished that last moment of freedom's fresh air.

Resigned to his fate, he faced Detective Daryl Watson. "I'm ready."

Chapter Eleven

Jail was no place for a lady, even one who knew herself to be less than a pillar of propriety. Nevertheless, Emma was there. Be it concern or plain old anger, she needed to see Paul Rousseau. With any luck, the turmoil of her heart and mind would be eased.

In deference to her social position Emma was allowed privacy for her visit. While waiting, she sat five, perhaps ten, minutes in Detective Watson's iron-barred small office in the calaboose. Finally Paul darkened the door. He wore the dark-blue uniform she had seen him in the previous day. It was as if he'd remained in the same attire to taunt her, but she realized he probably hadn't been afforded a chance to change.

Anger was written on every plane of his angular face. "What do you want?"

From a chair in front of the detective's desk, she pushed herself to a standing position. "To find out if you're all right."

"Ah. I see." His brown eyes were hard pools of black—as black as his hair. Paul picked up a chair

156

and with a flick of his wrist, turned it around. Resting an arm on its back, he straddled the seat. The pose was deceptively relaxed. "You can quit losing sleep. All things considered, I'm doing fine. No thanks to you."

"If you're trying to make me feel guilty, forget it." Irritated, she called up a haughty remark: "And I believe it's not considered gentlemanly to take a seat while a lady stands."

"We settled that gentleman-lady business a while back." Paul rubbed the stubble of his beard. "You've found out what you *said* you came to hear. What else do you want, Emma?"

"The truth."

"You heard it yesterday."

"Not all of it. If any." Emma walked to the barred window, stared out with unseeing eyes and whirled around. "After you left, I needed a hairbrush. I couldn't find one, so I searched through your belongings. I found the brooch."

"I figured as much."

"Be honest. It didn't find its way into that sea chest!"

"If you'll remember correctly, I tried to explain that yesterday. But you weren't listening." Paul shot from the chair and closed the distance between them. Curling his fingers around her shoulders, he said, "The explanation is simple. I saw a woman wearing it, and I bought it back."

"How convenient." She turned her head to the side.

"Does my scent bother you?" he asked, jeering.

"Not in the least." She wasn't concerned with the

157

smoke clinging to his coat; soap and water would take care of that. Poor character could not be rinsed out of a soiled soul. She was determined to get back to the prior subject. "You saw a woman on the street, walked up to her and asked, 'Madame, may I buy the jewels off your bosom?'"

"Basically. But I didn't see her on the street. She was in her house." He paused. "I know the people who stole it."

"Packert and Katie?"

"You knew their names. . . ." He frowned. "You would've saved us both a lot of trouble if you'd told me that."

"Well, how was I to know you were acquainted with the scum of society? On second thought, I retract the question. I'm sure your pirating background has opened to you the drawing rooms of many derelicts and thieves."

His anger rising, Paul snapped, "Shrew."

"Snake!"

He chuckled then, and grinned. "Beautiful . . ."

"Handsome," she replied, far too quickly, but meaning it at any rate. What was wrong with her that she continued to be attracted to him?

He slipped his palm to her nape, and his fingers slid through her hair. *"Chérie,* about the brooch . . . I told you the other night to forget it. I thought that'd be sufficient. That was an error in judgment on my part, and I apologize."

"For the error in judgment or for blackmailing me?"

"For both," he replied in a low timbre. His thumb, now at her shoulder, began to caress the dip above her collarbone. "I know you were, and are, angry with me over the brooch," he said. "So furious, I believe, that you cannot, for the glare in your eyes, see the truth about the fire. But I did not start that blaze."

"I beg to differ. You are the only suspect."

"Between black and white there are shades of gray." His thumbs bit into her flesh. "Search your heart, Emma. What reason would I have had to torch that factor house?"

"Because you still hate my uncle for defending his honor against your father."

"Think back to the night you appeared in my quarters. I told you I was set on righting the wrongs of yesteryear."

"And perhaps you have."

"Rest assured, Emma Oliver, I don't stoop to felony. Never. Dammit, I'd just left you at the hotel. Why would I want to set fire to your uncle's place of business?"

There was credence to Paul's words, but Emma was not entirely convinced of his innocence. Something didn't ring true. "My heart tells me you're not telling the entire story of what happened yesterday morning."

"Bien entendu." He removed his hands from her neck and shoulder. "The calaboose has many interrogators. You needn't add your name to the list."

"Fine." She gathered her cloak and reticule. "I'll leave it to the courts."

"It may not come to that," Paul said. "Not everyone in New Orleans believes I'm guilty. My

159

attorney certainly doesn't; Howard O'Reilly is on my side."

Emma rounded on him. "He's my mother's brother—my beloved uncle, just as Uncle Rankin is. Did you know that?" When Paul nodded she continued. "When he used his influence with poor departed James to get you off that ship, I had no qualms about it. But this is different. You stand accused of arson committed against Oliver property. Haven't you done enough without setting the Olivers against the O'Reillys?"

"Too bad you didn't inherit some of the O'Reilly mercy."

"O'Reilly idiocy you mean!"

"Are the Olivers so thirsty for my blood that they'd turn against Howard for performing a professional duty?" Paul's lip curled back. "Or should I replace the plural with the singular? Are *you* thirsty for my blood?"

"Yes!"

She swept out of the office, closing the door behind her. After whispering politely to the policeman who guarded the room, she made her way outside and past the Place d'Armes. Once inside her carriage, she fell to reflection.

What would she do if the Paul Rousseau matter caused a rift between her maternal and paternal families? Since Howard was only fifteen years her senior Emma didn't address him as uncle, but that was no indication of her feelings for him. She loved Howard. He was family, and kith and kin were an important aspect of Emma's life.

After all, Uncle Rankin was the wronged party in

this miserable affair. He had suffered a major financial loss, and a good many people he'd employed had lost their source of income. Furthermore, were it not for the swift action of the fire brigade, the fire would have spread—and the city of New Orleans could have been leveled.

Her conscience reminded Emma that Paul had seemed sincere in declaring his innocence. But the odds were stacked against him. When it came down to it, Emma was an Oliver.

"You Olivers are all alike," Marian said while adjusting the mourning veil around her shoulders. "Too pigheaded for your own good. I don't believe Paul is guilty."

On this somber occasion Emma thought her topic of conversation uncalled for.

Rain, steady and cold, darkened the afternoon as the black-draped carriage pulled away from Christ Church, lurching to the right in the muddy street, to follow the funeral coach to Girod Cemetery. Seated opposite from Marian and Howard, Emma was doing her best to ignore her uncle.

Howard observed his niece's frown, and wanted to tell her about the surprising development in Paul's defense, but professional ethics forbade it. "There's more to the story than meets your eye," he said evasively.

One side of Emma's upper lip quivered at Howard's smug words. The traitor! Even Uncle Rankin, who had returned only for the day to attend the funeral and to assess the damage to his cotton

161

enterprise, was peeved at Howard's alliance with Paul Rousseau.

"Howard dear, I'm so thankful you agreed to help poor Paul."

I'll just bet you are, Emma thought angrily. "Marian," she scolded, "we're on the way to your brother's burial. Surely you shouldn't be talking, or even thinking, about that man."

"You fear I'll fuss at you for going to his room."

Emma was taken aback. This was the dreaded moment! "How do you know about that?" She shot a dirty look at Howard, who had apparently informed Marian, but he merely lifted a hand.

"Now don't give Howard the evil eye." Marian reached under her veil and blew her nose on a handkerchief. "I overheard you on the morning when Paul and I were going to join you for a ride. I'd gone to check on Tillie, remember? When I came back to the stable, the two of you were arguing."

Her defenses on alert, Emma asked, "How long did you lurk about?"

"Long enough to find out that you and Paul are made for each other." The widow waved the handkerchief dismissively. "Oh, don't give me that round-eyed stare—I swear, Emma dear, you'd never make a poker player."

"Then I'll have to work on my expressions."

"Well, anyway, I'm not mad. Paul's too much for me. Too—I don't know—volatile? Though I do think he's an intriguing person . . . and so virile." She cast a sidelong glance at Howard. "I'm more inclined toward a gentler man."

This brought a satisfied look to Howard's face,

162

and Emma wondered about that, but not for long.

"Shall we tell her, darling?" Marian asked Howard. "I know you told me to wait a respectable length of time, but—"

"Don't fret, sweetheart. Emma is special to both of us, so I see no reason to keep it from her." He covered the back of Marian's left hand with his right palm before locking eyes with his niece. "Marian has agreed to be my wife."

"Well, that's wonderful," Emma exclaimed, forgetting her irritation with Marian and her fury at Howard. She was caught up in the good news.

"Oh, pooh, Howard O'Reilly! Tell the truth. I didn't agree to be your wife; I *asked* to be your wife." Marian dropped the handkerchief onto her lap and linked her right arm with his elbow. "On Carnival night." Her words were addressed to Emma, but her eyes never left her fiancé's. "He was *finally* paying attention to me, so I seized the moment. Oh, I was so happy! I couldn't wait to tell James, and—" She withdrew her arm and leaned back. "Poor James . . . God rest his soul. He was so pleased . . . and now he's gone." Her shoulders heaved, and she began to cry. "Those awful men—I hope Paul hangs them from the yardarm!"

Howard's tone was soothing as he patted her hand anew. "Don't fret, sweetheart. I'm sure justice will be served."

It surely will, Emma thought. But Paul won't be the one to hang the mutineers, if that in fact does come to pass. He'll be visiting the gallows long before James's murder is avenged!

On Liberty Street the carriage pulled to a stop at

the gate to Girod Cemetery. Emma peered out the window to the white-plastered brick tombs. They were eerie, those above-ground crypts. Regardless of her position, she shuddered to think of Paul's body being shoved into one of those ovenlike places.

Perhaps his punishment won't be that severe, she told herself. But why was she worrying about him? Had he concerned himself with her? No! That cad was the devil's own right-hand man. A person of that caliber didn't deserve sympathetic thoughts! It shouldn't be forgotten that he was a Rousseau, something she *had* forgotten of late.

She felt the carriage list as her companions alighted.

"Miss Emma?" Jeremiah offered a hand and held an umbrella in the other.

"Oh . . . uh . . . yes." She lifted her black skirts and stepped down to the muddy street. The heels of her shoes immediately became mired.

"Let me help you," a slightly Gallic-sounding voice offered.

Emma's anger rose in a billowing black cloud. "Get away!"

In full military regalia Paul Rousseau moved in front of her and took her arm, which she jerked away. His eyes met hers, and he doffed his hat, revealing his black hair. How, she wondered, had he gotten out of jail?

Howard was probably to blame. Emma took the umbrella from Jeremiah, and lifted her nose before side-stepping her tormentor. She'd show him just how little he meant to her!

In spite of his anger and her garb's severity, Paul

thought Emma was beautiful in black, even though her shocked expression had turned to one of disdain. He caught up with her. "Emma, wait a second. . . ."

When he reached out, she blocked his arm with the umbrella.

Paul chafed at her snub. If she wanted to be that way—fine! He had been truthful, for the most part, about the fire. She was just too much of an Oliver to accept anything other than what she wanted to hear.

Paul watched her grab Howard's arm and stand on tiptoe to whisper into the attorney's ear. Then Howard looked Paul's way, nodded, and turned back to Marian. Emma stomped off several feet.

She was angry, Paul figured, because her uncle had freed him from jail. The witch.

Well, two could play the snubbing game. He turned his attention to the carriage halting at the cemetery. Tillie Oliver, a woman of medium height and overabundant poundage, emerged. Rain soaking his high-crowned black hat and his equally somber cloak, Rankin Oliver was right behind her. With a flick of his hand, he dismissed his coachmen's umbrella.

It had been thirteen years since Paul had laid eyes on his father's killer. For all those days and nights he had imagined this face-to-face meeting. His fist ached to plow into Rankin's jaw, to inflict a modicum of the pain he himself had felt over those years. But his purpose was to gain justice, legally, against this miscreant. Bile rose in his throat, yet he forced it down as his archenemy marched toward him.

"Monsieur Rousseau," Tillie said, the courteous

form of address coming out like mon-sewer, "isn't it awful? I—"

"How'd ye get out of jail, Rousseau?" Rankin cut in, his green eyes drawn to slits.

Tillie pulled on her husband's arm. "Oh, Rankin—"

"Matilda Oliver, get over there to your daughter-in-law!"

Tillie obeyed her husband's edict, but shook her head and clicked her tongue as she did so.

"I asked ye a question, Rousseau."

"So you did." Paul swallowed the vile taste in his mouth. For too long he had waited to confront his father's killer, yet he wouldn't make a public spectacle of their meeting. "In view of the present circumstances, I'm sure you'll agree that this is neither the time nor the place to discuss the, uh, fire. Shall we meet tomorrow?"

"Can't do it. Just came for the funeral. I'll be leaving again in the morning. Answer my question *now*."

Unwilling to step to Rankin Oliver's tune, Paul strode past his tall blond enemy and took his place with the mourners. For two days he had been grilled, but no more.

The case against Paul had been strong before Lieutenant Seeger had come to his rescue. Before sailing for the Arcas the lieutenant had gone to the calaboose and had spoken with Detective Watson. Howard O'Reilly had been called in to hear his story, which the attorney had then relayed to Paul.

"Just before the crack of dawn, Seeger went

166

ashore with Throckmorton's body," Howard had said. "He docked at Rankin's wharf. That had to be minutes before the fire."

"What does that prove?" Paul asked.

"Nothing. But it weakens the case against you. Seeger said he saw a suspicious-looking character lurking about the factor house, and Rankin's skiff was at its mooring when Seeger rowed back to the *San Antonio*."

"But it wasn't there right after the fire," Paul put in.

"Exactly. So there's a good chance it was stolen by the guilty party."

"A very good chance." Paul paced the cell's small confines. "But Seeger won't be able to testify in my behalf. He's on his way to the south Gulf."

"We have his deposition. I daresay it's enough to free you until the trial, if not after."

"Then I can leave?"

"Yes. You're a free man, in a way. Until we go to court you're forbidden to leave Louisiana."

"Half a loaf is better than nothing."

After his release Paul had given thought to not attending Throckmorton's funeral, but he'd changed his mind. Though his views had not coincided with those of his late captain, he felt it was his duty to represent the Republic of Texas, and he owed Marian Oliver a few words of condolence. So he had come.

Rain continued to pour as the Anglican priest recited the appropriate chants over James Throckmorton's body. ". . . ashes to ashes, dust to dust . . ."

167

From the sidelines Paul, soaked but unmindful of it, glanced at Marian, who was clinging to Howard as if he were a lifeline. The three Olivers flanked them.

Her gray ringlets bobbing beneath a sheer veil of black, Tillie Oliver sobbed as if her own child had departed this earth. She had a tendency to over-dramatize situations, Paul recalled. Rankin Oliver, obviously bored with the formalities and just as obviously making it a point not to look Paul's way, shifted from one foot to the other while holding an umbrella for his wife. Emma, Paul saw in profile only.

No veil impeded his view, but a black bonnet, elegant and costly, almost covered her honey-hued tresses, which were upswept, save for an errant lock that lay curled on her neck. The aristocratic line of her throat was evident, for she held her chin slightly higher than normal. And though he had never thought much about it before, he found her straight nose to his liking. She held the umbrella high. Lowering his gaze to her breasts, he remembered how delicious they had tasted. He cleared his throat, hoping to turn his mind elsewhere, but was unsuccessful. As he took in the curves below her chest, he surmised she was wearing a whalebone—her tiny waist was cinched in to such minuscule proportions. Ah, corsets—an erotic time could be had with the unlacing. . . .

Paul felt an uncomfortable, inappropriate sensation settle in his groin. There was no disavowing he craved her, but he mentally credited that weakness to lust. Damn! Why hadn't he taken her when she

168

had offered herself? Better yet, why couldn't he forget her and get on with his life?

". . . in the name of our Lord, Amen." The priest closed his book of prayers and turned to whisper with Marian.

The pallbearers slid the coffin into the crypt. The mourners turned away. Rankin offered his arm to Tillie, and Paul ignored the curl of his archenemy's lip as Rankin stomped past him.

Marian extended a hand in Paul's direction, and he went over to offer his sympathy. "The people of Texas mourn your loss," he said, reaching out to hug her.

"You're very kind, Paul," she whispered. "I know you didn't get on with my brother, but I am certain your words are sincere."

"I wouldn't count on it," Emma muttered.

"Heavens to Betsy," Howard said, filling in the stony silence that followed. "Your skirts are sodden, ladies. I daresay if I don't get you back to the carriage, you'll catch your death—I mean, you'll catch a chill."

"I'm riding with my family—the Olivers—thank you, my dear Benedict Arnold uncle." Emma stomped away.

Go on and run away, Emma Oliver. But it'll do you no good. I will *have you,* Paul silently railed. He was determined to let the little witch know who had the upper hand. In the meantime he'd let tempers cool—his and hers.

Every time Paul thought of Emma, he envisioned

an accusing finger pointed at him. Yet by the time two weeks had passed, his anger had gone from a raging fire to smoldering embers. Why couldn't he get her out of his mind?

Shore-bound due to the upcoming trial, he had made the best of his situation. Eighteen experienced sailors had been recruited to replace the mutineers, and they'd been sent to the *San Antonio* by way of a merchantman. And Paul had petitioned the court to place the remaining culprits under the jurisdiction of the Texas Navy. Unfortunately the governor of Louisiana had demanded Sam Houston's signature before he'd release the mutineers.

Henry Packert was another matter. According to Katie, he had gotten a tip on the real shipment of contraband, and had set sail from Barataria the day of the fire. Paul took a bit of comfort from the woman's information. Packert hadn't given up the fight to put Rankin Oliver in his place. Still, there would come a day when Paul would have to deal with that single-eyed pirate.

Figuring the Navy could use a good dispatch carrier, Paul had purchased a single-headsail sloop. Now, as he checked the rigging, he gave thought to the letter that had been delivered to the hotel earlier that morning. Ed Moore had received Paul's first dispatch. The commodore, uninformed of the mutiny, expressed his deep concern for the sailors of the *San Antonio* and he mentioned that he intended to relieve Throckmorton of command as soon as he could sail back to northern Gulf waters. There lay the problem.

Paul retrieved the parchment from inside his shirt to reread the last part.

"... I've received President Houston's recall order, and I choose to ignore it. My reasons are twofold.

If the fleet sails back to Galveston, he will, using the excuse of lack of money, dismantle the Navy. Of this I am confident, even though I have Governor Barbachano's assurances the $8,000 per month will continue until the Quintana Roo treaty is ratified in Mexico City. Secondly, I refuse to leave our ally at the mercy of Santa Anna. (The Yucatecans are fools to trust him, just as Houston is a fool not to see his threat.)

We sailed the Austin by Vera Cruz, and the harbor is rife with Centralist warships. Though they did not engage us in battle, they know, by God, we are here.

They are setting the stage for war, against we Texans and their own rebel Peninsulares. Santa Anna, I believe with all my heart, only wishes to placate the Yucatecans with Roo's treaty; he's waiting for the right moment to squash a foe, all foes, under his heel.

If our fleet is placed in ordinary, the Centralist Navy will bombard our coastal towns and blockade the entire Gulf. While our Army has been cashiered, Santa Anna's stands ready to capture our inland cities and slaughter the citizenry.

Use all your influence, my fellow patriot and friend, to secure financial backing in New Orleans. This I cannot stress too strongly, for without money we have no ammunition to fight our enemies in both camps. May God protect us.

Yours faithfully,
E.W. Moore"

Paul was glad that he had sent the *San Antonio* back to the commodore. Though both he and Moore were in jeopardy of being court-martialed for dereliction of Houston's orders, Paul felt the end would justify the means.

And he had a mission: find money for the fleet. Where, he didn't know. With the arson trial pending, he had a blight on his reputation. No person of wealth, American or Creole, would trust an accused torcher with their gold.

His own resources were minimal, since he had purchased the little sloop. But what he had, he was more than willing to use for the Navy's benefit. Money was not important to Paul.

Crouching back on his heels, he hanked a forestay.

"You're a fine-looking one," a female voice said from wharfside. "Bet you'll make pretty babies."

He stretched to his full height of six-two and peered across the dock to the wrenlike woman standing on it. "What are you doing here, Cleopatra?"

"Came to see you. Mind if I come aboard?"

"Sorry. I'm leaving in a few minutes."

172

"That's all I need—a few minutes."

Paul lifted a shoulder. "As you wish."

"Funny name, *Virgin Vixen*," Cleopatra said after boarding. "Where'd you get it?"

"Who said I named her?" Paul had of course rechristened the sloop. The name had seemed appropriate for Emma.

"Never did cotton to a man who'd answer a question with a question." Cleopatra shook her head, then shot him a sly look. "Why ain't you been calling on my baby?"

"If you're referring to Emma Oliver, you ought to know why. Left up to the two of you, I'd swing from a tree."

"Wasn't right, you burning that warehouse, but Master Rankin hisself's done wrong by many. Ain't it funny, too, that he stays clear of New Orleans now that you're back in town?"

Paul inwardly agreed. "Do I detect a faint note of disenchantment from the Oliver slave quarters?"

"I ain't no—" Cleopatra kicked her slippers away. She was, it seemed, settling in for a long visit. "I seen enough of the master to know he's got two sides to his mouth. Couldn't be sweeter to those he loves, like my Emma, but he's got another side. Ain't mentioned it to her, though."

This was an astute woman. She knew Emma would even banish her mammy for disloyalty. "So, you've come here to tell me you don't like Rankin Oliver. Interesting." Warily he asked, "But what makes you think I have a problem with him?"

"Hmmph. I didn't just fall off the turnip wagon. I seen the vengeance in your eyes, Frenchie, that day

173

you come out to Magnolia Hall. Day after your daddy died, remember?"

"That was a long time ago."

Cleopatra wiggled her toes and leaned her head back to take full advantage of the sun. "Told my Emma you was ugly back then. Tee-hee. You weren't though. Needed a little drying behind the ears, but I got a feeling for men. You be one of those hot-blooded kind that keeps a woman sore between the legs."

Paul had never thought it could happen, but he felt his face redden. "You're a wicked old tart."

"I ain't old." She kicked his shin. Solidly. "Forty, that's all. I still got plenty of good miles left in this body."

He rubbed his sore leg.

"Where you headed?" she asked out of the blue. "Before I showed up, that is?"

"Barataria," Paul answered. He wanted to see if Packert had returned. More than anything, he yearned for the roll of water beneath him as he sorted out his strategies.

"Pirate's kingdom . . ." A dreamy look settled in her eyes. "I ain't a bad sailor, if'n a body needed one. Wouldn't mind sailing those forty miles myself."

"If you're hinting that I should take you out there, you can forget it."

But within five minutes they set sail. He was curious about her visit, so he decided to let her go along. And by the time the settlement's coastline was in sight, Paul trusted Cleopatra. Damned if he didn't like her, too!

Shading his eyes, he surveyed the line of ships

174

anchored in Barataria Bay. Packert's wasn't among them. Paul thought briefly about heading back to New Orleans, but reconsidered. After all, Cleopatra had expressed an interest in this pirate land.

"Well, is you or ain't you gonna say nothing about my Emma?" Cleopatra asked, arms akimbo.

The back of her skirt was tucked in the front of her waistband, having been pulled between her bantam legs, and her tignon having flown away, somewhere between New Orleans and the bay, her nappy hair headed in all directions. She had the steely determination of the world's wickedest freebooter in her brown eyes. Explosives, Paul knew, came in small packages. "All right, I give. What about her?"

"You gonna marry her?"

"Wh-what makes y-you ask that?" Paul queried, though he was not given to stuttering.

"You deflowered my baby—I gonna see she's done right by."

"Now wait a minute." So that was why she had sought him out. "If she told you that, she's lying."

"She tried to deny it, too. But I saw those bloodstains on your bed, Frenchie."

"My back was bleeding."

"Yes, and I'm white as snow." Cleopatra eyed him critically. "She could do worse than you."

"Thank you, madame, your kindness overwhelms me." He bowed low. "But there are considerations you've overlooked. I've no wish to marry, and, correct me if I'm wrong, the lady in question wishes to make medicine, not me, her career."

"A lady's got," Cleopatra said as haughtily as her name implied, "a God-given right to change

175

her mind."

"I see. And what about you, wicked goddess of the Nile?" Serious now, he walked down the deck to stand in front of her. "Will you change your mind about testifying against me?"

She picked up the mooring line. "If the State of Louisiana sees its way clear to call me, I wouldn't lie about what I saw." Raising a brow, she continued. "'Course I might be lenient if'n you was my baby's husband."

"If I weren't, would you give me the benefit of the doubt?"

"May . . ." Cleopatra's hand, the one which held the rope, froze. Watching the marshy shore, she stood straight and still. Then a wide grin split her face to expose beautiful pearly white teeth.

Paul's eyes picked up the object of her attention. At water's edge was a Goliath-tall pirate, his mouth dropped open. Ben Edwards, known for sheer brawn and canny intelligence, appeared to be dumbfounded.

"Don't just stand there, you big hunk of meat," the small woman called to the big man as she perched on the rail. "Get me off this tub, and *kiss me!*"

Never had Paul seen Ben move so fast, especially through three feet of water. Cleopatra yelped with delight when he caught her in his arms.

Paul cast the mooring line to shore, waded after it, and twisted the ropes around a tree. He quit thinking about Cleopatra nagging him to take Emma to wife.

Chapter Twelve

"You need a wife."

Frowning at Howard's statement, Paul reached into his coat to extract a cheroot. With slow deliberation he lit the thin cigar. Less than twenty-four hours had passed since Cleopatra had harangued Paul about marrying Emma. The mammy he could dismiss. His attorney was another matter. Of late, he had bombarded Paul with advice both legal and personal.

His palms planted on his knees, Howard leaned forward on his carriage seat and turned his head toward Paul. "As I've told you before, the sooner you marry, the better. In order to inherit your grandfather's sugar plantation near St. Martinsville, you must have a woman to share your name."

"I don't want his land."

"Don't be a fool, Paul. It's—"

"Why are you bothering me with this? We just left a hearing at the Cabildo, and in two weeks I'll face judge and jury."

"I'll thank you not to interrupt me, my good man. Now, where was I? Oh. At the end of one year,

177

provided you've lived up to the stipulations, the property becomes yours in fee simple. To do with as you wish."

Paul chuckled with irony. "Ah yes, the terms of dear old Grandpère's will. He never forgave me for those stolen moments of passion with the, um, shall we say, object of his affection."

"Far be it from me to second-guess Remi Rousseau's intentions." Howard grimaced as the carriage wheels hit a rut and jostled the two occupants. "My purpose is to see the terms of the will executed. And time is running out. If you're not going to accept his challenge, then I shall be forced to relinquish the property to one Miss Aimée Thérèse Goyette."

"The object of his affection."

Howard adjusted his now-lopsided beaver hat. "Be that as it may, Paul, you must make a decision soon."

Neither the property, nor his grandfather, nor Aimée Thérèse meant anything to Paul. They were past forgetting. "Managing canebrakes would jeopardize my naval career, provided the State of Louisiana allows me my freedom, and planting is not one of my desires, nor is marriage."

"A year, old chap, isn't forever."

"Marriage is."

"How many times over the past days have you said you're in need of money?" Howard asked. "This might be the answer to your prayers. The mansion and fields are worth a great deal. You could sell Feuille de Chêne, after clear title is granted."

Paul realized that temporary ownership to Feuille

178

de Chêne had advantages. The proceeds from its sale could be used to protect the citizens of Texas from Centralist aggression by keeping the Navy afloat, at least partially. But to wait a year for the money? Anything could happen in a year's time. And where would he find a temporary wife?

"Could the property be mortgaged?" Paul asked.

"There's nothing to say it can't." The attorney raised his eyes, making their whites evident. "Of course a year on the plantation might change a seadog to a landlubber."

"Not a chance. Not on Feuille de Chêne, anyway. Texas is the place for me." Paul glanced out the carriage window, and took a leisurely puff of the cheroot. "It's a new country, a good place to start over without the hindrances of the past."

"You'd know more about that than I, I suppose."

"No doubt. But that's not the issue, is it?"

"Not at the moment," the attorney replied. "About the plantation, do I hear a weakening of conviction in your voice?"

"Perhaps."

Howard raised a brick-red brow. "You're going to marry Emma?"

"*Emma?* What's she got to do with this?"

"Well, a marriage takes two people, and she seems to be the one dominating your interests."

"I didn't say I was going to marry." If Paul were to do so, she was the only person he could imagine sharing bed and hearth with. But . . . An awesome but. Emma had all the earmarks of a less than ideal wife. Setting his hesitation aside, Paul wondered why Howard was promoting such a match.

179

"I'm surprised you'd mention your own niece in almost the same breath as a temporary marriage." Chuckling, he ribbed Howard. "Is the family that desperate to get her off their hands?"

"That's hardly the case." Howard grinned slyly as the carriage hit another rut. "As for myself, I have my reasons."

"Being?"

"She couldn't testify against you at the trial."

Paul bristled. If he married Emma it wouldn't be for that reason. "I appreciate your help in handling my problems with the law, but I don't think you should offer to sacrifice your blood kin."

Howard sighed and shook his head. Several seconds later, he eyed Paul. "All right, I'll be honest—I think you and Emma could make a marriage that would last until death parted you."

"You sound like a romantic. Your engagement to Marian must've gone to your head." Paul stretched his legs as far as he could in the close confines of the carriage. "There's something you should know . . . in case I do take possession of the sugar fields. I'd mortgage them, sell them, whatever—and give the money to the Navy. That's no situation into which to bring a wife."

"Money isn't everything. Emma's never been one to covet the all-mighty dollar."

"What does she covet?"

"Being a doctor, having a home and—"

"I understand the doctor part, but having a home?" Paul flicked an ash out the window. "She doesn't strike me as the tapestry-by-the-fireside type."

180

"She might surprise you."

"Well, Howard, you're forgetting one thing— Emma wouldn't agree to it."

"Then you don't know the woman who visited my office after Throckmorton had you lashed. But I do. She may not admit it, even to herself, but she loves you."

Paul's suddenly weak fingers dropped the cheroot, and it burned a hole through the leg of his breeches. Grabbing the cigar and brushing away his pain, he said, "You're crazed as a loon, Howard. The woman is out for my blood!"

"Her Irish is up over this factor-house situation, but she's not one to carry a grudge for long. Convince her you're more important than Rankin's warehouse. Shouldn't be hard to do." Howard took out a cigar. "You haven't lost faith in your powers of persuasion, have you?"

"No, I haven't. But even if she did agree, and even though she couldn't testify against her husband, what about her mammy?"

"The courts won't take her word over yours."

"She deserves better than that," Paul said in defense of Cleopatra. "There's something wrong with a country that won't take the word of a good woman because of her race."

"You must admit it's to your advantage this time."

Paul contemplatively drew smoke into his mouth. Should he give up his bachelor state for the sake of Texas? It was a small enough price to pay; it wasn't as though he were giving up his life, and plenty of men had done that.

Hell, why don't you admit it, Rousseau? You want

181

to be with her. Paul pushed that weak-hearted thought aside. If he went along with Howard's suggestion, it would be for Texas, not for himself. Maybe he should marry her.

But, like all major decisions in life, it wasn't that simple. In order for the marriage to succeed at least for a year, Paul knew compromises would have to be made.

He'd be landlocked when the Navy needed every man it could get. Still, Texas would have his financial support, and that counted for something. On second thought, there was nothing to keep him from his duties at least part of the time. If the Navy needed him for a campaign, Paul would be there.

The last part of the compromise was the most bitter pill to swallow. If the marriage were to work for at least twelve months, he couldn't, in all conscience, overtly seek revenge against Rankin Oliver.

No! He wouldn't do it. For too long vengeance had propelled him. But could he sacrifice Texas? To do so would be selfish.

"I'm going to marry Emma." If he was making a mistake, Paul would worry about it later.

"I think I should warn you. Like you, she's a Catholic. Marriage is forever."

Forever? As in old and gray? As in a life contract? For several long moments Paul considered his predicament. His heart cried out, "Why not? You're crazy for her." His mind told him to pay no heed to that inner voice. This was a matter of national importance, pure and simple. He felt much more comfortable with that line of reasoning. "I'd better

182

start convincing the Oliver side of your family."

"Capital idea." The carriage stopped at the St. Charles, and Howard reached out to shake his hand. "By the by, Emma's decided to forgive me, I suppose, for taking your case. She's accepted my dinner invitation."

Paul nearly missed the step down from the coach.

Tapping a cane tip against the carriage wall to alert the coachman to depart, Howard said, "Be at my house at eight. Rankin will be there, too."

"I look forward to the challenge."

It had been fourteen days since Emma had seen Paul. She had passed the endless hours studying and gaining practical experience by helping Dr. Boulogne. He had given her enough work to keep her busy, and it was fine therapy for a heart in jeopardy. Paul's absence was a blessing, she supposed.

She had even mellowed to the point of accepting Howard's dinner invitation for that evening. Looking at it from her uncle's point of view, she acknowledged that his career put him in contact with the wrong element at times. She shouldn't blame him for taking the enemy's side.

"Mademoiselle Oliver, did you hear me?" Dr. Boulogne asked sharply, bringing her errant thoughts back to the women's ward of his clinic.

"Sorry, sir." Emma emptied a tray of used bandages into a bin and turned to face her mentor.

"May we have a moment of private conversation?" He gestured to the side. "Perhaps in that anteroom over there?"

She followed him to an austere room with white walls and wooden chairs.

"I'm pleased with your progress, Emma," Dr. Boulogne commented; of late he had begun to use her given name. "You have a deft hand with the patients."

She murmured her appreciation of his comment. Though he still categorized her as a nurse, Boulogne had given her tasks far beyond even an apprentice's expectations. Normally a physician in training could expect to do no more than mix medicines, observe the master, and sweep floors. Over the past weeks, however, Emma had set bones, treated burns, prescribed *materia medica* for various ailments, and on two odious occasions she had participated in bloodletting, which she preferred not to think about.

She forced a smile. "Doctor, you haven't yet allowed me to do more than observe in surgery. And I'm growing impatient over your lack of faith in my abilities. I really believe it's time."

"An ambitious *femme* you are." His face stern, Boulogne folded his arms across his chest. "It is folly, this way of yours."

"I beg your pardon?"

"A nurse should not chide the physician." He walked to the window and stared out. "There are your high-reaching demands, and you have fussed at me, about washing my hands with disinfectant."

Emma made no apology. "I meant no offense, Doctor. But I've read much on the matter. This new method kills the germs we see under the microscope, and that has to be good for our—I mean your—patients. It keeps infections from being spread from

184

one sick person to another."

"But you question my wisdom about the leeches!"

"I fail to see how draining blood heals a weakened body."

He chuckled. *"D'accord.* For a long while, this theory I have questioned. I will give up the practice."

Emma sighed in relief. No more would she punish a patient with bloodletting. And never again would she have to place her hand in a crock of wiggling, slime-coated worms. She was blessed with a stomach of iron, but she did have her weaknesses.

"How long have you studied medical books?" Boulogne asked.

"Even as a child I was interested in my father's work, and I mastered Latin then. But hard study? Going on four years."

He ran his fingers across the top of a chair. "That is longer than courses of study at medical schools."

She studied his profile. He was baiting her with something, and Emma had to know what. "Is there something you'd like to tell me, Dr. Boulogne?"

"As of today you are not my nurse," he said sternly.

Was he letting her go because she had questioned his methods of treatment? Disappointment edging each syllable, she said, "I'm sorry I've displeased you. Please give me another chance."

"Displeased me? Not so, Emma. As of today you are my apprentice."

Squealing her delight, she threw her arms around him. "You won't be sorry. I promise you! This is the most wonderful day of my life!"

Scarlet flames shot from his cheeks, and he pulled

Emma's arms from his neck and stepped back. "You would cause a scandal on your first day as a physician? Shame on you, Dr. Oliver."

Dr. Oliver! Oh how wonderful it sounded. Grinning, she raised her chin. "Decorum will be my byword."

"But warn you I must. Medicine is a difficult profession, one fraught with long hours and many battles sans reward. None but an *imbécile* accepts the situation."

"None but the dedicated," she corrected, now solemn. "I intend to be the very finest physician in America . . . after you of course."

He winked a blue eye. "You flatter me, Madame Docteur."

Madame Docteur. Paul had called her that. When she had attended to his wounds, he had shown faith in her, had encouraged her. Oh, why did he have to be so difficult in other matters?

"And now," Boulogne said, "we must return to our duties."

Emma brushed a stray lock of hair away from her temple. "The little girl . . . Surgery is hardest to deal with when it involves a child."

"A good physician cannot allow sentiment to impede his, er, *her* healing powers."

Facing him squarely, Emma said, "I understand that personal involvement is dangerous to a doctor's emotional well-being, but too many physicians are callous about the feelings of their patients. I make no apology for wanting to be different."

"That is your prerogative, but leave sentiment at the door of an operating chamber, you must."

"Did I go weak when I stood by during the amputations?"

"No, you didn't. And do not be defensive. This is a discussion I would have with any new doctor." He glanced her way. "Especially on the day he . . . or she . . . first assists in surgery."

Ready for the challenge, Emma's heart skipped a beat. "Your confidence isn't misplaced."

"Bon." He turned on his heel, making for the door. "Now we must save the life of a twelve-year-old girl."

Emma gave thought to the patient. Myrtle Ann Murray had been pulled by a fisherman from the jaws of an alligator. Huge chunks had been eaten from her right calf and knee. The wounds had turned gangrenous, and if the limb was not removed promptly, death was certain to follow.

As they walked toward the operating chamber, Dr. Boulogne went on to explain the procedures Emma was to perform.

"Doctor, there's something else. . . ."

He threw his hands upward. "Who might I ask is the teacher, and who the apprentice? Answer not. I fear your reply."

Swallowing a smirk, Emma smiled fetchingly, she hoped. "I, uh, I've done some experimenting on induced somnambulism."

"Oh?"

Thankfully he hadn't exploded in rage, as her father had. She took that as a good omen. "I'd like to use sulfurous ether to ease Myrtle Ann's discomfort."

"Where do you get such an idea?"

187

"I have two older brothers, both students of medicine. Several months ago I was a guest at one of their socials. It got rather out of hand, you see, and my brother Brian brought out a vial of sulfurous ether."

"A wicked young man he seems."

"No, just curious. Anyway, he sniffed it and got rather giddy. Drunk, if you will. Then he fell and cut his hand . . . and he felt no pain."

"A flesh wound has *petit* comparison to surgical shock."

"Granted, but watching him set my mind to whirling. He'd only taken a couple of whiffs, so I asked myself what would happen if a larger dose was administered." She paused. "As I mentioned, I did some experimenting."

"On who?"

"When they were injured, my dogs and cats. I discovered that deep sleep can be induced by continuous inhalation of ether." She added quickly, "While I tended their wounds they experienced not the slightest operative discomfort. I've used the method numerous times with no ill effects."

"Animals are not people."

"We're all mammals. I believe we should ease Myrtle Ann's discomfort by this method."

"I trust your theories not!"

"Please, Dr. Boulogne—please! She's so young and frightened."

He brought his fingers to his lips and studied the floor, then raised his head. "No sulfurous ether is in this clinic."

"Wrong. If you'll pardon my presumption, I distilled some last night after you left for home."

188

He shook his head and clicked his tongue. "Too determined, you are, for your own good."

"I don't think so." She straightened. "Will you allow me to use the ether?"

"No-o-o-o-o!" Myrtle Ann's bloodcurdling scream resounded through the room when she caught sight of the surgeons. The child flailed her arms and writhed about, but her small body was held down by four husky attendants. "Mama! Want my mama."

Emma carried the ether and its paraphernalia forward. "Shhh, little one," she cooed while brushing Myrtle Ann's brow. "Dr. Boulogne and I will make this so much easier."

"How?"

"We're going to help you go to sleep."

"Really?"

"Yes, really." Emma explained the canister of ether and the gauze pad's purposes. "And when you wake up, it will all be over."

Her chest still heaving in fear, the girl eased back against the table.

Emma scrubbed up to her elbows with a disinfectant solution, and draped a tent across the girl's abdomen. Afterward she repeated the washing procedure. Dr. Boulogne swabbed Myrtle Ann's thigh with iodine, then washed his hands. They moved to the table. The attendants bore down on the girl to halt her movements.

"That won't be necessary," Emma said. "Step back."

They did.

"Can you count to fifty?"

The child nodded, and was instructed to count

189

backward from that number while Emma uncorked the ether. Hurriedly she pressed a square of gauze over the bottle opening, turning it upside down. The rotten-egg fumes burned Emma's nostrils, so she held her head away from them as she placed the gauze over Myrtle Ann's mouth and nose, and used a dropper to place more ether on it.

"Fifty, forty-nine," came the girl's muffled voice. "Forty-eight, foh-se . . . sis . . ." She wilted.

"We can proceed now, Doctor."

Boulogne looked at Emma in amazement before collecting a scalpel from the tray of instruments. With the speed of lightning, he set to his skill, and fifteen minutes later, he raised his eyes to Emma. "Close."

Emma abandoned the dropper and ether to take up the needle that had been threaded from a skein of thin, iodine-soaked catgut. Deft fingers sutured fifty-three blood vessels at the girl's upper thigh.

Boulogne, working with No. 3 catgut, closed the incision at the base of the stub. Finished, he checked Myrtle Ann's pulse. "Make it, she will."

As the doctors wiped their blood-stained hands, the assistants, who had stood back during surgery, bore the child away.

Emma cleared the door and wilted against the jamb. "Saints be praised."

"*Mais non.* Dr. Oliver be praised." Chuckling, Boulogne shook his mop of strawberry-blond hair. "I believe that you, not I, will be the—how did you say it?—the best doctor in America."

She shot him a satisfied grin, then pranced away, calling over her shoulder, "You said it, I didn't."

Six hours later, seated in the drawing room of

Howard's Garden District home, Emma would have gladly renounced the Hippocratic oath so she could murder Uncle Rankin. Having just returned from his trip, and before she could speak to him privately about Paul, he had used Aunt Tillie's malady as an excuse to renege on dinner. If he hadn't, Emma felt certain he'd bring the man she wanted to hate to his knees, or at least get her out of this uncomfortable situation.

She stared at the blackguard Paul Rousseau. His frame dwarfing the high-backed Chippendale arm chair, he met her scowl and smiled. After she had warned him not to pit the O'Reillys against the Olivers, that despicable fire-starter had a lot of nerve flaunting himself in Howard's home!

Though she had this thought, Emma hadn't forgotten the feel of Paul's hair beneath her fingertips, the taste of his lips, or the sound of his slightly Gallic-flavored voice. But why, tonight of all nights, did he have to reappear in her life?

"Sailing here was horrendous. I had a deathly case of seasickness," Franklin Underwood admitted in his high-pitched voice. "But it was worth it. It's wonderful being with Emma."

Emma stole a glance at her former intended, whose pale face was framed by overlong hair and the ruffles at his collar. He had arrived on Magnolia Hall's doorstep late that afternoon, and her good manners had not allowed her to turn him away.

She had been worn to a frazzle from her day at the hospital, and her guard had been down. Now she regretted the Southern upbringing that had prompted her to invite Franklin to escort her to dinner.

Howard didn't appear too pleased by Underwood's presence, either. Neither he nor Marian offered much in the way of conversation.

"Not much of a sailor, huh, Underwood?" Paul asked, curling his lip.

"Give me the good green earth, rain or shine, over the sea."

Paul took a sip of sherry. "Planter, are you?"

"Why, no. I'm due to inherit a great deal of property from my father, but tobacco planting isn't for me."

"Then what do you do with your spare time?" Paul asked.

"Society keeps me busy—we have a marvelous set in Richmond." Franklin fingered his cravat's bow, subsequently scratching a thinly grown, brown sideburn. "And home is a comfort, too. Mother encouraged me, in my childhood, toward the classics and chamber music, and I shall be forever in her debt."

Emma ground her teeth together. She knew Franklin was a bore, but she had never before realized how boring he was. He had no purpose in life beyond the little world centered on himself. At least Paul was dedicated to the Texas Navy, and his conversation inspired more than yawns.

Taking a peek at Franklin's outfit, then at Paul's, she made comparisons. Paul eschewed the fripperies so many men favored; his clothing was tailored in clean lines, and his short, thick black curls just brushed his ears.

Franklin patted the area next to himself on the horsehair sofa. "Do come closer, Kitten."

Staying put in the far corner, Emma cringed at the

term of endearment. She cringed at Franklin!

"What an interesting endearment, 'Kitten.'" Again Paul lifted a glass of sherry to his now-arrogant lips. "I'd be fascinated to know how you arrived at such a name for Mademoiselle Oliver."

"Because of her green eyes. Aren't they lovely?"

"Quite so." Paul easily extended a black-booted foot on the Oriental rug. "Enough to make a man suffer and suffer. But a young cat's? No, they put me in mind of a tigress's."

"Now that you mention it—"

"That's enough!" Emma crossed her arms over her chest. "It isn't decent to discuss me as if I weren't in the room."

"Oh, I'm sure neither gentleman meant disrespect, Emma dear," Marian put in. She smoothed the skirt of her mourning frock. "Isn't it a shame Tillie has such a terrible headache tonight?" She received no reply. "Howard, would you excuse me? I'd like to check on dinner? It is getting late, and I'll just bet Mr. Underwood enjoys crab."

Evidently Marian had sensed the unease. Emma was glad for the switch in tempo, but she held her breath, hoping that Franklin, who eschewed seafood, wouldn't complain about the crab.

"Good of you, my dear." Howard helped his fiancée from the chair, then turned his eyes on Franklin. "I understand you're interested in sculpture, Mr. Underwood."

"Quite so. Mother and I toured Europe last year, and we—"

"Well, do come along, my good man. I've some interesting marble to show you."

"Marvelous!" Franklin jumped to his feet. "Join

193

us, Kitten?"

"I . . . I—"

"Mademoiselle Oliver looks as if she could use another sherry." Paul winked her way. "I'll do the honors, so you gentlemen may just enjoy yourselves."

At any other time Emma would have protested, but the thought of walking at Franklin's side called for another apéritif. Still, she hated to give Paul the pleasure of winning so easily. "Thank you, Mr. Rousseau."

Howard closed the French doors after he and the other two departed, leaving Emma alone with Paul. She clenched her fingers on her lap while he poured a glass of sherry and walked over to her. Instead of handing it over, he eased onto the middle of the sofa and took a sip.

"I thought that was for me," she said.

"It is." Paul scooted closer to hold the glass to her lips. "Have a sip, *m'amoureuse,* unless you're frightened—"

"I'm frightened of nothing."

"Then why are you hugging the arm of this sofa?"

Emma snatched the drink, downed it, and pressed her thigh against his. "Satisfied?"

"Not . . . quite." Paul lifted her chin with the edge of his forefinger. "I hope that fool doesn't expect to get you back. He'll be in for a disappointment. You're mine."

It was on the tip of her tongue to set him straight about Franklin, yet she didn't. Let him think whatever he pleased. She smothered a grin. He was jealous! She delighted in it. Paul Rousseau had been so sure of himself and of her after he had turned away from her heart and body that night in his room. This taste of sweet revenge went down smoothly and easily, like warm cider on a December evening. "Aren't you modest?"

"No, intelligent." His expression was worthy of an emperor's. "And delighted to meet the worldly Franklin Underwood."

"My, if you were a woman, I'd call you catty."

"Did I strike a nerve?" Grinning, Paul ran his thumb over the rim of her glass. "If I were a woman, I'd be scared witless to have children by such a fool."

"That's a nasty thing to say."

"Is it? Consider this. Do you want to be the mother to five or six little Underwood sons, all of them with leavened-dough faces and squeaking voices?"

"I'm sure I'd love my children no matter their appearance."

"Don't forget the begetting of those bundles from heaven." Not having received the comeback he'd sought, Paul welded his gaze to hers. "What do you see in that weak-kneed Mama's boy?"

"That's none of your concern."

"I'm making it my concern."

Those whispered words melted through her reserve. How could she despise and adore him at the same moment? Yet it was so easy to forget his evil ways. She wished she understood what had driven him to criminal measures.

"You want me, too," he murmured, "and I was a fool, a damn fool, for not making love to you that night at my hotel."

"If memory serves me right, you didn't because I was a virgin," she reminded him, perhaps in too self-

195

serving a manner. "I still am."

He traced the pad of his forefinger along her bottom lip. "Not for long."

"You're wrong." She fought against his mesmerizing effect. "That night was before you set fire to—"

"Shhh." He leaned across her lap to place the sherry on the table.

A shiver ran the length of Emma's spine when his body touched hers. Then his right arm slipped beneath her arm and up her back, and he pulled her close.

"Don't," she pleaded in a whisper.

"Don't do what? This"—he feathered a kiss to her temple—"or this?" His tongue flickered down her cheek. "Or this?" His mouth closed over hers.

She forced herself not to respond, and kept her lips sealed against his tongue. Yet through the materials of his shirt and her bodice, she felt the friction of his chest, and her mouth parted. As his finger traced a path along the edge of her ear, she lost all strength of will. Giving in to the fire that flashed through her, she ran her hands around him, to his back. "We shouldn't . . ."

"I know," he murmured against her lips.

"Emma!"

Slamming the door, Franklin stomped over to the two of them. Paul eased back to the middle of the sofa, and brought to her senses, Emma touched shaking hands to her mussed hair.

"Got a problem, Underwood?" There was a recklessness to Paul's demeanor; he might have been spoiling for a challenge.

Franklin said in a croak, "I cannot believe what I saw!"

"Believe it. She's mine now." Paul took Emma's hand. "And if you don't like it, do something about it. There are ways of defending one's honor."

Gulping loudly, Franklin recoiled. "I . . . I . . . I."

"I think you'd better tuck your tail between your legs and make tracks for Virginia, Underfoot. Excuse me—Underwood." Paul's words, as well as his eyes, goaded Franklin. "A coward's not well received in this town."

Franklin's Adam's apple was bobbing up and down.

Drat! Emma compressed her lips. Her former intended was such a coward that he wouldn't defend his own honor, much less hers. And what was the matter with her? Duels were horrid ways of settling arguments. The best way to handle the present situation was to get Franklin well away from it.

"Come along, Franklin," she commanded. "We're going back to Magnolia Hall."

"Don't do it, Emma." Paul clamped his fingers around her wrist. "Don't leave with him. You belong to me."

"I belong to no one save myself."

"We'll see about that." His eyes were hard as coal.

She chafed under Paul's possessiveness. No matter what her heart said, she wasn't his for the claiming. Emma pulled her hand from his grip and ignored his furious expression. Yet worry dogged her, as she and Franklin departed.

Had she, by her stand, pushed Paul Rousseau too far?

197

Chapter Thirteen

"How could you embarrass me like that?" Franklin said, pouting, as the carriage rolled down St. Charles Avenue.

"If you have anything to be ashamed of, it's your own behavior. You had no right to barge in on Paul and me, nor to act the spurned suitor." Emma didn't mention his cowardice. "Back home I told you in no uncertain terms that you and I were finished."

"Yes, Kitten, but I'd hoped by now you'd have changed your mind." He extended his stubby fingers to touch her arm, but she drew away. "I promised your parents I'd bring you home."

"Louisiana is my home now." As she said those words she grasped the honesty of them. She wouldn't skirt the truth by calling this an extended visit. Here was where her destiny lay. With Dr. Boulogne, with her career, with Paul. With Paul? What had made her think that?

"No self-respecting, unmarried lady of society would think to establish her own residence. Unless . . ."

Emma suddenly wondered what would she do

about living arrangements? She felt certain her uncle and aunt would offer to share their home on a more permanent basis, but that would be an imposition.

"By your silence, I take it you plan to marry Rousseau."

"That never entered my mind." Emma frowned. Why did everyone—Marian, Cleopatra, and now even Franklin—assume that she would cleave to Paul Rousseau? The scoundrel faced criminal prosecution; his future was uncertain to say the least. "He means nothing to me," she lied.

"My, my. You've certainly allowed your principles to deteriorate. First you allowed me to break our engagement, knowing your reputation would suffer for it; and tonight you behave in a most brazen manner with a ruffian you've no intention of wedding. How," Franklin lamented, "could I have fallen in love with a woman of such loose morals?"

"Oh, Franklin, you're such a prig and a bore that you need someone to shock you out of your dull, mother-entrenched existence."

"Emma!"

"And get something straight—I never, ever imagined myself in love with you. I only agreed to the engagement to please my parents. I have since realized marriage cannot be based on pleasing others. When I wed it will be because I want to live with that person. He's going to light a spark within me, and I'm going to do the same for him." She looked straight at Underwood. "Before I arrived here, I never knew that feeling. And I lied a minute ago—I do care for Paul. There's a fire between us, perhaps not enough of a one to base a marriage on, but by darn, it's . . . It's none of your concern."

She tapped on the carriage wall, and Jeremiah opened the sliding panel. "Drop me by Boulogne's clinic," she said, "and after you do, take Mr. Underwood back to Magnolia Hall. But don't turn in for the evening. He'll only be staying long enough to pack for his return trip to Virginia."

"Emma, how could you!" Franklin protested. "I won't go."

"Don't forget, Jeremiah, take Mr. Underwood to a hotel *tonight*."

The barouche stopped in front of the clinic, and Emma got out. Tending to the unfortunates of society, especially to poor little Myrtle Ann, would get her mind off her personal problems. And it did.

Three hours later, past the point of exhaustion, Emma returned to Magnolia Hall. Jeremiah had, after dropping Franklin at the St. Louis Hotel, returned and waited for her. She trudged up the staircase, then down the hall to her room. Closing the door behind her, she realized that someone, perhaps Betsy or Cleopatra, had left the French doors to the gallery ajar.

She was halfway across the room when Paul's voice stopped her. "Where've you been?"

"What are you doing here!" She turned to his voice, and saw the orange glow of what smelled like a cigar. Irritated, she ordered, "Get out."

Her eyes unadjusted to the dark, she heard rather than saw him extinguish the smoke. He stepped into the faint light that edged across the rug from the French doors. The knotted muscles of his arms and torso were cast in relief. He wore dark breeches, no shirt and no boots.

"Did you get rid of Underfoot?"

Remembering her words to Franklin about the spark between herself and Paul, she smiled. But she was weary, emotionally and physically, too weary to cope with this intrusion. She needed time to consider just how important Paul Rousseau was to her, and his presence had a way of blocking sound reason.

"I told you to get out," she repeated.

He advanced toward her. "So you did."

"I'll scream," she warned, meaning it. Unfortunately her room was in the opposite wing from Uncle Rankin and Aunt Tillie's room, and she had no idea whether Marian had returned.

"But you won't." Paul stopped in front of her, lowered his head toward hers. "You've been wanting what I'm here to give you, and if you scream, you won't get it."

Scrambling back, she whipped her arm in a wide arc, catching his jaw with the palm of her hand. Pain shot up her arm. He didn't move. "Get back or my knee will find your groin."

"Ah but, *chérie,* if you do that, I'll be no good to you tonight . . . and we can't have that." He wrapped his forearms behind her, and, lifting her, threw her over his shoulder.

"How dare you," she raged, and beat her fist against his back while he strode across the rug as if he bore no extra weight. He threw her onto the turned-back bed, and the wind left her lungs on impact.

"Get . . . away . . . from me. I . . . don't want you."

201

"Liar." Paul covered her with his heavy frame. "You were deliberately taunting me tonight."

He slanted his mouth over hers, the fire of his sherry-tinged kiss spreading down and through her. Then he eased onto his side and brought her with him. The scents of herbal soap and cigar smoke and lustful male assailed her, enticingly. His manhood was swollen against her leg. Moving his sculpted lips along her jaw, he trailed his tongue over the fleshy prominence at the front of her ear and whispered, *"J'ai besoin de toi."* Despite her limited grasp of French, she understood, and excitement raced through every bone, every nerve, of her being.

Saints above! How she enjoyed his breath in her ear. And she had need of him, too.

"We've both waited a long time for this," Paul said, "and I intend to get a good look at you." He pinioned her with a leg, propped himself on an elbow, and reached to light the candle on the night table. Her sharp letter opener was resting beside the taper; he picked it up. Then he straddled her hips, the blade reflected in the light.

Emma didn't fear him. For some strange reason she didn't believe he'd do her harm. There was something in his dark eyes, a fire of longing and passion and utter virility, that burned through her. She watched mesmerized as he brought the blade close to her chest.

One by one he sliced the buttons from her bodice. His free hand swept the material away, then lingered to caress her chemise-covered breasts. She moaned as he lightly pinched first one nipple and then the other. He slid the blade under her lacings and the steel point flicked free the ribbons of her chemise. Finally, his fingers never touching her flesh, he drew the thin white muslin from her bosom.

"You'd make an excellent surgeon," she murmured, smilingly and half teasingly.

"I'm"—he discarded the letter opener and worried her nipple with the edge of his nail—"a better lover than cutter."

Remembering her sister's words about her husband's unimaginative rutting, Emma murmured, "Yes . . . I believe you are."

Triumph gleamed in his eyes. "Then say it! Tell me you want me to make love to you."

She wouldn't give in that easily. "How can I when your weight is squeezing the life out of me?"

He lifted his body, moving to the side. "That better?"

"Oh, much . . ." She batted her lashes, Marian-style. "Let me get out of this dress. It does seem to get in the way." As she started to scoot from the bed, his palm touched her wrist. As his fingernails pulled at the minuscule hairs of her lower forearm, she shivered, a pleasurable feeling.

"Taking off your dress is my job," he said, smooth as honey. "The only thing you need to do, *ma bien-aimée,* is lie back and enjoy my attentions."

Considering the liquid heaviness that had settled in the core of her womanhood, Emma was tempted to acquiesce, but having gone this far, she resented being a sitting duck. Inching her leg to the far side of the mattress, she said, "Oh, but you're taking forever to undress me."

She lunged aside, hoping to get off the bed and

across the room, but he grabbed the back of her dress and undergarments, and yanked with all his might. The harsh sound of material ripping filled the air. Her clothing fell around her ankles; and she whirled around, instinctively covering the private parts no man had seen before.

"Brute!"

"Don't hide yourself, my beautiful one." He extended his hand, and his tone was deep, meaningful. "There are many names you call me, and many of them I deserve, but I must show you that 'brute' shouldn't be added to the list."

"Oh?" She moved one foot backward. "Then what appellation should I place on a man who breaks into my bedchamber, cuts the bodice from my gown, and then rips the garment to shreds when I don't lie back like a meek little mouse?"

"Try 'sweetheart.'" In slow, easy movements he rose from the bed. Taking her in his arms, he whispered into her hair, "It's not a difficult word. If you're not comfortable with that, try *amoureux*. Either one would make me happy."

She rested her cheek against his chest. The hairs tickled her nose, but she enjoyed the sensation. She savored Paul's unique essence as her palms grazed his back, resting on scars. *Oh, Paul, there's so little I know about you. What makes you happy? And what makes you sad?* She yearned to ask those questions, but realizing that would show weakness, she didn't.

He swallowed, as though her silence disappointed him. Then he stepped back, bringing her with him, and adroitly maneuvered her onto the mattress. She rolled onto her stomach, hiding her face. She sensed

204

him near her, yet he didn't touch her. Squeezing her eyes, she prayed for guidance. For days she had admitted, both to herself and to Paul, that she wanted this lovemaking, but wanting and admitting had naught to do with sanity.

She was simply too bone weary to make a decision that would change her forever. Virginity lost was a lifetime thing. But hadn't she relinquished it, emotionally, that night in his hotel?

"You seem very tired," he commented gently, much more gently than was his custom.

"I am."

"If you'll allow me to touch you, I'll relieve your tension."

"That, Paul Rousseau, is exactly what I fear."

"Don't," he murmured. "And don't jump to conclusions. You helped me when I needed it, and I'd like to return the favor. I'm going to rub your back till you fall asleep."

She didn't say yes, but no wasn't on her lips either. Feeling his roughened fingers brush aside the hair at her nape, she shivered with delight, and when his right hand, big and strong and callused, kneaded the muscles of her neck, she yearned to kiss those long fingers. With circular motions he attended to one shoulder, and then the other. Emma felt her weariness diminish as if by magic. Paul's magic. The tips of his fingers worked their way down her spine and over the rise of her hip—his thumb found the dimple at the top of it. She heard him swallow hard. Her pulsebeats resounded against her eardrums like waves crashing against the shore. She couldn't wait to make a forever change.

"I'm not going to fall asleep," she murmured, her face still averted, and edged her fingers to his chest. The back of her hand turned up, she flattened it against his skin, saying silently to him, *This is the sign*, amoureux. *I'm telling you I've made my choice. Don't make me put it into words. You've won the war, but give me this battle's victory.*

As if he had read her mind, Paul changed course. The hand she had offered him was taken to his lips for a gentle kiss. The caress shot straight to her heart. And the sweet ecstasy was only beginning. His lips . . . his tongue . . . caressed her from forearm to elbow. She tried to turn away, but he spread his arm across her shoulder.

His voice was a husky tremor. "Don't deny me my pleasure."

No other part of his body touching hers, he moved his lips and tongue ever so slowly, and lightly, across her back.

Tingles ran up and down Emma's spine. She was intensely aware of his soft touch and feathered breath. Never in her wildest fancy had she dreamed it could be this tantalizing, this pleasurable to be possessed by Paul. Every part of her responded to his erotic assault, and her primitive urgings overshadowed sanity and doubts and uncertainty about what the future, and past deeds, might bring.

"Would you deny me my pleasure?" she asked.

"You don't enjoy this?" He flicked his tongue across the rise of her hips.

"You . . . know . . . I do." She turned over, and settled on her back. "But my body cries for more. I yearn to see and touch you."

Brushing the curtain of hair away from her face,

she allowed her eyes to assess him as they had never done. Outward confidence didn't mask the need in his dark eyes. He was large and strong, like a mature oak—no sapling to be sure. There was sheer strength in his taut muscles and long limbs. And in his inner self. He was the kind of man a strong woman wanted to be sheltered by. She yearned to be held within his hirsute arms . . . to touch him . . . and to experience total fulfillment.

"The first time I met you," she admitted, "I wondered how far down the hair on your chest grows. I still wonder." She glanced at his lower section, then back to his face. "Take off your breeches, my darling. I long to see how God made you."

Paul's features tensed, as if he were held in check by a thin rein. "Your wantonness fires me, sweet witch."

"Do you not like it?" she asked, bending a knee and moving her foot up and down the sheet.

"That needs no answer. But I question your experience, virgin vixen. You behave much as a woman accustomed to a man's bed."

"This is my bed, need I remind you, and don't compare me to other women."

"I've never compared you to others, *ma bien-aimée.*" He grinned and eased himself off the bed. His fingers worked a buttonhole, freeing his waistband. "This . . . is only between you and me."

"Oh it's not between us . . . yet," she teased, centering her attention on the hard male thighs that were presented to her. The dark hair of his midsection veed in whorls to his navel, then spanned downward and cut across the only white skin of his body. His thick staff, thrusting upward above legs bunched with physical strength, was stiff and dark. In a moment fraught with lunacy, Emma remembered the photographic plates in her father's medical books; Paul was exceedingly different and superior to them.

And now she knew the purpose of those short-chopped breeches she'd found in his sea chest. His bronzed, olive skin was light only below his waist. "So this is what you're like. . . ."

"No, my beautiful Emma." The mattress sank as he levered himself above her. "This is what I'm like."

He lavished kisses, both tender and fiery, on her breasts, her neck, her lips, and with primitive need, her legs spread for him. She felt the tip of his sex at the entrance to her womanhood, yet knew no fear, the ache to sheath him within herself overpowering. Yet he gave her no solace.

"Please," she moaned. "Take me."

"No." His voice was strained with longing. "I won't take you. I'm going to make love to you. There is a difference."

"Show me."

"My pleasure . . ." He kissed her lips, and his ardent tongue explored her mouth.

Her hands wound beneath his arms, crossing at the wrists to allow her fingers to explore his scarred back. Neither he, nor she, could take any more. But he stopped at her maidenhood.

"Don't stop," she pleaded.

Clenching his jaw, he claimed what was only his to possess.

Pain, deep and searing, shot through Emma as he passed the point of no return. Her body torn in

208

agony, she bunched her fingers and beat her fists against his shoulders. "Stop it!"

His movements ceased. "I can't." He brushed his lips against her cheek. "The worst is over now, *ma bien-aimée,* all that's left is the better."

And it was. Within seconds, she began to respond to his thrusts; then she met them with ardent passion. She moaned, but these sounds were not the kind to elicit pity.

"So wonderful . . . so wonderful," he said, groaning, before he took her lips once more.

Her legs wrapped around him as the most heady feeling assailed her—a strange sense of euphoria she had never before experienced. A shower of pleasure, comfort, closeness, happiness, exaltation—all gathered into one climactic frenzy.

Her ankles digging into his hips, she rose to meet his final thrust. "Love it . . . love it."

And when it was over, Paul whispered, "You all right?"

Her love-swollen lips curved into a smile; her eyes were drowsy with satisfaction. "Does the sun set in the west, sweetheart?"

The endearment drew a smile from him. Unwilling to relinquish Emma from his arms, he kissed her eyelids closed, and felt her soft breath, in the cadence of sleep, against his chest. He placed a tender kiss on her forehead, his thoughts centered on being the luckiest man in the world.

None of that shy maiden business—not for his Emma. How he had relished her instinctive, wanton responses . . . and overtures. Their bodies had been in tune, as if God had created them for each other. She was under his skin, no doubt about that, and he realized it was going to take a long time to get his fill of her. Now, with the scent of her clinging to him, she was bonded to him spiritually; he was certain of it.

Emma was beautiful. And feisty. That lapdog Franklin Underwood wasn't worthy of trailing at her heel; Paul knew she could have her pick of men. But she had chosen him for her first lover. He smiled, and looked forward to their married nights.

A tickle of guilt nagged at him. His plan to use Emma to further the Texas cause made him a bit of a scoundrel. Well, he wouldn't abuse her. He'd be a faithful husband, which would be no difficulty; he wanted no woman save for her.

While he had had more than his share of women in the past, in only one of them, besides Emma, had he been interested in more than mere sex. That had been a long, long time ago, and he realized Aimée Thérèse didn't compare to the woman beside him now.

Emma moved in her sleep, sliding her leg across his thighs. He swallowed as her flesh touched his manhood, bringing him to instant arousal. Then he eased her leg to the side and brushed the golden hair from her temple.

"You aren't asleep," he said, drinking in her wide eyes.

The side of her thumb drew a circle around his nipple. "Not at all . . ."

"We'll have to do something about that." He drew her earlobe between his teeth, and felt her shiver . . . before making love to her again. Slowly, tenderly, reverently.

In the afterglow Emma was satiated. No thoughts were on her mind except for how enchanting it was to lie in Paul's arms.

His fingers grasped the top sheet and ran it between her thighs. Gently. Cleansing her as if she were a babe, he furrowed his brows.

"Don't be such a fussbudget," she said. "I'm fine."

A grin pulled at one side of his rugged face. "Ah yes, my Emma ... but you're more than 'fine.'"

"You, too." Stretching like a lazy Persian before a glowing hearth, she giggled. She never thought this could happen! But then, she had never thought a lot of things could happen.

"Vixen." He chuckled. "Are you thirsty?"

"For what? Another kiss?"

"Woman, I'm a man not a steam engine. And even a steam engine needs power." He slapped her delectable derrière. "I was talking about champagne!"

He leaned an arm over the side of the bed to produce a glass and a bottle of the sparkling wine. Not bothering to cover himself, he sat cross-legged on the bed. She followed suit.

There was something nice, she decided, about this shameless intimacy. "Imagine ... a picnic at four A.M. And in my own bed."

Paul uncorked the bottle and filled the glass. Holding the now-tepid refreshment to her lips, he said, "Why be conventional?"

"I agree."

A drop of champagne slid down her chin, and Paul leaned over to lick it away. He then took her face between his palms, tilting her chin upward with his thumbs. "But there are occasions, *ma bien-aimée,* when convention should be respected."

"This is a strange time and place to be speaking

211

so." There was no malice in her words. "And it seems even stranger that such a thing should be said by you."

"Hush up, Emma Frances Oliver. I'm trying to ask you to marry me."

This should have been the happiest moment of her life, for she loved Paul Rousseau. There. She had admitted it. And it felt good.

But the image of Paul running from the burning ruins of the Oliver Factor House clouded her happiness.

His hold on her tightened. "Marry me, Emma."

"Do you propose to all the virgins you deflower?"

"I won't honor that with a reply." He frowned, his expression dark and hurt. "Just say yes."

"I . . . I don't know."

"I won't stop you from being a doctor, if that's what you're worried about."

She was aghast. "You wouldn't?" Suspiciously she asked, "Why not?"

"I know it's important to you, and I wouldn't wish to take your happiness away."

"That's a rather strange thing for you to say. If I were to say yes, shouldn't I expect our life together to bring total happiness?"

"Does this mean you're not as dedicated to medicine as I had imagined?" he asked.

"Absolutely not. I intend to devote myself to the infirm of this earth."

"Tell me about your work," he urged.

"Perhaps another time." She was pleased by his interest, but at this moment she would not be sidetracked from the issue he had posed. "I question your motive in this proposal."

He seemed to study the pillow where her head lay. "Marriage doesn't keep two people in bed twenty-four hours a day. You'd have to have your own interests."

"And what would your interests be?"

"Sugar planting." He eased back against his own pillow, and slipped his arm beneath her shoulders to bring her to him again. "I'm set to inherit a plantation on the banks of the Bayou Teche. From my grandfather. I want to take you there as mistress of Feuille de Chêne."

"Ha! Being a planter's wife is a full-time occupation. Where would I find time for my medical practice? And besides, my apprenticeship has only begun." She gave him cursory details of her work with Dr. René Boulogne. "You'd take me up the bayou, and I'd find myself overwhelmed with the responsibilities of the mistress of Feuille de Chêne."

"Not so. I'll find adequate help."

Needing time to think, she pulled away from him and inched to a sitting position. She drew her knees beneath her chin. How could she fulfill her dreams in an isolated part of Louisiana?

Yet, she thought, people there got sick, they were hurt, had babies. If Paul stood by his word and relieved her of the mistress's responsibilities, she'd have ample time to pursue her career. But a niggling worry prodded at her. His proposal sounded like a business arrangement. There had been no declaration of love. She remembered her own words, spoken hours earlier to Franklin. She had talked of sparks between lovers and wanting to be with that other person. Those things, she knew, were true of herself and Paul. Yet . . .

213

She pulled the sheet up to cover her nakedness. "Have you forgotten you'll face judge and jury?" When would he? she wondered. "Very soon you'll answer to the State of Louisiana over the fire."

"I resent the accusatory tone of your statement." He quaffed more champagne, then looked her in the eye. His expression was sincere, yet wrought with hurt and anger. "The State of Louisiana will see me a free man, Emma Oliver . . . soon to be Emma Rousseau."

"Your confidence overwhelms me."

"I intend it to."

"What about the Texas Navy, Paul? Will you forsake your adopted country for marital bliss?"

"There are many ways to demonstrate patriotism. I will serve my country in the manner I feel best, have no fear." He grimaced. "Don't trouble yourself with my plans. You won't suffer unduly for them."

She buried her face against her drawn-up knees. "You must leave, Paul. Dawn's going to break soon, and the servants will be here."

"I won't leave until you say yes."

"I can't," she said, shaking her head.

"Can't is a different word from won't. You can. Why *won't* you agree?"

"I won't agree because I don't want to be your wife."

His ego bruised, he shot to his feet. Ironclad determination filled his eyes. "When I make up my mind to have something I get it. And, as I warned you before, I give no quarter in the getting. You *will* be my wife, and I intend to employ any means, fair or foul, to accomplish that end."

Chapter Fourteen

By ten o'clock in the morning Emma had cast aside Paul's threats about marrying her. She had done much since he'd pulled on his breeches and left. All evidence of his nocturnal visit hidden, except to her person and memory, she had dressed, had breakfast, and been driven into the city, had looked in on Myrtle Ann, who was progressing well, and was now walking down St. Peter Street toward the factor-house grounds. Mind in a turmoil, she asked herself: What do I really want?

Her quest to be a doctor was progressing well. And she had come to the conclusion that Louisiana was her home. Paul was the man she loved. Why fight him?

By marrying him she'd sacrifice nothing. He'd allow her the freedom to pursue her doctoring endeavors, though the backwaters of the Teche would be the setting for her endeavors rather than New Orleans. But she still had several months of apprenticeship under Dr. Boulogne. To leave now would mean losing an important part of her training.

Be that as it may . . . Under no illusions, she realized that fellow physicians would scorn, if not deny, her use of the appellation of medical doctor. Yet it was not uncommon for men of medicine to simply hang out a shingle. She shuddered at the thought. Many of those who called themselves healers were nothing more than unschooled charlatans who had never seen the insides of a textbook, never examined a specimen through a microscope.

She journeyed on. Less than a block separated her from Uncle Rankin and the building site—both reminders of the chasm separating her from Paul. If only he hadn't maligned her family . . .

"Oh, Paul!" A tug of longing pulled at her heart. She resented the inner fears that stood in the way of their happiness. Standing at the edge of what used to be her uncle's cotton warehouse, she forced herself not to think of her lover . . . or of his proposal.

Lumber, freshly sawn and pine scented, was stacked near the street. About thirty dark men, singing a tune flavored by the Gullah of their African homeland, toiled bare-chested in the humid sun. An overseer, wearing a wide-brimmed hat and carrying a whip, walked among them; he shouted an order. His raised voice disturbed the egrets perching on the ground, and the workers picked up their pace.

Emma caught sight of her uncle as he stepped out of the temporary office that had been erected.

"Uncle Rankin!" She waved a greeting when he turned and smiled. "Good morning."

"And it's a good one to see ye." A smile raked his weathered, yet handsome, cheeks as she stepped next to him. "What brings ye here, girl?"

"Oh I just wanted to . . . to check the construction progress," she said. "I thought a few minutes alone together would be nice."

A steamboat docked along the levee, and to announce her arrival, she blew her whistle.

"My sentiments exactly." He put his arm around Emma's shoulders. Surveying the site, he was full of enthusiasm. "Now that they've cleared the rubble," he said, "today we begin raising the new building. It's going to be bigger and better than the old one, Emmie," he said, using his pet name for her. "And I'm going to put up another. Think I'll add ship chandlering to my enterprises. I've been doing a bit of that in the past," he went on to explain. "On an informal basis of course."

"That's marvelous, Uncle. But aren't you spreading yourself a bit thin? Besides your cotton factoring, your sugar plantations keep you busy."

"I thrive on being busy, Emmie. And traveling does me good as well. Gives me breathing room." He paused. "Well, I enjoy being out of town."

"Between here, St. Martinsville, and the West Indies, how do you manage it all?"

"Come on in the office, and I'll tell ye." He guided her into the boxed room and took a seat behind an impressive mahogany desk.

Emma sat beside it. Still thinking about his comment, she urged him on. "I'm all ears."

"I keep my overseers indebted to me." He leaned forward to chuck her chin lightly, then laced his fingers behind his neck, pushing the brim of his hat forward. "And let me give ye another hint—I pay them well." He leaned back. "My managers stay

217

loyal because I keep them in my pocket. If ye've enough gold, ye can buy anything."

"Even love?"

"Especially love," he answered with a melancholy tinge.

Curious about that, Emma frowned. Several years earlier she'd asked her mother about the feud between Uncle Rankin and Étienne Rousseau. When Rankin was a penniless young man, Noreen had told her, he'd been in love with Angélique de Poutrincourt; but she'd married a French expatriate, not him. "Rankin made a fool of himself over her," Emma had been told, "and carried on in the most awful way. He never put the blame where it belonged—on the woman who had her choice, and made it, for money and position. Oh no, it was always the rich Mr. Étienne Rousseau's fault." Noreen had never liked her brother-in-law, for reasons her daughter didn't understand, so Emma had chalked her hostility to Rankin to sour grapes. Always, she had believed her uncle's version of events: Étienne had slandered Uncle Rankin's character for a petty insult that had occurred in St. Martinsville many years earlier.

Now she wondered if her mother had been right about the source of the feud. Did her uncle still pine for a woman long dead?

And what about Aunt Tillie? Surely he loved her. With no parental pressures, such as Emma had experienced, he had made his own choice. What other reason would he have had for marrying? "Did you buy Aunt Tillie's love?"

"Everything I've ever acquired has been through money."

Emma pushed herself off the desk and walked to the window. "Didn't you . . . do you love her?"

"Not as she deserves," he said tiredly. "But I respect her, and would never dishonor her with harsh words or a raised fist. She's been a loyal wife and a good mother to William, but if the"—he paused to stare at the ceiling—"if the spark is not there, a person can't force love on another person."

Unthinking, she said, "Too bad Aunt Tillie wasn't richer than you, then maybe you could've been bought."

Rankin's jaw slackened. "You wish to shame me?"

"Oh no, Uncle, not at all!" He was a paragon in her eyes, and deserved better than trite disloyalty. "I meant . . . in other words she tried to make you love her."

"Yes." He doffed his hat and studied the brim. "That's why she thinks she's sick all the time. But— ha!—if she were as sickly as she allows, she wouldn't be alive, much less be able to carry on with her duties."

"She's a hypochondriac."

"What is the meaning of that word?" he asked, and after Emma explained it, he said, "I agree, but her maladies get my attention, and they take her mind off . . . Well, I think ye understand, Emmie."

She was overwhelmed with love and pity for both Uncle Rankin and his wife. Wedlock should be based on love. How horrible marriage must be for both of them.

Her palms suddenly felt clammy. Never had Paul mentioned love. But some men, she knew, had a difficult time saying those words, and she hadn't expressed her love yet, either. With nothing to gain

219

monetarily by marrying her, surely Paul loved her! His fiery, though sometimes gentle, passions of the night before proved that he cared for her.

Their relationship in no way resembled the one between her uncle and aunt. She realized that Rankin had never gotten over loving Angélique Rousseau. From his startled expression, she realized she had spoken the thought aloud.

"How do ye know about her?" He pursed his lips. "Never mind—I think I know." To bridge the gap in the conversation, he finally added, "And I also know ye're involved with Paul Rousseau."

Emma was speechless.

"Don't give me that wide-eyed stare, girl. I'm not going to throttle ye, though I should."

"Your changing the subject so quickly says something for my statement about Mrs. Rousseau," she retorted, her equanimity gained. "And I'm not involved with Paul," she lied, unable to confess the whole truth.

"*Paul,* eh? Don't take me for a fool, Emmie. Your slip of the tongue speaks for itself."

Well, he had her on that. Now was the moment she had been waiting for. For weeks she had wanted her uncle's counsel about Paul. But why did the opportunity to get it arrive on the heels of losing her virginity? She blanched at the mere thought of Uncle Rankin knowing *all.*

"I've no wish to deny it—I know him. But don't try to imply anything beyond that." Emma confessed she had called on Paul in an attempt to thwart the match between him and Marian. "With you out of town, I was trying to protect the Oliver interests."

220

"I can see ye had your heart in the right place, but I don't condone your methods. Got in thicker than ye supposed, eh?" Not waiting for an answer, he said, "Cleopatra tells me ye spent the night in Rousseau's room."

"I'll strangle her!"

"Now, now, girl. Don't let your Gaelic temper get the better of ye. Though I know ye mean Cleopatra no harm," he tacked on, then steepled his fingers in front of his face, resting his chin on his thumbs. "I'm in a bit of a predicament, Emmie my girl. You tell me how should I handle the situation. I've got a dear niece who I love as if she were my own daughter, and she's slept with the man who torched my factor house. Do I call him out and avenge my loss and her fallen honor, thus taking the chance of her bringing a fatherless babe into the family . . . or do I turn the other cheek and prevail upon Étienne Rousseau's son to do right by my beloved niece?"

"He's the product of Angélique Rousseau, too," Emma reminded him, shaken. "And d-don't worry about unwanted babies." Oh, saints above, why hadn't she thought about that?

"I warned you not to take me for a fool, girl. Last night ye were caught in his embrace—right in Howard O'Reilly's drawing room, remember? And ye *did* share a night with Rousseau—the night before the fire." Rankin's gaze was speculative. "Or wasn't he man enough to perform in bed?"

Flying to Paul's defense and shocked at the bold question, she said, "Of course he was man enough!"

"Just as I thought. Well then, shall I call Paul Rousseau out?"

"Absolutely not! Don't make me a part of this lunacy you practice here in New Orleans. The courts will decide how to rectify the fire, and the . . . and what's between me and Paul is personal. I'll not allow a life to be lost over either issue!"

The door creaked open. "Which life concerns you the most, Emma?"

She whipped around. Cambric shirt sleeves rolled up to his elbows, Paul cocked his arm against the door frame. Her heart pounded, with both love and embarrassment at being caught discussing him. "Why, you—"

"Thank you. Now I know where your loyalties lie."

"Why you sneak, that's what I meant!" *You're right. You are more important to me.* She yearned to rush into his arms and declare her feelings. But here in this office, in the presence of the man Paul had done evil, she wouldn't do it. "Don't place yourself too high in what you believe are my sentiments. You'll be sorely disappointed."

"I doubt it." Pushing away from his stance, he said, "Remember early this morning, just before I left? You're the one who must be, mm, sore."

He was laying their whole affair open! "Drat you—you slimy, slithering snake!"

"Snake? Ah well. You, *ma bien-aimée,* should know."

"That's enough!" Rankin cut in, the slap of his palm against the desktop interlacing his demand. "What do ye want, Rousseau?"

Paul clipped a mock salute at Emma and then turned back to her uncle. "Work started today on your factory, so I'm here to lend a hand."

"The criminal returns to the scene of the crime, eh?" Rankin hunched forward, flattening his palms on the desk as he sneered at Paul.

"The innocent bystander returns to . . ." Paul straightened his shoulders. He wasn't without a certain amount of guilt over the fire, and he wanted to make inroads with Emma, to show sincerity. "I'm not spoiling for a quarrel," he explained. "You ought to consider granting me a few moments of your time before I join the workers outside. It could be to your benefit."

Watching her uncle's reaction, Emma held her breath. He was scowling, but as the moments ticked away his sharp frown eased.

Rankin nodded. "I'll grant you a few minutes. Sit down—both of you, sit down."

Emma took one of the two armchairs fronting the desk, Paul the other. She had to hand him one thing—it took courage for the accused to face his accusers. She respected that.

Not looking Emma's way, he crossed his arms over his chest. "My attorney's advised against it, but I want to clear the air about the fire. No pun intended. Secondly, there seems to be some doubt as to my former intentions toward your widowed daughter-in-law. Wait! Don't say a word till I'm finished. . . . Thank you."

Emma listened as he gave his version of the fire. His story hadn't changed appreciably, and she watched her uncle's expression change from skeptical to questioning.

"And ye only went in the building to tamp out

223

the flames?"

"I went in with only one thought in mind: doing justice to you. For too long the feud between our families has gone on. I want to have a free heart . . . after all these years," Paul said. "As for Marian, well, I'm prone to the charms of women, but I meant and did her no harm. And Emma can attest that I can *perform* in the bedroom. Isn't that right, *chérie?*"

Obviously he had overheard quite a lot of her conversation with her uncle, and she realized something else. Paul had made no idle threat about using fair means or foul. Well, two could play at that. "You lie!"

"Do I?" Paul reached for her fingers. "Can you say with all honesty that I'm impotent?"

"Rousseau!" Rankin exclaimed.

In any other situation, Emma would have throttled her lover. There was no end to the torment he inflicted on her.

"I am going to marry your niece." Paul eased himself from the chair. Standing tall, he said, "She may very well be *enceinte,* and she'll have the protection of my name."

"You've said nothing about love," Rankin prompted.

Paul swallowed hard. "Many marriages have started with less than what we share."

A dull throbbing began at her temples, and Emma's spirits sank. Had she been a fool to think he loved her? Had he proposed marriage only in the name of decency and honor? "Forget it. Your name and so-called protection mean nothing to me."

"Ah, *ma bien-aimée,* that's just what I expected you to say. Perhaps I should restate my words. I will give my child the protection of my name. Don't try to stop me."

She shuddered at her possible predicament, yet the thought of bearing his child wasn't repulsive. "Don't do this."

"Give it up, Rousseau. She says she didn't sleep with ye, and I believe her," Rankin said emphatically. "I may tend to agree with your story on the fire, but ye'll never receive my blessings to a union between an Oliver and a Rousseau."

"Your blessings are not what I'm after. I'm just stating facts. I'm going to make Mademoiselle Emma Oliver my wife; and if you don't like it, you can stew in your own juice."

"Ye bastard!" Spoiling for battle, Rankin grew white with rage. "I've had enough! Choose the weapons—because I'm challenging ye!"

Emma couldn't stop the pounding of her heart. Her anxiety over what might transpire was terrible.

"I accept your call to arms. St. Anthony's Garden it is. Rapiers at dawn."

Horrified, Emma begged them to be reasonable, but it was fruitless.

"Until tomorrow," Paul said as he departed. "And today I help build a factor house. *Au revoir,* my future wife."

The rest of that day and night, Emma prayed that something—anything—would happen to stop the upcoming duel. Emotionally she was in turmoil. She

225

was dedicated to preserving life, yet a life might be lost—because of her!

And what if the life lost was Paul's? She could very well be pregnant, and then would be without his protection. Her future was at stake. She didn't want to risk bringing a fatherless child into the world.

Just before dawn she went to her uncle's room to beg him to cease this madness. He denied her request, however, and forbade her to witness the duel.

But she was not to be denied. The landau carrying Emma drew up to St. Anthony's Garden, and she got out as the sun peeked through the clouds, ribboning the sky with muted orange and pink. Dew moistened the ground. A steam whistle sounded from the Mississippi River, nearly drowning out the bells of St. Louis Cathedral. The contest had not yet begun. Both men wore form-fitting white, Paul's dark coloring a contrast to the material.

"I told ye to stay home," Rankin shouted, as he stomped toward her.

Paul, confident and arrogant, held his ground while gripping a triangular foil. His wrist flicked, and sunlight reflected from the steel blade as he eyed Emma. A half-smile pulling at one cheek, he nodded recognition.

She lifted her eyes to her uncle, who now blocked her view. "What he said is true. I've been intimate with him. And I'm going to take him as husband."

Rankin's blond brows drew together. "Why did ye lie, Emmie?"

"Pride, I guess. I didn't want you to think ill of me."

"'Twould take more than weakness of the flesh for that."

His gloved hand gripping the handle, Paul held the point of his rapier downward and strode over to them. "Ready, Oliver?"

"Call off the challenge," she pleaded.

"No," Rankin said. "I will not."

She grabbed his arm. "Only yesterday you put the decision in my hands. Now I'm telling you I've made it—I want the protection of Paul's name!"

Displaying a gleeful smirk at her words, Paul said, "You needn't fear, *chérie*. I shall be victorious."

"Take your womanly whinings back to Magnolia Hall." Rankin pulled back from her grip and thrust the tip of his foil toward the arena. "And you, Rousseau, take your mark."

Confession had been useless, but Emma wouldn't run from the duel. She knew that swift medical attention might save a life.

Forcing herself not to hide her face behind shaking hands, she watched the pair square off. Her eyes were on Paul. His right foot angled toward her uncle, his knees bent slightly, he tipped the blade skyward with one hand. His left hand was held high, in balance. There was no stiffness to his pose; he was ready for instant execution.

"En garde, Oliver!"

Swords twanged as they thrust and parried— Emma lost count of the times. Paul withdrew his blade just far enough to clear the tip of the other foil. With lightning swiftness, he flexed his arm and wrist, cutting over and lunging forward to strike at the other man's chest. Rankin's right foot retreated, then the other. To her, they sparred for what seemed

227

like hours, but it must have been mere minutes. Her uncle made an attempt to feint, but Paul was too swift.

In one direct motion he executed a sharp, forward-striking action to the weak point of his opponent's blade, disarming the older man, and he lunged forward. Emma screamed, "No!" just as the tip of his foil thrust against Rankin's chest.

Paul stopped short of a mortal wound.

Panting and humiliated, Rankin bit out, "Finish what you started, Rousseau."

"I've no wish to kill you." Paul dropped the point of his blade and rubbed the bell guard of his victorious sword.

"Don't dishonor me."

"I have." He cast a meaningful glance at Emma. "But I'll not have my bride wearing mourning garb to our wedding."

He strutted to her, took something from his vest, and captured her hand. "With my grandmother's ring"—he slipped a delicate band of gold, one enhanced by emeralds and diamonds, onto her left ring finger—"I will thee wed."

Aunt Tillie had an attack of the vapors upon hearing of the match, yet she made a remarkable recovery in order to supervise the wedding preparations.

And the bells of St. Louis Cathedral tolled for the marriage three days later. Emma wore a white lace and satin gown that had been hastily, but beautifully, stitched by New Orleans's best dressmaker.

Isn't white supposed to be indicative of purity? she asked herself, feeling hypocritical as the priest recited the ancient rites of matrimony.

But that feeling of hypocracy didn't spoil Emma's frame of mind. She was resigned to the marriage, she loved Paul, and she felt certain he'd grow to love her.

The wedding party then descended on Magnolia Hall for the reception, at which champagne, and edible delicacies were served to the accompaniment of music.

"I believe it's traditional for the bride and groom to have the first dance," Paul said, pulling Emma into his arms.

She smiled up into his face. "And I thought you didn't believe in conventions."

"Don't hold me to words once spoken." He whirled her in step with the music. "Matter of fact, I'm thinking we should leave for the hotel right now. A glass of champagne and an armful of my naked wife, that's what I'm wanting and needing."

"I wouldn't be opposed. But—"

Wordlessly, Rankin tapped Paul on the shoulder and pulled Emma away. Paul winked at her, then stepped back.

"I don't trust him," her uncle said, easing into step with the tune. "Leaving here after Throckmorton's funeral was a mistake on my part." He shot an angry glare Paul's way. "I should've protected you against that bas—"

"Don't call my husband foul names." Emma exerted pressure on his hand. "It's too late for might-have-been's. Paul and I are married now, and we should all make the best of it."

Her uncle grimaced. "Would that I could.

Rousseau blood runs cold in his veins. Beware of his intentions."

"That's unfair. His intentions seem honorable enough. No one forced him to marry me, you know."

Rankin wasn't to be swayed. "What about the fire?"

"Paul says he isn't guilty, and I . . ." She disliked being selfish, but her present situation had to take precedence. There was no changing the past; she had to look out for the future. "I'd rather not discuss it."

"He'll hurt you, Emmie, and—"

"I believe I'm next," Howard cut in. "Must dance with the bride, you know."

Boulogne followed suit. *"Pardon,* but I wish you to know, I'm sorry you married another. I always thought that you and I might—"

"Doctor! I never thought such a thing." She smiled at her husband, who was patting Aunt Tillie's hand. "This is my wedding day, and you shouldn't spoil it."

"Forgive me. Out of line, I was."

Relieved, she said, "Now that you've signed my certification, I'm going to set up practice in St. Martinsville. My husband's allowed me to be very generous with my personal funds, so I've bought medical supplies rather than a trousseau to honor our marriage."

"A strange man he is. I would have bought you both the supplies and the trousseau."

The incessant tapping on his shoulder brought Boulogne to a halt. Emma turned into another man's arms. Over her shoulder, she saw Cleopatra laughing with Paul.

The mammy was exuberant with her own happiness; Cleopatra had found an old love, a man called Ben, and Emma was pleased for the two of them.

There was a tap on her partner's shoulder, and one by one, the other gentlemen took their turns at dancing with the bride. Emma smiled and laughed, and occasionally cast longing-filled glances at her husband. Uncle Rankin's prediction was filed into the back of her mind.

Dinner went smoothly, but lasted forever. She was aching to be in Paul's arms again. At least he sat beside her, his leg finding ways to twine with hers. As his hand canvassed her thigh, her heart beat wildly.

"Let's get out of here," he whispered in her ear, his breath drawing from her a delighted shiver.

"The cake. We'll leave as soon as we cut it."

He rose to his feet. "My wife and I thank you for this pleasant reception," he announced to the others at the table, "but surely you can appreciate that we need to get that cake divided up. Emma here has been begging me to take her to the bridal chamber, and—ouch!" He moved his injured foot aside. "Pardon me. I meant my bride grows weary from the festivities."

A round of laughter filled the air. Yet Uncle Rankin didn't join in; his face was set in a scowl.

Aunt Tillie rose to her feet, fluttering her hands. "Dear me, it is getting late. It's back to the ballroom for all of us. Come along, Rankin darling."

"Us too," Paul murmured in his wife's ear. "By the way, have I ever told you how much I like the way you shiver when I blow in your ear?"

"No."

"It pleases me, as I know it does you." His hand on

231

the small of her back, he herded her into the ballroom.

The wedding cake, a fruited concoction with white icing, was tiered into five layers. Paul's big palm, warm and powerful, covered Emma's small hand as they drew a silver knife through the bottom layer. As she fed him a bite, his teeth nipped at her fingers. Thinking about his lips on her bare flesh, she tingled with anticipation.

Cleopatra adjusted the many-feathered hat that dwarfed her petite body. "You gonna stand there all night, or is you gonna let an expert do the cake-cutting?"

Emma handed over the knife and leaned to place a quick kiss on her mammy's cheek. "Sometimes I think you're in collusion with my husband."

"Tee-hee." Cleopatra jabbed Paul's stomach with her elbow, as if they shared a private joke. "Why'd you think I told the master about what you and Frenchie done that night in his hotel room?"

Emma rolled her eyes. "Sometimes I think—"

"If he be mine, I'd be getting my clothes changed so's I could get him alone in that fancy room of his. Now don't you go to looking at me like that, missy. You be tired, remember?"

"Remember?" Paul put in, winking at Cleopatra. "Heretics!"

From the corner of her eye, Emma spied Aunt Tillie and Marian making an exit. They had offered to help her change into her traveling suit, so Emma surmised that now was the time to do as Cleopatra had suggested, and as both she and Paul wanted. "I'll just be a moment, *amoureux.*"

232

Bouquet in hand, she made for her room. After topping the staircase, she floated down the hall. Raised voices from behind her bedroom door stopped her.

"Someone ought to tell her!" Marian said.

There was a moment of silence before Aunt Tillie spoke. "Oh Lordy, my head is aching over this. Can't think straight."

"You never think straight, Tillie Oliver. But try this time for Emma's sake. One of us has to tell her about it."

Her hand shook. What was going on? Whatever it was, it wasn't good. She turned the knob and pushed the door open with the heel of her palm. "What do I need to know?"

Chapter Fifteen

"It's about Paul," Marian said slowly, too slowly, as she shook her head.

"What about him?" Emma crossed the room, stopping in front of her cousin-by-marriage. *"What about him!"*

"Now, Emma, I'm sure it's not as bad as it sounds," Aunt Tillie said. "Dear me, I need to lie down. My head is pounding."

"Well then, lie down," Emma said, abandoning her usual patience with her aunt. She turned back to the widow, and brushed a tear from Marian's cheek. "Tell me."

Marian sank into a chair and buried her face. "It's . . . Oh, I don't want to hurt you." Troubled sincerity was evident in each word. "I—I'm not a learned woman like you are, but my years with William taught me a few points of the law. His being a lawyer like Howard, you understand."

"Does this have to do with the fire?" Emma asked, and, from the bed, Aunt Tillie exhaled a sob.

"In a way." Marian rubbed her eyes. "Ever since you announced your engagement, I've been worried.

You see . . . well, it's just that . . . a wife can't testify against her husband in a court of law."

It was as if Emma were suddenly removed from herself. She felt hollow, bloodless. "H-he . . . Paul's not a lawyer. He doesn't . . . he probably doesn't know about it."

"I think he does. A few minutes ago, I asked Howard if it were true. He clamped his mouth shut—you know how he can be sometimes. Anyway, I put it to him as if I knew Paul was aware of that point of law. He . . . he admitted something when I pressed him about it. Days ago, he told Paul you couldn't testify against him if you two were married."

Her wedding ring suddenly heavy on her left hand, Emma dropped the bouquet.

"Paul's too nice to use our girl," Aunt Tillie said.

"I hope my fears are groundless." Marian raised her head and locked eyes with the bride. "I mean it."

"I'm sure you do." Emma shed her veil, throwing it to the floor. "But I would've appreciated your mentioning this before the wedding, not after."

"I wanted to be certain before I made accusations. I . . . I'm sorry."

"Not nearly as sorry as I am."

Unmindful that she hadn't changed from her wedding dress, Emma turned on her heel to stomp out of the room and down the stairs. Along with the other guests, Paul, smiling and expectant, was waiting at the foot.

"Let's go," she said tersely.

The wedding party gasped in unison.

No matter how much Paul tried to pry the

problem out of his wife, she refused to speak to him as they rode to the St. Charles. He was stymied. How could so warm a woman suddenly turn into an iceberg?

In the room that had been his, and was now theirs, she kept her mouth clamped. Her silence, Paul realized, was much more effective than the most fiery argument.

Posture straight as a poker, Emma sat down on a chair. He bent to take the dainty white slippers from her feet and tried to touch her ankle. She kicked his shin.

The kick added little to the physical discomfort he was feeling; he was suffering. And he was furious with her, but this was their wedding night, a time to hold and be held. He didn't want either of them to look back on it with regrets.

Watching her try to ignore him, he stripped away his coat, cravat, and shirt to place them neatly in the armoire. His evening shoes went in next.

"Perhaps," he said, going down on one knee in front of her, "if we discuss what's troubling you, we can work it out."

She shook her head and started to cross her arms over her chest, but he wrapped his fingers around her right hand. He felt her flinch at the pressure, but he placed his opposite palm over her wrist. Her hand was so small and delicate within his big, rope-roughened one.

Beautiful, that was Emma. His fair-haired wife. The spitfire who had enchanted him from the moment he'd laid eyes on her . . . in this very room.

"The management's gone to a lot of trouble to

236

make this night special for us. Candles, champagne, a plate of cold meats and cheese. Smooth silk sheets. Shouldn't we make use of those amenities?"

She gritted her teeth in response.

"You're right." He brought her palm to his lips, brushing it lightly. "Whatever is special has to come from us. Me and you." He released her small hand. "We'll have but one wedding night, and wouldn't it be better to make it one to cherish?"

At once, she yanked her knee upward between his thighs, striking his chin. He reeled with pain, and she pounced from the chair.

"There. Now you have a special memory of your wedding night!"

By degrees he uncoiled to a standing position. He had never struck a woman in his life, and he wouldn't now. But he was mighty close to doing it. "I'm going to ask you one more time. What's the matter with you!"

Hugging her arms, she stared out the window. "I hate you."

"No. You don't. Far from it. Hate is nothing but a word spoken in anger. Your body speaks a different language."

"That's just a weakness. I'm sure I'll recover from it." She paused. "But I don't know if I'll recover from what you've done." She whirled around, and her eyes were chips of green ice. "You used me."

"What!"

"You married me to stay out of jail."

The memory of Howard's suggestion washed over him, and he lowered his head. "Did Howard tell you that?"

237

"Never mind where I found out."

"It's not true. Whatever you heard. It's not true."

"The odds aren't on your side, Paul. But aren't we lucky? You have what you want—the prosecutor's case against you is weak. And I have a name for my child, in case there is one, though I pray there isn't."

She was lashing out due to her pain, he knew, and he understood her anger. "I'll admit Howard told me a wife can't testify against her husband, but I told him I wouldn't hide behind my wife's apron. I didn't set that fire, so I have nothing to hide." Well, not quite *nothing*. "My legal problems aren't related to why I asked you to marry me."

"Why—and please be honest—did you force me into this marriage? Surely you didn't do it just to give me protection from social censure."

"I wanted to be with you," he replied, half in truth. "You're . . . you're the woman I chose to share my name"—he grinned and motioned toward the tester bed—"and that, too."

Yearning for his lovemaking, Emma considered his answer. With all her heart, she wanted to believe Paul's tender words. She turned back to the window, raised the sash, and threw open the shutters. The slightly mildewed scent of the riverside city fluttered through the room. She thought about her own reasons for marrying.

Crazy though it was, she loved, and wanted to be with, Paul. But that hadn't been the primary reason for this match. In a way she was using him, too. If there was a child, she wanted it to have a father—a full-time father.

To make this marriage work, she had better show some trust. Placing undue emphasis on trouble was

238

asking for more of it. Why ruin their wedding night further? Now that she had given the matter some thought, Emma realized that Marian was a gossip—many of her tales lost credibility in the retelling. Paul might be speaking the truth.

Resting her palms on the sill, she said, "I shouldn't have taken my anger out on you physically."

"And I should've told you, before we wed, what Howard had to say."

She sighed, then glanced over her shoulder, a sorrowful quarter-smile easing her features. "Did you mean it . . . about marrying me because you wanted us to be together?"

"I won't repeat myself. You heard me the first time." Paul closed the distance between them, and clasped her elbows. Leaning to her ear, he felt her quiver as he whispered huskily, "Let's go to our marriage bed. I long to make you Madame Rousseau in fact as well as name."

Her cheek touched the hard strength of his arm. "I . . . I'd like that."

"Ah, my angel . . . thank you." Paul swept one hand beneath her knees, the other cradled her back; and he carried her to the foot of the bed.

As he released her to stand before him, their gazes met. She fingered his arm; he, her cheek. They both yearned to ignore the past and enjoy the present.

"As lovely as you look in your wedding gown, I ache to see you without it."

"It's your right . . . and my wish."

Slowly, treacle slowly, he unfastened the top button of her gown, then worked his way downward.

It was impossible for Emma, hungry with antici-

239

pation, to breathe. His fingers were lingering, caressing her flesh. As if she were a precious doll, he undressed her. As he freed each lace, he placed a kiss behind its hook, on the chemise's soft lawn. Finally, the corset fell to the floor at their feet, and he pulled the underdress over her hair, undoing the mass of blond curls. The ties of her pantaloons gave, and to steady her, he placed her palms on his back as he took that final garment from her ankles.

"Mine, all mine . . . You are so beautiful." Squeezing her hands, he stepped back.

"And so, my darling, are you." She stepped closer, felt the hardness of him. "Now it's my turn to undress you. . . ."

Her hands weren't nearly as steady as his as she worked the buttons of his breeches or as she bent to help him step out of them. Her face near the crisp hairs of his shins, she felt the urge to flick her tongue against his leg. Why not? They were husband and wife. She leaned forward. Why be inhibited?

Hearing his masculine moan, she smiled and looped her arms behind his calves. She felt his fingers comb through her tresses. Her tongue made tiny circles on a tanned, hirsute shinbone. His flesh tasted clean and manly, and the short black hairs tickled her nose.

"You fire me, *m'amoureuse.*"

Leaning her head back, she smiled again. Her vision was impeded—and she liked it.

"Enough of your teasing," he murmured, bringing her against his chest before placing her on the bed.

The mattress dipped as he settled himself into the cradle of her arms. It felt so good, so right to be there!

His kiss was at first gentle, but she urged aggression. She ached for their joining, yearned to drown in that place where there were no thoughts of yesterday or tomorrow.

"How about some of your . . . teasing? Now! I'm afire for you, husband."

Like a man possessed, he touched his lips to her cheek, her ear.

She quivered as he whispered, "Are you sure, *ma bien-aimée,* you want me to finish consummating this union?"

"If you don't, I think I shall cry."

"I've never seen you cry," he said, his voice low and deep, as he poised above her.

"I don't cry. Usually." She teased his legs with the inside of her ankle. "Are you going to force me to tears, Paul?"

Running his lips across hers, he said, "No!"

He pressed his manhood against her as she raised for him. Inhaling, she sheathed his bigness. "Don't be so reverent," she chided, her voice husky with passion. "You should know by now I won't break from your ardent touch."

He grinned before leaning to bite her earlobe. "Lusty vixen!"

Her nails dug into his shoulders, and her voice was laced with unbridled desire. "Yes . . . oh yes."

Losing control, they were wild for one another, neither able to get enough. He drove and drove and she wrapped her legs around his waist. Their rhythms meshed, completely attuned, as time swept onward. Once, and then again and again, explosions of euphoria radiated within her. And finally she felt his body tense even more as he gripped her hips.

Groaning a phrase in French, he reached his climax.

Still tangled in his arms, she asked, "What do you call it, Paul, when we . . . when that funny feeling assails us?"

"Lust."

"Not that. I'm talking about the explosion I feel . . . and when you become the most excited?"

"Ah, Madame Rousseau, in French it's *le petite mort.*"

"The little death?"

"Yes." He grinned and bent to kiss the rise of her breast. "And you'd better get used to it," he said, holding her.

"Is this any way to start a honeymoon?" Paul asked the next morning. In the afterglow of lovemaking, he lay on his back amid the rumpled sheets, Emma astride him. "You'd rather go to that chamber of horrors called a clinic than to be with your poor sex-starved husband?"

"You are pitiful." She chuckled and tickled his ribcage. "You promised before our marriage that I could pursue my career, as I remember, and I do have a good memory, you insatiable beast."

"You're a fine one to talk about insatiable, and if you don't stop tickling me, dammit, I'm going to renege on my promise . . . for today anyway." He insinuated his hips against her derrière. "On second thought, please don't stop."

"Have to. I should've been seeing patients an hour ago." She took her hands away. Combing her fingers through her hair, she swung her leg off Paul and jumped out of bed. Shamelessly, she lifted her breasts with her palms and moistened her lips. "Nevertheless, eat your heart out."

She had never seen him move so fast.

Two more hours passed before she set foot in Boulogne's clinic. In an understated frock of gingham and with her hair pulled back in a bun, she was cool and professional in her duties. Though perhaps the canary-eating cat's smile that kept curving her lips was a giveaway that she was newly married.

Emma rewrapped a bandage, moved to the next bed, and looked down on little Myrtle Ann. "Feeling better today, honey?" she asked while bending to check the dressing Dr. Boulogne had apparently already changed.

"Yes, ma'am. I guess. But my leg hurts—sorta like it's still there."

"That's to be expected."

Myrtle Ann's lower lip quivered. "Once I get a whole lot better, how'm I gonna get around without my leg?"

Did this sort of question ever get easier to answer? Emma wondered. "You'll be fitted with a peg. It's going to take a lot of practice and even more courage, but you'll learn to walk just fine."

"No! I can't. I don't want to. The other children'll tease me and call me Peg Leg. And boys won't like me."

"It won't be as bad as you think. Be thankful you're a girl—your skirts will cover the peg." Emma put a comforting hand to the girl's brow. "Besides, you're too young to be thinking about boys; and by the time you're old enough, you'll be a master at walking. I'll bet my bottom dollar some nice man

243

will look past your handicap and see the goodness inside you."

"Do you really think so?"

"Absolutely."

"How can you be sure?"

"My mother lost her leg when she was seventeen. My father was her doctor . . . they married a year later. Now she has a houseful of children."

"Well, I can't marry you." Myrtle Ann grinned. "You're a girl."

"Myrtie?"

"Katie!"

Emma looked around to spot the source of the interruption, and the blood rushed from her face. Standing beside the child's bed was the woman who had stolen the brooch! The woman Paul had retrieved it from. Katie!

Apparently she didn't recognize Emma. She merely nodded, set a basket beside the bed, and pulled a chair up to sit by Myrtle Ann. "I brought you something to eat, little one. Those fruit cakes you like so much."

"I'm not very hungry, but thank you." Myrtle Ann turned her eyes to her doctor. "This is my friend Katie. She used to take care of me sometimes, but she moved away and she's living too far from me to come by my house very often."

"I see." Emma was itching to get Katie the Good to the side so she could ask her a few well-phrased questions.

Myrtle Ann turned her freckled face toward her visitor. "And this is Dr. Oliver. She helped cut off my leg, but I'm not mad at her about it. She put a piece of gauze on my face and I had to smell some stinky stuff, but I went to sleep and didn't feel it when they chopped off my leg."

Katie's hazel eyes rounded. "Asleep?"

"Yes. The doctor, she's nice."

"You're a lucky young lady to have so nice a doctor," the visitor said while smoothing the girl's brow.

"Oh yes, I think so." Myrtle Ann then said, "Guess what! Her mother's a peg leg, too!"

There was no use getting into that, so Emma extended her hand. "Nice to meet you. I'm Dr. Emma Rousseau." The name sounded strange on her lips. Strange, yet nice. And the mention of it drew no reaction from the woman. "Perhaps I could have a word with you, after you've visited with Myrtle Ann?"

Having received Katie's polite consent, Emma moved on to the next patient, but she kept her within sight. Ten minutes later she spied Katie obviously dodging out of the proposed meeting. She followed her to the street, catching her a half a block away.

Grabbing Katie's arm, she said, "Remember me?"

"No. I've never seen you before."

"Then why were you running?" Emma received no reply. "Shall I refresh your memory? It was night. In front of the St. Charles Hotel. You and your—" Emma had been about to say accomplice, but had thought better of it. "You and Packert stole a brooch from my cloak."

"I don't know anything about it."

"That's not true. My husband told me he got it back from you. He's Paul Rousseau. Do you recall him?"

Katie's hazel eyes rounded. "You're married to

245

Monsieur Rousseau?"

Emma smiled despite herself. "Yes. As of yesterday."

"Congratulations. Um, I mean best wishes. My mother would be ashamed that I made such a blunder."

Emma was baffled. There was an elegance to this woman, a sheer majesty that belied her thieving ways. Why would she—young and beautiful and possessed of the social graces—have aligned herself with such as that old pickpocket Packert? And why had she become a party to his misdeeds?

Emma Frances, don't be naive, she chided herself. This Katie could very well be the instigator rather than the follower.

"Could we sit down and talk?" she asked.

Katie nodded, and they walked to a bench in a nearby garden. Bougainvilleas, just-budding roses, and evergreens surrounded them.

"This is a beautiful place," Katie commented.

"I agree. But—"

"Your husband is a very handsome man."

A thread of jealousy tightened in Emma. "How well do you know him?"

"Don't look at me askance. I met him but once." Katie smoothed the skirt of her tattered gown. "When he came to the house I share with Packert and discussed my fa— When he came to visit Packert."

"What was the purpose of Paul's visit?"

"I . . . I don't know."

Emma figured she wasn't getting the entire truth. "Who was my husband discussing before he claimed the brooch?"

246

"My father. An evil man." Katie's breath quivered. "The talk had to do with his misdeeds against the Texas Navy, I believe."

"Who is your father?"

Nervously Katie fiddled with her hands. "If you don't mind," she murmured, "I'd rather not discuss the man who caused my birth."

Realizing that this woman's history was none of her business, Emma didn't importune Katie, but she was startled when the beautiful brunette suddenly said: "Your husband isn't guilty of setting the Oliver Factor House aflame."

"Wh-what do you mean?"

"I read the charge in the *Picayune*." Katie wet her lips nervously. "But I know he didn't set fire to that warehouse. Packert did it."

"Packert?" Emma repeated incredulously. Paul wasn't guilty! Paul wasn't guilty! Her heart sang with that knowledge. *Oh, my beloved, I wronged you, and you told the truth.*

"Tell me the particulars," Emma urged.

"I don't know them." There was sincerity in the brunette's voice. "I only know what Packert told me later. He has . . . he has reason to hate the man who owned the factor house, and he was set on destroying the building."

Why would Packert hate Uncle Rankin? Telling herself not to be foolish, Emma realized that no person, no matter how strong in character, was without enemies.

"We'll have to go to the authorities. The culprit must be punished."

"That's impossible. Packert sailed away from Louisiana. But if he returned and found out

247

I'd . . . I'd served him ill, I shudder to think what he'd do to me. His temper is violent."

"If you fear him, why did you tell me about my husband's innocence?"

"Because . . . I . . . I like Monsieur Rousseau, and I yearned for a way to clear his name without accusing the man who owns me."

"Owns you?" Emma shook her head in bewilderment.

"I am a woman without rights—the blood of Africa runs through my veins. My white father sold me to Henry Packert."

"Oh, Katie . . ."

"I don't want your sympathy; I just stated a fact." The lovely brunette held her head high. "Despite his temper, Packert has treated me well, all things considered. In his own way he cares for me, and that is the first loving emotion I've known in my life." She paused. "As for Monsieur Rousseau, I—"

Emma baited her by saying, "If my husband's name can't be cleared, he'll most probably receive a prison sentence . . . if not the gallows."

"My conscience plagues me, for I don't want to see an innocent man suffer for a crime he did not commit." Katie sobbed. "I don't know what to do. I cannot tell the police, but if there were some way—"

Emma could taunt her no more. "Paul will not pay for Packert's misdeed. I am his accuser, or I was until our marriage."

The tall woman shook her head in confusion. "I don't understand."

"Rankin Oliver is my uncle. It was I who witnessed Paul running around the corner of the building."

"That would make you . . . I read in the newspaper . . . You must be . . ." A veil fell over her eyes. "You'd have to be Emma Oliver."

"Yes. Now Mrs. Paul Rousseau."

"Life has many strange twists and turns," Katie said with a touch of irony as she stood. "In spite of your connection to the Oliver family you've taken Monsieur Rousseau to husband, so you must have believed in his innocence."

Emma flushed.

Katie reached down to take her hand. "I know him not well, but I perceived his character at our one meeting. Your Paul is a man driven by his convictions, and he is relentless in his pursuits. But there is a gentleness within him, a kindness, as it were. Return his kindness, and you shall be rewarded with a lifetime of happiness." She smiled, but it was a melancholy expression. "I offer my congratulations, and this time there is no apology. Any woman who captures the heart and soul of Paul Rousseau has won herself a prize."

Poised and graceful, the unfortunate woman departed.

Emma walked back to the clinic to finish her rounds. That accomplished, she collected her reticule and thoughts. Katie had been right about Paul. Beneath his arrogance and his drive, he was a prize worth holding. Making for the St. Charles Hotel, she felt guilty for doubting him.

Now it was time to eat humble pie.

Chapter Sixteen

Humble pie turned out to be quite satisfying.
Emma was astounded. When she had confessed to
Paul, saying, "I know you're innocent, and I'm sorry
for doubting you," she had expected harsh words, at
the very least.

But he smiled and said, "I forgive you."

That had been a week ago.

Now aboard the *Virgin Vixen* for the trip to the
plantation, Feuille de Chêne, she took an adoring
look at her husband. His hands on his waist, he
stood before the mast. The breeze blowing through
the secret bayou pass into south Louisiana swamp-
land plastered the soft material of his loose-fitting
shirt to his muscular torso and arms, and ruffled his
curly hair. His tight breeches outlined his trim hips
in a most alluring way. From the top of his head to
the heels of his boots, he looked every inch a rakish,
swashbuckling pirate.

Marriage, she thought as he bent to man the
anchor, was the grandest situation on earth.

Paul thought so, too. How easy it had been,
though strange to his inner makeup, to forgive

Emma when she had blamed him for the fire. In a way he hadn't faulted her. She had believed him guilty, and had done what she thought right.

His callused hands stinging from his efforts to lower the anchor, he stood erect. Swamp, dark yet fascinating, surrounded the pass, and warblers' sweet songs mixed with the loose-banjo-string croaks of green frogs. Cypress stumps littered the banks, along with gently swaying Spanish moss. It had been years—possibly forever?—since Paul had felt such peace.

He turned to his wife. He could have, time allowing, stared at her for hours on end. She wore simple clothing today—a white blouse of soft cotton and a green linen skirt. And only the very minimum of underpinnings, he knew, was beneath those outer garments. Though he enjoyed unlacing her corset, he disliked the contraption for the discomfort it gave her, and had requested that she toss it overboard; she had been pleased to comply.

Mussed hair blowing in the breeze, Emma was leaning back against the rail, her breasts and slightly sprawled legs beckoning him. Vixen! Unvirgin vixen. God, how he adored her. She was the stuff fantasies were drawn from. But she wasn't a figment of his imagination. Emma was a wonder.

"I feel sorry for Katie," she said, slamming him out of his musings. "She seems to love that vermin Packert."

"Ah, my sweet, stranger things have happened."

One of them happened immediately when Emma said, "She said you'd called on that rat to talk about a man who was undercutting the Texan cause. Why

251

did you meet with Packert to discuss Katie's father?"

Katie's father? Paul dropped the line he was holding. He had visited the old sea rover to get the goods on *Rankin Oliver* . . . who had to be the octoroon's father! Apparently he was the one who'd sold Katie to Packert. Paul had difficulty swallowing his anger, and he now understood why the pirate hated Rankin. Did that murdering traitor have any good traits?

It was hard to believe that Emma was of the same blood. Though he had misjudged her at times—and she could be a true viper at others—he admired her ability to forgive and forget, as well as her stalwart convictions. No, he wouldn't hold her lineage against her. He would hold himself against her. . . .

"Ma bien-aimée, don't trouble yourself with Texas Navy business." Paul approached from behind, and wrapped his arms around her waist. "Warm enough?" He bent to nuzzle her ear. "I could make it warmer."

Her shiver was elicited by his nearness, not the chill evening air. "Please do."

She turned into his arms to accept, and return, his torrid kiss. As if there were no tomorrow, as if they didn't have a lifetime for lovemaking, he lifted her into his arms and carried her to the cabin below, to their honeymoon haven, where they were immediately enveloped in arousal, ardor, and wild loving. And, a long time later, breathless satisfaction.

Amid satin sheets spiced by the scent of them both, and to the gentle lap of water against the sloop,

252

Emma awoke the next morning. Sunlight radiated through the portholes; and Paul, dressed in black woolen breeches and soft shirt of cambric, stood with his back to her, one hand bracing the opposite elbow.

"What are you pondering?" she asked.

He turned and smiled. It wasn't his usual grin; it seemed rather grim. Stepping to the bed, he leaned down to brush a lock of hair behind her ear. "Today, Madame Rousseau, we arrive in St. Martinsville."

From his tone, she knew something was amiss. "I thought you were pleased to claim your grandfather's estate."

Paul sat on the edge of the wide bunk. "I vowed a long time ago never to return to Feuille de Chêne." He paused. "I disliked Grandpère."

"Tell me about him," she prompted as he fell to silence and studied the ceiling.

"He was unfair to my father."

"And to you?"

"I held my own with old Remi. But I blame him for turning away from my father when his help was needed most. Papa had lost heavily at the faro tables, and we were forced off my maternal grandparents' plantation. My mother was dying, so Papa asked Grandpère if he'd take us in. Old Remi wouldn't do it. I'll never forget the look of despair on Papa's face."

This vulnerability in Paul, so out of character for him, drew her closer. "You loved Étienne a lot, didn't you?"

"That goes without saying." Paul blew a stream of breath upward. "Anyway, since you're my wife I

253

thought you had a right to know about my grandfather."

She ached for her husband, yet she had never felt so close to him. "There's something . . . You know, we've never truly discussed what happened between your father and Uncle Rankin."

"Some things are better left unsaid." He turned to straighten clothing that did not need such attention.

Pressing him on the matter wasn't timely, she realized. But he had been willing to talk about Remi Rousseau. "The way you feel about your grandfather, I can't help wondering why you took the plantation over."

"Il me faut de l'argent."

"Paul! Speak English. What do you mean?"

"Money. I must have money." He grinned. "Anyway, you're in French-speaking territory, Emma. You'd better get used to a foreign tongue."

"The only foreign tongue I want is yours."

He leaned over to tweak her nose. "You hussy!"

She started to make a fitting retort, but it was not often that they enjoyed such moments of communication; she'd make use of this one. "What do you mean about money?"

"I'm not a rich man, Emma. I hope you didn't expect wealth."

"I didn't. Wealth wasn't a consideration." She'd married him because she loved him. Basically.

"Enough of this maudlin talk." Tenderly he slapped her derrière. "Rise and shine, madame. We need to make Feuille de Chêne before sundown tonight."

"Wouldn't you rather make love?"

On the brink of acceding, he stood stock-still. Half a minute later, he said, "Woman, you'll be the undoing of me, I swear. And what a sorry excuse for a second mate you are, lying abed all morning when we need to weigh anchor."

"Your sensitivity floors me," she shot back, laughing, and threw a pillow at his head. "And what happened to appreciation?" She held her palms aloft. "Just look at these poor hands. Surely I'm deserving of a little reward for helping you sail here."

He surrendered. "So appreciation and reward are what you're after?" Tickling her naked breast, he said, "Oh, insatiable temptress, I do believe I can handle that. . . ."

The next day they sailed the last leg of the journey.

Spiked cane, low-growing palmetto and moss-tented live oaks of mammoth proportions lined the banks. Everywhere were shadows as dark and mysterious as the deep waters of the Teche itself.

Paul told her about the Cajun migration from Canada to the area over a hundred years previously, and about the influx of Royalists after the Reign of Terror in France. And she liked the bayou. Despite the occasional grand home and lawn that cut through its untamed beauty, it was an unspoiled wilderness of flora and fauna.

An alligator sliced into the water, starting toward the sloop, but Paul, muscles straining, manned the sails and the *Virgin Vixen* outdistanced the reptile.

Shivering, yet relieved that the reptile was almost out of sight, Emma asked, "How did this bayou get its name?"

"The Attapakas Indians called it Tenche. Snake. Legend has it a huge serpent once terrorized these Indians, and they shot it full of arrowheads. When they ran out of those, they took to clubs. In its death throes the snake cut wide grooves in the soil that filled with water." He grinned. "Must've been one hell of a snake."

"I'll say." Emma went back to her sailoring duties.

Around the bend, Paul told her, was Feuille de Chêne. "I sent word to the overseer to put the place to rights," he added.

She was full of anticipation. This new home, so different from the James River of her past, was the start of a new life, but right now she looked forward to a good hot bath.

As the sloop's prow banked left to follow the wide, meandering river, shadows departed and sunlight fell on the *Virgin Vixen*. A weatherbeaten, sagging jetty angled into the water. Speechless, Emma eyed her new home and inhaled a sharp draught of air.

"What the! . . ." Paul grabbed the rail. "The damned thing's falling down!"

They hurried to land. Indeed the brick mansion of Feuille de Chêne was no longer palatial. The paint on the columns and the wide veranda was chipped and peeling, windows were smashed, and shutters sagged like rejected lovers' shoulders. Furthermore, vandals had sacked the house, stealing everything of value that could be carried away.

The overseer was nowhere to be found, and they learned that he had been gone for months. All but twelve of the fifty field workers had escaped. The canebrakes had not been tended and were overgrown.

256

Emma realized that making the home comfortable and the fields profitable would necessitate taking time from her medical endeavors, but she was willing to make the sacrifice. She had to. It was her duty, and she would be proud to expend the effort for Paul and herself.

Her spouse, it was glaringly apparent, wasn't so optimistic. After unloading the *Virgin Vixen*, he refused to discuss the plantation. He even refused dinner, and wrapped himself in the embrace of alcohol.

"Don't want any light," he said, his speech slurred, when she brought a candle into the library.

The scent of dust long settled, as well as the aroma of rice paper and aged parchment, bit at her nostrils.

Cobwebs hanging over his head, Paul sat behind a faded gilt desk, and his hands were clenched around a whiskey glass. "Go away," he bellowed. "Wanna be alone."

Stepping over the books scattered on the floor, Emma went to her husband. "Come to bed, darling. I'm sure everything won't seem so awful in the morning."

"Ha! It'll be worse." He poured spirits remaining in the bottle into his glass. "This place is worth nothing."

"We'll put it back in order," she said. "It'll take time, but we'll do it."

"I don't have time." Paul quaffed the bourbon. He was tired of subterfuge. She would know sooner or later about his intentions, and sooner was better than later. Yet he couldn't look his wife in the eye. "Need to sell this place."

"I can understand your wanting to get rid of your

grandfather's property, but why do you *need* to sell it?"

"The Texas Navy needs money."

"Come on, Paul," she scolded, perching on the desktop. "Surely you don't intend to give up your inheritance for some idealistic cause."

"Certainly do." He didn't expect her to understand. He didn't want her to! He lifted his eyes and hated the crushed look on her face. Right then he regretted bringing Emma into this mess, but there was no quitting now. "Nothing will stop me from furthering the Texan cause. Not you, not anything."

Wariness etched a line between her brows. "So you'll give yourself and your money selflessly to that nation of misfits and lawbreakers—"

"Spoken like a true Oliver."

Wondering about it but ignoring the comment, she went on. "Till death do us part is a long time, husband."

"I married you for better or for worse. You're just getting a taste of what's to come."

"And what is that?"

"Who knows? Maybe I'll go back to sea."

Emma felt as if she had been slapped. The ring on her finger was a reminder of the vows they had spoken. Why would he give her this heirloom, his name, and protection if he was so eager to go back to sea?

She forced herself to face whatever truth he was, in his drunken ramblings, trying to convey. "Are you asking for a divorce?"

"What's"—he lifted a shoulder—"the use of staying married?"

"I seem to recall you've found several uses for

me," she bit out, lacing each word with emphasis.

"So right, *chérie*. Many uses. But the one I married you for is . . . well, it's in ruins."

"Get to the point, Paul."

"I needed a wife to inherit this property." His voice was surprisingly sober. "It'll take a year to get the title. In the meantime I'd planned to mortgage it. Now it's not worth a plugged nickel."

Through a haze of emotional agony, she asked, "You married me . . . for a year? And just to get your hands on this place?"

"That's what I said. Just to get my hands on this place."

Hurt turned to fury. "You've not been trustworthy since the day we met," she retorted, "but I never dreamed you had no respect for the vows we spoke before God."

He ducked his head. "I never said anything about divorce. You can go back to Virginia or New Orleans or wherever you please, and tell everyone you're a widow." He tossed down the half-inch of whiskey remaining in his glass. "I'll stay out of sight."

"How convenient. You've got it all signed, sealed, and delivered." Chilblains seemed to throb in her hands and feet. "And if I do take off for parts unknown, what does that do to your neat little scheme? Won't you need a legal wife for the next year?"

"Scheme's over."

Emma's fury turned to disgust. "Uncle Rankin tried to warn me about you. I should've taken the word of a good man."

"Good man? Ha! You wouldn't know one if you

saw one. Your uncle, paragon though you make him, is nothing but a murdering traitor." Paul chuckled mirthlessly. "He murdered my father in cold blood. Conspired with Papa's second to tamper with the pistol's firing mechanism. I couldn't prove it—Rankin hustled the man out of town that same day. Thirteen years, Emma—thirteen long years I've been out to get him."

She couldn't believe what she was hearing. Paul did bear a grudge against her uncle!

"Last January in Sisal I thought I had him," he was saying. "Your darling uncle's mistress was gathering evidence to prove he'd sold arms to the Centralists. But he smashed her skull to keep her quiet." His face and fists whitened. "I held her dying body, and her blood mingled with my hatred. She looked into my eyes and murmured 'Oliver' just before she died."

Emma abandoned the desktop and backed away. "Lies! You've made a mistake. Those things can't be true."

"Oh but they are, *chérie*. And someday I'll prove them."

Immediately, he regretted those last words. He had promised himself not to seek revenge as long as he stayed married to Emma, which might be forever. On second thought—muddled though his thinking was—wasn't he releasing her from this farce? But in the depths of his soul he didn't want her to leave.

"What do you plan to do?" she asked in a hoarse voice.

"Nothing right now."

"Well, that's obvious. Right now you're not capable of doing more than passing out!"

He deserved that jab. "Emma," he said quietly. "You're my wife, and I don't want to hurt you. I promise I won't seek to discredit your uncle."

"What if you don't have to search for evidence?" she asked, believing such would not be the case. "What if it falls into your lap?"

"I hope that doesn't happen."

"I'll tell him. I owe him that much."

"Be my guest. But rest assured, Emma, he knows. As we speak, I'm sure he's covering his tracks."

Hurt and anger ran rampant throughout her heart and mind. She ached to strike out at him, to inflict a modicum of the pain she was suffering. But regardless of her threat, she couldn't go to Uncle Rankin. To do so would damn her husband. And her pride wouldn't allow that. Furthermore, that same pride wouldn't allow her to give up. She'd stay here, and she'd help Paul come to grips with his insanity.

He wanted the property, and it would take twelve months to clear the title. She had a year to change his mind. But now she had one more question that begged an answer.

Folding into a chair, she asked, "Feeling the way you do, why didn't you run him through when you had an opportunity?"

"I couldn't." He raked unsteady fingers through his curly hair. "We'd just made love for the first time. You'd broken through my guard, and touched me in a way my heart doesn't care to be touched."

Her spirits rose. For all the ugliness of the situation, maybe it was salvageable. Her eyes blazing into his, she watched him, seeing sadness, deep and tormented, reflected in his eyes. The proud lift to his shoulders sank, and he buried his chin against the wide chest she had taken comfort from over the past few days.

"What do you mean?" she asked. "About me breaking through your guard."

He yearned to shout out the truth. He loved her. It had to be love, this strange mixture of heaven and hell that had been with him since the moment they'd met. But he couldn't be honest. She needed to be protected from him and from the miserable existence he offered her.

He spoke slowly. "What I feel for you is like this bottle of whiskey. In the beginning it's full and fulfilling, but when you get to the bottom it's empty. I just haven't gotten to the bottom of you."

"You rat!" Her heart was shattering into a million sharp pieces. She wouldn't cry—wouldn't! It took all her strength not to. "Well, at least I have one thing to be thankful for," she said facetiously. "You certainly didn't marry me for my silence in court."

He lunged to his feet, the chair toppling behind him. "Right. Now leave me the hell alone." Spinning around, Paul slammed the heel of his fist against the bookcase. "Leave this place, Emma. Go home. I won't stop you."

She brought a shaking hand to her lips. Lies. Deceit. Manipulation. Paul was guilty of those three sins. Despite the vow she had made to herself only minutes ago, her instinct was to run, to flee as far as possible from this nightmare. But she wasn't going to run.

"I won't leave," she stated. "I'll give you a year, and I won't stop you from selling Feuille de Chêne. But when you've sobered up I think you'll see there's

262

something here, be it our relationship or the fields, worth cultivating."

"Don't be a martyr. Show some of that independence I admire in you."

"I wear no crown of thorns." She jumped to her feet and advanced toward him. "I told you not long after we met that I don't run from anything or anyone. I'm not going to start now, either. You wanted a wife, Mr. Rousseau, and you've got one. Now reap the harvest."

Forcing composure on herself, she left the library and made for the master suite. Once inside, she turned the lock, to be alone with cobwebs, dust, and inner anguish—except for Paul's fierce pounding at the door.

Huddled into the musty sheets, she squeezed her eyes shut. What had she agreed to! She had promised to remain his wife for the next year. Anything might happen in a year. Including—God forbid—a child. Perhaps one grew in her already.

That realization lashed through her with the sting of a cat-o'-nine. When she had made her pledge in the library, there had been only three points to this triangle of misery: herself, Paul, and Uncle Rankin. She wouldn't bring a fourth, an innocent child, into this!

For what seemed an eternity she listened to fists hammer against the door. Finally Paul ceased to torment her, and a nightmare-laden sleep took her away from the burning caldron of reality.

His head pounding and his stomach queasy, Paul awoke on the library's faded satin sofa. Empty bottles lay around him, his mouth tasted like dirty cotton, and his knuckles were scraped and sore. He took a moment to clear his head. Where was Emma, and why wasn't she with him? A partial replay of the previous night dawned on him. *Mon dieu,* he had told her everything!

"No," he moaned, despising himself.

Had she left? He fought for remembrance and recalled pounding on the bedroom door until his fist bled. Serves you right, he told himself.

Staggering outside, he inhaled restorative air. *You're a bastard, Rousseau. You've just ruined the only good thing that's ever happened to you.*

What could he do to rectify his actions? Apologize and try to make a home for Emma. The best one he could manage. It would take time and money to set this place to rights, but he was up to the challenge. He'd find the money somewhere.

If only Emma would forgive him . . .

In the tall grass to his right, Paul heard a puppy whine. That sound roused his curiosity, and he set aside his recriminations, momentarily. Wetting his cracked lips, Paul descended the veranda steps and walked toward the pup.

He parted the reeds to find a small white creature with long black ears. The pup quit gumming a piece of wood and looked up at him with limpid eyes. The dog appeared to be about six or seven weeks old. Paul picked it up by the scruff of the neck, holding it before his eyes.

Looking about for its mother, he brought the pup close to his chest and began to stroke its floppy ears. "Been abandoned, huh, fella?"

The dog found Paul's finger and began to suckle

it. "Let's see if we can't find you something to eat."

Remembering what Marian had said weeks ago, about Emma loving strays, Paul stared at the house's upper floor. A dog wouldn't be much of a peace offering, but at this point he had nothing to lose and maybe something to gain.

"Put that smelly hound down," Cleopatra ordered, wagging a finger at her husband.

"You be an ol' grunch, Cleo honey. He be cute," Ben Edwards said as he cuddled Woodley even closer to his broad chest. The big man was rewarded with a fast-widening wet spot on his shirt. He grinned and set the pup on the ground. "Sorta cute."

Emma laughed. It felt good to chuckle. Since Paul had presented her with the young dog two weeks previously there hadn't been much merriment at Feuille de Chêne. Then Cleopatra and Ben had arrived with the rest of her trousseau, and the medical equipment and supplies she had purchased with the remainder of her personal funds.

Woodley curled up at her feet. Emma had wanted to take Paul's gift of the pup as an affirmation that they still had a future together. When he'd gotten on his knees to apologize, she had been on the edge of giving in, but drunken truths were difficult to sweep under the rug.

In the aftermath she'd maintained a cool facade, and had kept her bedroom door locked against him, but her heart was aching. If there was anything to be thankful for, it was her monthly. She had gotten it the morning after their argument. In a way, though, she regretted that there'd be no child, and that regret was selfish!

"It be getting on noon, Ben," Cleopatra said. She wagged her finger in the direction of the cane field. "If you want your dinner you'd better go help Frenchie out there—you know you been wanting to talk to him. And take that mangy dog. My baby don't need no more messes around this house."

"You gonna pay for that bossy talk," Ben said wryly, and scooped Woodley back in his arms. "Tonight I gonna teach you a little obedience."

Cleopatra smiled and grinned. In the blink of an eye, she kicked his behind. "You the one gonna be taught respect."

"Whoa-key." He landed a kiss on his wife's cheek and headed for the canebrake.

Emma yearned for the kind of love Ben and her former mammy shared. Trusting, loving, teasing.

Her eyes dancing, Cleopatra shook her head. "Gotta tell men ever'thing."

"Not so with Paul." Emma turned to the pail of soap and water. Scrubbing woodwork with a passion, she knelt on the gallery floor. "He knows what he wants and goes after it."

"You ain't happy, are you?" Cleopatra touched her shoulder. "I know you be disappointed about the state of this place, but it ain't like you to let something get you down. What is it, baby?"

"It's not the place. I've no doubt that Paul'll get it squared away in record time—he's been working from sunrise to sunset with the field workers. And he spends the evenings repairing the house and working on the books." Emma dropped her chin. "Cleo . . . he tricked me. Tricked me in the worst way. He was lying from the beginning. He honestly believes there

266

was foul play involved in the duel between his father and my uncle, though he says since he's part of the family now he's not actively seeking revenge."

"Now listen here, missy. If your Daddy had been carried away from the dueling arena, you'd be saying the same thing. That's human nature. Nobody be wanting to believe their blood kin less than perfect, or less than victorious."

"Oh, Cleo, I realize that. I'm not so simpleminded that I went into this marriage with my eyes closed. I figured, as an Oliver, there might be problems marrying into the Rousseau family. And I can sympathize with Paul over his father's death, though by no stroke of the imagination do I believe Paul's version." Emma got to her feet and hugged her arms. "The most hurtful aspect is . . . He married me . . . Oh, there's no easy way to say this. I thought he loved me. He never said it, yet I thought he did. But he needed a wife to get his hands on this property. He's planning to sell it, and use the money for that ragtag Texas Navy."

"You gonna let him?"

"I can't stop him." Emma cast her eyes toward the brakes where Paul and the others toiled. "But that's not the whole problem. I need him to return my love. You know how he pursued me, and well . . . I was foolish enough to take lust for love."

"What about your feelings for him? Did you mistake lust for love?"

"Of course not."

Cleopatra placed a hand on her hipless form. "Then tell me what you *like* about him."

The initial images forming in Emma's mind could be attributed to sexual attraction. But that wasn't

267

the issue. There were a number of qualities she admired in Paul.

"He's brave—he doesn't back away from a challenge. He can be kind. He's lied to me . . . a lot, but I think he's prone to telling the truth. And he's not selfish; every cent he has, he's spending on refurbishing the house, and on clearing and planting fields. Even if it's only to make it salable, he's not doing it for himself. He really has a feeling for Texas and its people, though I don't agree with him. And he doesn't complain about my cooking."

"He *hasta* be in love."

Emma ignored the barb. "He has the makings of a decent man."

"I got faith in Frenchie; he loves you, I know it, but he probably ain't admitted it to himself yet. And lust ain't a bad way to start out. Love's been known to grow in the bedroom. Never knew nobody who started the other way around."

"What about my father and mother?" Emma tilted her head. "Their love didn't grow in a bedroom."

"Hmmph. Maybe your daddy started out by pitying Miss Noreen, but I be there at the time. I can tell you, she had plenty of lust in her big blue eyes!"

"Oh, hush. And I might as well, too. Arguing with you has always been an exercise in futility."

"You just know I'm right, but you be afraid to admit it."

Emma made tracks for the kitchen, which was separated from the big house by a breezeway. "It's time to fix lunch. Are you going to help me or not? You know I'm all thumbs in a kitchen."

Catching her arm, Cleopatra said, "I ain't much better. My job always been taking care of you. But I got something to say. Ben and I been thinking. Now that we's married, he ain't got the itch to take to sea. And I ain't interested in going back to Virginia now that you be settled in Louisiana. We want to live here at Feuille de Chêne. My Ben be asking right now about it. Frenchie be needing an overseer, and you"—the usual superior look played across Cleopatra's face—"you can't run this place without house servants."

Emma called up a superior look of her own. "You run a house? Don't make me laugh. You're not a scrub woman."

"Didn't say I was. I'll fire up those two lazy gals in the quarters. You can get back to your doctoring— crazy though the very idea is."

"Oh, Cleo, you're the best thing that ever happened to me."

"Second best thing. You just ain't reconciled to the best thing yet."

Preparing the noon meal, Emma gave thought to her confidante's words. She wanted Paul. Wanted his heart, his soul, his body. Was she cutting off her nose to spite her face by keeping him locked from her bedroom?

Her monthly had given her a reprieve. She might not be as lucky the next time. But she wondered how long she could keep Paul at bay. How long would it be before he tired of a door separating them and enforced his husbandly rights?

Chapter Seventeen

Emma retired for the evening to ponder her predicament, but no sooner had her head hit the pillow than someone pounded against the bed-chamber door.

Woodley left his post at the foot of the bed and flew across the room. "'Ufff! 'Ufff!" He had a habit of dropping his *R*s.

"Come quick," Cleopatra shouted. "There's an old man in your office. He's sick as a dog and be wanting you to help him."

"I'll be right down."

Emma hurriedly got back into her clothes, and pulled her hair into a twist. Poking the last hairpin into place, she hurried past the dog and on to the quarters above the carriage house serving as her office.

The man, who was wheezing and coughing, was indeed ill. Holding a blood-streaked handkerchief to his mouth, he was doubled over in a straight chair. Sweat beaded his wrinkled forehead.

"You Miz Rousseau?" he asked, croaking.

"Yes." She led him to the examining couch and

began to check his vital signs. "How long have you suffered with phthisis, Mr. . . . I don't believe I caught your name."

"Dyer. Simon Dyer." He hacked out another blood-spittled cough. "Had this consumption nigh on two years."

Emma blended a tonic of honey, lemon, and laudanum. She held a spoon of it to his lips, but he forced her hand away.

"Elixirs don't help," he said.

"If I'm to treat you, you must follow my advice."

He nodded and quit resisting. "Your husband home?"

There was no menace in his weak voice, so Emma had no reason to fear such a question. "No, he's in New Orleans."

Paul had left Feuille de Chêne four weeks previously. Since Ben was overseeing the fields, Paul spent much of his time away. Business, he told her. Neither of them had mentioned it, but Emma knew he was looking for excuses to go afield. A man's pride—and Paul was full of it—wouldn't allow him to stay in the proximity of his wife's locked bedchamber.

"Do you know my husband?" she asked, while bathing Simon Dyer's clammy brow.

Dyer closed his eyes. Should he lie and say no? he asked himself. He had been the accomplice in Étienne Rousseau's death. Étienne had been his best friend, and he'd betrayed him. Paul Rousseau had searched far and wide for Rankin's second in the duel's aftermath, but Oliver had spirited Simon and his wife out of the country for two years. By the time

271

he and Lois had returned to their Feliciana Parish cotton plantation, Paul had bid farewell to Louisiana.

'Tis folly, your being here, you old lackey for Rankin Oliver. If Paul were to catch him, Simon figured the young man would finish off what Providence seemed to be set on doing, taking his life. Simon gave consideration to purging his soul, but if he told Paul—or his wife—all he knew . . . No, he couldn't yet. Not until he had dealt with Rankin Oliver. If he lived that long . . .

"No, I don't know your husband. I'm here in St. Martinsville on business." Simon felt the familiar clawing in his lungs. "Heard about"—he expelled phlegm—"about the painless lady sawbones. Take my suffering away, good lady."

Emma loosened his shirt buttons. Could she comfort this helpless old man? The properties of sulfurous ether brought painless intoxication before total somnambulism. Could the brew soothe Simon Dyer? She thought it could.

"Maybe I can help you," she said, "but there are no guarantees, and I've never tested my theories."

His pleading, rheumy eyes beseeched her. "If you'll try, ma'am, I'd be thankful."

She placed a gauze mask over his nostrils and mouth, and unstoppered a small vial of ether. Holding the bottle away from her face, she poured one drop of the alcohol-and-sulfur distillate onto the mask.

Dyer's eyes widened at the rotten-egg odor, and he flailed his arms, catching Emma's forearm with the side of his wrist.

272

The ether flew out of her hand. She tried to catch it, but the bottle shattered at her feet. The powerful stench overwhelmed her, and she swayed. For a drunken moment she half focused on Dyer, who was slumped back on the couch.

Then she fell backward as induced sleep brought blackness.

Paul was in a dark mood as he shouldered his way toward the O'Reilly box at the Orleans Theatre. His fund-raising activities for the Navy had so far been for naught. During intermission at the opera, he had explained the cause to several of the gentlemen in the narrow lobby, but the stigma of "torcher" still clung to his name, even though he had been cleared of the charges.

It figured. His place was not here, it was at sea. Would he ever get back to his first love? And what was his first love? The sea or Emma? For the first time in his life, Paul was in a quandary.

He seated himself in the box. Marian and Howard—now Paul's aunt and uncle by marriage—sat next to him. Damn, he'd never have thought the Widow Oliver would become his aunt! Well, several months ago he had never imagined a lot of things.

The last seat was empty, and it seemed to say to him: "This chair should be for your wife. You've no business being here without Emma." It dawned on Paul that he was growing weak in the mind.

"I say, old chap, news doesn't sound good from Texas. I read an article in the *Tropic* today, said San Antonio's fallen to General Vasquez. Made mention

273

that Sam Houston moved the capital from Austin, too."

"That's what I hear. Apparently Houston's not taking any chances on the capital falling into enemy hands." Paul rubbed his eyes. "Yet he still refuses to stand by the fleet."

"My guess would be," Howard said, "he's furious because you and Moore haven't followed his orders."

"You may be right. But there's a chance you're not. He's sent no arrest party, so I take that as a good sign."

Marian pursed her lips. "You two hush all that war talk. Let's enjoy the opera. I'm feeling awfully mistreated."

"Now, now, sweetheart. You know we don't mean to ignore you, but our nephew and I have so few opportunities to chat." Howard patted her hand before proceeding. "And, Paul, there's a rumor Commodore Moore has quit the Yucatecan waters."

"True. Governor Barbachano thought we were impeding Quintana Roo's peace treaty, but Ed departed for another reason as well: our ships are unseaworthy. He couldn't stay in tropical waters any longer."

"Is he tacking for New Orleans?" Howard asked.

"No. For Houston. He and I are going to make a last-ditch appeal to the President for money—and his support."

"Meeting Houston in Houston. Formidable. Good luck." The attorney reached into his frock coat and brandished a check. "In the meantime, I've

274

something for you. Do use it for the Navy."

Paul was taken aback at the figure. By no means would this money cover refitting the fleet, but it would provide food for the men. The aid was appreciated.

He bent his eyes on his benefactor. "You are a friend, indeed. Thank you. This is going to help."

"Call me benevolent. Marriage to Marian"— Howard brought her hand to his lips and was rewarded with a giggle—"has softened me, I'd say."

"Isn't he wonderful, Paul darling?"

"And how is marriage treating you?" Howard asked quickly.

Marian put in: "You're treating our Emma famously I trust?"

"She's getting along." *Rousseau, you're really a bastard. She's miserable, and you're the cause of it.* "Not a word of complaint has escaped her lips." *That's because she's just too proud to complain.* "Seems to be taking bayou life quite well."

Paul was too embarrassed to admit that he had failed Emma. Though he refused to think beyond the next nine months, when the title to Feuille de Chêne would be cleared, he hadn't wanted Emma to suffer. Yet she had. Oh, she hadn't gone hungry, but her circumstances weren't those to which she was accustomed. Revitalizing the plantation had taken Paul's reserve of funds, and there was much yet to do. Still, Emma hadn't complained about the lack of finery and glitter. Ah hell, he thought sourly, what is the matter with me? He felt he was going soft in the head thinking about her, that he was in quicksand of the soul.

"Well," Howard said, "I do believe you two are as happy as"—he suddenly gasped as Marian touched him intimately—"as Marian and I."

"Stop that blushing," she cooed.

Paul fidgeted in his seat. His aunt-by-marriage had no compunction about displaying her ardor for Howard. In truth, Paul was jealous. He wanted Emma to be touching him with the same unbridled ardor. He ached to have her stroke him, soothe him, take him past the point of awareness.

But he realized that wouldn't happen unless their lives changed. She had little regard for his vehement leanings toward Texas. He didn't expect her to love the place—no strings bound her there—but to give up his work was unthinkable. He was tied by choice to the Republic.

Leaning back in the chair, he closed his eyes as operatic strains filled his ears. In addition to her doctoring, Emma wanted a husband at her heels. At least that was what she thought she wanted. Paul remained convinced she wouldn't be happy without a challenge, and he'd rely on that until his own mind was clear. But deep down he wondered just what in hell he was going to do about Emma.

"Folk's be calling our Emma a witch doctor. You gotta do something with her."

Paul shook his head and lifted his palms, both gestures of exasperation. He raised his eyes to the summer sky. "Doing something with" his wife certainly had its merits. But that something had nothing to do with Emma's medical practice. He was a man possessed by the need to break down the door

276

separating them.

"Cleopatra," he replied, "Emma's the most stubborn woman alive. You've wasted your breath trying to talk sense into her, and I've done the same."

"Well, something's gotta be done." The small explosive bundle stamped her foot. "She's got the slaves scared outta their wits. They think she's gonna sneak up on 'em with that stinky concoction she brews and put 'em to sleep."

"And the people in town are divided into two camps," Paul supplied. He looked across the sugar-growing brakes to the *garçonnière* cum doctor's office. "Some of them want to try this miracle of ether, but the majority say she's mixed up in voodoo."

"If'n she don't stop this business, she gonna be shunned by the people of St. Martinsville."

"I doubt that would bother her. Emma doesn't care what people say about her practice. She believes in what she's doing, and we both should admire that in her. I know I do."

Cleopatra swatted away a mosquito as if the pesky fly were a vulture. "Well, see if you admire this!" She clenched her hands on her hips. "Last week while you was in New Orleans she got too much of a whiff of that stuff. She was trying to ease the suffering of some old consumptive so-and-so. Fell down, she did, and hit her head on a table. Bled like a stuck pig and didn't even know it."

"Why didn't you tell me before?" His concern was evident. "Never mind all the pestilent diseases she might contract from patients, she could've killed herself!"

"Said she'd turn me and Ben off this place if I told.

277

But my conscience told me you needed to know, and I ain't gonna let her temper get in the way of what's right."

"Believe me, I won't either." Paul tossed his wide-brimmed white hat to the ground, then stomped toward the neatly blocked sign reading Madame Docteur E. Rousseau. He was giving serious consideration to delivering a good spanking. "Anybody rides up here," he bellowed over his shoulder, "you tell them the doctor is *out!*"

Emma heard the clomp of feet on the staircase and whipped around when the door nearly flew off its hinges. Paul yanked the curtain closed over the glass in the door.

At Emma's side, Woodley, sensing a threat, raised his hackles and bared his teeth. It didn't matter that he adored Paul and had spent many evenings curled on his lap, the dog was her protector.

"What's the meaning of this?" she asked, her heart beating wildly. There was murder in her husband's eyes. What had she done now? And what was he planning to do?

Head forward, Paul started for her. "You and I have to talk."

"'rrrr!" The half-grown pup leaped across the room and went for Paul's ankle, fastening his fangs around the bottom of his left leg.

"Get off!" Paul tried to shake the ball of white fur away, but Woodley growled around his tusks and held on for dear life. "Call off your damned dog, Emma Rousseau!"

All she could do was laugh. A small pup was getting the better of her big, tall husband!

Paul changed tactics. "Good doggy, good doggy," he crooned to no avail.

In a swish of voluminous skirts, Emma stepped to the rescue. At a gentle word from her, Woodley eased up, and she took the pup in her arms. "Naughty boy. You scared Papa."

"I'm not that dog's papa, and I wasn't scared." A frown pulled at his features. "Put Woodley outside."

She did, and he scratched the door after Paul slammed the bolt into place and charged over to the long sofa.

He dropped like a sack of potatoes onto it, and folded his arms over his chest. "Come here."

"No."

"Come here."

She was determined not to do as she was bid, and kept distance between them. "You look just like Woodley when you bare your teeth like that."

"The trouble with you, dear wife, is that you've put too much emotion into that dog."

"Why shouldn't I? He's the only living thing on this earth that loves me, as you French would put it, *sans peur et sans reproche.*"

"Don't start spouting chivalry, madame. I'm not going to be put off by a damned canine's attributes."

"Jealous?" she goaded.

Paul's eyes blazed. "You put too much of your time into this doctoring thing." He leaned forward, ready to spring. "Now you get your derrière over here right now, or I'll come get you."

"Why should I?"

"Because I'm going to take a look at your head. I've been told you fell down and cut it last week."

"Cleo."

"Yes, Cleo." He squinted and eyed her menacingly. "Let me warn you. If I leave this sofa to get you, you're going to get the spanking you richly deserve. Now, what's it going to be?"

Five seconds later she was adjusting her skirts across his lap. His thighs were like bricks beneath her, his sex was even harder. Yet his hands were gentle as he parted her hair to expose the wound at the back of her crown.

His lips touched it, and he whispered, "My mother used to kiss away my hurts when I was a boy. It always made them better."

Emma's face was buried against the soft cotton of his shirt and the warm strength of his chest. The feminine part of her, the part that had been so long denied satisfaction, ached for him.

"Is your hurt better?" he asked, his voice deep and low.

"Yes. . . ."

She nestled against him, weary of holding her mate at arm's length. Over these past months she had questioned her own wisdom. She yearned for him to love her and for them to reconcile their differences. Matters of the heart couldn't be resolved with a closed bedchamber door between them. If there were only some way to prevent a child . . .

But maybe . . .

Just this once . . .

He had tantalized her before, often. He had given her every opportunity to change her mind. And, she thought, just this once . . .

If they conceived a babe, she'd love it. Raising a child didn't frighten her, for she had a lot of love to give. But a babe deserved a father's care. Although many children had been reared by one parent, Emma felt it was self-serving of her to yearn for Paul. The child would pay for any stolen moments of rapture.

Her mind overrode her passion, and she pulled herself to her feet. "We can't. The result might be a baby."

"Why, Madame Rousseau, shouldn't we take a chance on a baby?"

"Because it would be selfish of us. Soon you'll have title to this plantation, and it'll be sold." *To further your idealistic cause!* "You'll have no more need for a wife. And I've no desire to bring a child into a world with neither a father nor a home to call its own."

"That wouldn't be the case."

She doubted him. "I promised to remain your wife for a year. I didn't promise to bear your children. If we settle our differences about Uncle Rankin and the Texas Navy, fine . . . we can then look to the future."

"That's blackmail, Emma."

"I don't see it that way."

"There are a lot of things you don't see clearly." He tucked his shirt into his breeches. "Which brings me to the crux of this little idyll." He turned slightly to point a finger at her beakers and bottles. "This sleeping potion hocus-pocus is going to stop."

"It will not! I am pledged to ease the suffering of

281

surgery patients, and I won't allow you—as I've told you several times before!—to stand in my way."

"Surgery patients? Ha! Cleopatra said you were treating a consumptive with that god-awful gas."

"I was trying to give a terminally ill old man just enough ether to ease his discomfort and get him giddy. Drunk, if you will. That's all."

"Yes, and you fell and hit your head." Paul bent over her. "I've had one woman die in my arms from a head injury, and I won't allow the woman I—" He swallowed the word love. "I won't allow you to die that way."

Emma was touched. If he didn't care for her, he wouldn't be concerned. "Are you talking about that woman in Sisal?"

"Yes. Karla. Karla Stahl. Your uncle's mistress who died at his hands."

Her breath caught at his sincerity. Was Uncle Rankin guilty as charged? She chewed her upper lip. No! He couldn't be—he couldn't! Yet a niggling doubt had been planted in her mind. It was best, she decided, to avoid this line of conflict.

Maybe she should make a few concessions on her doctoring. In truth, the accident had scared her. Ether was dangerous. She had to improve on its administration and in the meantime, she needed assistance.

"Sweetheart," she said, not realizing she had murmured the endearment, "I'll meet you fifty-fifty on my work with ether. I'm going to train an assistant to help me."

"And who do you think would be crazed enough to fall in with your scheme?"

"Cleo."

He rolled his eyes. "That'll be the day."

It took seven.

"How did I get talked into this?" Emma muttered under her breath. Weeks had passed since that confrontation in her office. Weeks of verbal sparring with nothing settled.

"Careful where you step," Paul said, taking her elbow. "This mud is bottomless."

"Really."

Emma thumbed her nose at this border of civilization. Houston, Texas. Paul had been ordered here by Commodore Moore, and in turn he had insisted she accompany him. Not stopping in Galveston, the *Virgin Vixen* had carried them up the narrow, magnolia-lined Buffalo Bayou to the temporary capital, a frontier town fifty miles inland from the Gulf of Mexico.

"We're nearly there. That's the Capitol Hotel at the end of the street. It's the best in town."

"The Capitol?" Emma eyed the two-story frame building. "Isn't that a pretentious name for a dilapidated hotel?"

"Careful. Your snobbery is showing."

Her face colored. "You're right."

She still wasn't impressed after they took a look at the interior. The lobby was a large room with white walls. An iron stove dominated the middle, and a few broken chairs were the only furnishings. The atmosphere wasn't improved by the "guests," who were expectorating tobacco juice into chipped spittoons. If this was the best Texas had to offer, she shuddered to think about the worst.

Thankfully, the upstairs parlor and the dining room were more pleasing. Behind a screen in their Spartan bedchamber she dressed for dinner. Thinking about the hotel had kept her mind off the reason for their visit. The Texas Navy. She resented the idea that a band of seafarers kept her apart from Paul.

And he was obsessed with Texas's dire situation. Several days earlier he had received word from Ed Moore, asking him to meet with the commodore in Houston. Due to Mexican aggression, the Big Drunk had softened toward the commodore and the Navy, and had requested that the fleet sail back to home port for further orders. This time it seemed as if the vacillating Sam Houston would support his naval forces.

Confident in that thought, Paul got into his brass-enhanced dress uniform. He was ready ten minutes before Emma stepped from behind the moldly screen. He took her hand—it was chapped by chemicals—and led her toward a small private room. Tomorrow he'd purchase a tub of ointment for those hands!

"You're especially beautiful tonight, Madame Rousseau," he commented, taking in the upsweep of her blond hair, the rosy tint to her cheeks, the emerald green satin gown that dipped low at the bodice. "Though I don't know if I want the Commodore and the President to see quite so much of your attributes."

"I don't want to see Moore or Houston at all, so why don't I just go back to our room? Then we'll both be happy."

At the top of the staircase he stopped and drew her into the shadows. Despite her icy demeanor she was warm against his body, and he grew hot. "Is there a fraction of you that can concede?"

"To what? To playing the good little wife in front of your compatriots? Or to— Stop that!" When he took his hand from her behind, she said, "Just as I guessed. You want me to let you into my bed."

"We share one tonight. And there's no guard dog to protect you."

"Because you forbade Woodley to accompany us, and . . . well, your pigheaded pride wouldn't allow you to rent two rooms." She straightened her creamy shoulders. "I didn't make a scene in front of the desk clerk, but don't make too much of that. I've no desire to argue in front of outsiders."

"What do you desire, *ma bien-aimée?*" He took her hand and touched it to what hurt the most. "This perhaps?"

"Is that all you think about?"

"I wouldn't be a man if I didn't think, daily and hourly, about holding you in my arms." His words were sincere. "You're under my skin, and my thoughts are on you constantly. When we're apart, you're on my mind. I remember everything about you. Your scent and your hair. Your skin. The way it feels to be inside you. My mind draws a sketch of the places where we've made love."

"Don't . . . please don't," she moaned and dropped her cheek to her shoulder.

Paul gentled his lips against her neck. "You're trembling. I remember how you shivered when I used to blow in your ear."

"There you are!" Commodore Edwin Ward Moore said, walking up to them and slapping Paul on the back.

Emma silently thanked the saints above for the interruption as Paul made introductions. She had been near—so near—to succumbing to her husband's magic.

"The devil you say," the commodore said. "How did an ugly fellow like yourself win such a lovely wife?"

Paul was not ugly. But Emma realized this was the usual bantering males engaged in. "Oh, Commodore Moore, believe me, he can be very persuasive."

"Ed. Please call me Ed."

She gave him a once-over. The commodore's hair was parted at the side, and his long square face was elongated further by the beard growing below his chin. He, like Paul, wore dress uniform—white stockings, white breeches, and dark blue fitted jacket with gold epaulets. He carried a tricorn hat. Trim but not slim, he wasn't a tall man; her husband topped him by half a foot. Yet Ed Moore's bearing commanded attention, as did Paul's.

"My best wishes for your continued happiness."

We're going to need a lot more than best wishes, she thought ruefully. "Thank you, sir."

"Paul, before we go in . . . let me brief you on the mutineers. They're still fighting extradition. The governor in Baton Rouge flatly refuses my requests to give them over without Houston's signature."

"Add one more demand to our list," Paul replied dryly.

Emma sighed and took her husband's arm.

"Enough of that. We shouldn't keep the President of Texas waiting, gentlemen. I suggest we repair to the dining room."

Ed hiked a brow. "Woman of spirit, eh?"

"Oh yes," Paul replied dryly. "Woman of mighty will."

Holding her head regally high, Emma led them to President Sam Houston, who waited in the dining room. He was big, dark and handsome. Charming and magnetic described him, too. Though probably in his fifties, he looked younger. From what she had heard his third wife—his first had divorced him; the second had been a now-deceased Cherokee Indian—was several decades his junior. *He had to be a rake,* and was almost, she thought, as appealing as her husband. Almost.

Though she didn't care much for the Texan cause she was drawn to its leader. He gave no quarter and asked for none either. Neither did Paul.

She could tell, despite Houston's polite conversation over dinner, that he liked neither Commodore Moore nor her husband. A pained expression never left his face.

Houston waved the serving woman away. "No more food for me, thank you."

"Our President has a hole in his stomach," Paul explained. "An Indian's arrow pierced his gut years ago."

"Cease your indelicate talk." The President scowled. "You'll have your lady fainting at the table."

"Emma doesn't faint. She's a physician. A good one."

"Is that so?" Houston commented, leading the

conversation to her medical pursuits.

"Mr. President, we're not here to discuss the science of Hippocrates," Paul said. "Are you, or are you not, going to sign those extradition papers?"

Houston frowned before saying, "I will."

Placated, Paul asked, "What orders do you have for us?"

Taking a long draught of Madeira, which Emma figured couldn't be good for his delicate stomach, Houston said, "With Mrs. Rousseau in our presence, I don't believe military talk proper."

"Mr. President," she said, "I live in the backwaters of Louisiana. My hearing this conversation won't jeopardize security."

Paul agreed and so did Ed Moore.

"All right." Houston leaned back in the chair, which creaked under his weight, and eyed his subordinates. "I'll be honest. In the past I've thought seriously of having you and your men branded pirates, Moore. You ignored my recall order, and that is a court-martial offense."

"We sailed out last December under your orders, sir," Moore reminded him. "And I didn't receive word to the contrary until mere weeks ago."

"I'll turn a deaf ear to your insubordination . . . as long as it doesn't happen again."

"And what guarantees do we have that you won't rescind more good-faith orders?" Paul interjected.

Houston refilled his wine glass and downed its contents. "I'm sure you men are well aware of the present situation. The Santa Fe expedition was captured to a man, and marched to Mexico City in chains."

"I know," Moore said. "While our Navy was in the

Gulf—unauthorized, I might add—I received word Frank Lubbock had escaped from a Mexico City dungeon, and I dispatched the *San Antonio* to Laguna for his rescue."

Houston shifted, obviously in discomfort. "You're to be commended."

Moore pushed his plate forward and braced a forearm on the table. "We don't want commendations, Mr. President. We want your support."

"No doubt." The former Indian fighter grimaced. "You Texas Tars . . . well, as I was telling Andrew Jackson, I don't like the idea of fighting on the high seas."

"You don't believe in navies?" Emma asked, confused.

Houston cleared his throat. "Not particularly."

"I don't need to remind you, sir," Paul said, "that General Vasquez and his troops captured San Antonio."

"Somervall retook the town."

"Yes, but you've invited shipowners to apply for privateering commissions," Moore said. "You've moved the capital to this place and evacuated your wife to safer territory. Yet you've made no move to retaliate against the Centralists."

"I've heard lynching parties are out to get you." Paul brushed his jaw. "Over your hesitation to follow up on our people's mistreatment."

"I've never allowed public opinion to stand in the way of what I believe right," Houston announced.

"Is it right to place our citizens in jeopardy?" Paul appraised the president coolly. "Sir, what are you after?"

"Statehood for Texas."

"Don't tell me you're hoping the U.S. will intervene in all this!" Moore appeared aghast. "I've nothing against joining the Union, but annexation is years away."

"And you believe all the answers are yours, Moore? I beg to differ. You may be a superlative naval leader, but *your* navy is comprised of nothing but brawlers and duelers. Diplomacy, not fists and swords, will bring peace to our Republic."

The air was electrified with tension. Like a satisfied Cherokee after a coup, Houston waited for a response. Moore clenched his fists. Emma's eyes flew to Paul, who rose slowly to his feet.

"Mr. President, Santa Anna is a warrior not a statesman. Several months ago Ambassador Ashbel Smith warned you that two new powerful Mexican warships were being laid down in England," Paul added. "The Centralists won't use those ships for mackerel fishing." He stood straight and tall. "They're taking on a rented crew, sir. Well provisioned and keenly supported.

"The *Guadalupe* and the *Moctezuma* are standing for the Gulf of Mexico. With their guns mounted . . . to invade our waters, and crush our people." He leaned forward. "Will you allow the Republic of Texas to go without the 'brawlers and duelers' who can keep those war steamers from our shore?"

Chapter Eighteen

The air remained tense in the Capitol Hotel's private dining room. Paul waited for President Houston's response. Moore was trying to hide his smirk. Emma feared her husband had pushed the president of Texas too far.

Houston rose from the table. "All right." He was less than enthusiastic. "Reinforce the Gulf blockade."

Emma sighed in relief. Paul wasn't in danger of a court-martial. Yet she didn't notice an appreciable amount of gratitude on the naval men's side. She should take her husband's stand in the matter, but she couldn't help thinking that President Houston was an experienced leader. Surely he knew what he was doing. If he didn't like the idea of using the Navy, he might be justified.

"We can't renew the blockade," Paul said at last. "The entire fleet is in dire need of refitting. Some of our vessels should be scrapped. We can't confront the enemy with disabled ships."

Moore scratched his beard. "Another thing. An extended cruise with fo'c'sles full of short-timers is folly. Without the support of our President *and* money to back it, we cannot recruit new sailors. Issue funds to put the Navy to rights, and we'll go. Posthaste."

"Perhaps," Houston said, condescension in his tone, "the two of you could learn something from the Indians. They finance their battles from the spoils of their last victories."

"Until lately we imposed upon our allies in the Yucatán for cash," Paul reminded him, a muscle working in his jaw. "The Navy has sailed by its own devices."

Moore's face had turned florid. "Lieutenant Rousseau has gathered some financing, and he and I have both used our own reserves to keep the fleet provisioned. There is a limit, though, sir, to what we can do."

"The Treasury is bankrupt," was the presidential reply.

"Sir," Paul said, "freedom is on the line. Will you have your infant son wearing the yoke of Mexican oppression?"

Silence fell. Emma's eyes went from Paul to Houston and back again. Though she was ambivalent toward the fate of Texas, she had never respected her husband more.

"You'll have your money," Houston replied, each word strained. Acceding to the men he despised was not an easy thing. "Bring the Navy up to snuff. Then renew that blockade."

"Thank you, sir," said Paul and Moore. They both clipped a salute.

"But I'd suggest you keep something in mind."

Houston's eyes gleamed. "I'll be watching you, and I'll allow no further disobedience. Follow my orders, or I'll see you both punished."

Emma's heart pounded in fear, for she knew that Paul would follow his convictions whether or not they coincided with Houston's. She prayed he'd be obedient.

Later that night she lay on her side of the bed they shared, her body not touching Paul's, yet she felt his presence as fully as if he were lying atop her. He radiated heat. She yearned to turn and see his tanned face, his brown eyes. It would be so easy to reach out a hand to him. She heard his breathing, even and sure. Feigning sleep, she rolled onto her back and deserted her marked impassiveness by opening one eye slightly.

"You're not asleep," Paul said.

"Neither are you." She indulged in a full appraisal of him. He was nude, no part of the sheet covering his maleness. Her fingers had to be restrained from reaching out.

He started to touch her, but spread his fingers through his ebony hair instead. "How can I? I want you, you know. More than anything."

"More than your quest for the Texas Navy?" She knew that had been a nasty thing to say.

"I've been falling-down drunk once in my life," he said. "That night we claimed Feuille de Chêne. Are you going to send me to my grave regretting the words spoken by a liquored tongue? A tongue that should've stayed in the back of my mouth."

"This has nothing to do with that." She slid her arm behind her neck. "I'm worried about what's going to happen with Houston."

"There's nothing to fear." He punched his pillow, wadded it into a more comfortable shape. "He's given us what we desire."

"And what if you don't kowtow to his wants?"

"You're borrowing trouble." Touching the pad of her ring finger, he whispered, "If I didn't know better, I'd think you don't want anything bad happening to your husband."

"I don't."

"What"—he took that finger to his mouth—"do you want?"

She was unnerved by his touch. She should be strong and get up. But how could she? He was nibbling her neck now, and her senses were honed in on him. She was weak with desire.

He repeated his question. "What do you want?"

"Peace of mind, the joys of being married in spirit, a home for both of us. Children."

"The last part's easy enough to accomplish."

"But selfish to consider until the others are a fact."

"A naval wife has no peace of mind, Emma. It doesn't go along with the territory. It's only a matter of time till I'll be looking down the business end of a Centralist cannon. If you can accept that, I'm willing to make a few concessions."

"Like?"

"While I'm here, I'm all yours. My spirit will be totally married to yours."

"Where's your promise not to sell our home and livelihood?" she asked, bunching the sheet's hem

294

with her hand.

"If Houston makes good on his word, it won't be necessary." He pulled away. "But I don't trust him. I'm going forward with the mortgage plans."

"I see," she said, but she didn't. "What will we do after you've sold the plantation? Live in the gutter and beg for alms?"

"Thank you for the vote of confidence."

Her heart cried out for a better answer. "What about Uncle Rankin? Can you promise with all honesty that you'll never seek to discredit him?"

"I wish I could."

She rolled to a sitting position and hugged her knees. "Then there's not much hope for us."

"I think there is. Once your eyes are opened to the truth, you'll understand what I've been going through since my father's death."

"There can be only one person right, the other wrong, in that feud. But what difference does it make at this point? Your father is gone, Paul, and nothing will bring him back."

"It makes a difference to me, and nothing will change the way I feel." He turned to her, then slid his arm around her waist. "But you are my wife, and . . . I can't stay celibate forever."

Longing to be his woman, she savored the moment. His free hand was working the ribbons of her nightgown; his breath was hot against her cheek. If she allowed herself this pleasure, at dawn she would still face today's stumbling blocks.

She eased from bed, went to the window, and hugged her arms. After a long moment she turned to him again. He was sitting on the bed's edge.

"I can't accept your terms," she said. "But I'll live up to the promise I made. I'll be your legal wife until Feuille de Chêne is free." Whirling around, she stared with unseeing eyes out the window. "And then you'll be free. I'm going to divorce you."

Immediately she regretted those words. And they haunted her through the rest of their time in Houston, on the trip back to Feuille de Chêne, and for weeks to come. Paul made no attempt to touch her. It was as if two strangers resided under the same roof.

Yet day after day life went on. She gained a modicum of inner peace from watching the house become lively and the fields green with sugar cane. And there were patients to heal, a plantation to be managed, slaves to feed and clothe. If her marital woes were gone, Emma would have been happy. She had grown to love Le Petit Paris, the bastion of expatriate Royalists. Despite its location in the wilds of south Louisiana, St. Martinsville was resplendent with old-world charm. It was home.

"Will that be all, Madame Rousseau?" the burly shopkeeper asked, tallying up the cost of the bolt of calico, the flour, and the salt Emma was purchasing.

"Yes, thank you, Monsieur Broussard. Please have that put in my buggy."

In spite of her request, she wandered through the cornucopia of treasures in the store. Smells, there were many. Cayenne, cinnamon, and cloves. Fresh coffee was being brewed. A counter held bottles of bay rum and French perfume. She lifted stopper after stopper, inhaling the scents of patchouli, cassia, and heliotrope.

But she put her desire for these extravagances away. Whatever extra money she had in her reticule was needed to replenish her dwindling medical supplies. Though she had a fairly steady line of patients seeking her services, many were poor Cajun fishermen and their families. They bartered for health care. Not that she minded. Fresh crawfish, chickens and vegetables were always welcome.

It was then she caught sight of a curvaceous brunette, turned out in purple silk and finery, fingering a skein of exquisite lace.

"I'll take ten yards," the woman said in a voice as smooth and creamy as her complexion. "No. Make that twenty."

"As you wish, mademoiselle." The shop girl took up measuring tape and shears.

Sloe eyes turned to Emma. A smile dimpled one cheek as a jeweled finger tipped up the skein. "Did you see this beautiful lace? It's from Alençon."

"I'm not in the market today, thank you."

The brunette murmured something to the shop girl before floating over to Emma. She extended that bejeweled hand. "Allow me to present myself. I'm Aimée Thérèse Goyette."

This was the female Cleopatra had recently told Emma about. Paul's mistress in his youth! Gossip from the slave quarters said she had bedded both Paul and his grandfather . . . and she would have inherited Feuille de Chêne if not for Paul's idealism.

"Pleased to meet you," Emma lied. "I am Madame Rousseau. Madame Paul Rousseau."

"Yes. I know."

"And how is that?"

"I've seen you on the street. Little in St. Martinsville escapes me."

"How nice for you." Emma stepped back. "I must be leaving. . . ."

"Wait a moment, please." Aimée Thérèse swept her hand to a deserted corner of the store. "May I have a minute or two of your time?"

Emma's natural curiosity got the better of her, and she agreed.

"Your husband and I have been friends for a very long time," Aimée Thérèse announced when they had privacy. "Did you know this?"

"Paul has many friends in this area. I'd be surprised if you weren't among them."

"And you aren't jealous?"

"Of course not," Emma lied.

"I love your husband."

"What, Mademoiselle Goyette, is the purpose of this?"

"While you are tending the sick, he tends me. I'm warning you, madame, that he is mine. Always has been, always will be."

Emma was the sick one. "If that were true, why didn't he marry you long ago?"

"I refused. Remi Rousseau was my protector, you see, and I had no wish to become the wife of a poor young man."

"He's still poor."

"Yes, but I no longer need his money. I have Remi's."

"Well, aren't you the lucky one?" Emma said facetiously. "But I really don't care how my husband's grandfather wasted his money."

298

"Do you care about Paul?" Aimée Thérèse asked, her hand going to her bodice. "If you do, you should pay attention to him. If you don't, let me warn you; he is lonely. I'm content for now to have him in my bed, but I want more. I intend to be the next Madame Rousseau."

A strange thought penetrated Emma's shock. What would Marian do in this situation? Fight for her man, that's what, and make no bones about it.

"It'll be a cold day in July when you marry my Paul." Emma stomped away, grabbing a bottle of heliotrope perfume as she went and taking it over to Monsieur Broussard. She was not going to let that hussy have Paul. Not without a fight!

On the way home she made plans. She had vowed long ago to make him love her, and he was going to! She had been a fool to keep him at bay. A lustful man like Paul needed an equally lusty wife to warm his nights—and days. She would find a way to stop a pregnancy, but his bed she intended to share.

However, Paul was gone when she arrived back at Feuille de Chêne. Texas Navy business. As usual.

He had yet to return from New Orleans on the dog-day Saturday when Uncle Rankin's fine sloop docked at Feuille de Chêne.

Wearing a white linen suit and white-brimmed hat, Rankin walked back and forth across the lawn separating the house from the bayou. "I knew this place had fallen into disrepair, but I hadn't realized how bad it is."

Emma had known it was only a matter of time before her financial situation became known to her family, yet she had filed that worry in the back of her

299

mind. Now that it was out, her pride wouldn't allow her to make an unkind statement about Paul.

"I don't know about that." Provided she'd had them, Emma's feathers would have ruffled. She pridefully eyed her home and the flower gardens. "I think we've done wonders with it. We've installed new windows; scrubbed and painted the woodwork; repaired the furniture. In case you don't know, Remi Rousseau was in failing health for years and wasn't able to supervise the upkeep. And no one's lived here for almost a year."

"I didn't mean to criticize ye, Emmie. Matter of fact, I'm not surprised ye've made something out of nothing. It's our good Oliver blood that flows through yer veins. Yer father and I were born to poverty, but look how much we've both accomplished?"

"Born to poverty, huh? That doesn't say much for the industriousness of our ancestors."

"Don't be impertinent, girl." Rankin went round the corner of the house and waved toward the fields. "That is a disgrace. Sugar cane should be growing high this time of year."

"Cane takes two years, you know, to mature. Weeds were the only things growing high when we arrived. And I'll thank you to know there's nary a weed in the brakes now."

"Is that so?" He cocked his head. "Word has it a bunch of his slaves escaped. Successful cane-raising takes many men not few."

"We're doing all right. Paul's hired a few freedmen."

"Be that as it may, Emmie," he said, baiting her,

300

"why doesn't your husband visit the block and bid for more slaves?"

"To tell the truth Paul doesn't care much for the idea of slavery." That was certainly true. He had told her he planned to free his chattels when he sold the property, and he wouldn't bring in more unfortunates in the meantime.

"Abolitionist bas— Is that why he took a mortgage on the place? To hire workers?"

She was nonplused. How did her uncle know about the note? What Paul did, or didn't do, with Feuille de Chêne really wasn't Uncle Rankin's business!

"Now, don't look askance. It wasn't my intention to rile ye." Rankin took her hand. "Emmie, I'm here for a purpose. We all know—we being yer parents and I—that Rousseau is, for all intents and purposes, broke."

"That's not true," she hedged.

"Don't be proud. All of us are financially embarrassed, come one time or another." He waited a moment before saying, "Yer father's sent a dowry. And I've added a bit myself."

"I can't take it."

"Yes ye can. All brides deserve a tocher, but I wasn't in the best of moods to offer one at yer wedding. Yer father's a mite upset that ye married without his consent, but he's willing to forgive and forget. Don't insult him, or me, by turning yer back on what's rightfully yers."

"My husband takes care of our needs," she replied defensively.

"Then allow him to take care of 'needs.' Quentin

and I want to offer you luxuries."

She couldn't take the money for two reasons. Pride being the first, and the second . . . there was a shadow on Uncle Rankin's character. Until she knew for sure . . . "There's something I need to ask."

"Yes, Emmie?"

She hesitated to speak, yet she squared her shoulders and did so. "Did you conspire with Étienne Rousseau's second? Did you get him to tamper with the firing pin?"

Rankin's face slackened. "How can ye ask that? Do ye think so little of me?"

"This has nothing to do with the love I bear you. You're as precious to me as my own father." One of his hands still in her grasp, she took the other blue-veined one. "But each day I'm faced with another side to the story. Please, in the name of love, answer truthfully. My marriage's success hinges on your being straightforward."

Her uncle, his jaw clenched, studied the sky. Finally leveling his eyes with hers he said, "At St. Anthony's Garden on a July dawn in 1829, I met Étienne Rousseau's challenge. He chose the arms— pistols. Yes, his gun misfired. But I took my rights. I felled him. But I did not," he lied, "conspire to kill him."

Emma watched for telltale signs. There were none. Shouldn't she be happy? She wasn't. Paul was wrong about his father's death. What could she do to help him see the light?

She now saw no reason to ask Uncle Rankin other damning questions, about a murdered woman in Sisal or about arms sales to the Centralists.

302

"Are ye satisfied, Emmie?"

"Yes. And I'm sorry for asking. But I had to hear it from your mouth."

"I can understand that." He smiled. "Now, back to the purpose of my visit." He released her hands and stepped back. A look of pride lit his features. "I've deposited, in my own name, the sum of twenty-five thousand dollars in the St. Martinsville bank. Ye, and ye alone, are authorized to make withdrawals. Any time, for any purpose. No questions asked, no reports made to me or to Rousseau. 'Tis yers, Emmie, to do with as ye see fit."

"Twenty-five thousand dollars is a world of money."

"A fortune, it's true. But I've many hundreds of thousands, and yer father's no pauper himself. Our gift is but a raindrop in a storm." His leathered face and hard dyes softened. "Take the dowry, Emmie. Buy frippery or champagne or throw it in the air and run under it, whatever pleases ye. But don't insult our gift."

Put that way, she had no choice but to accept.

"Good girl! Now come along, niece of mine. I must introduce ye to the bank manager up in town."

She had the buggy readied for the trip into St. Martinsville, and they rode there. The banker, Pierre Ravel, was overjoyed to meet her—not many depositors had such a grand account. All the while they were talking she wondered what to tell Paul. Would he demand she turn her funds over to him to use for that blasted Navy? Should she tell him about them?

It wasn't that she didn't wish to share her windfall;

under other circumstacnes she would have had no compunction about turning over the money to her husband. A dowry, by rights, belonged to the husband. If Uncle Rankin had given her cash, or if the account was in her name, then Paul would have a legal right to it. But her uncle had insured it would remain Oliver money. And her family's money, she decided, wouldn't be used to further the Texas Navy.

"I'd be honored if you'll be my guest at *déjeuner,*" said Pierre Ravel, rising from behind his desk.

"No thank ye. Another time. Appreciate yer offer, but it's been months since I've seen my fair niece, and I'm looking forward to a quiet lunch—just the two of us."

"But of course. Another time."

Emma and Rankin took their leave. They strolled toward the hotel where they planned to partake of the noon meal. As they neared the inn she stopped short.

Paul. He wore close-fitting, biscuit-colored trousers and shirt, the latter scandalously unbuttoned to the middle of his hairy chest, its sleeves rolled up to his elbows. Paul. Who was supposed to be in New Orleans. The scoundrel had his hand braced on a pillar and was talking to a tall, shapely brunette! Miss Sloe Eyes Goyette.

The beauty gazed up into his eyes and flashed her white teeth. Paul's lips were very near those of Aimée Thérèse. Emma was green with jealousy and red with fury.

"What have we here?" Rankin said.

Emma slammed her reticule under her arm and marched forward. "I don't know, but I'm going to

304

find out."

At that moment the brunette caught sight of Emma. In a familiar fashion, she touched Paul's arm. Slowly he turned, as though he hadn't been caught in an indiscretion, and said a curt hello to Rankin.

"Well," he then declared, "now the mystery of my missing wife is solved. She's been entertaining her favorite uncle, and left her husband to arrive home to an empty house."

How dare he take the offensive? Emma's determination to win back her husband, by fair means or foul, was now at full tilt. "Come on, darling," she said while taking his arm. "Let's do go to *our home.*"

Apparently ignoring her demand, Paul said, "What brings you to St. Martinsville, Oliver? Mumbo jumbo?"

"See here, Rousseau—"

"How are you, Rankin?" Aimée Thérèse put in quickly.

Emma shot a glance at her uncle.

He smiled strangely, evidently choosing to ignore Paul's insult. "Fine, Aimée Thérèse, and you?"

"I'd be much, much better if I could convince Paul"—she grinned at her prey—"and his wife to join the festivities tonight. My birthday fête, you see. And now that you're in town, Rankin, I hope you'll attend."

"I'll be leaving for Magnolia Hall this afternoon, but happy birthday nonetheless, gal," the older man said. He turned to Emma. "I'll meet ye at Feuille de Chêne. Got more business to conduct here in town."

"Well, Paul," Aimée Thérèse pressed, "will you

305

help wish me a happy birthday?"

"Which one is it?" Emma unsheathed her claws. "The fortieth?"

"Thank you," Paul interrupted. "But we have other plans."

Emma was more than willing to meet the enemy in her camp. "Not true, and I don't see why we can't come. Thank you for your gracious invitation." Mentally, she dared Paul to make a contrary statement. He didn't.

"Then I'll see the two of you at Salle de l'Union tonight. Nine o'clock, don't forget. *Au revoir.*" Aimée Thérèse waved her gloved fingers and turned away. Swaying her behind, she glided off.

"Bloody hell, Rousseau," Rankin said, taking his niece's arm. "Don't ye have the decency to hide yer ogling from yer wife?"

Paul continued to watch Aimée Thérèse's every move. "What I do, Oliver, is none of your damned business."

Now that it was done, Emma regretted accepting the invitation. Why play with fire? Paul was a hot-blooded man denied his husbandly rights, and the birthday "girl" was a woman who granted his desires.

But Emma, wise in the ways of Paul's passions, felt she could do something about his needs.

Chapter Nineteen

Paul hitched his steed to the rear of Emma's buggy, and they rode away from town. He was glad she had caught him talking with Aimée Thérèse. Anything that might spark a reaction from his wife had to be good.

And she was reacting. She spoke in the low, tender voice he hadn't heard since their honeymoon; he forced his replies to be insouciant. On the leather seat beside him, her hips were much closer to his thigh than usual. Fanning herself, fanning him, her tiny hand worked the ivory-handled ornament. The scent of heliotrope assailed him. Emma hadn't worn perfume in months. The buggy bounced, and her hand shot through the curve of his elbow. Emma, he decided, was fighting Aimée Thérèse's fire with fire.

As for fire, though the heat of his body might be attributed to the hot August day, actually his wife caused it.

Come hell or high water, he wouldn't let on that Aimée Thérèse was past history. He had run into her a few times and his former mistress had made it

307

obvious that she was available, but he hadn't been taking.

Soon Emma would know how much he loved her. Soon. But the message wouldn't come from his mouth. A surprise would be delivered from New Orleans. Before he'd left the crescent city this last time, an idea had germinated. Now it was in full bloom. As soon as the surprise arrived she'd understand.

"Oh look," she said, pointing to the side of the roadbed. "Cattails. Cleo loves making mats out of them. Could we stop so I can pick some?"

From the look in her leaf green eyes Paul could tell the last thing on her mind was flora.

"Don't see why not," he replied, his nonchalance evaporating. They were on Rousseau property, land he knew well. He pulled back the reins, and guided the gelding to an oyster-shell lane. "Matter of fact, there's a bayou branch just a couple hundred yards away that's growing high with, um, cattails."

Helping her from the buggy, Paul gave himself a mental pat on the back. He was going to get her all worked up, then let her have a taste of rejection.

It wasn't going to be easy. They were alone in an isolated neck of the woods. Very alone. Her honeyed locks were swept into braids and curls—his fingers were itching to free them—and she wore a white organdy frock trimmed with aqua satin that contrasted with the green surroundings. Stooping to the side rather than bending at the knees, she flicked his knife across a cattail stem. He caught a glimpse of a well-turned ankle above a satin slipper. He swallowed hard.

"Look," she said. "A squirrel. Isn't it delightful?"

"Exceedingly."

She turned and straightened, the cattails near her bosom. "Would you hold these for me, please?"

He swallowed again. "Just, uh, put them down."

To retreat from the disappointment that dashed into her April-leaf eyes, he made a volte-face and strode to a spreading oak. Squatting back on his heels, he broke a blade of grass, sticking it between his teeth. And tried to ignore the swelling in his groin.

Emma placed the load of furry reeds on the ground, then swept over to him. "Are you having an affair wih that sloe-eyed hussy?"

"Might be."

"Yes or no?"

"Might be."

Her fingers shook. "You are."

"I never said that." He relaxed against the broad tree trunk. "But I will say this: some of these hot summer nights get mighty cold."

She lowered her eyes and moistened her lips. "They wouldn't if you were sleeping with me."

"Is that an invitation?"

"Yes."

"No thanks," he replied, yearning to say the opposite. "It's best we do not."

"Why? Because I said I was going to divorce you?"

"Could be."

"I don't want a divorce."

"What do you want, Emma?"

She stepped closer, the hem of her skirts touching his forearm. "A reconciliation."

"The terms haven't changed."

"I know." She knelt beside him. "But . . . I can't stand living without you."

He was at the brink of succumbing, but she wasn't going to win that easily. The tips of his fingers moved to rest at the juncture of his thighs. "Or is it, you can't stand the thought of Aimée Thérèse having this?"

Anger flushed Emma's cheeks. Her shoulders drew back. For a moment he thought she'd flounce away, but she didn't. As she straddled his hips, he surrendered.

"Tell me you've missed this," she implored, pressing her pelvis against him.

He lifted his legs on her derrière, bringing her face to his. His words were rife with meaning. "I've missed it. Every hour, every day, I think of our couplings. I remember how good it feels to have you tight around me." He framed her adored face with his hands. "But most of all, I've missed you. Your sharp tongue, your god-awful ways. The angel you are at other times."

"Let me be your wife again," she whispered.

"Gladly."

They parted for just enough time to dispense with one another's clothing, which fell in heaps on the leaf-strewn terrain. If there would be regrets later, Emma wouldn't consider them now.

All she wanted was his embrace . . . and she had it. She watched him as his amber eyes devoured her naked body. Basking in his worshipful gaze, she took in his male perfection. Her fingers itched to comb through the black chest hair that grew in

310

whorls to his stomach . . . and downward. His olive skin was hard with muscle.

She raised her arms to his neck. "How about a hot kiss, husband?"

He complied. All the while his fingers were loosening the confines of her hair. After it fell to her shoulders, the two of them dropped to the bed of oak leaves, Emma atop him. As her nails found the crisp hair that fascinated her, the pads of his fingers trailed across the swollen peaks of her breasts. Then his mouth replaced those fingers, which moved to the most sensitive nub of her womanhood. Gently, rhythmically, he imparted exquisite torture. A wave of agonizing pleasure crested within her.

Throwing back her head, she murmured, "Oh, darling, I've missed you so much."

"Amoureuse . . ."

His strong hands spanning her hips, she lifted herself upon his turgid staff, enveloping him. His groan of pleasure elicited a moaning response. At this moment he was hers, and she was his, and there was no yesterday or tomorrow.

Light-headed, she set the pace, moving slowly, then faster. His hands cupped her breasts, his fingers thrumming her nipples. She heard him moan *"Mon dieu,"* as another wave of orgasmic euphoria peaked within her. This power she wielded was wondrous.

She felt him tense, and knew his own satisfaction was near. And she was frightened. Semen could beget a baby. Her heart despised what common sense bade her do, but she lifted herself away.

He surged to a standing position and towered above her. "Why did you do that?"

She gulped before stuttering, "I . . . we . . . it's—There could have been a child."

Turning his back, he stuck one leg, then the other into his trousers. He buttoned them. "We'd better get on to the house. Your uncle will be wondering where we are."

"Paul . . . please understand—"

"Get dressed." His eyes guarded, he tossed her pantaloons onto her lap. "I don't want to be late for Aimée Thérèse's birthday fête."

She deserved his anger, and she tried to make amends, but he was close-mouthed and grim for the rest of the afternoon—even while he dressed in his finest attire . . . for Aimée Thérèse.

That night they attended the birthday extravaganza. No matter that Emma had spent months in the area, she remained amazed at grandeur amid wilderness. The Salle de l'Union, a brick building of two stories and a dormered attic, sat high above the oak-lined west bank of the Bayou Teche. A place of elegance for certain, resplendent with chandeliers, gilding and finery. The residents of St. Martinsville were proud to call their town Le Petit Paris, and the Union Building did much to further that image.

The local aristocracy was there in full force, but Emma's arrival caused a stir of excitement. Her two-seasons-old gown, teal silk and low cut, enhanced her blond good looks; she knew it and was glad. She wanted—no needed—to be appreciated on this night. But that need could be assuaged only by one man who paid her no heed. Paul.

312

Emma turned her attention to the festivities. The honored Mademoiselle Goyette had not yet made an entrance. Holding delicate Oriental fans in their equally delicate hands, the women present wore satins and lace and twinkling jewels. Liveried footmen passed delicacies and champagne to the ladies, which they sipped while cooing at the gentlemen, and the objects of their attention were served liquors of the first quality. Under swinging, ceiling-fastened fans manned by small black boys, they danced to the music of great composers.

Men of all ages and levels of attractiveness sought Emma out. She consented to dance with each one: waltzes and reels and minuets. Her laughter and chatter were forced, but no one sensed how insecure she felt.

A blond man, Philippe St. Jacques, bowed low as the last chord of a waltz faded. *"Merci beaucoup, madame.* I'm honored by the pleasure of your company. May I have another dance?"

"Actually, *monsieur,"* she said, eying her husband who was engaged in conversation with an elderly gentleman and a dour-faced woman she knew to be Monique Carteaux. "I do believe I should see what my dear husband is up to."

"As you wish. Thank you again for the dance."

Emma strolled up to Paul and took his arm. He turned, and for a moment she thought he was pleased to see her. But a guarded look crossed his face.

"Hello, Emma," Monique said.

Emma responded easily to the greeting. Monique was an unmarried schoolmistress, a no-nonsense

313

person, and she had done much to ease the townspeople's minds about Emma's "witchdoctoring," though she and Emma were but passing acquaintances.

"May I present my grandfather Louis Carteaux?" Monique asked. "A duke and formerly military adviser to Louis XVI."

Emma dropped a curtsy. "Pleased to meet you, your grace."

"And you, madame, but I'll have none of that 'your grace' business," he said, resting his arthritic hands atop a silver-handled cane. "This is Louisiana, not France."

"As you wish, sir."

Paul offered no conversation, merely stood with Emma's arm looped around his elbow.

"How are you liking St. Martinsville?" Carteaux asked.

"It pleases me. Before my marriage, I'd never been to this area, but I've grown quite attached to it." Emma meant those words. "It's home, and our future. I'll be forever thankful my husband brought me here."

Carteaux smiled. "It warms me to hear this. For many years I've hoped Paul would return to St. Martinsville."

The subject of their discussion cleared his throat before arching a brow at his wife. "I know you'll be interested in what the three of us were discussing. It's a topic near and dear to your heart, the Texas Navy."

"Discussing?" Monique said. "You mean debating."

"Debating," Paul conceded.

"Are you, like your husband and my grandfather, a supporter of Texas? I would assume you are, but I've learned over the years never to rely on assumptions."

Emma wouldn't publicly embarrass Paul with the truth. "I respect my husband's opinion," she responded. In matters not pertaining to Texas, that was true.

From the corner of her eye, she saw puzzlement in her husband's face.

"I've followed the Navy's activities through the newspapers," the old duke said. "I'm interested in all that goes on. But, with your lovely lady in our presence, we must change the subject."

"Oh no." Paul raised his crystal glass; its brilliance caught the gleam in his eye. "Do go on. My loving wife has shown much interest in the fate of my adopted nation. I'm certain she wants to hear all about it."

Emma did not correct this brash falsehood. "Oh yes, Monsieur Carteaux. Please tell me more."

"I was explaining to Paul here that I am concerned about the situation in the Gulf. The Centralist vermin in Mexico City have invaded the Yucatán, and we shouldn't allow them to get away with it."

"I don't see why the two of you worry so," Monique said, her thin lips drawn into a line. "The Mexican peninsula is far from our shores."

The ancient royalist's grooved face took on a perturbed expression. "All far-thinking residents of Louisiana must be concerned, Monique. President

315

Santa Anna seeks victory over the Gulf of Mexico and if his goal is accomplished, we'll all feel the repercussions. There'll be no shipping in or out of our State."

"Perhaps"—the schoolteacher strung out the words—"you worry too much."

Carteaux's face took on a purplish hue. "As usual you use me for sport, Petite-fille."

Emma was uncomfortable with this exchange between the duke and his granddaughter, and something strange happened. She suddenly felt the urge to defend the Republic she had visited but once.

"Santa Anna must be stopped before he takes any more lives in the Republic of Texas," she declared.

Paul turned his head in her direction, astonishment on his face.

"I doubt it will come to that." Monique sipped her glass of champagne.

"You are young and haven't known the horrors of war," Carteaux said. "Almost fifty years have passed since I was forced out of my homeland by the Terror, but even if it were ten times that number of years, I wouldn't forget how it feels to be crushed by an enemy."

"Alarmist," his granddaughter retorted. "Did you ever stop to consider that Texas might do well to capitulate to a stronger power? After all, the revolution of '36, no matter how venerated in most American minds, was led by upstarts who'd sworn allegiance to the Mexican flag. They stole that land."

"Whether or not you speak the truth, Texas was victorious at San Jacinto." Emma was quivering with anger. "Nothing gives the Centralists the right to capture Texas towns or to terrorize and kill their citizenry. Yet Santa Anna's forces have done that.

"His navy is aimed toward the Yucatecan peninsula, but the Texas Navy has vowed to keep them at bay. Its presence occupies Santa Anna in those waters . . . and keeps him away from ours. At least for the time being."

"Thank you, Emma. I appreciate those words," Paul said. Then he added, "Forgive me, Monsieur Carteaux. I'm afraid I skirted the truth. You see, my wife didn't share my views on the Navy to which I've sworn allegiance. In the past she scoffed at the cause, and I merely wished to rile her." He exerted pressure on her arm and stood taller. "It pleased me to hear her speak those words."

Emma was thrilled. She had made her husband happy, and that made her happy.

"I see." The elderly man clicked his tongue. "I'm glad you've come over to our side."

Yes, Emma was on their side, but the sacrifices Paul was making for Texas remained a point of contention between them.

Carteaux imparted a smile to Paul. "My fortune is not what it was, but I'm willing to give my fair share for freedom."

Paul grinned triumphantly at Emma. "Thank you, sir. Now I have two financial backers for my cause—you and the honorable Howard O'Reilly of New Orleans."

"My uncle Howard has always been your supporter." Emma wanted to support him, too. Suddenly, a decision was made. Uncle Rankin's money was going to be spent on the Texas Navy. It would free Paul from fund-raising, and might save Feuille de Chêne from the sale block. As soon as they were home she'd tell her husband. "I must praise Howard at our next meeting."

"For that I'm thankful," Paul responded.

Apparently Monique knew she was outnumbered. "Grandpère, you're looking a bit tired. Shall we sit down for a few moments?"

The elderly Carteaux agreed, and they walked over to a table.

Then the music stopped, and all eyes turned to the entrance. Emma watched her husband's face; it was unreadable. A round of applause and a tribute from the orchestra filled the room.

Mademoiselle Goyette had arrived. Dressed in jewels and silks, she nodded at the assemblage, then swept into the ballroom, her head held regally.

When Aimée Thérèse caught sight of Paul, she changed course, making straight for him. "Paul"— she held her jeweled fingers aloft—"I'm so glad you could attend. You, too, Madame Rousseau," she said, almost as an afterthought.

"Happy birthday."

Emma kept her eyes on Paul. The words he had spoken to Miss Sloe Eyes had been murmured sweetly. Was he simply being cordial? Or was he, in truth, having an affair with her?

"You know I'm expecting a present from you, *chéri*," Aimée Thérèse said. "Later perhaps?"

Jealousy stabbed Emma as he kissed the woman's hand in a gallant manner. Would he go from an unfulfilling bed of leaves to one of satisfying down all in a single day?

An even stronger emotion tore at Emma's heart when she got an eyeful of her rival's bodice. Angélique Rousseau's brooch was pinned to it!

Baffled, Emma stepped back, her fingers going to her lips. Then realization dawned. After all the heartache Paul had given her over that despicable brooch, *he'd given it to that strumpet!*

Horror gripped Emma. This proved how little Paul cared for her and what a mockery their marriage was.

She forced an "Excuse me . . . I need a breath of night air" past her dry throat and whipped around.

"Of course," said Miss Sloe Eyes, and she turned to acknowledge the greetings of another.

Several feet from where they had stood Paul caught Emma's arm. "We need to talk."

"Leave me some pride," she whispered, hoping no eyes would turn toward them. "Grant me a moment alone. And don't follow me."

He leaned toward her ear. "I'll give you two minutes. Then we're leaving for home."

His breath roused an involuntary tremble within her. "Two minutes, Paul. That's all I ask."

Her back stiff, she cleared the French doors, glancing over her shoulder to make sure his word was good. She had to get away! Putting distance between them was the only way she could sort through her heartache.

Blindly she hurried to their pirogue, took up a paddle, and rowed south toward Feuille de Chêne. She strained her eyes to navigate, for it was dark, deep dark, on the bayou. Night sounds mocked her over and over again. Yet she had nothing with which to light the lantern that could have helped to guide her. Lost on the bayou, she also felt lost regarding her future.

Something snapped at the wooden boat. An alligator? Her heart jumped into her throat, and she rowed harder. Suddenly realizing she might be paddling in circles, she cried out in exasperation. "Why, Paul . . . why?"

Drat him! Hadn't he known, or at least suspected, that Aimée Thérèse would wear the brooch on this night? Was it his way of showing that he'd never accept her terms? Or had he, like the night sounds, simply mocked her?

Pledging that he wouldn't get the best of her, Emma again took up the paddle. By her leave-taking she had shown him how much he had hurt her, but never would that happen again.

Paul was frantic. Emma had no business being alone on the Bayou Teche—she knew that—and he was concerned about her emotional state. He had to make her understand about Aimée Thérèse.

With swift, sure strokes, he guided a borrowed pirogue through the bayou. A lantern was hooked to the prow. Caws and coos filled his ears. He heard an alligator flop into the water and glide toward him.

His heart and mind screamed reproaches for allowing her those two minutes. Another five had been added to them before he'd secured this pirogue; most attendees had arrived at the fete by carriage. And his progress wasn't as swift as he would have liked. Each foot of the way required careful study.

Her pirogue could be overturned at any bend or tree stump, her body . . . *What would he do without her!*

It seemed like hours later, yet it was only minutes, before Paul cleared the last bend separating himself from home. *Please let her be there!* As the lantern's glow illuminated the pirogue tied to the quay, he exhaled and his shoulders wilted with relief. In the same breath heart's ease was replaced by aggravation.

"You scared the life out of me," he yelled up the lawn, all the while shaking and staring at the light that poured from one lone window of the big house. "You could've been killed!"

Stomping up the incline, he gave serious thought to shaking Emma until her teeth rattled. He yanked the front door open and continued his march toward her. But the moment he opened the library door, irritation left him. He wanted to take her into his arms and rain kisses of joy on her face.

"Emma . . ."

She sat at the desk, calmly making notes with quill and paper. "You've returned, I see."

The icy chill of her voice brought Paul back to their problem. He had a lot of explaining to do. Cutting across the rug, he said, "About the brooch, I—"

"I'd rather not discuss it." She put the quill down. "There's something I must tell you."

"We are going to discuss that damned pin. It was—"

"Pardon me for interrupting, Paul, but I really don't care what you do, or don't do, with your personal property. And that's what I'd like to discuss with you. Personal possessions. This afternoon you asked me why Uncle Rankin was in town, and now I'm going to tell you. He and my father have given me twenty-five thousand dollars."

The figure hit Paul like a ton of bricks. "You can't be serious," he said in French, then caught himself and repeated it in English.

"But I am. The money is mine, to do with as I please."

Deciding he'd return to the brooch later, Paul asked, "How do you plan to spend it?"

"After taking care of necessities and indulging in some luxuries here at home"—she wanted to hurt him, bruise him to the core of his being, just like he had wounded her—"I'm sending a tidy amount to the government in Mexico City, with the proviso that it be used for the poor," she lied.

"Traitorous *Oliver* bitch!" He'd be damned before an explanation about the brooch would pass his lips now.

The words he had pridefully heard her say in defense of Texas had been nothing but lies. She had been trying to make up for the afternoon's disaster. That was all. He was totally disgusted.

"You'd do that, wouldn't you? You'd send money to our enemy."

"Your foe, not mine." She despised herself for continuing this farce, but she couldn't control her temper. Avoiding his angry eyes, she said, "I fail to see how the poor of any country could be tagged as the enemy."

"If that's the way you feel, why don't you send an equal sum to Texas?"

322

"Perhaps I will, but maybe I won't." She lifted her shoulder in forced nonchalance. "I fear some of my money might fall into the hands of war-thirsty Texans."

"You speak in paradoxical terms. Perhaps you should listen to yourself," he gritted out, then cleared the desk's edge to capture her elbow. "You're a naïve fool if you think your money won't fall into Antonio López de Santa Anna's coffers."

She pulled away from his grasp. "Drat you! Yes, I'm a naïve fool. What else could you call a person who is foolish enough to base her future on the likes of you?" Her chest was heaving. "But you, dear husband, have played me for the fool for the very last time! You'll never—ever—get your hands on my money. Not one red cent of it will go to the Texas Navy!"

"I wouldn't take your filthy lucre if you begged me to do it," he said, meaning those words. "Why would the hungry and ill-armed but courageous men of Texas need alms from a vicious, self-centered seed of the Olivers?"

"You're one to talk, spawn of *Étienne Rousseau!*"

"That's right. I'm his son and proud of it. But your tainted blood runs thick through your veins, Emma *Oliver*. You're no better than your slime-hearted uncle who slayed my father, cracked the skull of an innocent woman, and sold arms to the bastards who, among their other heinous deeds, marched my fellow Texans in chains."

Emma drew her hand back to slap him, but he caught it, twisting it behind her. She cried out in pain.

Furious, he fastened his lips to hers. She squirmed beneath him, and as quickly as he had seized her, he let her go. She fell to the floor, her legs sprawled before him. Paul fought the urge to place himself between those thighs, to bury himself deep within her.

"Leave me alone," she said with a hiss. "Don't put your filthy hands on me."

Towering above her, he said, "You needn't worry. I've no wish to lay a finger on your comely flesh. If I did, you might get the child you fear so much, and I won't take the chance of poisoning Rousseau blood with an Oliver's."

Chapter Twenty

Paul stared down at the floor, at his wife. Her sharp intake of breath shamed him. He hadn't meant to be so harsh. But her pronouncement about furthering the Centralist cause had angered him beyond the point of rational behavior.

He had to free her, and himself, from the cruel web of deceit that had started when he'd deceived her into marrying him. Nothing in Remi Rousseau's will stipulated that either of them had to be chained to Feuille de Chêne. Until those twelve months of marriage were over, Ben could manage the fields, Cleopatra the house.

"Go back to Virginia, Emma. Or New Orleans. Or wherever you wish to be. This place can never be our home."

Her anger was suddenly replaced by anxiety. "What will you do?"

"Leave."

"Please don't."

He left. Left Louisiana. Left his heart. His soul.

He needed time to think, probably lots of it, and in Emma's presence clear thinking was not possible.

When he reached Galveston, the *San Antonio* was ordered to the Yucatán, and Paul, now Captain Rousseau, was at the helm.

Emma did not leave Feuille de Chêne. And she did not send money to Mexico City, although she anonymously gave a sizable sum to the missions of San Antonio.

She was tormented by Paul's betrayal. He had slept with Aimée Thérèse, had given that strumpet the despicable brooch. Emma was too angry, too hurt, and too disgusted to put those thoughts out of her mind.

Summer waned to autumn. Each night she slept in her lonely bed, her arms equally empty. Thanksgiving passed. Christmas, that time for family and loved ones, came and went. She neither visited her relatives nor invited them to do likewise. To let them see how much she hurt was unthinkable.

Of course Cleopatra was full of reproval mixed with closely guarded compassion. Woodley, the mostly white pup, had grown into a fluffy dog, and proved a comfort. His limpid brown eyes seemed to understand Emma's loneliness and sorrow, and he faithfully cuddled on her lap or followed at her heel. It was as if he wanted to take the hurt from her, wanted to make her whole again. Yet woman's best friend was no substitute for husbandly love. But then, Paul's love had never been a part of the bargain.

Through Howard's letters, which held no mention of Paul, she was informed of the goings-on in Texas.

A hurricane had battered Galveston, destroying two of Texas's warships. The *Zavala* was so worm-eaten that she was an embarrassment, and the remaining vessels were fast deteriorating. Crews had been skeletonized, both by desertions and by lack of money to pay them.

In September General Adrian Woll's Centralist troops had overwhelmed the city of San Antonio—its second capture in six months. There had been no easy recapture this time.

The people of Texas were in trouble. Congress had appropriated funds for a full naval campaign; then, strangely, President Houston had vetoed the bill, and had instructed Moore to apply for credit with New Orleans ship chandlers, though credit wasn't their method of doing business. Sam Houston's popularity in the Republic was next to nil.

The citizens, Howard had written, feared it was only a matter of time before the Mexican flag replaced the Lone Star.

Her husband, Emma realized, must be beside himself. What was he doing and what measures had he taken to stop the aggression she had scoffed at?

Where was he? Why hadn't he at least sent a letter informing her of his whereabouts? Despite her anger, she longed for news—any news—about him. It was pure curiosity . . . wasn't it?

The first year of their marriage was drawing to an end. Spring came early in the warm climate of south Louisiana. New leaves bloomed on the trees in which birds nested with their young. Flowers blossomed. The canebrakes grew higher.

Would Paul go through with his plans to dispose of Feuille de Chêne? If so, he'd be forced to return to St. Martinsville. Emma didn't want to see the two-timer, yet he filled her thoughts. Drat him.

The sun was in descent when the supply boat arrived, to a round of Woodley's barking, at the plantation dock.

"Have a delivery for Madame Paul Rousseau," the captain said. "Two crates of medical supplies."

"Please explain," she implored, holding the dog's velvet leash tight.

"Your husband bought medical supplies for you. Asked me to keep it a surprise till they were delivered."

Emma was at a loss to understand. Why had Paul purchased medical supplies?

The captain ran his fingers across his bald pate. "Sorry we didn't get these to you sooner, ma'am. The lieutenant, your husband, asked us to deliver 'em straightaway, but the suppliers up North delayed freighting 'em down here. Then I was down on my back till after Christmas. Started over here finally, but my boat sprang a leak and had to be repaired." He flushed. "Well, excuses have a way of sounding hollow. But I pray you'll accept my apologies."

"No harm done," she said, taking the letter he offered.

"Where do you want these crates?" the man asked as he reached down to pet a now tail-wagging Woodley.

Absently Emma motioned toward her second-story office. She was on pins and needles, so eager was she to open the letter inscribed "Emma" in Paul's bold, manly script.

In the privacy of her bedroom she ripped a letter opener through its top. It was dated four days prior to the argument that had sent him away. As she read the contents, she choked out, "Oh no . . ."

"What's the matter with you?" Cleopatra stuck her head through the doorway.

Emma dumped Woodley off her lap. "Read this."

Cleopatra wiped her hands on her apron and picked up the letter, reading it. "Well, I tried to tell you."

"Couldn't you find a little mercy in your heart," Emma pleaded, "this one time?"

"Oh, baby, I am sorry."

"Read it aloud, Cleo. Read it to me. I want to hear it again so my foolishness will be reinforced."

Reluctantly the tiny woman did so. *"Chère Emma, I've racked my brain trying to think of a way to make up for the hardships you've endured since our marriage. I thought of giving you my mother's brooch—she would've wanted you to have it, and I'd be proud for you to wear it—but you probably wouldn't want the blasted thing. It might bring back memories best left in the past, right? So I've sold it (hope you don't mind) to a woman in St. Martinsville whose intelligence stops at baubles and gewgaws. Anyway, I thought you might appreciate medical supplies instead. You're a fine doctor, ma bien-aimée, and my fondest wish is for your success. I take that back. That's almost my fondest wish, but we'll get to my fondest desire after you've opened these gifts!"*

Cleopatra wiped away the tear that rolled down her brown cheek. "'I love you, Paul,'" she croaked.

Emma felt certain that this letter hadn't been written by a man who'd cheated on his wife! "H-he didn't give it to Aimée Thérèse. He sold it to her. For me. For what he thought I wanted. Oh, Cleo, didn't he know I just wanted him?"

"You made it kinda hard to see at times."

"He never said he loved me. But he wouldn't have . . . wouldn't have signed the letter that way if he hadn't meant it."

"Baby, baby, don't cry." Cleopatra hugged her close. "You ain't cried since you was five and fell outta that big old mulberry tree and broke your arm."

"This is a lot worse than fracturing an ulna."

"Well, missy, what you gonna do about Frenchie?"

"If I knew where he was, I'd go to him."

"Something that insignificant ain't never stopped you before. Find out where he be, and even if you have to collar him, bring him back! Go on, girl, before I take a switch to your tail end!"

Emma stuck her tongue out. "I don't need your prompting." Cleopatra at her heel, she hurried to the storage room to find her traveling trunks and the dog's wicker carrier. "You and Ben mind the store— Woodley and I are going after the merchandise!"

The obvious place to seek word of Paul was St. Martinsville. The home of Louis Carteaux, with its rococo furnishings, was where Emma headed. The old duke, whom she hadn't seen since the night of

330

Aimée Thérèse's birthday fête, greeted her warmly.

Refusing to let foolish pride stand in her way, Emma said, "This is going to sound strange, sir, but do you know how I can get in touch with my husband?"

The white-haired nobleman swayed forward on his silver-handled cane. "Left the night I met you, right?"

"Yes, sir. We had words, and"—a flush spread over her face—"I haven't heard from him since."

"That's not right of him." Carteaux grimaced. "I've known Paul since he was a boy—knew his parents and grandparents, too, but that's not important at the moment. Anyway, I've never known him to behave in such an ungallant manner."

"I provoked it."

The old man shook his snow-thatched head. "To leave and send no word, he must be very angry with you."

For the first time since she had hatched this scheme to find her husband, Emma was assailed by doubts. Yes, Paul was angry. Very angry. Furious. He had written that he loved her, yet that was before . . . This was now. Had she destroyed his love? She had to keep her spirits up. They *would* be able to put the pieces of their marriage back together again, she told herself.

"Yes, he's upset. But I love him very, very much and I seek to heal his wounds."

"It pleases me to hear this, madame. Paul is dear to my heart—I've never had a grandson, you see. I do hope for the success of your marriage."

Emma uttered the proper words of appreciation,

then pursued her goal. "But I still need to know his whereabouts. Is he in Texas?"

Carteaux swayed. He studied the toes of his shoes. He was taking a long, long time to answer. Finally he raised his tired old eyes to her anxious ones. "Initially, yes. He was in Galveston. But he left for Sisal late in July. On the *San Antonio* I understand." His cane shook under unsteady hands. "You've received no word from the Department of War and Marine?"

"None. *Monsieur,* please don't keep anything back. Tell me what is going on."

"Commodore Moore sent him down there to offer renewed help to Barbachano's rebels."

Fear sliced through Emma. "So long ago! Have they engaged in war?"

"I don't believe so."

"Please don't hedge. Please tell me!"

The valleys in his face deepened. "There's been no word from the *San Antonio.* It's"—he closed his eyes—"listed as missing."

"No! It can't be true. Paul could be . . . could be dead." The words sounded odd, as if they did not come from her. Emma sank onto a settee. Why, oh why, she railed silently, did I drive him away?

"He thought I didn't love him." Her voice was a monotone of grief. "Thought I'd taken the enemy's side."

"Don't punish yourself."

"I can't help it. He gave his all for the country that embraced him after his own grandfather turned him away. Yet I degraded his convictions, and led him to think I'd turned against him."

332

"There's no proof the ship went down," Carteaux was saying, evidently trying to infuse hope.

"If there's been no communiqué from the schooner, there's only one explanation—it sank."

"You owe your man the benefit of the doubt. I know Paul, and he wouldn't wish you to give him up for dead. Not until it's a proven fact."

She stared at the wise old man. "You're right. He wouldn't want my sympathy. He wants my support, and I'm going to give it to him. I'm going to Galveston. When Paul returns, he'll go there."

"Well, give him my best regards," Carteaux said, pushing aside his own inner doubts.

Despite her show of optimism, Emma feared for her husband. If I am lucky enough to have one more chance, she thought, he will know how much I love him. She was now determined to stand by his side, for better or for worse, and without doubts.

If she got the chance.

Chapter Twenty-One

This was a flat place, near sea level. No native trees like the majestic ones of south Louisiana. No points of prominence. But it was not without natural beauty. Lagoons and marshes boasted rushes and reeds, and tall grasses swayed across the flat horizon. Graceful pelicans and flamingos perched on the wharf.

Emma, with Woodley at her feet, held on to the rail as the merchant brig docked in Galveston Bay. She was holding her breath in the hope that Paul would be in the coastal town.

To her right, she saw a forlorn Texas Navy steam side-wheeler. The *Zavala*, weatherbeaten and tired-looking, and aground. Yet its red, white, and blue ensign waved proudly and brightly, as if to say, "I'm down but not out."

That was exactly how Emma felt. Down but not out. She feared for Paul's life. And if he was alive, would he forgive her? But she had confidence in his written words of love, and she'd never give up—on his life or his forgiveness.

"Mrs. Rousseau, will you be taking accommodations at the Tremont House?" Captain Faracy asked.

She turned to the middle-aged man. "I don't think so, Captain. From what you've told me, that hotel is much too bustling for my taste. I hope to find my husband here, and we'll want peace and quiet. I'll search for a house to rent."

Faracy chuckled. "Well, that's fine and dandy, ma'am, but you'll need a place to stay in the meantime. Unoccupied houses are few and far between on the island, and the rooming establishments are crowded as a rule. Perhaps I could make a suggestion?"

"Please do."

"There's a Mrs. Lightfoot you might call on. She lives a block north of the Strand. I can't guarantee anything, but she's been known to let a room, provided the renter is the upstanding sort." Faracy winked in his good-natured manner. "I think she'll find you to her liking."

"Thank you, Captain."

Emma took Woodley into her arms, and he slathered a kiss on her chin. She murmured a "no, no" while tapping his little black nose with her forefinger.

"Saving your kisses for the mister, eh?"

"Exactly."

"Mr. Rousseau is a very lucky man." Captain Faracy bowed politely. "Mrs. Rousseau, if I may, I'd be honored to introduce you to Mrs. Lightfoot."

Emma realized that an unaccompanied woman might not be welcome. Add Woodley to the package, and chances were he'd be the coup de grace. But why was she concerned? Paul might have accommodations here in Galveston. She should look for him first.

No. That wasn't a good idea. She needed to freshen up; he must see her at her best, provided he was in town. She accepted the captain's offer.

Minutes later they were walking into Galveston. A babel of voices filled her ears, and warehouses and shops advertising drugs and chemicals lined the streets, which were hard-packed sand. She noted that all the buildings were constructed of wood.

Woodley stopped to lift his leg on an acacia shrub fronting the Come Inn grog shop. His deed done, he growled, tugged at his lead and pushed his nose beneath the thorny bush. An earless, tail-less pig oinked once, and made a run for it. The dog tried to give chase, but Emma laughed and scooped a squirming ball of white fur into her arms.

"Naughty boy. Leave that pig alone. She looks like she's had a bad enough time as it is."

"Swine run wild here on the island," the captain explained, "but they keep the refuse cleaned up, so nobody minds. Least of all the dogs. Ergo, missing ears and tails."

From the Come Inn a man threw a bucket of food into the street. As if materializing from nowhere, three pigs—round and pink, and devoid of ears and tails—pounced upon the heap and began rooting.

"They are a strange-looking lot," Emma commented and fell in step with Captain Faracy.

Her eyes took in the town itself. Strange was the best adjective to describe this seaport. Why, she wondered, was Paul so fond of it?

Two more blocks and they arrived at a two-story white clapboard house with green shutters. On the sill of a front window rested a small, neatly painted sign reading Mrs. A. Lightfoot, Proprietress to the Discriminating.

Emma had expected a delicate woman of decorum and snobbish airs. She was shocked. Anthaline Lightfoot had a voice as huge as her body, which was big, tall, almost manly. She wore breeches and boots, and her carrot-red hair was cropped close to her ears. Her blue, wide-set eyes were her best feature, and they softened her pielike face. She said she didn't like dogs.

"Now, Anthie," the captain cajoled, "this here's a nice little feller." Faracy bent down to scratch Woodley's brisket; the dog was giving Mrs. Lightfoot a dubious twice-over. "He's been aboard the *Winsome Lady* for days, and I never received a complaint about him."

"Can't have no dog bitin' the guests or peein' on my floors."

"Anthie, you're being crude."

Emma gave serious consideration to thanking the woman for her time, and leaving. She was not about to be insulted or grovel for a room. After all, the Tremont House was just down the way, and surely its management was more hospitable than Anthaline Lightfoot.

Faracy directed a sympathetic smile at Emma before saying, "I gave you my word about his behavior. And, Anthie, you know my word's my bond."

Anthaline Lightfoot propped her roughened, oversized hands on her mile-wide hips and said, "Well, Faracy, I know you wouldn't lie to me. If that dog's housebroken, he can stay. Dollar a day for room and board for the young lady, and two bits extra for the dog. Can you afford it, girl?"

Emma did a quick mental calculation. "You may have to evict me . . . after about fifty years."

"So—you're a rich un, huh?" Those big blue eyes smiled down at Emma. "Well, that's neither here nor there, long's I get my money on time."

That was all Emma could ask. If Paul had a house, her stay at Mrs. Lightfoot's establishment would be short. Very short. And if he didn't, she intended to find suitable private accommodations.

Captain Faracy flipped his cap to his head. "Well, Mrs. Rousseau, it seems you're all set, so I'll take my leave."

"Thank—"

"Rousseau did you say? Any kin to Paul Rousseau?"

Emma brightened and turned to Mrs. Lightfoot. "Yes. I'm his wife."

"Paul never said nothin' about havin' no wife."

"I'll be going," Faracy put in, and hastened out the parlor door. "One of the hands will deliver your trunks straightaway," he called back. "Goodbye, ladies."

Emma turned back to the prior subject. "Paul and I were married a year ago this month."

"Oh." That one little word was heavy with meaning. "No use in us standin' on ceremony. Name's Anthaline, so call me that. What's your first

338

name, girl?"

Emma didn't know whether she liked this Anthaline, but she had a grudging respect for her forthright behavior so she wasn't contrary. Mainly, she wanted to find out what the woman knew about Paul.

"Emma. My given name is Emma."

"Had a sister named Emma." Anthaline allowed Woodley to smell the back of her hand, then she patted him. "Injuns scalped her."

Woodley's tail was thumping against Emma's ankle as she murmured sincerely, "Oh, I'm so terribly sorry."

"Aw now, wasn't goin' after your sympathy. Them's one of the hazards of livin' in the wilds of Texas. Wild Injuns, deserts, rattlesnakes, nasty Mexs wantin' to fly their Buzzard and Snake over our land. Yep, we gotta lotta hazards here—it ain't New York, that's for sure."

That was for sure.

"Where you from?" Anthaline asked.

"Virginia originally."

"My ma's from Virginie. Ever heard of the Smiths outta Williamsburg?"

"I don't think so."

Woodley forsook his mistress to sniff the giantess's leg. Tongue lolling, he sat back on his haunches.

Anthaline's mouth curved into a smile as she patted his head again. "He's a right cute little whippersnapper. Even though I don't like 'em on the place, dogs like me. Always heard they're a good judge of character."

Emma's ear was being talked off as surely as the town swine were losing theirs, but she warmed to Anthaline. After several more of the big woman's comments and questions, she asked, "Have you seen my husband lately?"

A question mark seemed to loom over Anthaline's broad forehead. "How . . . how long's it been since you heard from him?"

"He returned to his duties in July. We live in Louisiana, you see." Emma took a fortifying breath. "The last I'd learned he'd gone to sea on the *San Antonio*."

"Yep."

Emma's face drained of blood.

"Now hold on, girl. Let me finish. He sailed out on 'er, but he was put off down on one of them islands."

"Thank God!" That was the best news Emma had had in days. Paul wasn't on the missing ship. "Why was he put ashore?"

"Took sick. 'Course he's well now, but it took him a spell of time to get back to these parts."

Paul had been ill! "Do you know where he is?"

"Nope. Ain't my week to keep up with him." Anthaline turned on her heel and motioned toward the staircase. "Come along, girl. I'll show you to your room."

"Are you trying to keep something from me?" Emma asked, halfway up the narrow stairs, which barely provided space for Anthaline's hips.

"Nope." After huffing and puffing to the top, Anthaline turned to a door on the right. She opened it and disappeared inside.

Emma and Woodley followed her. The room was

340

painted white, and lacy curtains were at the lone window. A lantern rested atop a rough-hewn table, and Emma noted that the bed was wide enough for two, and long enough for Paul Rousseau's legs.

"Breakfast's at six; dinner's at one; and supper's at seven. Don't be late. I don't like it when people keep my help late. Effie and Mildred have families of their own to take care of." Anthaline went over to the bed and poked it hard. "You'll sleep like a rock here."

Sleeping was Emma's last consideration!

"Guess I'll have to scare up a pallet for your dog there. What's his name, anyway?"

"Woodley. And he has his own bed. It'll be arriving with my belongings."

"Should of known. Poor people have to sleep in the streets, but rich dogs bring their own beds. What's this world comin' to?"

Emma flushed at the statement's truth. "Does seem unfair."

"Aw now, 'tain't your fault, the world bein' what it is. Little scamp means a lot to you, don't he?"

"Yes. He's been fine company since Paul's been away." Was she ever going to get a straight answer about him from this woman? "Anthaline, if you know where I can find my husband, please tell me."

"I don't like to meddle in other people's business."

"Please."

Anthaline rubbed her palm over her mouth. "Try the Blow Fly Inn over on the Strand. Ask for Carl— he might know where Paul's at."

Ten minutes later Emma and Woodley were

341

within two buildings of the Blow Fly Inn, which appeared to be a disreputable establishment. On pilings, it leaned to the side. If a paintbrush had ever touched its clapboard siding, it hadn't been in that century.

Woodley halted, sniffed the ground, pointed his tail, and howled. Picking up a scent, he dragged Emma toward, and up, the eight steps leading to the grog shop. A crudely lettered banner at the entrance read Ment Jewleps 10 Cints. The sound of a tinny piano came through the door. She opened it, and a haze of tobacco smoke enveloped her.

As the dog lunged across the sawdust floor, Emma's eyes followed his course—and stopped. Paul was trying to disengage a blond floozy from his lap!

Emma swallowed her ire. She was here to make amends, and sugar was a better husband-catcher than vinegar.

"Get up, Evelyn," Paul ordered through gritted teeth, but the tart held on to his neck.

All eyes, most of them bleary, were taking in this scene. The music stopped.

Emma hadn't expected Paul to rush to her arms, and he didn't. But she wished he had. Even from a distance, she realized he was pale, had lost weight. And despite the woman clinging to him like ivy to brick, she decided she was going to make him better!

Head high, she walked over to the two. "Hello, darling."

"Hello, *chérie*. What brings you to Texas?"

"Who're you?" interjected the blonde, turning her green eyes on the intruder.

For a moment, Emma was struck by the physical similarity between herself and this Evelyn. But her competitor's eyes were outlined with kohl, her cheeks with rouge. Emma's were only ringed with worry.

Paul rested an elbow on the table. "She's my wife."

"You never said nothin' about bein' married, honey."

"Evelyn, get up. And I do mean now," Paul said, none too gently.

"Well, I swear!" The painted one huffed to her feet and half stumbled over Woodley, who was running rings around Paul's chair, 'oofing and begging for attention.

The barkeep lumbered over. He was round, dark, and had a square face. Polishing a glass with a dirty towel, he asked, "Can I be gettin' ya anything to drink?"

"I'll leave that to my husband." Emma's gaze went to her beloved's guarded amber eyes. "Would you like me to have a drink with you?"

Did the sun rise in the east? Paul was elated by his love's appearance, but caution had to prevail. Too much had been left unresolved between them. Still, he wouldn't tell her no. "Do as you please, you always do."

"Then I'll have a mint julep. And would you please bring a dish of water for my dog?"

"Don't got no water."

"Then a dish of ice will do."

"Set 'em up, Carl," Paul drawled, dragging a chair over to him with the toe of his boot. "Sit down, Emma."

She did, and her furred companion jumped into his master's lap.

"I think he's missed me," Paul said, warding off a slathering tongue. Even though the tavern was packed with its faithful, no one existed for him except Emma . . . and Woodley, who wouldn't be denied. His family.

"We've both missed you," she said. "Me in particular."

He searched his heart and soul for the right words. He loved her, yearned to hold her in his arms and never let go! But that night in Louisiana haunted him.

"Seems we've had a similar discussion. Didn't lead anywhere."

"I've changed. I'm ready to give as much as it takes to get you back. If there's a baby, I'll—"

Like lightning, his fingers shot forth to cover her lips. "Don't say it. Not in this place." He removed his hand. "Let's get out of here."

"Where to?"

"Somewhere private. A drive along the beach?"

"That sounds wonderful."

Paul rented a cabriolet from the livery, and they set out, Woodley yowling from the floorboard, for a ride along the hard-packed sand of the island's surf side. The sun streaked orange and blue through scattered clouds above the ocean. It was no accident Paul headed the horses toward a deserted part of the island.

Emma spoke first. "It's beautiful, the way the waves tumble over each other."

344

Not as beautiful as you are. "I agree."

A trickle of sweat ran down Paul's neck as he held the reins. It was an airless evening. Too airless.

"I arrived early this afternoon, in case you're wondering," she said. "I've taken a room at Anthaline Lightfoot's house."

"Salt of the earth, that's Anthaline."

"I didn't like her at the onset, but I've changed my mind."

"She has that effect on people." Paul wasn't about to admit the effect Emma had on him. "Why exactly did you come to Galveston?" he asked, fed up with chitchat.

She turned her light green eyes to him. "I'm sorry for those awful things I said. And I didn't send money to Mexico City. I never meant to in the first place. My temper got the best of me, and I knew that was the only way I could hurt you. I'm sorry, so sorry."

He reached for her hand. Sorry was the most difficult word to utter, but saying it always had a healing effect. He realized a few words from him might heal old sorrows, too. "And I'm sorry for what I said, too."

"Then we have something to draw from." She returned the pressure on her fingers. "I was so scared, so frightened. I heard the *San Antonio* was missing, and—"

"It's not missing. It's gone. Davy Jones's Locker. Sunk." He reined in the team, stopping near the shoreline. Agony assailed him as he leaned back against the seat. "And they're gone, Emma. Montgomery and Tampke and all the rest. Dead." He swallowed the lump in his throat. "It was my ship—I should've been with them."

"Don't do this to yourself."

He rubbed his grim lips. "Guess it goes with the territory. A captain should go down with his ship."

"But you were sick!"

"Who told you that?"

"Anthaline."

"It figures." He laid an arm across his bent knee. "Yes, I was sick. It started out as a cold, but it settled in my ears. It messed up my equilibrium."

"Paul, that cold caused you to be seasick!"

"That's about the size of it." A sheepish look blanketed his face. "Just like dear old Underfoot."

She laughed and punched his arm. "Serves you right for taunting him!"

"Probably. But luck's with me—my one and only bout of seasickness is gone." He captured her hand, bringing it to his lips. After he dusted a kiss on it, he said in French, "From the moment we met I've adored you. You've been the center of my universe. I've wronged you, but I want to make amends."

She answered in the same language.

"You know French!"

"I've been studying." She grinned. "A lot."

"Ah, *bien-aimée,* I love you."

Her heart was pounding. For so long—forever— she had waited for this moment. "I love you, too."

"Love means forever."

"I know," she murmured.

A gift from heaven, that was what she had given him. But he had to be sure, absolutely positive, that she realized what they were getting into. "I'm the

346

same man who left Louisiana."

"And I'm the same woman. Basically. But do you think there's a chance we could start over—forget the past, and go back to that night in the St. Charles?"

"If we did, we might end up with a baby." Memories of that last night in Louisiana nagged him. "Emma, I didn't mean what I said about a child of ours. We shouldn't consider our bloodlines or the misdeeds of our kin, we ought to just raise our children right. Give them love. Dedicate our lives to the future, not the past."

She leaned against him. "You're not a scoundrel —you're wonderful!"

His chest puffed. "Never thought I'd hear you say that!" Then he became serious. "There are some parts of the past that are worth remembering." He touched her cheek. "Let's pretend. Let's go back to that night we met. I'll tell you what I was thinking, and you tell me your thoughts then."

"Agreed." Gently she bit down on his thumb. "I saw you, and I was threatened. You were a rake."

"Still am."

"I was ignorant, but I wanted your kisses— probably more."

"I gave up my quest for Marian upon laying eyes on you."

"Why didn't you tell me!"

"Maybe I should've."

"You were threatening my family," she said.

"You were threatening my sanity."

"None of that matters." She slid closer to him. "But I'm glad I stole that pin. It gave you an excuse

347

to badger me."

"Whoa, *m'amoureuse*. I would've found an excuse."

"You really were a scoundrel."

"Still am." He bent his head to hers, brushing her lips with his tongue. "Admit it—you like a scoundrel."

"Guilty as charged."

There were a couple of points he had to get out of the way. He brought her hand to his groin. "But I'm not guilty of giving this to Evelyn—I know you must be wondering. Nor am I guilty of doing the same with Aimée Thérèse—not since I was seventeen, anyway. You're the only woman I've wanted, or needed, since that night in the St. Charles."

A full smile lifted her cheeks. "I'm happy for that."

"Enough about the past. Let's concentrate on now." He eased away. "Have you ever taken a twilight walk in the surf?" he asked, hoping she hadn't. As he had been the first man to make love to her, he wanted to be the first to introduce her to this experience.

"No, never," she whispered.

"Then there's no time like the present. Come on, sweet angel, we're going swimming!"

Woodley jumped across his lap and onto the beach without further ado, running for the water's edge, and Paul took hold of Emma's waist. He pulled her forward, and slid her body over his growing heat. Bending his head, he nuzzled her ear. And felt her shiver. Her arms wound around his back. Her breasts were flattened against his chest as he claimed her honeyed lips. This was home, this was what he wanted and needed and ached for. This was Emma.

His hands, as well as hers, moved quickly to dispense with clothing. Naked. They were both nude—the way they were meant to be. Nothing between them.

He stepped back to drink in her loveliness. "All these months we've been apart I thought I remembered every detail of your body, but seeing you now . . . You're more beautiful than I imagined. So blonde. So well formed. Your figure's so smooth and sleek. No scars. No sags. Yet I'd love you however you came to me."

"That goes for you, too. For always."

On the sand, with the ocean's roar in their ears, he took her in his arms and buried his face in a cloud of blond hair. Their lovemaking was sweet and tender, wrought by the affirmation of eternal love.

Holding Emma in his arms, Paul savored the afterglow. Despite their pledges to one another in the past, he realized their basic problems hadn't been alleviated. Nonetheless, he prayed their differences would never again separate them.

Chapter Twenty-Two

Viewed through the eyes of a woman in love,
Galveston was a wonderful place. Uncivilized
perhaps, and a town where grandeur was a foreign
term, yet Emma gained a whole new appreciation of
its charm. The climate lacked Louisiana's oppressive
heat and rag-wringing humidity. People, rugged and
jovial, drank grog by the gallons. They ate johnny-
cakes by the stacks, seafood by the bushel. The
beach was for running barefoot . . . and for making
love. Most of all, this was the Texas Paul loved.

And Emma was determined to live there! That in
mind, she had enlisted Anthaline's assistance in
finding a house. Now, standing in the yard of the
only one available for purchase, Emma gave it an
uncritical eye. It wasn't a mansion like Feuille de
Chêne, but it was cozy. A few flowers here and there
would do wonders, and a fence would keep Woodley
in and the roaming pigs out. Mostly, this was a place
to put down the roots Emma craved.

Inhaling the sea breeze, she laced her fingers with
Paul's big ones. "Do you like the house?"

"It's a shack on stilts. Don't look at me like that!"

He turned her into his arms to kiss the top of her blond tresses. "It's nice. But we have a home in Louisiana."

"Paul, aren't you going to sell the plantation? The year's up now."

"No, I'm not going to part with it. I won't take your home away from you."

She should have been ecstatic. He was willing to sacrifice his goal for her comfort. "Anywhere you are is my home."

"Until Santa Anna gets it through his thick skull that Texas belongs to Texans, my home is at sea." Paul squeezed her shoulders. "And Louisiana is where you need to be, not in a frame shack here in Galveston."

"It's not a shack, and"—she turned to get another look at the house—"I'm going to have it put in tip-top shape. Since it's on the Strand, it'll make a wonderful location for my office."

"Oh, Emma . . ." He wanted to make her happy, craved having her at his side, but he quailed to think about involving her in war. He stepped back, flattening his palm on a weather-beaten hitching post. "I want you to go back to Louisiana. With the Centralist Army moving overland, you aren't safe here."

"We're over two hundred miles from the territory Santa Anna wants."

"And less than a mile from the coast he'll invade if we don't stop him."

"Why do I get the feeling this is the prelude to, 'Emma, I'm leaving Galveston'?"

"Ah, the intuition of my woman . . . !" He stepped

forward to cup her chin. "General Peraza's in Campeche. I'm sailing there tomorrow. I've got to renew our alliance. Santa Anna's ready to attack. The Yucatecans first, us second. Mark my words."

A frisson of fear ran the length of her spine, but she had to be brave. "Paul, I know the Navy needs money. I have quite a bit left from my dowry. Take it."

"No. This is Texas's battle, not yours."

"It's for *my* Texas. This is my home now, and I want you to take the money."

Paul chuckled inwardly at the irony of using Rankin Oliver's money to protect the Lone Star republic from the aggressors who had battened his wealth. "I refuse."

Nothing she'd said had changed his mind. She quit arguing. "While you're gone I'll take care of matters at Feuille de Chêne—find a buyer, close my practice."

"And free the slaves."

"Of course."

"Yoo-hoo!"

Both Paul and Emma turned to the booming voice of Anthaline Lightfoot. Walking up the sand-packed street, the bearlike woman held Woodley under one arm and waved a greeting with the other. The dog's tail thumped against her hip as he barked a greeting.

Paul leaned over to whisper in Emma's ear. "And while I'm gone you'll have him to warm your feet at night."

His words were drowned by Woodley's enthusiastic barks.

352

"Hush, you scalawag." Anthaline touched the dog's nose with her fingertip, and he nipped it playfully. "And as for the two of you, are you going to buy the house?"

"Yes," Emma replied, turning to her husband. "I'm going back to Louisiana for a while, but this is our home. Our future."

His eyes held love and a trace of uncertainty. "Yes, wife, our future," he said as if he wondered just what fate had in store for them.

Five days later and with night as cover, Paul skirted the *Virgin Vixen* around the Centralist Navy blockade of Campeche bay. He dropped anchor line in a protected cove away from the town, then dressed in black and rowed the dinghy to shore.

Into the walled city—past shacks, haciendas, and the Cathedral of La Concepción—he stole, slipping through the streets and making for the fort. Two sentinels stood watch at the stone fortress. Luckily, one of the men recognized Paul as friend not foe, and he opened the creaking wooden gate and led him through the arched courtyard to Colonel Martín Peraza of the Yucatecan Army.

"Word has it General Barragan's army is bombarding the coast at Telchac," Paul said.

"*Sí*. And General Ampudia's men are advancing on this city. Commodore Marin's navy supports them . . . you saw his ships in our harbor." Peraza, a man of medium height and dark complexion, rested his right elbow on the palm of his left hand, and paced back and forth across the Spartan command

353

room. "I must be frank with you. I fear the end is near."

"Don't give up now," Paul said. "Their armies are divided. If we can keep them that way, they won't win."

"Ah, *mi amigo,* that is wishful thinking."

"No. It's planning. Commodore Moore and I want you to know that we are willing to drive off the navy that supports those foot soldiers. We've done it before, and we will again. Your peninsula and my Republic both have a vested interest in keeping the Centralists in their own bays."

"Your president doesn't agree."

"It is, as usual, a point of money. Sam Houston issued Exchequer notes to support our fleet, but unfortunately he didn't release the cash." Paul grimaced. "To his way of thinking, Texas cannot afford another war. We are, as you know, a bankrupt nation. Houston hangs on to the idea that diplomacy not salvos will bring peace."

"Then he is a fool." Peraza folded into his chair. "My fellow Yucatecans were foolish, too, to trust Santa Anna's peace initiatives. If he had wanted peace, he'd have sent emissaries not armies to this peninsula."

"Exactly." Paul leaned over the desk. "Moore and I want to help you . . . and help ourselves. I hope you can appreciate our predicament. We need money. You have money. Give us sufficient funds to outfit our fleet, and we will chase the *Moctezuma* and the *Guadalupe* out of these waters. Then your army has a fighting chance at winning."

"How much do you need?"

354

"Twenty thousand U.S. dollars now, and our usual monthly stipend thereafter."

"All right," Peraza said. "The money is yours."

"Thank you, sir."

They exchanged salutes, and Paul turned on his heel. The future had never looked brighter. It was time to return to New Orleans to oversee the provisioning and manning of the fleet, what was left of it—time to return to Emma.

"Don't be hasty, Captain Rousseau. I give you the money with stipulations. You must stay here in Campeche for a while. Governor Barbachano and I need your advice on dealing with the Centralist Navy. I will send the *Aguila* to your commodore, and he can see to manning your ships. Is that agreeable?"

Paul nodded. Emma would have to wait.

Emma was proud of all that had been accomplished at Feuille de Chêne. The new owner was on pins and needles to take possession. Sugar cane grew high and stout. And the big house, plus all the surrounding buildings, sparkled from elbow grease and new paint. But she missed Cleopatra and Ben, who had returned to New Orleans. More than anything, she missed Paul.

Her medical practice was winding down, with the exception of one patient. In her office, she collected the paraphernalia necessary to ease Simon Dyer's discomfort. The man, who looked to be seventy but was in his fifties, was lying on the examining couch. He was a rack of bones; his face was gray and sunken; his chest heaved for breath.

She had fashioned a cone from a metal cup, had attached a short length of tubing to it and a valved bottle of sulfurous ether. Placing the cone over his mouth, she released a small amount of the rarified fumes. Within moments the tenseness of his body eased. Breathing easier herself, Emma closed the valve and stepped back.

Simon giggled. "Magic, gal. You're magic."

"I've been accused of working magic."

"Ah, gal," he said, throwing his arms wide, "'tis a wonder you are. If I were young and didn't have this consumption, I'd steal you from Étienne's boy."

Étienne's boy? "I thought you told me you didn't know my husband. Apparently you knew his father."

Drunkenly Simon swayed to his feet. "Course I know 'em. Know 'em both. Was Étienne's friend. Was his second in the duel that killed him."

Emma's pulse raced. "Then you can attest there was no foul play involved in his death?"

"Give me another whiff of that rotten-egg concoction of yours," Simon demanded, his chest rattling, as he lay back, "and I'll tell you the whole story."

She replaced the cone, then took it away. "As you were saying . . ."

"I'm a dying man, so I've got nothing to lose." He laughed. "Oh, there was foul play all right. Your uncle blackmailed me into being part of his evil scheme. Threatened to tell my wife and the world about me. Couldn't let that happen, so I went along with his plan. Fixed the firing pin. Étienne took aim at Rankin, but his trigger finger got nothing."

Emma shuddered and closed her eyes. Paul had been right! She recalled the slurs that had been made against his father, and she ached to right the wrongs of the past, to soothe her husband.

A wash of cold reality froze in her veins. To do those things would implicate Uncle Rankin! What should she do? She was caught between the two men she loved beyond reason.

"Hate Rankin Oliver," Simon was saying. "Used me all these years. Made a puppet out of a man. Hate him."

"What do you mean?"

Simon curled back his lip. "I fixed him up with that woman in Sisal. His mistress. He liked her, maybe loved her, and he never liked anybody. I went to her hacienda and took a club to her head, that I did! Just afore I did I told her, ''Tis a greeting from your lover. He sent me to kill you.'"

Emma was horrified by this confession of murder. "What . . . what were the two of you doing in the Yucatán?"

"Selling guns and ammunition to the Centralists. Ha-ha! Rankin didn't have a part of it, not really. 'Twas me who was making a profit, but I made it look like he was to blame. He was trying to catch me at my own game. Using himself as a decoy, letting the woman think he was involved. After she died, he wanted to stop the shipment, but it was too late. Too late. I had the papers she was going to turn over to Paul. Papers that had Rankin's handwriting all over them."

"Those papers implicated my uncle as the guilty party in the arms sale?"

"Oh yes. Implicated him good. Real good. Never thought I could trick him, but I did. Got him to sign a stack of legitimate papers—I'd stuck the agreement between them, you see. Made sure he was in a hurry, so he didn't have time to read them all." Hatred, deep and evil, was reflected from the depths of Simon's soul into his eyes. "Then he couldn't stop me. The weapons and powder reached the Mexs. Ha-ha! Old patriotic Rankin—his only good quality, I might add—stands to be blamed for supplying arms to the people who will crush their way across this land."

Stunned into silence, Emma's hand went to her lips. She tried to sort through Simon Dyer's confession. Uncle Rankin was guilty of blackmailing this man into helping murder Étienne Rousseau. And apparently he had used Simon in the ensuing years, until his accomplice had had enough of it. Her uncle had suspected Dyer of selling arms to the Centralists, had gone along with the plan in order to trap him. A woman had died as a result, and the Centralists had received the shipment of arms. None of that said much for Rankin Oliver's character.

Nevertheless she loved her uncle and he returned that love. His crimes didn't diminish those facts.

What about Paul? He had been right all along about his father, and he deserved to know the truth. She must tell him!

All of a sudden a warning bell pealed in her brain. Her father's office flashed into her thoughts. Behind his desk was a tapestry stitched by Emma's mother, a reminder of those things symbolizing the physician: the caduceus, a staff with two entwined serpents and two wings at the top; and the Hippocratic oath.

As a girl Emma had read the latter over and over, committing each word to memory, and when Dr. Boulogne had signed her certification, she had raised her right hand and recited that solemn pledge.

And now the last passage preyed on her conscience. ". . . Whatsoever things I see or hear concerning the life of men, in my attendance on the sick or even apart therefrom, which ought not to be noised abroad, I will keep silence thereon, counting such things to be as sacred secrets."

That oath would keep Emma from telling Paul, from telling *anyone*. An ethical doctor could not under any circumstances relay a confidence uttered by a patient.

Caught between the two men she loved plus a code of honor, Emma was tied to the past. A past that needed to be cleared for future happiness. As long as Uncle Rankin's misdeeds went unknown, there would forever be a gap between her and her husband.

"Gotta go." Simon swayed to his feet again. "Feel better now."

On knees weakened from ill health and induced intoxication, he made for the door. Twice he stumbled on the stairs leading down from the office, but Emma bolstered him.

The cool night air was sobering. Simon's gnarled hand went to his forehead. My God, what had he done!

He mounted his gelding and rode away. Far away.

Emma didn't know what to do or which way to turn. Her uncle was to sail to Feuille de Chêne at the crack of dawn the next day. She had to find some way to get at the truth.

She used their mutual enjoyment of a morning ride as an excuse to get Uncle Rankin alone. Astride a chestnut mare she followed his bay as he rode past the slave quarters and into the marshy woods adjacent to the plantation.

"Wait up, Uncle!" she called through the thicket. "We need to talk."

He glanced backward, pulled in on the reins, and dismounted. He walked toward her. "What's on yer mind, Emmie?"

As he helped her from the sidesaddle, she said, "How do you feel about Santa Anna's campaign against the Yucatecans?"

His fingers stiffened momentarily, but he called up nonchalance. "Not much of anything."

"Even if it affects me?"

"Why would it affect ye?"

"I'm married to a Texan. I'm a Texan myself . . . now. If Santa Anna conquers Texas, I'll be in danger."

"Then stay in Louisiana. Ye have a home here. Either here or at Magnolia Hall. Ye're always welcome."

"I love my husband, and I love the Republic. My place is there, and that's where I intend to be."

"Ye've really cleaved yerself to him, Emmie?"

"With all my heart and soul." She paused. "Have you ever loved a woman . . . besides Angélique de Poutrincourt?"

360

"Never."

"Have you ever taken a mistress?"

"Watch that impertinent tongue."

Unable to repeat the information Simon had confessed, she grappled for the right words. "I've heard you kept a woman in Sisal. Didn't she mean anything to you?"

"I know nothing of a woman in Sisal. Yer husband's been filling yer head with slanderous tales about me."

"The same way his father spread lies?"

"Yes."

Cold washed over her. She believed he was lying. "Then you didn't murder him? Didn't conspire with Étienne's second to fix the firing pin?"

"I'll tell ye like I told ye before—I did no such thing!"

Emma walked away and tied the mare's reins to a tree. She faced him. "Paul says you sold arms to the Centralists."

"Another falsehood."

"Well, I'm glad to hear your denial," she responded. "I knew you wouldn't lie, but my own ears needed to hear it."

"That's my girl." He quickly changed the subject to Magnolia Hall. A smattering of horsetalk followed.

Guiding the conversation away from that, Emma said, "I appreciate the money you gave me; it's provided supplies to treat those who can afford my services and the indigent of this area."

"Glad ye've put the money to good use."

She launched into a dissertation on her patients.

"There's a man who comes by the office from time to time. A consumptive. He used to live in the vicinity, but doesn't anymore, so I don't see him regularly. I've always been intrigued by him, though. He's rather a mystery. But he mentioned your name the last time I saw him. How do you know Simon Dyer?"

Rankin inhaled sharply, and blanched.

His expression spoke louder than a thousand words. Simon hadn't lied. *Paul* hadn't lied! Yet she couldn't be pleased. No matter what her uncle had done to others, he had been good to her. That was difficult to put aside. Being torn between two loves was a hurting thing.

She agonized over what to do. Should she turn against her criminal kinsman?

Chapter Twenty-Three

"Do you know Simon Dyer?" Emma repeated.

Rankin pulled his bearings together. "Of course I know him. But I haven't seen him in years."

Emma was sick at heart. She couldn't openly accuse her uncle of wrongdoing. To do so would unearth the source of her information—Simon Dyer. Professional ethics wouldn't allow that. The hardest part was, she couldn't tell Paul of Simon's confession or of this conversation. If so, she'd have to make explanations.

"I think we should head back," she said.

Once back at the stable, Rankin made a hasty excuse to leave, and she was glad for it.

That same afternoon a communiqué for Paul arrived from Commodore Moore. "Meet me at the Balize pilot station posthaste," it stated.

And at twilight, Cleopatra sashayed into the bedchamber. "There be a body tying up a sloop to the jetty." She pursed her lips in a smug smile. "You best look out the window, missy, 'cause your man be home."

Paul! Emma forgot everything in her elation. She

ran down the stairs, threw open the door. Her legs couldn't carry her to the dock fast enough. Arms akimbo, he stood, smiling, watching her. He wore black leather boots, dark breeches, and a shirt of soft white cotton. A slight breeze tousled his short black curls. This was how she had pictured him as a privateer before the mast. Rakish, swashbuckling, sensuous.

He started to swing off the *Virgin Vixen*, but Emma flew into his arms, knocking him to the deck. Inhaling salt air, tobacco, and male warmth, she landed atop him.

He laughed with joy. "I've fantasized about coming home, *chérie,* but I never thought it would be like this."

"Hush up. You talk too much." Her mouth came down on his, and she kissed him soundly.

Returning her embrace, he ran his hands over her back and down her legs. Clothes were dispensed with as the last ray of sunlight vanished, and the two lovers explored the wonders of each other's body and conquered the loneliness of being apart.

Their euphoria didn't diminish. Even though Emma's heavy heart was a mighty weight to carry. Even though Paul, at a loss to understand why Ed Moore hadn't sailed for Campeche, carried dire tidings from the Yucatán.

"I'm going with you to Balize," she said, and he finally agreed.

They sailed at dawn for the pilot station at the mouth of the Mississippi. Fog as thick as pea soup met them. They caught sight of the flagship *Austin* and of the *Wharton*, which was the brig under Paul's command. He didn't have long to wonder why the two ships were stalled there; a longboat carrying Commodore Edwin Moore and Naval Commissioner John Naylor rowed up beside the *Virgin Vixen*.

Colonel John Naylor, elderly yet vital, stepped aboard. His thick gray brows were knitted. "There you are, Rousseau."

Behind Naylor's back Ed Moore raised a hand to signal problems. "The commissioner has been with us in New Orleans for some weeks. He's—"

"I'll tell him, Commodore Moore." Naylor dusted his sleeve. "Perhaps we could go below."

Oh no! Emma thought. The cabin was a wreck; her unmentionables were everywhere. "Oh, but it's a lovely day, gentlemen. You don't want to go down there," she said quickly.

"Colonel Naylor"—Paul cleared his throat— "may I present my wife Emma."

"Charmed." He took her hand and gallantly kissed her fingers. "But it's not a lovely day, Mrs. Rousseau." As if on cue, foggy vapors swirled between them. "Please lead the way."

Emma took the only recourse. She stepped down the companionway, kicking clothes out of sight as she crossed the salon. Then she sat squarely on the chemise that lay on the bunk. However, her concern about the cabin's appearance vanished when Naylor turned to Paul. "I bring bad news, Captain Rousseau."

"Our Navy is no more," Moore said gravely.

Naylor nodded. "At the behest of President Sam Houston and under the powers granted me by the

Seventh Congress of the Republic of Texas, I've disbanded the Navy."

"Commodore Moore was suspended from command and ordered to report to the Department of War and Marine at once. The same goes for you, Captain."

"Why?" Paul's voice was strained.

"We've entered a period of naval pacifism. The government plans to sell the fleet."

Emma's eyes went to Paul. She could see the fury boiling in him. For months—years—he and Ed Moore had struggled to keep the Navy afloat, and now the Centralists were moving overland, committing atrocities against the citizens of the Yucatán peninsula as well as in the hills of central Texas. The Texan naval patriots were being forced ashore by the very Republic they had pledged their hearts and lives to.

"There's something you should know," Moore said. "I'd planned to join you in Campeche, but after the commissioner arrived—"

"Why the delay?" There was a sharp ring to Paul's tone. "And what does our esteemed naval commissioner plan to do with our two last ships? Let them sit here at Balize until the highest bidder comes along?"

"No," Naylor said. "The commodore convinced me to let him command the fleet until we reach Texas waters."

"As well he should. To abandon our ships in a foreign port would be treason on his part."

"Paul, please . . ." Moore waved a hand in gesture of caution. "It's too late for recriminations."

"Too late. That seems to be the watchword of our times." Paul pulled a cheroot from a humidor. He pinched off the end before saying, "May I beg your tolerance for a moment, gentlemen?"

"I'm interested in what you have to say," Naylor said.

"General Martín Peraza entrusted a large amount of money to us. He gave it in good faith, and in equally good faith I promised we'd drive off Santa Anna's Navy. Peraza was on the verge of surrendering." Paul struck a lucifer, raised it to the cheroot, then took a long draw of smoke, exhaling it slowly. "Now Peraza and his men are going to surrender to the Centralists. And when they do, they'll be forced to fight against our Republic."

Naylor had the grace to appear shocked. "Surely it won't come to that."

"But it will. The Yucatecans intercepted an intelligence report. As soon as they're brought to heel, Commodore Tomás Marin has been instructed to sail his formidable fleet north." Paul allowed that to sink in. "To sack the city of Galveston."

"Good God!" Naylor didn't enjoy his mission. Never had. He had left retirement and ease at the earnest solicitation of President Houston. "Something has to be done to bring those rebels to heel," Sam Houston had said, "and I want you to do it. Moore respects you. He's never respected me or my authority. It's your duty as a citizen of Texas to curb the violations of authority that Commodore Moore and Captain Rousseau perpetrate against my administration." Then, as now, John Naylor had difficulty understanding Houston, but a call to duty was a call to duty.

Rubbing the tense muscles in his neck, Naylor studied the two men in question. They weren't rascals. They were fighters with love of freedom and country in their souls. And they were willing to give their lives for the cause. He appreciated their will and wisdom.

His graveled voice rose. "We can't let Santa Anna get away with it."

"My sentiments exactly, Colonel." Paul knew an advantage when one was presented. "So . . . do you still wish to send us like whipped pups back to Galveston, then drydock the *Austin* and *Wharton* until you can find a buyer?"

"No, for God's sake. No! We must save the Republic." Naylor's gray eyes rested on Moore, then Paul. "Do you have any suggestions?"

"I'd like to hear what Paul has to say," Moore said.

"I understand the *Moctezuma* is planning to move Santa Anna's troops from Telchac to Campeche. I suggest we make a detour on our way to home port. If we engage in some well-placed salvos against the ship, then we'll be in a good position to attack the Centralist squadron guarding the port of Campeche. With the *Guadalupe* whipped, too, Santa Anna's armies would receive no reinforcements or supplies—and they couldn't be united. The Yucatecans could reorganize their land forces, defeat their foe . . . and ours."

"Brilliant!"

"Then we have your consent, sir?" Paul asked. Moore looked to Naylor.

The colonel, arch Texan and proud of it, fell to contemplation. He was alarmed by Captain Rousseau's words. For too long he had lived in a state of complacency, expecting that nest of Centralist rattlesnakes to strike the western regions of Texas. He had been resigned to that, but he had never given full thought to what would happen if a coastal invasion were to take place—near his plantation!

And he, John Naylor, had plenary power to do with the Texas Navy as he saw fit. It wasn't too late to exercise his authority, but he had no say over Moore and Rousseau. Their hides belonged to Sam Houston.

"May we have your answer, Colonel?" Moore asked.

"There's something you need to know," Naylor replied solemnly. "I haven't been totally honest with you." He slipped his hand into his frock coat, and withdrew the secret document that might stand in the way of Texas's freedom. "I think you'd better read this."

Moore took the parchment. His eyes widened as he read it. "May God have mercy on us! Has this been published?"

"No, and it won't be. Provided you do as told and sail into the port of Galveston."

"What does it say?" Emma asked, unable to keep quiet.

"Houston plans to brand us pirates!"

She gasped. Paul went white beneath his tan.

"This proclamation," Moore explained, "invites the nations of the world to . . . seize us. We're to be arraigned and sentenced by a legal tribunal." A

369

muscle worked in his throat as he read aloud the closing sentence. "'The naval powers of Christendom will not permit such a flagrant and unexampled outrage.'"

"I couldn't tell you before," Naylor said. "And I shouldn't now. That document is to be published only if you give me any trouble."

"It's underhanded trickery on his part." Ed Moore stood his ground. "He won't do it. Public opinion is too strongly against him."

"If we sail on our course to honor our commitment and to protect our citizens against invasion," Paul said, "it'll be without the sanction of our government. In the eyes of the world we'll be regarded as those who put to sea under the skull and crossbones."

"I'm willing to take that chance, and the men under my command will feel likewise," the commodore said.

Paul nodded. "Absolutely."

"I appreciate your apprising us of the situation, Naylor." Moore took a step forward. "And now I ask you—are you with us or not?"

Naylor brushed a palm across his lips. "I'm with you."

Emma shuddered to think of it. On one side was right; on the other, Sam Houston's law. Provided they didn't perish in the campaign, they'd face the wrath of their Sam Houston—and punishment by court-martial. She longed to run to Paul, to plead sensibility and self-preservation.

But what was sensible? Abiding by Sam Houston's dictum put the whole Gulf in peril. Emma realized that Paul would never be able to live with the knowledge that he hadn't done everything in his power to preserve the lives of his countrymen, even if it meant the loss of his own.

She resigned herself. She might lose him, but she wouldn't tie him with her own selfish fears. He was a Navy man, first and foremost, and her love was strong enough to grant him his freedom. But there was a hurting, aching tear in her heart.

The three men put their heads together to plan their strategies. While they did so Emma shaped her own plans. She was not going to stand by while Paul sailed away, possibly forever. The *Wharton* needed a surgeon, and she intended to fill that need. Most of all, she wanted to be with her husband. There was no use arguing about her decision. She knew Paul; he'd have her put ashore, and there'd be no stopping it. But she'd be aboard that brig when it sailed. She didn't know how yet, only that she'd have to be crafty.

Day broke to cerulean skies and a fine tail wind. Sailing conditions were perfect, so the *Austin*, with Naylor aboard, and the *Wharton* made for Telchac.

Paul grasped the rail and watched the *Virgin Vixen* head west. The sloop carried a letter to the editor of the Galveston newspaper. It stated Commodore Moore's intentions in the Yucatecan waters, and declared that he had the consent and full concurrence of Naval Commissioner John Naylor.

The sloop also carried Emma. It would make a detour on its way to Texas to put her ashore at Feuille de Chêne. A tug yanked at his heart. Would he ever see her again? There were no guarantees that

371

the *Wharton* wouldn't go to the bottom, or that a shot wouldn't fell him. He wasn't afraid to die. But never holding Emma in his arms again, that thought scared the hell out of him.

"I love you," he mouthed across the waters.

In truth he was surprised she had put up but a modicum of resistance at being sent back to the plantation. So little, in fact, he became suspicious now. She wouldn't dare conceal herself on this brig, he told himself. Even Emma wouldn't do something that harebrained.

And it would've taken an accomplice. Moments from the previous evening flashed into his mind. After he had said goodbye to Emma, he and Naylor were piped aboard the flagship to assess a ticklish situation. Then Naylor discovered he had forgotten the piracy proclamation, and the longboat was sent back to retrieve it from the *Virgin Vixen*. Reese McDonald had been the oarsman.

"McDonald," he shouted down the deck, "front and center."

The young marine stopped polishing the pivot gun, handed the rag over to a weathered old salt, and made his way to his captain. His footsteps still echoing on the planks, he saluted snappily. "Sir?"

"Are you certain Mrs. Rousseau's aboard that sloop?"

"Begging your pardon, sir, but I can't guarantee her whereabouts at this moment." McDonald squared his wide shoulders. "She was on deck when I boarded the longboat."

Though McDonald's faithfulness and character were both proven, Paul wasn't convinced. "She

372

wouldn't by any chance be on this brig, would she?"

"No, sir!"

Paul was of a mind to row the longboat after the *Virgin Vixen* and make certain Emma was on board, but he'd never catch her. The notion of tacking westward was dismissed by him also.

A delay wasn't justifiable. Tomorrow a painful duty had to be performed on the flagship. The *San Antonio* mutineers would be punished. Sam Houston had signed the extradition papers—finally —and the men had been released to naval jurisdiction. Before Naylor had arrived in New Orleans a tribunal had been convened, and the *Austin* had been transporting the prisoners to Galveston. The warship wasn't on course for home port presently, but Moore was adamant that sentences be read on the morrow. And he wanted both ships in the middle of Gulf waters when justice was carried out.

No, Paul couldn't run after Emma. For now, he had to trust in her word and McDonald's obedience. "Dismissed."

But he couldn't dismiss the suspicion that she had something up her sleeve.

Hair tucked beneath a sock cap, Emma tugged at her scratchy sleeve. She had borrowed her garb from Reese McDonald. Bless him! Naturally her shirt and breeches were too long and way too big, but she had negated wearing feminine finery. A stowaway needed practical garments.

At present, she was hiding in the *Wharton*'s longboat, beneath a tarp, and that was where she

373

intended to stay until the North American coast was long over the horizon. Perhaps tomorrow she'd make an appearance. In the meantime, she'd make do, twiddle her thumbs and eat the jerky Reese had provided.

At half-past nine the next morning the *Austin* signaled the brig to hove to. With heavy heart Paul acknowledged the message. This was the day sentences would be read to the last of the *San Antonio*'s mutineers. Remembering Seymour Oswald's kindness to him after his lashing, Paul was grateful that the sergeant wasn't among them. This was going to be difficult enough, and he was worried. Without governmental sanction, he felt they shouldn't act on the sentences. Moore, however, believed it should be done forthwith.

He descended the ratline to the longboat. Two seamen accompanied him. George Williams took up one oar, Bobs Bates the other. Ruminating on the mutineers' fates, Paul sat in the stern. Damn! He hated this aspect of duty. Piracy proclamation or not, he didn't want to be a part of it, despite his respect for the now-deceased patriots who had defended the luckless schooner. In frustration he kicked the tarp.

"Ouch!"

Paul groaned and squeezed his eyes. Emma. He'd know her voice anywhere. He whipped the canvas cover away. There she was, face covered with grime and wearing a man's garb. Undoubtedly McDonald's. "Get up."

"Who me?" Wide-eyed, she had a look of innocence. "Are you talking to me?"

374

"Coquettishness doesn't become you, Emma Rousseau. Especially in your present garb." It was all he could do not to swat her behind. "Let me guess. You've decided to see for yourself what it's like to engage in battle at sea. And that's exactly what you're going to get—a sea battle with me!"

Grinning sheepishly, she tucked the hem of her shirt into the breeches. "Well, I didn't expect you to be happy."

"Why, in the name of all that's right, can't you behave like an ordinary woman? Why can't I ever depend on you?" He didn't mention her timing, which couldn't have been worse. "Think back to the time we met. You came to my room. You thought nothing of stealing. You've taken up a profession that rightfully belongs to men. Now you've stowed away on a ship of war!"

"I thought we decided not to talk about the past. Oh, never mind! Anyway, you didn't complain when I was in your room. You got that plagued brooch back. You appreciated my doctoring when your . . . when your, mm, wonderful back was sliced to smithereens." She derived a degree of satisfaction from the half-grin that he was trying to hide. "And your men deserve a surgeon's services."

Silently he conceded the first part. But if the Mexican snake-and-buzzard didn't get him first, this woman was going to be the death of him. "You're right. Our men do need a competent surgeon. But my wife isn't going to be the one wielding a scalpel. You, madame, are going back to Louisiana!"

"How? Surely you won't turn this brig around. I'm a good swimmer, but you can't expect me to swim ashore."

"A shark nipping at your ankles would serve you fair." He balled his hands into fists. "Your trouble, Emma, is you should've been born a man."

She stepped forward, looking up at him and flattening her palms against his chest. "That wouldn't please you, would it?"

He'd have his tongue sliced out before admitting it, but she was slowly, and successfully, drawing him into her net with her sexual powers. If they were alone . . . But they weren't, and the longboat was near the flagship.

He yanked the tarp aloft. "Get under there."

"No. My muscles are cramped."

He addressed her sternly. "Today the mutineers' fate will be determined. I beg you—don't do anything to disrupt order."

Wordlessly, she scooted under the canvas. She now understood his edge of temper. For over a year he had been troubled over those mutineers. She knew he was torn between sympathy and duty.

Paul turned on his heel and marched over to the oarsmen. "Not a word of this, Bates, Williams. Stay at your posts, and make sure she stays hidden."

"Aye, aye, Cap'n," they both replied.

The longboat's prow thumped against the *Austin*'s wooden hull. "Ahoy!" a boatswain's mate called down as the rope ladder was thrown over the side. Agilely Paul climbed aboard, yet his heart was a leaden weight.

Solemn and pensive, all 146 Texas Tars in service

to the *Austin* stood at attention. The prisoners were brought forth in shackles from the quarterdeck's prison box.

Paul watched the mutineers. Their faces evinced no fear, for they believed they'd be pardoned. With the *San Antonio* gone forever and the chief prosecution witnesses at the Gulf's bottom, they figured the case against them was weak. They were unaware that Seaman Sheppard had turned state's evidence.

His eyes troubled, Moore took a scroll from Fourth-Lieutenant Quartermain. The commodore unrolled it and swallowed with difficulty. "It is my awful and painful but sacred duty to perform this sentencing. May God save your souls."

Paul despised yet respected what had to be done. A lesson had to be learned by all assembled. The strength of naval martial law must be maintained; no matter how difficult the conditions or how callous the commanding officer, respect for authority must reign. But he and Moore were going against their superior's authority.

While Moore read the articles of war and the charges against each of the mutineers, Paul's jaw was clenched. Sam Houston might brand all the good men of these two ships as pirates, and their fate might not be any more noble than that of the men shackled beneath the fore yardarm.

"John Williams," Moore said, "guilty as charged. But in consideration of informing Captain Throckmorton at the last moment that mutiny was about to take place, your sentence is lowered to one hundred lashes of the cat."

"Will Barrington, Edward Keenan. One hundred lashes each."

The cook, Keenan, moved his mouth in silent prayer and looked to the heavens above. Barrington smiled.

"Captain of Marines William Simpson, Seamen Isaac Allen and James Hudgins, Marine Antonio Landois. Guilty of all charges. You are to be hanged at the fore yardarm. You have twenty-four hours to prepare for your deaths."

"No!" shouted Landois. Simpson and Allen closed their eyes and dropped their heads.

Hudgins shouted, "What about Sheppard?"

"Frederick Sheppard," Moore said, "in view of the testimony given at the tribunal in New Orleans, you are acquitted and released."

"You son-of-a-bitch!" Hudgins screamed at the traitor. "May your bloody soul burn in hell."

Paul hated his own cowardice, but he was relieved that he wouldn't be forced to view the executions.

"Secure Williams, Barrington, and Keenan to the number-nine gun," Moore said, rerolling the scroll. "Commence sentencing."

The lash cracked through the air as Moore turned troubled eyes to Paul. "This is the most difficult day of my life. And tomorrow will be worse . . . I've never viewed an execution."

"Nor have I."

"I'd better board the *Wharton*," Moore said. "I've got to do some explaining to your men."

"Aye, aye." Feeling an invisible noose around his own neck, Paul did an about-face. Now Emma had to be dealt with.

378

Chapter Twenty-Four

Howard O'Reilly settled in for an evening of marital conviviality. As Marian's excellent meal rested comfortably in his stomach, he chatted about the weather, the social season, and other amenable topics.

Finally his wife yawned and stretched her arms above her head. "Think I'll take a bath before turning in, sweetie."

Frowning, Howard picked up the *Tropic*, which was folded on the table beside him. She never allowed him to watch her while bathing, no matter how much he begged.

His attention centered on the headline. "Wait!"

"Whatever's the matter? Do you need a bicarbonate for your stomach? Oh, I shouldn't've had Cook put all those onions in the jambalaya."

"Stop fretting about the food. Paul's in trouble."

Marian hurried across the drawing room and snapped the newspaper from her husband's hand. Her eyes rounded with horror as she read the article. "Oh . . . no!"

"Oh yes." Howard shot from the wing chair and

ran a hand through his red hair. "That miserable fool Sam Houston's branded the brave and courageous men of the Texas fleet as pirates. He's invited all nations in treaty or in amity with the Republic to seize them."

"Do you think anyone will take such action?"

"I doubt it, but this does mean Paul will be in trouble when he returns to Galveston. He may be hanged for this."

"He'll need a lawyer," Marian said. "You'll have to help."

"If he comes to us."

"He will." She lovingly touched the brush of a rust-hued sideburn. "We should take comfort in one thing. How did the *Tropic* put it? Oh, yes. The Texans are 'a race in whose veins never flowed the blood of cowards.' If our Paul dies, it'll be courageously. Doing what he believes in. We should all be so fortunate."

"I daresay you're right." Winding his arms around her, Howard buried his face in her hair. "But our poor Emma . . ."

It took a lot of hard convincing to sway Ed Moore to Emma's way of thinking. "A woman has no place aboard a ship of war," he had said, but she had adroitly listed the pluses in her favor. As to the issue of gender she was not faint of heart, and she was determined to do her part for the Navy. The *Wharton* lacked a surgeon, and she had both training and experience on her side. Most of all, she intended to stand by her husband, through thick or thin, and no one was going to parcel her off to Louisiana. No one.

That evening, in the captain's cabin at the stern of the *Wharton*, Paul grimaced—and it wasn't because the brig hit a trough and dropped sharply, bow first. He was aggravated on several levels; he didn't want his wife involved in the battle that was certain to come.

"Drat." As water sloshed onto the wood planking Emma grabbed the edge of the iron tub in which she bathed. "Rough seas, huh?"

"Yes, Madame Rousseau, there're rough seas now, and even rougher ones ahead."

Her blond curls were pulled up into a knot, but a loose tendril had escaped and was plastered to the rise of her breast. He couldn't tear his gaze from it, or from the pink crests that pouted at the waterline. Having no sense of right or wrong, anger or happiness, his manhood stiffened.

Paul forced himself to be stern. "I've had enough of your charming every man you meet. Ed Moore would've never agreed to your scheme if you hadn't batted your lashes at him. And there's no telling what you said or did to poor puppy-dog-eyes McDonald to get him to let you steal aboard the longboat."

"Sometimes being a woman has its advantages."

"Mighty sure of yourself, aren't you?" he asked, wanting no reply. In two steps he was across the cabin. He pulled her, protesting, from the water. "It's about time you learned some obedience."

"Stop that!"

Taking her under his arm, he stomped toward the

bed, then turned her over his knee and began to swat her wet, naked bottom.

"Ouch!"

He rubbed the reddening imprint of his hand before spanking her again. Hearing her moan, this time in pleasure, he squeezed that shapely cheek and slid his thumb between her legs. She opened them, and he turned his attention to her womanly delight. He ached for release.

She slid back, unbuttoned his breeches, and stroked him. When he pulled the pins from her hair, a blond shroud fell in a tent around him. His hands shook. Gnashing his teeth in agonizing ecstasy, he fell back to the covers. The feel of her lips and tongue around him was more than he could take. Remembering her firm derrière, he pulled her from him and turned her onto her stomach. After sliding a pillow beneath her, he teased her. He wanted to be strong, to be capable of pulling back, to be able to teach her she didn't have control. But she beckoned him with her wriggling legs. He could take no more. Curving his fingers around her hipbones, he thrust into her.

A kaleidoscope of pleasure-coated pain exploded within Emma, and the bed groaned as Paul drove harder and harder, faster and faster, she met his pounding with her own passion. Never before had their lovemaking been this wild. Time after time he plunged into her, but she wanted more . . . more . . . more.

"You love it," he whispered.

"No," she lied.

"Yes, you do." He started to withdraw, but she reached back to stop him, and he thrust himself once more into her hot moist haven. Leaning forward, he slid his palms under her breasts and squeezed the nipples. "Admit it, *m'amoureuse.*"

"You're a brute."

"You bring out the beast in me . . . so tell me what I bring out in you. Tell me you love it."

"I love it."

At least, Paul figured, he was master of a small part of their destiny. Yet they were both slaves, each to the other's desires, and he wished that would never change.

With one final loving lunge of ecstasy he spent himself in the woman he adored. In the afterglow he covered her throat, her temples, her lips with kisses. There would come a day, he hoped, when Texas would be at peace. Then the proceeds from the sale of Feuille de Chêne would go a long way toward establishing a livelihood for them—a shipyard, perhaps. They would make their home in Galveston, create and raise children, grow old and fat together.

He would never grow tired of her. Never. Getting enough of Emma was as impossible as the sun rising in the west. His life would be a void without her. He'd never allow her to grow tired of him!

Would they have a chance at all those dreams? The *Wharton* was bearing down on the coast of Telchac, bearing down on the Mexican Navy. The Texans would be victorious, Paul couldn't doubt that, but they still might face the wrath and fury of Texas's Big Drunk.

"Paul," Emma murmured, tracing her fingertip along the scar on his jaw, "could we do it again?"

"I think something can be arranged. . . ."

*　　*　　*

Paul's plans didn't come to fruition. By the time they arrived in Telchac the *Moctezuma* had left. They came abreast of a merchantman sailing for New Orleans, and Paul cleared passage for Emma, but she flatly refused to leave the brig. He realized that when she made up her mind there was no unmaking it.

He ordered full sail, and the *Wharton*, along with the flagship, stood for Sisal.

"When we're engaged in battle you'll remain below," he warned. "If I have to chain you there, that's where you'll stay."

"Chain me? What happens if this brig goes down? Would you have me drown?"

"Why do you always have an answer for everything?"

Sisal proved a silver lining to the cloud. Paul, along with Commodore Moore and Colonel Naylor, called on Governor Barbachano and soothed his ruffled feathers, explaining that the fleet had not reneged on its commitment. They were there to stop General Ampudia.

"For that I'm thankful. We had given up hope," Barbachano responded; then he informed them that the *Moctezuma* was with the Centralist armada. At Campeche.

"My navy stands ready to assist in this battle," the governor said. "But our gunboats are small and slow and poorly armed. I have only the schooners *Siselano* and *Independencia* to help you. It will be sail against steam, *mi amigos*. Good luck."

384

They exchanged salutes and gentlemanly hand-shakes, and the Texans rowed back to the commodore's vessel. Paul then listened to Moore's plan of attack, and interjected his own ideas here and there. Nothing was to be left to chance.

Soon the two-ship fleet of the single-star Republic was headed for the Bay of Campeche. When night fell, the *Wharton* unfurled her sails. Tomorrow they would face the enemy. Tonight they would ready themselves, spiritually and emotionally, for battle.

The officers' mess was amidships on the gun deck. Emma, dressed in breeches and shirt requisitioned from a diminutive marine, sat down to the right of Paul, who was positioned at the head of the long table. The cramped cabin smelled of weathered wood, tobacco, and cooking. Twelve officers lined the table. Guy Frost, the cook, brought forth a pot of stew and a jug of rum.

Ashes from Frost's cigar fell into the pot, but he made no mention of it. No one else did either. But Emma's usually sound stomach was queasy.

Deciding it was nothing more than nerves, she concentrated on the cook. He was about forty, and had a stomach that could only be categorized as a belly. Bristly brown hair, streaked with gray, fringed his incredibly small ears. He was a jovial sort.

"Eat up, laddies," Frost said, he being the only enlisted man who had the gall to address his superiors as such. "Me stew's getting cold as a witch's teat." He colored. "Sorry, ma'am. Guess I been at sea too long."

"No harm done, Mr. Frost. I expect to be treated in the same manner as the men."

This comment drew a snigger from two of the officers.

Paul slapped his palm on the table and cutlery jumped. "That will be enough!"

Emma had sensed their animosity, and she intended to face it. "Thank you, Paul—um, Mr. Rousseau. If you don't mind, I'd like to hear what Lieutenants Massar and McGilberry have to say."

Massar bent his eyes on his commanding officer. "If it's all right with you, sir . . ."

Taking a swallow of rum, Paul glanced sharply at his wife, then at Daniel Massar. "You have my permission."

"Mrs. Rousseau, some of us don't like the idea of having you on this brig." Massar, a young man built like a steam engine, frowned. "It's bad luck."

"You won't think so when I'm available to doctor your wounds," Emma replied. "I'm a qualified physician. I've had quite a bit of experience with . . ." She hesitated, unwilling to say amputations. "You won't find my training lacking."

"We don't want a woman doctoring us," McGilberry said.

"You'll change your mind."

Massar sneered. "I doubt it."

"What if one of us takes grapeshot twixt his legs?" The older of the two protestors, McGilberry, quaffed his mug of grog. "What will you do then?"

"Cut away his breeches and tend the wound."

Paul shut his eyes and groaned.

"Well, let me just tell you something, little lady." McGilberry shoved away from the table. "If I take grapeshot twixt my legs, you keep your sweet little

386

hands off my private parts or there'll be hell to pay."

"Mc—"

Emma kicked Paul into silence, under the table. This was her skirmish, and she wouldn't allow him to fight her battles. "Lieutenant McGilberry, I don't frighten easily. If you're in need of my services, rest assured, you'll get them. If I have to gag and tie you, you'll be treated. And hell to pay? That doesn't worry me one bit. I'm a"—she cast a sidelong glance at Paul—"master at paying hell."

The light of respect now shone from Massar's eyes, but McGilberry retreated to lick his injured pride.

Paul had never been more proud of Emma. She was an ally worth having. He was almost convinced she could, and would, take on the entire Centralist squadron by herself—with no more than a switch.

At three that morning the *Wharton* made sail and maneuvered to pick up the sea breeze. Paul felt like a turncoat for not being topside, but he was unable to pull away from Emma's arms.

He kissed her throat and ran his tongue along the edge of her ear. "Vixen, you should be ashamed of yourself, keeping the captain away from his men." He felt her slide a silken leg across his hips. "Forget I mentioned it," he croaked.

Surrendering to her mighty forces, he chained himself to the irons of pleasure. Yet there was a poignancy to their meeting. No words were spoken, for that might have given credence to their fears. It was, Paul figured, as though she realized, as did he,

387

that this might be their last act of lovemaking.

He lingered long after their mutual satisfaction to hold her. He yearned to take her within his body and shelter her from the hell that dawn was sure to bring. Damn her! She didn't want protection. Didn't require it. He ached for her to need him.

That was the trouble with strong women: they didn't need their men. He wanted her to listen to reason when the occasion warranted it. She ought to be safe in Louisiana right now. He longed to be the dominant one in their relationship, at least when the going was tough. Situations beyond his control weren't to his liking.

Emma just didn't know what the fires of war could, and probably would, bring. But Paul realized all the things he craved ran counter to the things he loved and admired in his wife. Damn, life was funny.

"You're awfully quiet," she said.

"Can't think of anything to say."

She pulled away and swung onto her feet. "Go." She pointed upward. "Get up there and do your duty . . . sweetheart."

He went after her, pulling her back, and bent to kiss her cheek. "Please, Emma, please stay out of the line of fire."

"You, my beloved husband, are turning out to be a real seek-sorrow."

"And you've turned out to be a real pain in the arse."

"Oh, really?" she teased. "Well, turn around, honeychile, and let the doctor make it all better."

He groaned with exasperation before he pulled on his uniform and departed.

388

As the brig listed to larboard, Emma clutched her queasy stomach. She had done a good job of hiding her seasickness, a malady that had never troubled her before. She admitted aloud that she'd be glad—darned glad—when they returned to terra firma.

At dawn, his back to the slight breeze, Paul read the wind. East by southeast. The absence of good strong gusts was troubling. To be becalmed would be the ultimate . . .

He raised his spyglass to look across the bay, toward the village of Campeche. The Yucatecan fleet was nowhere in view. In his line of sight was the Centralist armada. Five small supply ships hovered around four sailing vessels. Exhilaration mixed with uncertainty washed over Paul, for he saw the snake-and-buzzard's crowning glory. For months he had heard of them. Like proud Aztec warriors they were, those two new steam frigates built in England to annihilate the people of North America. Vapor from their stacks billowing toward the sky and awesome Paixhans guns mounted, the *Guadalupe* and the *Moctezuma* beat toward them.

The odds were against the Texans but Paul couldn't allow anything but victory. Without President Sam Houston's sanction, they were sailing outside the dictates of international law. If they were captured, every man jack under Commodore Moore's command would be strung from Centralist yardarms.

Paul shared the commodore's view. If worse came to worst, they'd put matches to the powder magazines and send the fleet, with all its crew, to the bottom. But he was not about to let that happen. Emma was aboard. They had to be victorious.

Paul cupped a hand to his mouth and shouted, "Starboard tack!"

When they hove into range of the Centralists, he signaled to hoist additional colors to the single-star ensign at the mizzen. The English flag was raised at the foremast. This was a psychological maneuver, for the captains of both steamers were British.

But the enemy wasn't to be outdone. Spanish and English ensigns went up their foremasts, and they commenced firing. Paul did the same, concentrating on the *Guadalupe*, while the flagship pummeled the *Moctezuma*.

The *Wharton* rocked from the explosions of her guns. Grapeshot struck the steamer broadside, yet she continued her assault. Shot—some overhead, some in front of the prow—whizzed past the brig. Other pellets fell short, landing in Campeche Bay.

The *Iman* tacked forward, and Paul signaled to Reese McDonald, who captained the pivot. The gun's carriage creaked as it swung to the right and aimed. The enemy gun-brig caught grapeshot in the beam, but hove around and made sail.

Suddenly the entire Centralist fleet stood southward and away, the steam frigates covering the retreat of sail.

"Cowards," Paul yelled.

It was then the Yucatecan flotilla, sorry though it was, came abreast at the larboard quarter. Cheers were exchanged before Paul ordered the brig to beat for the Santa Anna's Centralists.

They chased them for half an hour. Then fate turned against the Texans. The breeze died to dead calm, and the enemy's steam squadron, on the starboard side, was propelled out of range and into Campeche harbor.

"What I wouldn't give for one steamer," Paul muttered to no one in particular. "Even that rotten wreck *Zavala*. Just one, and we'd drive those bastards to the bottom."

Emma burst through the open hatch and rushed to her husband. She had heard screams from the enemy, had been told of the gaping holes in their vessels' hulls. She was frightened, but she wouldn't admit it.

"Did we win?"

"No. It was only a running brush."

"Do we have any injuries?" she asked.

"Nary a one. So far." He raised his fist in the direction of the *Guadalupe*'s stern, and raked his wife with a grin. "But in the words of John Paul Jones: 'We've only begun to fight.'"

For days on end they chased after the enemy's navy. The Centralists took a pounding, yet they didn't return fire, and they didn't return to their home port of Vera Cruz.

Commissioner Naylor went ashore to confer with Governor Barbachano. He was piped aboard the *Wharton* late that night, hours after Emma had turned in for the evening.

"Ampudia and his men are scared," Naylor said to Paul. "And they've suffered numerous losses."

"How many?"

"The limey captain of the *Moctezuma*, for one—

Charlewood. Twenty others. Thirty injuries."

"Good." A smile etched Paul's grim lips. "Let's have a drink, good fellow. We'll toast Galveston. Our fair city that won't be attacked by the Aztecs' Eagle and Serpent. Or shall I say Chicken and Worm?"

"Suits me fine. I like your analogy much better than Buzzard and Snake." Naylor chuckled. "Let's go below, Captain. And all I've got to say is hip, hip, hooray!"

The commissioner and Paul, joined by five of the other officers, gathered around the mess table. As a bottle of French brandy was brought forth for their toast, the cook prepared a midnight supper of leftover pinto beans and cornbread, and he kept pot after pot of steaming coffee at the ready.

As that evening in May extended into the predawn hours, Paul grew to like and respect the naval commissioner. He was a fair man dedicated to Texas, and his steel-gray eyes danced with merriment when the occasion allowed.

Suddenly Reese McDonald tromped into the room. "Cap'n, the Mexs are steaming for deep water!"

Naylor's cheerful expression turned to one of dismay.

Paul shoved his coffee mug aside. "Men, Antonio López de Santa Anna's navy is ready for battle. Let's show them our teeth!"

Chapter Twenty-Five

Emma awoke to darkness. Yet the brig was asail. She heard men shout as hammocks were piped up and they began to run the guns out. She hastily got into her man's garb and rushed up to the bridge. Battle was upon them.

Paul half turned to her. "Get below."

"Not this time. Not until my services are needed."

He shook his head. "This is a helluva time for me to wish for injuries."

Fearing for all the men aboard the *Wharton*, and especially for her husband, Emma watched and listened as he shouted commands. He was sure of himself, and she was sure of his capabilities. She believed they would win.

The wind with them, the brig plowed through the blue waters. Guns were loaded. The decks were a scurry of activity. As sunlight brightened the sky, the enemy was in sight. In the schooner *Austin*'s wake, the brig maneuvered to a larboard, broadside position.

As much as Emma wanted to witness the battle, common sense reminded her to abide by the promise she had given both the commodore and Paul. She was Ship's Surgeon. She needed to ready her equipment and supplies. After taking a last loving gaze at the man she loved, she descended to the sick bay.

Paul was relieved when she left the bridge. He couldn't allow himself the luxury of personal worry. "The *Guadalupe* is ours today, men. Commence firing!"

Salvos burst from the long guns, taking their marks. A shot sliced off the enemy's flagstaff, and it fell overboard. The Centralists hoisted an ensign on the steamer's main gaff.

Suddenly the schooner *Eagle* turned her guns on Paul's brig. Thirty-two pounds of shot struck. Screams of pain burst from the gun deck, and the ship rocked beneath his feet. "Keep firing!"

Both steamers bore down; the *Guadalupe* steamed to starboard.

"Man all batteries!" Paul ordered, having no fear of attack from both sides. "Run between them!"

Enemy fire caught them, and all hell broke loose on the Texas brig as the main topgallant, breast backstay, and aftershroud toppled. Grapeshot struck Lieutenant Daniel Massar, killing him instantly. He fell at his captain's feet.

Paul reached down to pull him away from the bridge, but pain lanced his thigh as shrapnel hit him. Blood surged from the wound, so he tore off his shirt and wrapped it around the gash. He wouldn't allow a flesh wound to stop him.

For hours the battle raged. Shells exploded, large chunks of the wooden hull flew. Cries of pain and determination mingled with the sounds of destruction. Men died, others were injured. Thomas Norris, assisting McDonald on the pivot, took a wound, but returned to his station as soon as it was dressed. Five minutes later his left arm was blown away.

Steven McGilberry, the lieutenant who had taunted Emma, fell, injured. He was carried to sick bay.

Still, the battle did not end. The brig gave as good as she took.

Uncharacteristically sickened by the carnage, Emma wanted to clutch her stomach, but didn't. She had to be strong! She couldn't allow this queasiness to get the better of her. Sick bay, where she toiled, was littered with moaning men, and she had no sulfurous ether to ease their suffering.

Laying a cauterizing knife on the red-hot, pot-bellied stove, she shouted instructions to her two assistants. "Wind another tourniquet around Davis's foot. Open that keg of rum, and fill some tankards. These men need all the spirits"—and spirit, she thought—"they can get!"

"Yes, ma'am," her helpers replied, setting to work.

Emma held a cup to Norris's purple lips. He turned his head away, but she forced it back. "Take another drink."

He did as ordered. "My arm," he groaned, his words edged with despair, and he stared at the bloodied rag that was wrapped around the gap at his shoulder.

"Think of something else," she murmured gently.

"Do you have a woman, Seaman Norris?"

"Aye. A good one."

"Think about her. And how happy she's going to be when you return to her."

His suffering face eased, somewhat.

Emma took up the glowing-hot knife with one hand, and pulled away the makeshift bandage with the other. Blood gushed and spurted forth, staining her cheek. She laid the flat side of the knife against the tattered flesh where an arm had been. Norris screamed, a piercing wail that bounced off the walls.

His flesh sizzled, a cloud of smoke rising from it, and the sickly sweet stench of scorched skin and bone sank into the pit of Emma's weak stomach. Not breathing for fear of fainting, she forced her tongue to the roof of her mouth.

The cautery took, and the flow of blood from Norris's shoulder stopped. He fell into blessed unconsciousness.

Emma breathed a sigh of relief and turned to the next patient. Davis's foot, several toes blown away, was cleaned and stitched. Then, for what seemed like hours, she dug out bits of metal from injured men. Finally she came to McGilberry—the man who had challenged her not to tend his wounds looked up with untrusting eyes.

"Don't want you touching me," he said.

"Be reasonable, Lieutenant McGilberry. We've got to get that shrapnel out of you."

"I don't want no woman quack touching me." He motioned toward a youthful attendant. "Let Ellery do it."

Emma frowned. Wayne Ellery's face was even

396

greener than Emma imagined her own to be. He had been pressed into her service that morning, and he lacked experience and probably fortitude.

She picked up a pair of shears from the instrument tray. "He's busy right now. And unless you want an infection to spread and kill you, I suggest you shut your dratted mouth."

Grasping the ducking of his breeches, she started to cut the material. McGilberry jerked his leg aside, and his face went whiter from the effort. But Emma leaned against his leg, bore down with all her weight, and continued to trim away the bloodied material.

He gave up the fight.

The Centralist Navy regrouped and its captains conferred. They knew when they had been whipped. Ships battered, they ran signals up the masts, conceding victory to the Tars of Texas.

Several English sailors in service with the enemy then rowed over to the Texan fleet. One of Santa Anna's schooners lifted a white flag of surrender, and hove to alongside the *Wharton*. Her captain came aboard and told of their many casualties and injuries, and of the extensive damage to ships and morale.

The Texans went below to celebrate their victory.

Yet Paul took no overt delight in it. When the night's fog rolled in, he left the bridge, stopped by the galley to order a tray of food, and then went to the sick bay. To Emma. Lovingly she bandaged his slight wound, but when he urged her to retire for the evening, she wouldn't. Within minutes, he had had enough of her stubbornness. Though she was past the point of exhaustion, he couldn't cajole her into taking a rest, so he scooped her up and carried her to their cabin.

"You have to eat," he said, once food had been brought.

"Not hungry." Her words were spoken quietly, too quietly, and she grabbed a ceiling-secured bedpost. "Just tired."

Paul was not going to give up. He lifted the silver lid from the tray Guy Frost had prepared, and steam rose from the plate of stew.

Emma recoiled, her face turning white, then gray.

"Don't tell me you're going to be sick. After all you've seen to— *Emma!*" He pushed the tray aside and grabbed her just as she folded to the floor. "Emma?"

A curtain of blond hair hid her face, and he brushed it aside. Her eyes were closed, her breath shallow. She had fainted—cold!

He carried her to bed and, holding her in his arms, sat down. Rubbing her cheek with the edge of his thumb, he kicked himself inwardly for allowing her to be a part of the sea battle. It had taken its toll on the strong woman who was his wife. On Emma, who never cried, never turned from sickness or injury, never shied away from bad smells or blood or fights. She was the stuff valiant warriors were made of.

"Why," he wondered aloud as he tightened his arms around her, "did she faint now?" For several minutes he rocked her, whispering soothing words and reassurances, loving her with all his heart.

Slowly she began to open her eyes. "Wh-what happened?"

"You fainted."

"Let me up. I don't need coddling. I'm not a baby." She inhaled a sharp lungful of air, then tried to sit up, but he wouldn't allow it.

He watched her green eyes flicker, and suspicion dawned on him. "Are you with child?"

"I guess it's possible."

"More than possible, Emma Frances Rousseau. There hasn't been a night since I sailed back to Feuille de Chêne that we haven't . . . I'd say it's probable."

"Probable." A hint of a smile lifted her lips.

"Then it's true?"

"I don't know."

"Damn it, you're a woman . . . and a doctor to boot. Surely you'd know. Have you had any other signs?"

"Now that I think of it, yes."

Male pride burst in Paul's chest. "A baby. Think of that? Oh, *amoureuse,* I love you!"

Yet now he had another worry. Though the Centralist Navy had beat a retreat, she and the child could have been killed during the fighting. Victory was theirs, but Emma was across the Gulf of Mexico from a safe haven, and the Englishmen who had come over to their side had informed him that Sam Houston had published the piracy proclamation. With "the nations of Christendom" on the lookout for the Texan fleet, they might have to run the gauntlet.

A staccato knock at the door reverberated through the cabin.

"The captain of that Mex schooner wants a word with you," Reese McDonald said a few moments later.

Hat in hand, the vanquished man stepped around McDonald. "I've been told you've a surgeon aboard, Captain Rousseau," he said, his intonation clearly English. "Could you spare him? My men . . . My men are suffering. I beg of you . . ."

Paul opened his mouth to demur for the time being, but Emma interceded. Now appearing to be in the bloom of health, she stepped determinedly between him and the Briton. "I'm this ship's surgeon, sir, and I'm at your men's service."

"Thank you, good woman."

"Just a minute." Paul clutched Emma's elbow. "Surgeon Rousseau has my permission to go aboard, but she is going to eat her dinner and rest for a while. If she goes against my orders, Surgeon Rousseau will be locked in the hold of this ship, and she *will not* leave there until we reach Galveston." He exerted pressure on her arm. "Surgeon Rousseau, I'll not tolerate insubordination."

"Aye, aye, sir," Emma said and turned toward the food tray. "I do need my strength." Her eyes on the Centralist, she then added, "I'll be with you in thirty minutes."

Paul didn't believe a half-hour was proper rest, but she had made a concession and that stood for something.

*   *   *

At midnight the Bay of Campeche was quiet. Stars shone down on the surrendered schooner, but for safety's sake Paul went aboard with Emma and her two assistants.

While she tended the injured he inspected the ship. It was still seaworthy, and with Moore's permission, he intended to turn it over to the Yucatecans. However, any munitions aboard might be needed on the journey back to Galveston, so he strode toward the powder magazine. Anger, old and painful, whipped through him as he eyed the crates that lined the storage room.

They were stamped COPPER PIPING—OLIVER SUGAR MILL, HAVANA.

Rankin Oliver's munitions had killed and maimed men both Yucatecan and Texan. At long last Paul had damning proof that was sure to convict his old enemy.

Emma, in her delicate condition, didn't need to know about it. Not now. Maybe never. A strange feeling filled Paul. He almost wished he hadn't found evidence of Rankin Oliver's misdeeds. "Get some of the crew and have them load these crates into our longboat," Paul demanded of Wayne Ellery. "Have them taken back to the *Wharton* and hidden in the hold."

"Aye, aye, Cap'n. Anthing else?"

"Yes. Round up four or five of the officers." Paul's eyes never left the evidence. "They are going to attest in writing that these crates were stored on this schooner."

The deed done, Paul went to the schooner's sick bay. He pulled Emma aside. "Let's go."

"I can't leave. There's so much yet to be done."

"Our own men need you. I'm going to do what I should've done in the beginning. I've ordered a longboat to take the injured into Campeche. They'll get medical attention there."

"It goes against my principles to leave until these men are under another doctor's care."

He touched her cheek. "Do your principles extend to putting our child in peril? He needs his mother to think of him."

"She."

"He."

"She."

"*Sacre bleu!* Your daughter needs you. Let's go." She did.

In Campeche the *Wharton* and the *Austin* were made seaworthy. The Centralist Navy, after signing an armistice agreement favorable to the Yucatecans, finally sailed for its home port in Vera Cruz. A day in advance of the flagship, the *Wharton* slipped out of Campeche harbor and set a course for Texas.

Two days out of Galveston, Paul spied a strange sight. Through his scope he saw Henry Packert's corvette tacking into the wind, making for the *Wharton*. A signal of peace went up her flagstaff.

In the many months since the factor-house fire, Paul hadn't laid eyes on Henry Packert, and he was itching for a few answers. He called from the bridge, "Weigh anchor." The hawseholes groaned as the anchors were dropped. Though he wanted those answers, he wouldn't trust the pirate. "Man the larboard batteries," he ordered.

"Why did we stop?" Emma asked as the black-hulled *Barbara Elaine* came abreast. "Isn't that a pirate ship?"

"Yes. But I know this particular pirate. I'm going to talk with him."

Emma shook her head. "That's dangerous! Houston's invited the world to seize us."

He grimaced. It was more perilous to allow Henry on the *Wharton*. Emma knew him—he had stolen the brooch from her, and his ladylove had been the one who had told her of Paul's innocence in the fire. Questions—there would be plenty.

Paul strode from the bridge and made for the longboat. "Keep a keen eye on that corvette," he said to his second mate. "If anything looks amiss, fire."

Emma hurried behind him. "Paul, don't go."

"I'm going."

The *Barbara Elaine* creaked as if she had an old man's joints. Her crew, ragged and cutthroat, eyed Paul as he climbed the ratline. Wearing worn boots and a red-and-white striped shirt that exposed two inches of his snow-white belly, Henry Packert stood on the poop deck. A black cloth was wound around his head at a rakish angle so that it touched the crusty patch he wore over one eye, yet he was anything but a rake. Reprobate was a more fitting term for him. And Paul noticed something else. A certain defeat in the man's expression.

"Ahoy, if it ain't me old mate Paul Rousseau. Long time, no see, matey."

403

Paul eyed him warily. "I beg to differ on the 'mate.' Our alliance ceased last year. At the factor-house. When you set it afire and attacked me with that crowbar. Remember?"

"Sorry 'bout that. 'Twas a fit of mad-dog on me part." One side of Packert's mouth pulled into a grimace. "You ain't of a mind to take a pound of me flesh, are you?"

"I ought to."

"Well, I'm sorry for what happened, laddie." Packert crooked a thumb over his shoulder, point-ing downward. "Whaddya say we share a bottle o' rum and talk it over? Got a few things to tell ya," he added to sweeten the pot.

"Lead the way."

The old salt's cabin was in a general state of disarray. Soiled clothing and linen littered every surface, and the rancid stench would have gagged a maggot.

Clearing only the seat of a chair, Packert motioned Paul to it. Then he picked up two mugs and blew dust out of them. After filling the mugs with rum, he said, "Hear that ol' Raven in Texas is after your hide."

"That's what I hear."

"I'm in the same predicament. Almost. The Brits are after me and me lads," Packert confessed. "They was out looking for you and Moore, and we saw an opportunity . . . sacked one o' their merchantmen, we did."

"If you're wanting me to help the likes of you, you can forget it."

"Never said nothing 'bout that." The corsair

404

seated himself on one of the wooden chairs. It groaned under his weight. "'Twould be worth me while to capture that brig of yours, and take 'er back to Galveston. Might get those Brits off me tail."

"Since the entire Centralist Navy couldn't take her, I doubt you and your motley crew could do it."

"Aw now. Don't get on the defensive." He waved a thorny thumb. "'Twas only voicing a thought. If I'd o' been set on them ideas, I wouldn't o' offered me hospitality."

"What is on your mind?"

"Just thought you might be interested in a piece of gossip that's come down the pike."

"That being?"

"Simon Dyer's dead. Killed hisself. His body washed up on the bayou a few weeks back."

A smile of satisfaction broke over Paul's face, but he said, "Come now. You didn't stop my brig just to tell me that my father's turncoat second did away with himself. Let's hear the real reason."

"Our mutual *compadre* Rankin Oliver's headed for Campeche. Word has it his merchant ship's loaded with ordnance."

"Don't fiddle with me, dammit. I've heard that before."

"Yes, me as well. But this time, ol' mate, he ain't gonna get away with it."

"Wait a minute. Something doesn't ring true. You've said, and I know, that Oliver doesn't leave his scent. Why would he personally accompany contraband meant for the Centralists?"

"Getting lax in his old age is me guess." The old man lifted a fleshy shoulder. "But I'm gonna find him . . . and kill him. With me bare hands, if me Bowie knife don't do the trick."

"And you needed to tell me?"

"Naw. Was hoping for your help. Whaddya say we team up, make a run down to Campeche and catch him?"

At one time Paul would have jumped at this opportunity. Now he hesitated. The *Wharton* was on a course for home port, with Emma and their unborn child aboard. Paul would not put her in further danger nor would he cause her undue distress.

"Can't do it, Packert."

"You gone soft in the head?"

"Perhaps." Paul took a sip of cheap, esophagus-burning rum. "You're not the patriotic sort, the kind to stick his neck out for nothing. Tell me something. Why do you hate Rankin Oliver?"

Dropping his chin as if to stare at the tips of his worn-out boots, the weathered seafarer flattened his wrinkle-folded lips. He refilled his chipped mug and guzzled the contents, then wiped a shaking hand across his mouth. He belched.

"Did he cut you out of a deal?" Paul prompted.

Packert took a long time answering. "Has to do with me woman. Katie. Remember her? She be his daughter."

"I know. Kathryn told my wife. She also told her you'd set that fire, not me."

Paul expected a heated response, yet none came.

Painful memories dulled the pirate's eyes as he rolled a cigarette and brought a candle from the table to light the smoke. "Kathryn," he said, speaking the name with a sentimental sweetness that took Paul aback. "Me Katie. She liked to be called Kathryn."

"So you hate Rankin Oliver because he is Kathryn's father."

"Started out that way. Yea, it did." A fiery piece of tobacco fell onto Packert's belly and burned through his shirt, yet he didn't flinch. "Afore I bought her, he whipped her regular. Put her on the auction block for any buzzard to buy. Like she was a piece of meat." A tear meandered down the wrinkled troughs of Packert's right cheek. "That was a hurting thing for her. She'd been raised by her ma— a good woman o' high training, I understand. They both deserved better than to be put on the block. He sold them both."

"Why?"

"'Cause the ma wanted her freedom. Just the rights most octoroons enjoy in New Orleans. A place o' her own, a chance to introduce Katie to decent white men at the Octoroon Ball."

Was there no end to Rankin Oliver's evil? Paul shook his head in disgust. Murderer, consorter with the enemy, uncaring father and lover. How many people had been hurt by him?

The older man blew his nose on a gray handkerchief. "I would o' turned to the pulpit for me Katie . . . me Kathryn."

"It's not too late," Paul said dryly.

Packert snuffed out his cigarette, placed his forearms on the table and looked him squarely in the eye. "Yes, 'tis. She's . . . she's dead."

Remembering the beautiful, regal young woman

407

he had met in Packert's shotgun shack—the woman who had told Emma of his innocence—it was no mere platitude when Paul declared, "I'm sorry."

"The fever took her," the wretched man explained without being asked. "I was holding her in me arms when she passed. She died calling for 'Papa.'" What had been a tear was now a stream of them. "She was the only good thing ever happened to me. Afore I just wanted to make that bastard suffer for hurting me Katie. Now I'm going to kill him. And there ain't nobody gonna stop me."

Paul thought of Emma, and his mind's eye drew a picture of her. In that vision she was etched with pain.

Could he allow Packert to continue on his quest? Kathryn was gone. The munitions had already done damage to the Texans. Karla was gone. Nothing would bring Étienne back from the grave.

At that moment a sturdy young buccaneer burst into the cabin. "Trouble, Pack! That Brit frigate is headed this way."

"We'd better both make a run for it, matey," Packert said.

Already Paul was charging up the companion-way. Rankin's fate was left to the wind. The *Wharton* had to be saved.

Chapter Twenty-Six

At that same moment Rankin Oliver rested his head of graying blond hair on a wealth of satin-covered pillows. He was two days out of Campeche, and his cabin aboard the *Ransomed Princess* was lavish, befitting his station in life. He had everything money could buy. Yet he was miserable.

His wife was a twittering piece of rippling flesh, yet for some reason she continued, despite his indifference, to love him. William, his only child, was dead. And all the women he desired were out of his life, one way or another. Angélique had become Étienne Rousseau's wife. Estella, his comely high-yellow chattel of fonder days, had made unmeetable demands on him; he might have granted them if she hadn't lied to him over the years. But no matter what Estella had said, her daughter Katie was not his child. So he had sold them. And then there had been Karla. Teutonic and infinitely desirable—a Valkyrie amid the brown-bellied peasants of the Yucatán peninsula—yet gone now, too.

Yet there was Emmie. The light of his life. She should have been his daughter, instead of his brother's. Quentin had always ignored her or had thwarted her ambitions; he didn't deserve such a treasure. Life wasn't fair. Quentin had all the happiness in the world—marriage to the woman he loved, fine sons to follow in his footsteps, three daughters to love and cherish. And what did he, Rankin Oliver, have beyond riches?

"If Emmie were mine," Rankin bemoaned to himself, "oh, how different my life would've been."

But he *had* made her his daughter in spirit. He was the one who had been her buoy during the storms of life. Until Paul Rousseau had taken her away. And now . . .

Defeated, Rankin buried his face in his hands. Always he had wanted her to think only the best of him. Yet she knew his feet were made of clay.

He squeezed his lids shut, remembering. . . .

Simon Dyer—the wretch!—had come to Magnolia Hall. Coughing and spitting blood, he had laughed in Rankin's face. "Your beloved niece knows about you. I told her about our deal with the Mexs."

Emmie! Rankin's muscles had tensed. The last time he had seen his niece, he had suspected as much, but he had figured Paul had filled her head with suspicions. Now it was Paul's and Dyer's word against his.

"Got nothing to say, Rankin?"

He had had his fill of this blackmailer's fourteen years of harassment. "That was *yer* deal with Santa Anna, not mine."

"But your name was on the cargo manifest."

"Put there by ye." Rankin didn't give a damn if

410

Simon knew the whole truth now. "I went along with it to set a trap, to catch ye, then turn yer stinking hide over to the Texans."

"Well, old partner in crime," Simon wheezed, "it didn't work. I got the ordnance to Vera Cruz before you could catch me." His mean eyes hardened. "And aren't you the noble one? Turn me over to the Texans? Ha! You don't give a tinker's damn about them."

"True. But I care less about ye, Simon Dyer, ye miserable extortionist. I was, and am, sick of yer money-sucking."

Simon was eager to pour forth more venom. "Let's get back to our neighbors south of the border, I'm the one who killed your Sisal lover gal. Told her I was doing the deed for you."

A niggling of pain clutched at Rankin's chest, yet he spoke each word with forced indifference. "Karla was expendable. Tell me something that isn't a surprise."

"Your niece, the honorable Mrs. Paul Rousseau, knows we killed Étienne. I told her, and I'm glad I did."

Rankin's previously controlled anger burst forth. "Bloody bastard!" he shouted, and went for Simon's throat. "I'll kill ye, too!"

"Do it," Simon croaked, his face reddening and spittle oozing from one corner of his mouth.

The two men stared at each other. It was obvious Simon wanted his own life to end. Suddenly Rankin yearned to rectify his mistakes with the one person who had believed him above reproach. Emmie.

He thrust Simon from him, and his nemesis fell to

the ground. "I won't do ye in. Ye're not worth the effort."

Turning away, Rankin decided to change his life. Someway, somehow he'd do a good deed that would show Emmie his love, so he traveled to Feuille de Chêne. She wasn't there, and he learned she had accompanied her lawless, pirate husband to the Yucatán! . . .

Rankin opened his eyes to the present. The wide-hulled *Ransomed Princess* listed to larboard, and the lamps on his cabin walls swayed to the left. He rose from his bed to stretch his aching muscles. Beneath him, in the hold, were supplies sufficient to replenish the Texas Navy. The finest sailors and fighting men money could buy manned Rankin's merchant vessel, and her guns were mounted.

Armed and ready for battle at sea—for Emmie's sake—Rankin Oliver and his crew were sailing to the aid of Paul Rousseau. He had no idea his help was too late and not needed.

The *Wharton* outdistanced the British frigate. The next day Paul rendezvoused with Moore, and they sailed side by side toward home port. Dropping their anchors south of the Galveston sandbar, they were on the threshold of their next battle—that with President Sam Houston.

Emma yearned to take Paul's hand, but she hesitated to make a gesture of affection and reassurance in front of his men. So she watched emotions—anger, anxiety, pride—play across his face.

A boat cut through the Gulf, advancing toward

the *Austin*.

"Houston's men?" Emma asked, her heart in her throat.

"No. It's the pilot, that's all. He'll guide us across the bar." Several minutes later Paul lifted his scope and honed in on the flagship's bridge. "I'll be damned. . . ."

"What is it?"

"The pilot's shaking Ed's hand . . . and our men are—why, they're celebrating!"

Indeed there was cause for celebration. Ed Moore sent his longboat to the *Wharton* with good news: The citizenry of Galveston, led by Mayor Allen, were waiting at Menard's wharf for the gallant men of the Texas Navy. A full-fledged jubilee was planned in their honor. In the eyes of the Galvestonians, the pirates were returning home as heroes.

Twenty-one guns saluted the fleet as it entered Galveston harbor, and the honor was returned. Sails furled, the men went ashore to cheers and salutations.

A party stood on the wharf, awaiting Emma and Paul. Marian, dressed to the nines, clung to Howard's elbow and blew kisses toward the ships. While Cleopatra, wearing a feathered hat that dwarfed her, looked very happy. Ben was grinning, and Anthaline, in a mountain man's buckskins, was trying to restrain a tail-wagging Woodley by hanging onto the end of the rope around his neck. The dog broke free and leaped into Paul's arms when he stepped onto the jetty.

"Hey," Emma scolded. "He's supposed to be my dog."

As if he understood, Woodley squirmed and

jumped for her, wetting her cheek with kisses.

"We've got a celebration dinner all cooked up," Anthaline said. "Right in my own kitchen."

"We've fixed all your favorite foods, Frenchie." Cleopatra patted Paul's arm. "Yours too, missy.'

Emma smiled. Cleopatra was her dearest friend, and she was pleased that her former mammy loved Paul.

Ben, usually a man of few words, grinned self-consciously. "Cleo and me, we was wanting to be here when you showed up. We be staying here, too. Got me a blacksmithing shop." He cast a loving glance at his wife. "She ain't ornery unless she be around you . . . and I like her ornery."

They all laughed, save for Cleopatra, who kicked his shin. Ben then grabbed her about the waist, and she cuddled against him.

"It's good to be home," Emma said, smiling and happy. "But tell me. Why are you here, Howard . . . Marian?"

"We heard about Houston's piracy proclamation" —Howard reached out to shake Paul's hand—"so I'm here to act as your attorney."

"And I wouldn't dream of letting him travel here without me," Marian explained.

The local militia formed an honor guard to lead the heroes into town. Women, smiling and happy, pinned ribbons and badges on the crew's jackets. Kegs were tapped, music played; and girls begged dances from the Texas Tars, especially from the handsome sailor Reese McDonald, for they were attracted by his cobalt-blue eyes and thick, dark hair.

Emma was somewhat light-headed due to the show of support, both from her loved ones and from the Galvestonians.

Moore motioned Paul aside. "We've got the people on our side, Paul, so let's fight Sam Houston for our honor."

"I'm with you all the way. I suggest we surrender to the sheriff."

Colonel Naylor jumped on the bandstand to make a speech. "Ladies and gentlemen, you do our naval men proud, as they have done you. Thanks to Commodore Moore, Captain Rousseau, and their valiant men, freedom is yours." He clapped his hands, and so did the townspeople. When the roar died down, Naylor said, "Their foray was a courageous one, and I want to make something perfectly clear: it was I who sanctioned it. I am the one to blame, and I stand behind the commodore and Captain Rousseau." Naylor raised his hands. "Let's all show them our gratitude."

The crowd went wild with enthusiasm.

Paul and the commodore stepped back from the festivities, and Emma followed. She didn't want her husband in jail, but she knew he would choose to be vindicated by a legal tribunal. Within five minutes they had found Sheriff Smythe.

The commodore and Paul held out their wrists, and Moore, by right of command, spoke. "Sir, we surrender to the charges of piracy against the Republic of Texas."

Emma held her breath.

The lawman hitched up his breeches and shook his head. "Arrest you? Not on your life."

Emma watched Paul's reaction. There was disappointment in his eyes. He needed a court-martial to clear his name and Moore's, and to clear the tarnished repute of the Navy.

Paul was preoccupied during the dinner that Anthaline had prepared in his and Emma's honor. He wasn't worried over his fate insofar as Sam Houston was concerned. The public had vindicated the Navy men. Houston was sure to abide by public opinion; he'd either drop the charges or assemble a panel of judges.

But the crates that had been off-loaded in secrecy weighed heavily on Paul's mind.

He was considering his next step. Should he turn them over to the Department of War and Marine? That was his desire, for Paul could not condone Rankin's treachery against the Republic of Texas.

He glanced at his wife. She was engaged in animated conversation with her friends and family. Oh, how he loved her! Could he destroy her by turning that evidence over to the authorities?

Anthaline's serving girl pushed the swinging dining-room door and popped her head through the opening. "There's a sailor here to see you, Mr. Paul. Reese McDonald, he says he is."

Paul excused himself and rose from the table.

Emma put down her fork. Reese was a dear fellow and should be included in their private celebration! "Pardon me for a moment," she said, and she, too, quit the dining room.

In the darkened hallway leading into Anthaline's

416

parlor, Emma opened her mouth to speak, then closed it to wait for a break in the men's conversation.

Paul paced the room as Reese, speaking, stood with hat in hand. "A British frigate sailed into harbor a couple of hours ago. Thought you might want to know about it, sir. They captured Henry Packert and his crew."

Henry Packert? Emma stepped back and out of sight—behind a potted palm—but not out of eying and eavesdropping range. Why would that pirate be of concern to Paul?

"What happened?" Paul asked.

After we outran the British, apparently the *Barbara Elaine* fired on them. Packert was outclassed." Reese lifted a palm. "The corvette sank, and Her Majesty's men rescued the survivors."

As she watched a pensive expression come to her husband's features, questions and a realization came to Emma's mind. The *Barbara Elaine* was the black-hulled corvette that Paul had visited not two days earlier. He had said that the pirate captain was known to him, but Henry Packert had never been mentioned. Not then, not subsequently. What secret business had gone on between Paul and the miscreant? She told herself not to jump to conclusions.

Paul rubbed his fingers across his grim mouth. "What have they done with Packert and his men?"

"Turned the lot of them over to Sheriff Smythe."

"Guess the Brits don't want the bother of punishing Packert and his men." Paul rubbed his furrowed brow. "I think I'd like to talk with him."

417

"Uh, before you go . . ." Reese caught his arm. "The crates are taken care of."

"Them," Paul muttered, as if the subject were belladonna. "Did you put them in the shed?"

"Yes, sir. The one behind your house. It's secured with a lock."

"We'll have to move them tomorrow. I don't want my wife getting suspicious. Damn! It would've been better to leave them in the *Wharton*'s hold."

"I agree, sir, but as you reminded me, Houston's men are liable to confiscate our brig. And you wanted the evidence in a safe place."

What evidence? Emma wondered. She started to step forth, to demand explanations, but thought better of it. Paul would make excuses. She intended to find out for herself what was in those crates.

"I've made arrangements for a safer hiding place," Paul was saying. "In the stable behind Ben Edward's blacksmithing shop. See that they're moved tomorrow. Say around noon. I'll steer Mrs. Rousseau away from the house."

"You can depend on me, sir." A questioning look filled Reese's blue eyes. "How long are you going to keep those boxes hidden?"

"Haven't decided yet. Right now I want to have a talk with Packert."

"Aye, aye, Cap'n."

"Good. Now I'm off to city jail." Just short of the door, he turned. "Tell my wife and the others . . . tell them the commodore needs me. I'll meet Emma at home."

Though the conversation between Paul and his young aide could have been innocent enough,

418

Emma felt there was more to it than met the eye. She turned away and retreated to the dining room. After Reese made his hollow excuse for Paul's absence, she finished her dinner quickly and, pleading a headache, bid her hostess adieu.

Opening the door to the home she had bought in Galveston wasn't the joyous occasion she had imagined. Paul should have been with her. But he wasn't. And she was determined to find out why.

She lit a lantern, found hammer and chisel, and departed for the shed. Wedging the chisel behind the lock's iron hasp, she pounded the hammer down. After three tries the wood splintered, and she opened the creaking door.

The lantern's orange glow honed in on two wooden crates, which were each about four by four. She crossed the straw floor. Black stenciling on the boxes read COPPER PIPING—OLIVER SUGAR MILL, HAVANA.

Why did Paul have possession of her uncle's goods? What did Packert have to do with them? And most of all, why the intrigue? Suspicion crawled up her spine, and a sinking feeling settled in the pit of her stomach. Paul still sought revenge against her uncle. Apparently Henry Packert, the man who had fired the Oliver factor house, was mixed up in this, too.

She tried to wedge the chisel between the top of a crate and one of its side boards. Her diminutive size and the awkwardness of the situation worked against her. The shed was empty save for the crates, and with no stool available, she was unable to get the needed leverage.

Finally, in anger and frustration, she gave up the physical struggle. She could have gotten a stool from the house, could have returned to try again; but she had decided against it. What did the contents matter? The bald fact was that Paul was keeping something from her, and whatever it was, it would probably bring suffering to her marriage.

Yet she didn't relinquish her determination to find out why those boxes were important to her husband. She would confront Paul—and he had better be honest.

Chapter Twenty-Seven

"Don't lie to me, Paul." Emma curled her hands into fists as the first light of dawn peeked through the windows of their house on the Strand. "I've broken the lock off the shed door, and I've seen those crates."

Paul knew a strong offense was the best defense. "So you were eavesdropping on me and Reese."

His feelings were in turmoil. While he wanted Rankin to suffer for his wrongdoings, he yearned to put the entire matter aside, for Emma. Yet he couldn't. The agony of his father's untimely death had haunted him for too many years.

"Didn't your *maman* teach you it's naughty to snoop?" he hedged.

"Don't talk to me as if I'm a child. I'm your wife. Your partner. Your equal partner."

"We are partners." He rubbed his brow. "And I hope this partnership is strong enough to weather the storm that's brewing. . . . When we went aboard that Centralist schooner I found those boxes."

She advanced toward him. "You lied to me. You're still seeking revenge against my uncle."

"He's an evil man, Emma."

"He's human. In humankind lie good and evil. I'll admit he has his faults. But who are we to pass judgment? I do not have a sterling character, and neither do you."

"Granted. But have you sold munitions to the enemy? I haven't."

No matter how much she wished to keep Simon Dyer's drugged confession a secret, her future with Paul depended on total honesty. But, in her mind, if she betrayed a patient's confidence she'd never be able to doctor again.

She turned away. Around her, and within her, was her life to come—Paul, their child. But what kind of future would they have if she allowed his vindictiveness to go on? She had to sacrifice professional ethics to heal her husband.

She took a deep breath, and spoke out. "My uncle didn't sell arms to the Centralists."

Angered and unbelieving, he lashed out. "Spoken by a woman who believes no fault could possibly lie with her blood kin."

Emma rounded on him. "I speak the truth. I know Simon Dyer, and he told me *he* was the mastermind behind that shipment of arms, not Uncle Rankin."

"Simon Dyer?" Bewilderment etched each syllable. "How do you know him?"

"He was my consumptive patient in St. Martinsville. Under the influence of ether he told me about his dealings with my uncle."

She became silent, and Paul waited in vain for her to speak again. Finally he asked, "Would you care to explain?"

Emma's green eyes were clouded with agony. "Apparently Mr. Dyer wanted to get even with Uncle Rankin. He was the one who . . . Paul, he killed that woman in Sisal."

"How convenient. You conjure up this story, making Dyer the guilty party. Pardon me, *chérie,* but I don't believe it."

"I didn't suppose you would."

"There's something you need to know, Emma. When I went aboard the *Barbara Elaine*, Packert told me something. Your uncle—"

"Wait just a minute!" Emma poked Paul's chest with the tip of her forefinger. "Your friend Henry Packert brings up another point. I think you were in collusion with him regarding the factor-house fire."

"In a way," Paul confessed. "He told me a shipment of arms—your uncle's illicit goods—were stored in the warehouse. I went into the building to see for myself. I intended to turn the evidence over to the authorities. But Packert figured out what I was up to, and he attacked me. My physical condition wasn't good, if you'll remember."

"You didn't find what you were looking for?"

"No. I expected the building to explode, but it didn't. Apparently that was a dummy shipment."

"Exactly," she said. "Arranged by Simon Dyer . . . the guilty party in the deal."

"Even if what you say is true, I cannot—will not—put aside my hostilities."

"You never could forget and forgive."

"Oh, really? If you'll remember, Emma, I've done a pretty good job of it when it comes to you."

"I'll concede that. But I can't condone your quest

for revenge against my uncle."

"Why don't you forgive and forget?" Paul asked. Receiving no response, he added, "I'm not out to hurt your family, at least not now. But Rankin Oliver must pay for his misdeeds."

"I've told you—he's not guilty of helping the Centralists."

Paul took a contemplative breath. "Since Simon confessed his crimes, did he tell you they murdered my father?"

Emma moistened her lips and squeezed her lids. "Yes."

"Then as long as there is a breath in my body, I'll seek revenge against Rankin Oliver."

"It's revenge or me," she said quietly.

"Is that an ultimatum?"

"Yes!"

It was on the tip of his tongue to tell Emma about Kathryn. Yet he wouldn't. He had made his arguments, and Emma was either with him or she was against him. It was as simple as that.

He stepped forward and took her elbows. "You'd give up all we have for your uncle?"

Considering all that she—they—had to lose, she was tempted to reconsider . . . to accept his touch . . . to forget about everyone and everything that worked against them. But she couldn't. "And you, Paul? Would you give up all we have to right a wrong long since done?"

He didn't answer, and his lack of response spoke louder than words.

As if in a daze, Emma collapsed onto a chair. This was the end. Paul was diseased with vengeance;

there was no fighting it. Her devotion had its limits. She would not throw herself on his emotional funeral pyre in an act of suttee.

From the battle in which there was no victory, and from which there could be no escape, she made an honorable retreat. "I'm going back to New Orleans. Possibly forever. There are a lot of things I need to think through." She backed away. "And if you try to stop me, I'll never return. Do you understand?"

Hope faded in his eyes. "I won't stop you, Emma," he whispered in defeat. "Take our child and run."

Valise in one hand, Woodley's lead in the other, Emma stood on Menard's wharf. Three hours had passed since her ultimatum to Paul. Her instincts told her to go home, either to New Orleans or to Virginia, yet she hesitated. To run like a spoiled child to the embrace of her family didn't seem right. Perhaps it was pride that kept her from it. Probably, she figured, but she wanted to face this upheaval in a mature manner.

Yet she felt so alone in the world. She had lost everything—home, future, career. Paul. Most of all, Paul. Behind her was the town she had come to love, the man she loved beyond life itself. How could she face living without him?

You have to be strong, she told herself. You haven't lost everything. You have a baby to think of.

And as long as she had the child, she had a part of Paul. The best part. The product of their love.

She also had many other blessings to be thankful for. Memories of the good times, of the love they had shared. She was young and healthy. Thanks to Uncle Rankin she wasn't destitute. Her line of sight swept across Galveston Bay. Birds were singing out their early morning calls. The salt breeze blew. People were boarding the New Orleans-bound ship. Life went on.

The ticket agent cut in front of her. "Miz Rousseau," he said, "if you don't hurry aboard, the ship'll leave without you."

"Thank you, Mr. Upton, but I'm not leaving."

She turned and walked down the jetty. For her child's sake, and for her own, she first needed to work through her emotions. Neither New Orleans nor Richmond was the place to do it. She'd stay here in Galveston, not with Paul of course, but she wouldn't run away.

Anthaline agreed to rent her a room, and Emma was thankful the dear woman didn't ask too many questions. Undoubtedly Paul was aware she hadn't left Galveston, but he didn't seek her out. It was best this way.

Two days later, Cleopatra told her that Paul had left the port city. He was traveling to the new capital, Washington-on-the-Brazos. He and Moore planned to meet with Sam Houston. Emma hoped all would go well.

A week after she had left their little home, and her husband, she had a caller—Uncle Rankin.

"Simon told me ye know about . . . about all I've done," he said, his head dropping toward his chest. "I'm wanting to make amends."

From the rocking chair beside his on Anthaline's front porch Emma watched him. In the past, she had

426

never seen him like this—humbled.

"In your lifetime you've hurt a lot of people, Uncle."

"I never wanted to hurt ye."

"By maligning those around me, especially the man I love, you have played me false."

"Do ye . . . could ye— Is there anything I can do to get yer forgiveness?"

"I cannot absolve you," she replied. "The past can't be undone, but can you change your life?"

"I'm trying." He shuddered. "Do ye still have a place in yer heart for me, Emmie?"

"I love you. I can't stop loving you, and I don't want to."

He lifted his head, and hope sprang to his eyes.

"But it would do me proud," she added, "if you'd do yourself proud."

In slow measured words, he explained his intention to help the Texas Navy . . . to help Paul. But his gesture had been too late in coming.

Pleased by his efforts, she said, "That was good of you."

"When I arrived in Campeche the governor told me ye'd been the ship's surgeon. At first I was furious that yer husband had allowed ye into that mess, but then I realized—knowing ye and the way ye are—that it had been yer own decision."

"Exactly."

"Anyway, I had to come here. I wanted to face ye, and beg forgiveness."

"You should be begging Paul's forgiveness, not mine."

"Then I will." Rankin stood and brushed his lips

with the back of his hand. "Where can I find him?"

"He's gone to the new capital. I have no idea when he'll be back." She steepled her hands on her lap. "Go home for now. Go back to Magnolia Hall—you have a woman there who loves you. Aunt Tillie needs your affection."

"She does. I've many years to make up for."

"And try to give her your love." Truly believing that her uncle had changed, Emma smiled. "Then come back to Galveston. Make amends with Paul."

"I will."

They embraced, and he departed. Yet Emma was left with her own insecurities. For so long she had imagined her future melded to Paul's, had assumed she'd continue her medical practice. But she had forfeited the right to call herself physician. All was gone now. Except for the child growing beneath her heart.

After four weeks had passed, Cleopatra showed up, for the tenth time, at the boarding house. "There be a slave girl over to the Morgan place," she said. "Her babe's aborning, and she be needing your help."

"This town is full of doctors. Ask one of them to help."

"She don't want them. She heard about your magic, and needs you to take the pain away."

"Is she having complications?"

"No, but she's asking for you."

"Cleo, since the beginning of humankind women have been birthing children without the benefit of sulfurous ether." She yearned to go to the slave woman and ease her suffering, but she wasn't worthy of doctoring. A good physician abided by a code of

428

ethics. "Call one of the other doctors, and leave me be."

Cleopatra huffed up. "Listen here, missy, folks be needing your skills. You cain't quit—not after all you done gone through to be a doctor."

"I can't call myself a physician anymore. I betrayed a patient . . . for my own benefit."

"That's about the dumbest thing that's ever come outta your mouth, gal!" Cleopatra wiggled her forefinger in front of Emma's nose. "A quitter, that's what you is. Nothing but a lowdown quitter!"

"Exactly. Now go find help for that woman. I need to take a nap."

"Then you oughta be taking it in your own home, not in this durned boardinghouse!" Cleopatra shook her head in disgust. "You be pea-brained as a huntin' dog to let that man have your home. If'n you don't want him for a husband, least you should do is protect what's yours. But you quit on your work, quit on him, and hole up here in Miss Anthaline's place. I'm plumb ashamed of you."

"Hush, Cleo. The house isn't important. I want a home, not a mere roof over my head."

"Then go home to Virginie. Ben and I'll go with you if'n you're worried about making the trip alone."

"You two have followed me from New Orleans to St. Martinsville to Galveston. You have your own home here, and a good life. Ben has his blacksmith shop, and for once you're living as you should—for yourselves. There is no way I'll tear you two from your home."

"Ain't you got no sense? Home's where the heart is."

"Well, my heart isn't in Louisiana or Virginia."

"Then you haven't given up on Frenchie?"

Emma sat down on the bed. A tiny flutter, like butterfly wings, tickled her abdomen. The baby! It was moving for the first time.

"I guess I haven't given up on my husband. It's foolish of me, I'm sure. And I'd appreciate your not agreeing."

"I ain't agreeing to nothing." Cleopatra perched beside her, taking her hand. "Now don't you lie to me, baby. I know you be worried about this business with Sam Houston."

"Yes. I know Paul must be hurting."

"Cain't blame him. That was a dirty trick that ol' Raven did to him and the others."

"No man wants to live with the disgrace of a dishonorable discharge," Emma explained, "especially without the benefit of a court-martial."

Cleopatra pursed her lips. "Be pretty hard for a man to face all that without his woman backing him."

Refusing to succumb to her old friend's emotional blackmail, Emma went on. "I know Paul, and the commodore. For honor's sake they need that trial."

"Well, you cain't say they ain't trying to get ol' Houston to change his mind."

Emma recalled the events of days past. The president of the Republic of Texas was furious upon learning that the Navy men had been given a hero's welcome in Galveston. Immediately, he had issued dishonorable discharge papers to the commodore and to Paul. The next morning the men of the Texas Navy, led by Reese McDonald, had resigned in protest. Each and every one of them.

430

Paul had to be hurting. After fighting for Texas's freedom he had been branded an outlaw and pirate.

What could she do to help? Emma remembered his words: *Why don't you forgive and forget?*

"Cleo, I'm going to talk to Sam Houston myself."

Paul returned from Washington-on-the-Brazos a week later. Again Houston had denied his and Moore's requests for their day in court. Paul was determined to forget the shame of it and to get on with his life.

He stepped around the boards that littered the banks of Galveston Bay. Workers, twelve of them, were building a sloop. The first fruit of the Rousseau Shipyard's loom. But he was miserable.

He knew Emma was staying with Anthaline Lightfoot, and he yearned to throw himself at her feet and beg mercy—but he wouldn't. His stubborn pride wouldn't let him admit how wrong he had been to let her leave.

Yet the crates were still hidden in the shed. Paul had put off a decision about them. He realized he was delaying, stalling for time. When it came right down to it—no matter what he said or implied to Emma—he couldn't bring himself to turn the ordnance over to the Department of War and Marine.

"You're doing a fine job, Reese," he told McDonald, who was in charge of building the vessel. "She's a beauty."

"Thank you, Cap'n."

"Don't call me that. I'm Mr. Rousseau, a private citizen. Paul to you."

431

Reese shook his head in exasperation.

Paul turned away. "All of you go home for the evening."

The workers departed and he ducked into his office. Closing the door, he started across the small room. Suddenly he felt something hard and blunt hit the back of his neck.

"Traitor!" he heard, as if from very far away as pain exploded in his head—into fiery stars of white, orange, and blue. His knees buckled, and he pitched forward into darkness.

The office was dark, night having fallen, when his senses returned. Lying on the cold floor, he smelled dust, tasted it. A stabbing pain throbbed in the back of his head, which felt as if it were twice its size. His muscles twitched, and his throat was dry. *What . . . who? . . . Where am I?*

"Emma," he croaked, half-dazed.

"She ain't here," Henry Packert imparted wickedly. "It's just you, me . . . and me gun."

Paul pushed himself up by an elbow and shook his head, hoping to clear the cobwebs from his brain. "Damn you . . . wh-what's going on?"

The pirate lurched forward. Sticking the pistol barrel in Paul's face, he hunkered down. "You double-crossed me. And I'm gonna kill you for it."

"You're mistaken."

As Paul stared down the barrel, panic stabbed him. He didn't fear dying, but he was terrified of going to his grave without righting things with Emma. He desperately wanted to mend their broken fences. Right now, though, he had to get control of himself and of the situation.

"How'd you . . . get out of jail?" he asked.

432

"Broke out." The old corsair waved the gun. "Get up."

His stomach rolling with nausea, Paul shakily pushed himself to a sitting position. Then he took a deep breath of fortifying air. "I don't know what you mean about a double cross."

"Rankin Oliver's back in New Orleans," the pirate said. "If you'd gone with me, we'd o' got him. But you hemhawed around till that limey skipper come for me. Stalled, didn't you? I bet you knew all along that Brit frigate was on its way!"

"The *Spartan* was after me, too."

"I ain't believing you! You wanted to make me pay for swatting you back at the factor house."

They had had this discussion before, when Paul had visited Packert in jail. "Not true."

"Blimey, you were out to save your own skin— don't try and deny it. You always wanted Oliver to answer to the law, and you was just giving me lip service."

What was the use of replying?

"Now me *Barbara Elaine*'s gone to the bottom," Packert moaned. "Me crew's thrown in jail. And you're gonna pay for the insult!"

"Get another ship. Another crew."

Even as he said those words, Paul realized the futility of them. Henry Packert had never been a reasonable man, and the pirate wasn't going to trust him.

The tables had turned, and Paul fought to keep his head clear. He was dizzy, but he had youth and physical strength on his side. Nevertheless, there was a gun pointed at his nose. In the next moment, his luck changed—there was a noise outside.

Deciding on trying the oldest trick in the world, Paul motioned to the door and shouted, "Come in, Sheriff."

Packert turned his head. Paul's left hand shot out and up, knocking the gun to the floor. At the same instant he flung his right arm against the weapon, and the pistol slid away behind him.

"Damn you," the pirate screeched, diving for it.

Paul drew back his fist and slammed it forward into his attacker's nose. The heavyset man reeled backward, his nose flattened, as blood spurted over Paul's hand. Jumping to his feet before Packert had time to recover, Paul grabbed his opponent's right arm, wrenching it to the man's back, and put a strangle hold on his thick neck. Packert yowled in pain.

Paul kicked his leg to the side and the gun flew into the corner. He then further twisted the pirate's arm. He heard a gasp, a struggle for air. He felt a bone crack. Packert lost consciousness and Paul let him fall to the ground. Yanking the scarf from the pirate's head, he wound it around the man's limp hands.

He had fettered him for the moment, so he grabbed a skein of twine from his desk and wrapped length after length of it around Packert's feet. He then dragged the unconscious man to the lumber dray, swung his heavy body onto it, and set out for the jail. By the time they reached it, Packert, still unable to talk, was choking into consciousness.

"By golly, you caught him," the sheriff shouted. "I was just rounding up a posse."

Sheriff Smythe and his deputies surrounded the

434

dray. Lifting Packert from it, they carried him into his cell. A doctor was called for the old pirate, and the lawmen slapped Paul's back and thanked him for apprehending the escapee. One of the deputies offered him a snort of rotgut, but he declined and left.

Paul had gotten little satisfaction from taking the pirate back to jail. The man was sick in the mind. Had been for a long time.

"You've been sick in the mind, too, Rousseau," a voice in the back of his skull called out as he leaned a shoulder against the outside corner of the jail. With his thumb and forefinger, he rubbed his eyes and thought back on the promise he had made himself while tangling with Henry Packert.

What could he do to rectify his problems with his wife? The answer was simple, unfortunately. Rankin Oliver stood between them, and as long as Paul bore a grudge against Emma's uncle, there would be no reconciliation. To reclaim the woman he loved, he'd have to close the door on the past. Now and forever. For their marriage—and for himself—he'd do it.

Over time he had come to believe what Emma had told him, that his archenemy was innocent of killing Karla and of selling munitions to the Centralists. But Paul still had to come to grips with Étienne's death, to realize in his bones what Emma had said so long ago, nothing could be done that would bring his father back to life.

Deciding that life was for the living, Paul walked down the Strand, toward Anthaline's boarding-house. He was bent on having Emma back in his arms. If it wasn't too late . . .

435

Chapter Twenty-Eight

"Emma ain't here," Anthaline said, starting to close the door in Paul's face.

He wedged his foot between the jamb and the barrier. "Where is she?"

"Gone."

"Where did she go, and when will she be back?"

"If she wanted you to know, she'd've told you."

"Anthaline Lightfoot, you and I have been friends for a long, long time. In—"

"I'm her friend now, you sidewinder!"

Undaunted, Paul went on. "In the name of our friendship I'm asking you—where is my wife?"

Anthaline's tone softened. "Why do you want to know? You ain't out to hurt her, are you?"

"I love her, and I promise I'll never again do anything to cause her pain. I need her, and she needs me."

"I reckon she does." Anthaline released the pressure on the door. "Come on in, Paul. I'll make us a drink."

Over a glass of Madeira, Anthaline said, "She left a week ago. Went up the Brazos River to the capital.

Gonna have a showdown with Sam Houston. Over you."

After he had hurt her, she was championing him? Paul wanted to think she was doing it in the name of love, but . . . She was being loyal, that was all, he told himself. "Why?"

"Because she loves you, fool that she is. She's got some crazy notion you need your honor protected, and she's gonna see that ol' Raven gives you, and Edwin Moore, the court-martial you've been wantin'."

His ego bruised, Paul put his drink down. "I don't need a woman fighting my battles."

"Men! You're all alike. You say you need her, but I reckon it's just for makin' your home and babies. Wake up and smell the coffee, Paul Rousseau. You got a woman who loves you despite your faults— they're many, I shouldn't have to remind you—and she's set on walkin' beside you through the garden of Gethsemane. You outta be glad, not mad, she's willin' to help you with the Raven."

Remembering the time Emma had rescued him from the *San Antonio*'s hold, Paul realized he did need, and appreciate, his wife's support. Before he ruined what they'd shared, they had had a good partnership going. A partnership of love. But who had done most of the giving? Not him. Not even on the final issue that had torn their marriage asunder.

"You're a wise owl, Anthaline Lightfoot."

"You bet I am." Anthaline leaned forward. "And there's somethin' else you ought to know. She needs you real bad, too. And it ain't for spoutin' sweet nothin's and double-talk." She paused. "She's lost faith in herself as a doctor."

"That couldn't be true. Emma is above all dedicated to her work."

"Was. Was dedicated. Somethin' happened that changed her way of thinkin'. It's time you learned to give instead of takin' all the time. Get off your arse and go after her. Find out what the hell's the matter, and fix it!"

He got off his posterior and made for the door. "Rest assured—I will."

"I won't take no for an answer." Emma, having given up on charm, folded her arms under her chest and stared down her nose at Sam Houston's aide-de-camp. "I've traveled all the way from Galveston to see the president; surely he's gentleman enough to spare me a few minutes."

Theodore Spivey frowned and shuffled a stack of papers. "Mrs. Rousseau, you've been here to the capitol building every day for the last week, and every time I've mentioned your presence to our leader, he's refused to talk with you."

Emma leaned forward, pushing her face close to Spivey's. "You tell him this. If he doesn't see me, I'll inform every newspaper in Texas, Louisiana, New York, London—you name it!—that President Sam Houston is too much of a coward to speak with Captain Paul Rousseau's wife."

"Uhh, have a seat. I'll, uh, be right back."

Spivey almost toppled his chair in his eagerness to quell another scandal. Within two minutes, he returned from the President's office. "Go right in."

"Thank you . . . sir."

Sam Houston rose from his seat and side-stepped the huge desk that suited his large frame while smiling as if he were greeting a friend. "Mrs. Rousseau, how nice to see you again.

"And you." She lied, too.

"Do sit down." He took her arm, and led her to a leather chair. "To what do I owe the honor of this visit?"

"Let's don't beat around the bush, sir. I'm here on my husband's behalf."

"I'm surprised Mr. Rousseau sent you. He strikes me as a person who slays his own dragons."

"Don't be facetious, Mr. President. Captain Rousseau didn't send me. I'm here because of the public's belief in what is right and what isn't." Emma's pulse was racing. If she wasn't successful . . . "The Navy stopped an invasion of Galveston, and the people of Texas appreciate the sacrifices *your* naval men made."

"They're pirates who went against my orders."

"With the approval of Commissioner Naylor, they did what their consciences told them to do."

Houston waved a hand in dismissal. "Moore and his scalawags misappropriated money."

"That's not so. Private funds, plus the financial help of the Yucatecans, kept the fleet afloat."

"By sailing for Campeche instead of Galveston, they embezzled public property, neglected their duty, and they disobeyed and defied not only my orders but the edicts of congress," Houston retorted. "And they murdered those mutineers."

The first part of his statement wasn't even

439

debatable. That was for a court to decide. "Your correspondence with the Secretary of War and Marine will attest that you sanctioned punishing James Throckmorton's murderers. Commodore Moore merely carried out your request. Though he put himself and my husband in jeopardy by doing so, both of those men make decisions and stand by them!"

"They're traitors."

Emma fought the urge to slap the smug smile from Houston's mouth. "Then the cause of freedom needs 'traitors' like the commodore and Captain Rousseau."

"Mrs. Rousseau—"

"I know you work for our annexation by the United States. But the glory of our flag is in question. We are a proud people, sir. The United States laughs at your handling of this situation. Do you enjoy having the Republic of Texas shamed before the nations of the world? Our people have suffered to create this Republic. Many gave their lives for it. Remember Goliad? Remember the Alamo?"

"I, last of all, need a reminder of those battles!" He purpled with anger. "And you shouldn't mention those sacrifices in the same breath with those scalawags Moore and Rousseau."

She ignored the dig. "Will we join the United States of America with our President branded as unfair and dictatorial?"

"That is *not* the case."

"I think it is. Let's face it, Mr. President, your popularity is at an all-time low. If you grant the court-martial, you'll show our citizens that you are a reasonable man who believes that *a man is innocent until proven guilty.*"

Sam Houston furrowed his brows in thought. "I'll take it under advisement."

"Do that." Emma squared her shoulders. "And while you're thinking about it, remember something else. If Commodore Moore and my husband aren't given their legal rights, I will use every means at my disposal to further discredit you."

"Are you threatening me, Mrs. Rousseau?"

"No, sir. I'm stating a fact."

Emotionally drained, Emma departed the modest clapboard building that served as Texas's capitol. She had done her best. Now she would wait and see what would happen.

Paul couldn't wait to see Emma. A man possessed, he had sailed the *Virgin Vixen* up the Brazos to the new capital. The town, no more than an outpost thrown together in haste, had but a few businesses and homes. His first stop was the stagecoach inn, and luckily he learned that Emma was registered there.

"She's not here, though," the innkeeper said, then spat a wad of tobacco in the general vicinity of a spittoon. "Been gone a couple of hours."

Paul passed him a twenty-dollar gold piece. "How about a key to her room?"

The man scratched his thatch of unruly hair and smiled, displaying a mouthful of tobacco-stained teeth. "Seein's how ya put it that way . . . here ya go."

Fighting the urge to grab the unscrupulous

441

hosteler by the lapels for taking no precautions on behalf of a lone woman, Paul ordered a bath and a tray of food and drink sent up.

Hell, Emma didn't need protection, he thought as he ambled toward her room. She was capable of protecting herself. But he'd protect her from now on . . . if she'd let him.

After the bath and food arrived, Paul closed the curtains, took several candles from his traveling bag, lit them, and turned back the bedclothes. Stripping out of his travel-soiled clothes, he then settled himself in the tub. If nothing else, he was going to seem confident when she arrived.

As he lathered himself he took a look around. Emma's clothes were neatly hung on wall pegs. A bottle of perfume, her hairbrush, and two gold hairpins rested on the bedside stand. Beside them was one of the ribbons that had been pinned to his chest on the day they had arrived in Galveston. He felt a tug at his heartstrings. Though he had hurt her she still carried a reminder of him.

A key rattled in the lock, and he grinned before beginning to whistle a lively tune.

"Paul!" Emma's face lightened into a wreath of sunshine, but she glanced away to compose herself. "What are you doing here? How did you get in?"

"Slipped a gold piece to the . . . well, I hate to say concierge, but it'll do. It's a trick I learned from a beautiful blonde." He rested his elbows on the tub's edge. "And as for why I'm here, I'm waiting for you."

She looked away, but not before he caught her grin. "Well," she said, "if you've traveled all this way just to get your back scrubbed, you're in for a disappointment."

"That wasn't exactly what I had in mind, though the idea does have merit." The familiar tightening in his groin wreaked havoc with his determination to settle their differences before settling between her legs. "Aren't you curious about why I'm here?"

"No."

"You've always been the curious type, *ma bien-aimée*. You know it, I know it, and—"

"All right. Tell me why you're in my hotel room."

"Anthaline says you've given up medicine."

She crossed the room and sat down on the bed. "That's right."

"Why?"

"Because I betrayed a patient's confidence. A doctor without ethics has no business practicing medicine."

"This has to do with Simon Dyer, doesn't it?"

"Yes."

"He's dead. Was when you told me about his involvement with your uncle."

"How do you know that? Oh never mind! What difference does it make? I didn't know he was dead when I spoke of it." Emma rubbed her forehead with the tips of her fingers. "His death doesn't absolve me from blame."

"Medice, cura te ipsum."

"Paul Rousseau, that's Latin! I didn't know you understood the language."

The water was growing cold, and Paul was turning into a wrinkled mass of flesh, but he remained in the bath. Had to. Sex was not going to cure what ailed them. If it could, they would have been living in harmony a long time ago.

443

"There are a lot of things you don't know about me, my sweet and precious wife, but that won't be so for long. However, the point right now is—physician heal thyself."

Dropping her chin, she shook her head. "I can't."

"You can and will. I didn't fall in love with, and marry, a quitter."

"Don't you have the sequence of that all wrong? You married me for Feuille de Chêne. As for love, that happened later. And you've never loved me enough to put it before your desire for revenge against Uncle Rankin."

"You're wrong. All the way around. I loved you the moment I laid eyes on you—I just couldn't accept it at the time. And yes, the plantation was at stake when we married, but I wanted to be with you because I love you. I couldn't admit that either. For fourteen years the pain of losing my father has been clouding my reasoning, and I . . . well, I guess I couldn't see the forest for the trees." He held out his hand to her. "I've been a scoundrel, a blackguard, a snake—all the names you've called me. But—"

"You forgot blackmailer."

"All right. Add blackmailer to the list." His heart went into the next words. "But I've learned a lesson. If we're to be man and wife—and to raise our child in the loving home he or she deserves—I've got to close the door on the past."

"Then no matter what Uncle Rankin has done, you're willing to forget it—once and for all?"

He locked his gaze with hers. Total honesty went into his answer. "Yes."

"I never thought I'd hear you say that."

"I said it. And I mean it. I want you back in my arms . . . for always."

"And I want you back in mine."

"That's easy enough to accomplish. But unless we work through our differences, it wouldn't be for long, and I want it to be forever. Please forgive me, Emma."

She blinked. Then a tear rolled down her cheek, the first one he had ever seen her shed. "I forgive you, Paul."

"Together we can face whatever life has to offer," he said as she wiped that tear away. "We're a team, you know."

"I agree." She got to her feet, put her hands on her hips and smiled playfully. "I'm all for teamwork. As long as that deal doesn't include scrubbing your back!"

"You rub mine, partner, and I'll rub yours."

"Where's the cloth?"

Epilogue

Washington-on-the-Brazos, August 21, 1844

The sweltering-hot courtroom was packed with people. A panel of military judges sat solemnly behind a raised table, while attorneys and defendants, as well as onlookers, waited with bated breaths for the verdict.

The cry of a baby broke into the hush. The infant was comforted into silence by its mother.

The jurist at the center of the table spoke. "Will the defendants Edwin Moore and Paul Rousseau please rise."

Howard O'Reilly smiled confidently at Paul, who winked in return and rose to his feet. Commodore Moore was already standing.

Holding a piece of parchment in his hand, the judge said, "To the charge of misapplication of money, the defendants are not guilty."

The spectators cheered.

"Order in the court!" The judge pounded a gavel. His demand for silence granted, he continued. "To the charge of embezzlement of public property, not guilty. To the charge of neglect of duty, not guilty. To the charge of contempt and defiance of the law, not guilty. To the charge of treason, not guilty. To the charge of murder, not guilty."

Someone at the back of the room applauded.

The judge pounded his gavel again. "To the charge of disobedience of orders . . . guilty as charged." He smiled. "As punishment this court orders . . . no punishment."

Paul closed his eyes, thanking the saints above for clemency.

"This court is dismissed."

Joyful pandemonium reigned. Paul clasped his attorney's hand, and Howard O'Reilly muttered, "I knew it would go this way." Ed Moore then shook Howard's hand.

Rankin Oliver, his wife at his side, leaned across the rail to extend his congratulations. Paul took his hand. He'd never be overjoyed at seeing his former archenemy; but in the months since Rankin had first made conciliatory overtures, Paul had grown to appreciate the steps taken by this very proud man.

Tillie Oliver patted Paul's hand before smiling up at her husband. "Rankin and I are so pleased this went well."

"Thank you," Paul replied, knowing those words were spoken in truth.

Emma, smiling in relief and joy, and holding their son, broke through the throng around her husband. "This is wonderful," she said as he held her and the child close. "I'm so happy."

"I second that." Paul kissed the top of her blond head. "Let's go home."

Home to Galveston. That seaside town where they had lived in peace and contentment. Where the Rousseau shipyard thrived. Where the Rousseaus thrived.

Emma linked her free arm with his. "Lead the way, darling."

All of a sudden, a frantic woman burst through the courthouse door. "Dr. Rousseau, Dr. Rousseau, come quick! There's been an accident. A horse threw a boy, and he's hurt bad!"

Emma passed young Étienne to his father. "Take care of him, partner. I'll meet you back at the hotel." Her hand on the doorframe, she stopped and turned back to her men. "And, Paul, from the looks of your son he's going to need a diaper change. Soon."

Paul raised the boy to eye level. Étienne's face was red and screwed up. Suddenly his father's nose wrinkled at the powerful stench.

"Well, Son," Paul said, "there's something you've got to learn about partnering with women. It does have drawbacks."